The Scout

Unabridged Adventure Story from Mexico
of Karl May's Original Manuscript,
first published in German
under the title 'Der Scout'
in Deutscher Hausschatz in 1888/89

Travel and Adventure Tales
by
Karl May

Translated by
Herbert Windolf

Original German text by Karl May [1842 – 1912]
First published under the title 'Der Scout'
in Deutscher Hausschatz 1888-1889

English translation by Herbert Windolf

ISBN: 978-0-9821427-8-3

This book is printed on acid free paper.

Nemsi Books - rev. 02/28/2010

Acknowledgements

I gratefully acknowledge the availability to download this original Karl May story from the web site of the Karl May Gesellschaft.

My thanks go to Felipe Morales and Manfred Wenner for edting my translation of The Scout.

Herb Windolf, Prescott, Arizona

Karl May – translated by Herbert Windolf

Foreword

The narratives *Der Scout* (*The Scout*), together with *Deadly Dust* are, in some sense, forerunners of the later Winnetou novels. This volume presents the translation named, *The Scout*.

Karl May saw his narrative *Der Scout* published in the magazine 'Deutscher Hausschatz' (German Home Treasures) in 1888/89. Between 1881 and 1889, Karl May had successfully produced his *Oriental Odyssey*, following which he proceeded to accomplish the same for the Wild West of his imagination. In so doing, he incorporated some aspects of *The Scout* in Volume II of his Winnetou Series.

May's *Scout*, a first-person narrative, plays before a historical background, shortly after the American Civil War and the battle for power between the forces of Juarez and Maximilian, supported by the French, in Mexico, in the years 1865/66. He, furthermore, uses the opportunity to insert and express his beliefs about the then recently founded Ku-Klux-Klan.

The Scout certainly holds a special position in May's Wild West stories in that the first-person narrator is still a novice to the trials and tribulations encountered. Although the young man is capable, he is still encumbered by the trappings of civilization, and has difficulties dealing with his new environment. Still a *greenhorn*, aptly described here, he is familiarized with the rules of the West by the story's other protagonist, his mentor, the Scout, going by the frontiersman's name of Old Death.

In this narrative, the storyteller is still far removed from the later, always competent and experienced frontiersman, but is described as a fallible human being with a long way to go to become the Old Shatterhand of the Winnetou Series and other Wild West novels of May's. However, he also meets and defeats Winnetou in this story and is befriended by the Apache chief, who, in this early epic, is vengeful and is yet to become the noble human being of May's later writings.

The Scout is thought to be one of Karl Mays best travel stories, into which the author wove, as it appears, some of his early personal experiences from his incarceration, which find expression in the poem 'The Night Most Terrible,' and remarks of Old Death about his misdeeds.

So, if you have read the Winnetou Series, go back in time to meet the, not-yet-so-named, 'Old Shatterhand' when he was still a *greenhorn*. Enjoy!

Herb Windolf, Prescott, Arizona

Karl May – translated by Herbert Windolf

Contents:

Karl May – translated by Herbert Windolf

The Scout

Karl May – translated by Herbert Windolf

1. A Poem

Greenhorn – it is an annoying and disrespectful designation for a person to whom the word is applied. 'Green' implies immaturity and 'horn' refers to the young buds on certain ungulates, used more for feeling obstacles, etc., than for defense or combat. Hence, a greenhorn is a person who is new, and thus still inexperienced in the ways of a country, and ought to act circumspectly if he does not wish to expose himself to ridicule. The term is widely used by Yankees, but even more so by the residents of the Wild West: the frontiersman, the trapper, the cowboy and others who are well-versed in the ways of the West.

To clarify the concept: a greenhorn is a person, who does not rise from his chair when a lady comes to stand nearby; who greets the master of the house before he has bowed to the ladies; who knows nothing of firearms and who puts the cartridge into the chamber the wrong way 'round, or first pushes in the stopper, then the bullet and lastly the powder. A greenhorn speaks either no English at all, or conversely, a very stilted and affected form; to him Yankee-English is an abomination, which wouldn't come to his mind nor cross his tongue. A greenhorn thinks a raccoon to be an opossum, and considers a fairly attractive mulatto a charming quadroon[1]. A greenhorn smokes cigarettes and detests the tobacco-juice-spitting gentleman, and after having his ears boxed by a Paddy[2], runs to the justice of the peace, instead of simply gunning down the fellow like a true Yankee. A greenhorn thinks the footprints of a turkey to be the tracks of a bear and takes a sports yacht for a Mississippi steamer. A greenhorn is much too shy to put his dirty boots on the knees of a fellow-passenger, and to slurp his soup like it were the panting of a dying buffalo. For cleanliness, a greenhorn lugs a washing sponge the size of a pumpkin and ten pounds of soap onto the prairie, and packs a compass that keeps turning into every direction except to point north. A greenhorn writes down eight hundred Indian expressions, but when he comes across the first redskin, he finds that he sent his notes home in his last envelope, when he actually tossed the letter into a fire. A greenhorn – well, a greenhorn is simply a greenhorn, and once, I too, was one.

But one ought not think that I was convinced, or at least had an idea that this insulting designation would apply to me! Oh no, for, isn't it the outstanding characteristic of a greenhorn to think that everyone else, but never he himself is *green*?

And so it was with me. I was of the self-serving opinion that, despite my youth, I had experienced and learned much, very much even. I rubbed well-scented oils in my hair and delighted in the nice, small foot in my tight,

---

[1] Child of a Mulatto and a White, one-fourth black
[2] Irishman

1

lacquered, shiny little boots. I wore rubber stirrups on my pants and carried three kinds of beard wax in my toiletry bag. From my chest hung a conspicuously wide golden watch chain – but let me tell you in private, it was only a cheap imitation and had cost me just one taler and ten silver groschen in Bremen. Added to this was a *chapeau claque* and a silken umbrella with a heavy, elegant ivory handle – except that the latter was only bleached bone – in this way I was putting my century and thus also the United States in its place.

Mind you, with the afore-mentioned items I have not fully described my entire outfit. My actual equipment was kept in my suitcase. It consisted of several suits of various types, several wigs, many false beards and other illegal items, which were nevertheless required by a policeman. Should one conclude from the possession of these items that I was a traveling burglar, then let me assure you that this was by no means the case. And should some of you still shrug your shoulders questioningly, I wish to assure you confidentially that I was a dutiful enemy of all rogues and was after them as a detective.

This had come to be as follows:

After completing my studies, I had entered my profession with great enthusiasm; soon, however, I found I had enough. Empty heads, whose sole merit was having an old influential aunt, agile hypocrites whose position was derived from quickly taking advantage of a *milch cow*, and who had trained themselves in servile bows before a mirror, had been given preference over me. My immediate superior demanded that my work should benefit solely him, but I was certain that it was injurous to the well-being of my subordinates. When I discretely inquired with my higher-ups about the problem, they conceded that I was correct, but was told with a shrug of shoulders that abandoning my conscientious viewpoint would result in faster advancement. The man, my immediate superior, was surreptitiously informed of my report and now pursued me with a vengeance that could not be assuaged by anything. We had an open breach, he calling me an incautious fool, to which I responded with a silent, deep bow. I resigned my position and left – for America, a daring step, which I, however, did not regret. Much later, to my great surprise, I met this honorable sir again as a Mormon missionary. He had found subordinates less considerate than myself, had been removed from his position, and also gone to America, where, being an apostate to his previous activities, he was paying for the salvation of his soul among the Latter Day Saints.

Concerning myself, I learned that the United States does not receive everyone with open arms. However, just when my meager savings were depleted, I succeeded in finding employment which, however, had nothing at all in common with my former occupation. Following a very thorough examination, I was accepted and contracted as a member of the, at the time, famous private detective corps of the honorable Mister Josy Taylor. I became the sole German among my colleagues. My boss did not consider Germans very useful in this occupation, but I succeeded in gaining his trust through several successful ventures, for which I had to thank chance more than acumen, so that, in a weak moment, he even told me confidentially that he was actually of German origin. His grandfather had been called Schneider, but he had changed this name to the English Taylor.

Nevertheless, the goodwill this gentleman extended me did not make him forget that I was a greenhorn. He did not entrust difficult cases to me since he did not think I was smart enough, not by a long shot. But if there was a case that promised certain success and, in addition, good compensation, he assigned it to me, and had the great affability to, so to speak, put my nose onto the tracks by giving me detailed instructions.

I might have worked this way for about half-a-year for the good name of his organization when, one day, he called me to his room where a worried-looking gentleman was waiting. Upon our introduction I got to know him as the banker Ohlert, who had come to seek assistance in a private matter. As distressing as the case was to him, it was as dangerous to his business.

He had a son by the name of William, age twenty-five and not married. His business rights and dispositions had the same validity as his father's, who was married to a German woman and was himself of German birth. The son, more dreamy than energetically disposed, had occupied himself more with scientific, esthetic and metaphysical books than the business ledger, and had thought himself not only to be an important scholar, but even a poet. The acceptance of several poems by one of the German newspapers of New York had confirmed this opinion of himself.

Somehow, he developed the idea of writing a tragedy whose hero was to be an insane poet. To be able to do this, he thought he needed to study insanity and, for this purpose, had acquired some of the relevant literature. The terrible result was that, little by little, he had identified with this poet and now believed himself to be insane. Recently, the father had met a doctor who claimed that he intended to establish a private clinic for the insane. The man had been an assistant to some famous mental doctors for some time and had been able to so gain the trust of the banker that the latter had asked him to meet his son in order to see if his attention to the ill son might have some positive effects.

From the first day, an affectionate friendship had developed between the doctor and Ohlert junior, which had the unexpected result that both disappeared suddenly. Only now did the banker inquire more closely about the doctor and learned that this man was one of these medical quacks who, by the thousands, plied their trade undisturbed across the United States.

Taylor asked what this supposed mental doctor called himself. When the name Gibson and his address were given, it turned out that we were dealing with an old acquaintance, whom I had kept under close observation on some other matters for some time already. I even had a photo of him. It was kept at the office, and when I showed it to Ohlert, he immediately recognized his son's dubious friend.

This Gibson was a first-class swindler and in various disguises had traveled the States and Mexico. Yesterday, the banker had gone to the man's landlord and learned that the renter had paid up and left, where to, no one knew. The banker's son had taken along a substantial amount in cash, and today a telegraphic message from a connected banking house in Cincinnati had arrived, informing that William had withdrawn five thousand dollars, then had traveled on to Louisville to pick up his fiancée. The latter was, of course, a lie.

It could be assumed that the 'doctor' had induced his patient to escape with him, a covert kidnapping, in order to gain possession of large amounts of the banker's money. William was personally known to many prominent bankers in the field and could obtain funds from them as much as he liked. This made it necessary to catch the seducer and to return the ill son home. I was entrusted with resolving this problem and received the requisite authorizations and instructions, as well as a photo of William Ohlert, then steamed off to Cincinnati. Since Gibson knew me, I took along those items required to disguise myself, should the need arise.

In Cincinnati I paid a visit to the relevant banker and learned from him that Gibson had truly been with William. From there I traveled to Louisville, where I found that both had bought tickets for St. Louis. Of course, I followed them, but was able to pick up their tracks only after a lengthy search. They had taken a Mississippi steamer to New Orleans to where I now followed.

I had been in New Orleans for four days without the least success in finding the two. Ohlert had handed me a list of business establishments he had connections with. In Louisville and St. Louis I had gone to the respective addresses and learned there that William had stopped by to withdraw more money. He had done the same with two of Ohlert's business friends in New Orleans. I warned the others and asked them to inform me at once should William still come to see them.

That was all I was able to learn. Now I was stuck in the midst of crowds of people flooding the streets of New Orleans, with the humbling feeling of not being a man up to the task. Obviously, I had also contacted the police and could now only wait for whatever results these people's efforts would have. So as not to be totally idle, I roamed the crowd searching faces. Maybe I would experience some lucky coincidence.

I was for the first time in the south of the country, which is why I was greatly aware of the differences between the activities of New York and New Orleans. New Orleans has a decidedly southern character, especially in its older sections. There one finds narrow, dirty streets and houses with porches and balconies. It is to these places that life retreats when it shies from the light of day. One sees there all kinds of complexions, from a sickly, yellowish white to the deepest Negro black. Organ grinders, roving singers and guitar players produce their ear-shattering feats. Men shout, women scream; here an angry sailor pulls a Chinese by his pigtail; over there two Negroes fight, surrounded by a circle of laughing spectators. At a corner, two porters run into each other, immediately dropping their loads to beat at each other angrily. A third arrives and attempts to make peace, but inadvertendly receives blows from the two.

The many small suburbs give a better impression, consisting of pleasant country houses, all surrounded by neat gardens where roses, holly, oleander, pears, figs, peaches, oranges and lemons are grown. Here, residents find the longed-for peace and quiet once they leave the city's noisiness.

Of course, the port is the busiest place. It teems with ships and vessels of all kinds and sizes. Giant wool bales and barrels are stored here for loading with hundreds of laborers busy among them. One could imagine being on one of the cotton markets of East India.

Thus I was wandering the city keeping my eyes open – in vain. It was about noon and very hot. I was wandering the wide, beautiful Common Street, when I noticed the sign of a German beer pub. A sip of Pilsner in this heat didn't sound bad. I entered the place.

From the large crowd one could see how popular this beer had become. Only after some searching did I see an empty seat in a corner. There stood a small table with two chairs, one of which was taken by a man whose appearance was such that it could drive a potential customer away from the second seat. I went there after all and asked permission to drink my beer with the man.

An almost pitying smile crossed his face. He looked me up and down with an almost scornful look and asked:

"You've got money on you, mister?"

"Of course!" I replied, wondering about the question.

"Then you can pay for the beer as well as the seat you want, right?"

"I think so."

"Well, then, why do you ask for my permission to sit with me? I figure you are a Dutchman, a greenhorn in the country. The devil should get anyone daring to prevent me from taking the seat I like! Sit down, therefore, and put your legs where you please, and box the ears of anyone who'd forbid you to do so!"

I honestly admit that I was impressed by the man's style and felt my cheeks reddening. Strictly speaking, his words had been insulting, and I felt that I ought not to let it slide and make at least an attempt of defending myself. This is why I replied, while I sat down:

"If you think me to be a German, you hit it right, mister, but I must object to you calling me a Dutchman, for I would be forced to prove to you that I'm no Dutchman. One can be polite, yet remain a crafty fellow."

"Pshaw!" he answered calmly. "You don't look so smart to me. Don't make an effort trying to get angry; it wouldn't get you anywhere. I didn't mean to cross you and wouldn't really know how you'd succeed in putting yourself into a better position. Old Death isn't the man to lose his equanimity by a threat."

Old Death! So this man was Old Death! I had often heard of this well-known, yes, even famous frontiersman. His name was mentioned at every camp fire west of the Mississippi and had even penetrated to the cities in the east. If only the tenth, the twentieth part of what was told about him was true, he was a hunter and scout for which one had to take one's hat off. He had roamed the West for his entire life and, despite the dangers he had encountered, had never been injured. This is why superstitious people thought him to be bulletproof.

Old Death was extremely tall, and his bent-forward figure truly seemed to consist of only skin and bones. His leather pants literally sloshed about his legs. In the course of time, his leather shirt had shrunk, so that its sleeves came not much farther down than to half his forearms, on which one could, like on a skeleton, clearly differentiate between the two bones, the ulna and the radius. His hands, too, resembled those of a skeleton.

A very long, deathly looking neck in whose skin the larynx hung like a small leather bag, projected from the hunting shirt. And then the head itself! It seemed to be covered by barely five ounces of flesh. His eyes sat deep in their sockets, and there wasn't a single hair on his skull. The terribly haggard cheeks, the sharp jaw, the prominent cheek bones, and the rising snub nose with its wide, forward-pointing nostrils truly made for a skull one could be horrified of if one were to face it unexpectedly. The sight of this head truly affected my nose: I felt as if I were smelling the odor of corruption, the odor of hydrogen-sulfide and ammonia. One could totally lose one's appetite for eating and drinking.

His seemingly long, skinny feet stuck in some boot-like fittings, cut from a single piece of horse leather. He wore truly giant spurs, whose wheels had been cut from Mexican silver peso pieces.

Next to him lay a saddle and bridle and one of those yard-long Kentucky rifles, which can rarely be seen these days, having given way to breechloaders. His other weaponry consisted of a Bowie knife and two large revolvers, whose grips peered from his belt. This belt consisted of a leather skin in the shape of a so-called Geldkatze[3], the belt being decorated all around by palm-size scalps. Since these scalps did not appear to have come from the heads of palefaces, one had to assume that their owner had taken them from defeated Indians.

The waiter brought my beer. When I wanted to take the first sip, the hunter held his glass up against mine and said:

"Hold it! Not so fast, boy! Let's clink glasses first. I heard it's the custom in your fatherland."

"Yes, but only among good friends," I replied, hesitating to follow his request.

---

[3] Little decorated bags for coins or small items, customary in ancient times

"Don't make a fuss! We now sit together and don't need to, even in thought, break our necks. So, let's toast! I'm no spy or fraud, and you can safely give me a try for fifteen minutes."

This sounded different from his earlier remarks, which is why I clinked my glass to his and said:

"I know what to think of you, sir. If you're truly Old Death, I needn't fear of finding myself in bad company."

"Then you know me, and I needn't talk of myself. Let's talk of you then! Why did you come to the United States?"

"For the same reason that brought others here – to make my fortune."

"I believe it! Over there, in old Europe, people think that one simply opens one's pockets here to have shiny dollars drop in. If one man is lucky, all the newspapers write about it, but of the thousands who sink in their struggle and disappear without a trace, no one talks about. Did you find your fortune, or are you at least on its tracks?"

"I believe I can confirm the latter."

"Then make sure to keep looking sharply for it so that you don't lose its tracks! I know best how difficult it is to hold onto such tracks. You may have heard that I'm a scout who can take on any other frontiersman and yet, to this day, pursued fortune in vain. For a hundred times I believed that I only had to grab for it, but as soon as I reached out it disappeared like a castle in the air, existing only in the imagination of Man."

He had said this in a dismal voice, then gazed silently ahead. When I did not comment, he looked up after a while and said:

"I don't understand how I come up with such words, but, maybe, there's a simple explanation. I'm always a little concerned when I see a German, a young one like yourself, who will most likely perish. You must know that my mother was German. From her I learned her mother tongue, and if you like, we can also speak German. Before her death, she set me up so that I could see my fortune before me. But I thought myself to be smarter and ran off in the wrong direction. Mister, be smarter than I! One could see that you might end up the same as I did."

"Really? How so?"

"You look too nice. You smell of fragrances. If an Indian would see your hairdo, he would collapse from fright. There isn't the least spot or fleck of dust on your outfit. That's not the right way to find one's fortune in the West."

"It isn't my intention to look for it there."

"So! Would you be kind enough to tell me what your position is or in which line of business you are in?

"I studied."

I said this with a certain pride. He, however, looked at me with a slight smile, which resembled a disdainful grin coming from his skull-like features, shook his head, and said:

"Studied! Oh my! And you are even proud of it? Precisely your kind is least able to make their fortune here. I've seen this much too often. Are you employed?"

"Yes, in New York."

"What kind of employment?"

He asked his questions with such a peculiar voice that it was impossible to deny him answers. Since I could not tell him the truth, I explained:

"I'm here on a banker's assignment."

"A banker's? Oh! Of course, then your path seems to be smoother than I thought. Hold on to this position, sir! Not every studied man finds employment with an American money man. And in New York even? Then, considering your youth, you enjoy quite some trust. Only someone who can be relied on is sent south from New York. I'm glad I was mistaken about you, sir! Then it is some monetary transaction you must handle?"

"Something like that."

"So! Hm!"

Once more he glanced at me inquisitively, smiled as before and continued:

"But I think I can guess the real reason for your presence."

"I doubt it."

"I don't care, but would like to give you some good advice anyway. If you don't want anyone to find out that you came here looking for someone, better watch your eyes. You clearly checked everyone here in the pub and have continuously looked to the windows to observe passersby. You are looking for someone. Did I guess right?"

"Yes, mister. It's my intention to find someone whose whereabouts are unknown to me."

"Then turn to the hotels!"

"That was for naught, just as were the efforts of the police."

Now this seemingly friendly grin crossed his face again; he snickered, snapped his finger and said:

"Mister, you are after all a greenhorn, a real, true greenhorn. Don't take offense, but that's how it really is."

At that moment I realized that I had said too much. He confirmed my insight when he continued:

"You came here concerning a matter which has something to do with a money transaction, as you told me. The man in question is, at your request, being looked for by the police. You yourself run through the streets and beer pubs looking for him, and my name wouldn't be Old Death, if I didn't know who I'm facing now."

"Well, who, sir?"

"A detective, a private police man, who's to solve a task that's more of a family-related than of a criminal nature."

This man was truly the epitome of acumen. But how was he able to guess my intentions? Should I admit that he had guessed right? No. I was simply a greenhorn. It didn't occur to me that this man could be of great help in accomplishing my plans. His educational level was much, much lower than mine; it would dishonor my dignity to make him a confidante. That is why I made an effort to produce a fine, diplomatic smile, and replied:

"You are sharpsighted, sir, but this time you seem to have miscalculated."

"Don't think so!"

"Oh, sure!"

"Well! It's your business whether you want to admit to it or not. I can't and don't want to force you. But if you don't want anyone to see through you, you ought not act so transparently. We are clearly dealing with a money matter. The task was assigned to a greenhorn, and intended to be treated carefully. Therefore, the person sought is a well-known acquaintance or even a family member of the injured party. But there must be some criminal aspect to it, otherwise the local police would not have agreed to assist. It can be assumed that the person sought is in the company of a seducer, who is out to exploit him. Yeah, yeah, just look at me like that, sir! You are surprised by my fantasy? Well, a good frontiersman, from a couple of foot prints, can put an entire trail together, maybe even all the way to Canada, and it's unlikely that he would be mistaken."

"You certainly develop an exceptional imagination, mister."

"Pshaw! Keep on denying it! It doesn't hurt me. I'm fairly well known around here and could give you some good advice. But if you are of the opinion that you'll reach your goal faster on your own, then this is laudable, but whether it is smart, I doubt."

He got up and pulled out an old leather bag to pay for his beer. I thought I might have hurt him with my mistrust and to compensate for it, said:

"There's some business one ought not to reveal to someone else, least not a stranger. It wasn't my intention to insult you, and think . . ."

"Aye, aye!" he interrupted me, while he tossed a coin on the table. "No one's talking of an insult. You struck me well and, despite the beard wax in your mustache, there's something about you that stirs my goodwill."

"Maybe we'll meet again!" I replied.

"Hardly. Today, I'll head for Texas and from there to Mexico. It's unlikely that your little excursion is in the same direction, so . . . farewell, sir! And on occasion remember that I called you a greenhorn! You can easily take that from Old Death, since he's not meaning this to be an insult. It also doesn't hurt a newcomer if he thinks a bit more modestly of himself."

9

He put on his wide-brimmed sombrero that had hung behind him on the wall, put saddle and bridle on his back, reached for his rifle, and left. But after only a few steps, he once more turned, came back to me, and whispered:

"No offense, sir! I, too, did study, and today I'm still pleased thinking back to what a conceited fool I was for a time. Goodbye!"

He now left the pub without looking back. I looked after him, until his conspicuous figure, smiled at by passersby, had disappeared in the crowd. I would have loved to express anger towards him, but realized that I felt none. His appearance had caused a kind of pity to arise in me, and while his words were harsh, his voice had been simultaneously soft and well-meaning. One could hear that he truly meant well, and the content of his words had awakened a kind of shame, a deficiency in my value, which I was loath to admit to myself.

I put my elbow on the table and my head on my hand and looked pensively ahead. Greenhorn! I couldn't quite get over this expression. Did I look and act so immature? Of course, I had been more transparent than a Yankee would ever be. Did I really have the makings to catch a sly fellow like Gibson? I felt some doubt arise, but – no! I was quite the man to take care of the task assigned to me, and, yes, I had the wherewithal for it. I felt an enormous energy in myself, and – at that moment the door opened and Gibson entered.

He stopped at the entrance and scanned the patrons. Thinking that he would spot me, I turned to have my back face the door. There was no other vacant seat but the one Old Death had occupied. Thus, Gibson had to come to my table and sit with me. Silently, I enjoyed already his shock when he would recognize me.

But he did not come. I heard the noise of the door closing and quickly turned around. Really, he had recognized me and was fleeing. I saw him step outside and walk briskly away. Quickly, I put on my hat, tossed payment to the waiter, and rushed outside. There, to the right, he tried to disappear in the crowd. Turning, he saw me and doubled his pace. I followed at the same speed. When I was past a group of people, I saw him disappear into a narrow side street. I reached it, just when he turned a corner at its end. Before he disappeared, he turned once more towards me, drew his hat and waved it to me. Of course, I was annoyed, and without wondering whether the passersby would laugh at me, I fell into a trot. No policeman was visible. To ask some of the locals for help would have been in vain; none would have assisted.

When I got to the corner, I found myself on a small plaza. On both sides rose serried rows of small houses; ahead of me I saw villas with beautiful gardens. There were plenty of people on this plaza, but no Gibson. He had disappeared.

At a barber's door leaned a Negro. He seemed to have stood there for a while, which is why he must have noticed the fugitive. I walked up to him, politely pulled my hat and asked whether he had seen a white gentleman come hurrying from the lane. Baring his long, yellow teeth while laughing at me, he replied:

"Yes, sir! Did see him. He run very fast. Went in over there."

He pointed to one of the small villas. I thanked him and hurried to get to the building. The iron gate to the garden was locked and I may have rung the bell for five minutes until a man, again a Negro, opened it. I told him my request, upon which he slammed the door shut in my face and told me:

"First ask massa. Without massa's permission, I will not open."

He left, while I waited as if standing on hot coals, for at least ten minutes. At last he returned with the message:

"Not allowed to open. Massa forbade. No man come in today. Door locked all the time. You quickly go away; if you jump over fence, massa will shoot with revolver."

There I stood! What was I to do? I could not enter by force, certain that the owner would use his rights and shoot at me, for the American means business when it comes to his home. There was nothing else to do than to go to the police.

When I angrily walked back across the plaza a boy came running towards me, holding a scrap of paper.

"Sir, sir," he shouted. "Wait a moment! You are to give me ten cents for this note."

"Who gave it to you?"

"A gentleman, who came from the house over there." With these words he did not point to the villa, but to the opposite direction. "He pointed you out to me and wrote the note. For ten cents you'll get it."

I gave him the money and received the slip of paper. The boy ran away. There, on the cursed paper, torn from a note book, was written:

"My dear Mister Dutchman.

Did you, by chance, come for me to New Orleans? I guess so, since you followed me. I thought you to be silly, but not stupid enough to try to catch me. Whoever has more than half an ounce of brain ought not to attempt it. Go ahead and return to New York and there give my sentiments to mister Ohlert. I took care that he won't forget me and hope that you, too, will at times remember our meeting today which, of course, did not end gloriously for you. You'll remain a greenhorn for as long as you live!

Gibson."

One can imagine the delight I felt after I had read this kind epistle. I bunched up the note, put it in my pocket, and resumed my walk. It was possible that I was being secretly observed and so did not want to give this man the pleasure of seeing my embarrassment.

Yet, simultaneously, I looked across the plaza. Gibson could not be seen. The Negro in front of the barber shop had disappeared, and there was no sign of the boy to ask him about Gibson. In any case, he must have been told to disappear quickly.

Once more had I been called a greenhorn! Even in black and white! While I waited for entry to the villa, Gibson had found time to leisurely write me a letter of twenty-three lines. The Negro had fooled me. Without doubt, Gibson was laughing at me, and the boy had made a face as if he was aware that I was a fellow to be conned.

I was in an absolutely miserable mood. I had been shown-up, fooled to the highest degree, and couldn't even tell the police that I had come across Gibson. The police, too, would have thought me a greenhorn, even if not to my face, and secretly poked fun at me. I, thus, walked silently off feeling like a man who had boasted of being an excellent sailor, and had the first breeze capsize his boat.

Without walking across the open plaza again, I searched the lanes entering it, of course without success. A more experienced and crafty man than myself would not have needed to do this, since it was obvious that Gibson would have left this now dangerous section of the city as quickly as possible. One could even assume him to use the first opportunity to leave New Orleans.

I arrived at this idea in spite of my only half-ounce brain and, therefore, headed for the harbor and the site of today's departing ships. I gained the support of two policemen in civil attire, but our efforts were in vain. The anger of having been fooled so much did not let me rest, which is why I wandered the streets and all kinds of restaurants and taverns until late into the night. When I felt totally tired out, I went back to my lodging place and fell asleep.

My dream took me to an insane asylum. Hundreds of insane people, thinking themselves to be poets, held thick manuscripts out to me, which I was to read. Of course, they were all tragedies with a crazy poet being the hero. I had to read and read, for Gibson stood next to me, his revolver cocked, threatening to shoot me the moment I stopped. I read and read so that sweat ran off of my forehead. To wipe it off I pulled out my kerchief, stopped reading for a second and was thus shot by Gibson!

The shot's crack woke me, for it had not been an imaginary, but a real bang. In my dream's excitement I had tossed back and forth in bed and, in my attempt to pull the revolver from Gibson's hand, had slammed down the lamp standing on the bedside table. Next morning I was charged eight dollars for it. That's what happens if one wants to catch a scoundrel without having the talent for it!

I had woken up, totally bathed in sweat. I drank my tea, then drove out to beautiful Lake Pontchartrain, where I took a refreshing bath which also improved my low morale. Then I went anew on my search. In my walks I happened to pass the German beer pub again, where I had met Old Death yesterday. I entered without any thought of coming across some tracks. At the moment, the pub wasn't as full as on the previous day. Yesterday, not a single newspaper could be had, but today, several lay on a table and I picked one up, this being the 'German

Newspaper' as it was named, published in New Orleans. By now, it may have changed ownership and editors many times, following the American pattern.

Without intending to study it, I opened it, and the first item to draw my attention was a poem. When perusing a newspaper I either read poems at the very last or not at all. Its heading resembled the title of a horror novel, repelling me. It was called 'The Night most Terrible.' Ready to turn the page, I noticed the two initials the poem was signed with 'W.O.' These were William Ohlert's initials! For so long, his name had been on my mind that it was no wonder I immediately connected it with these two letters. Ohlert thought himself to be a poet. Had he used his stay in New Orleans to bring his jingling rhymes to the public's attention? The publication might have been so quick that he must have paid for it. Should my assumption turn out to be true, this poem might put me on the tracks of the sought-after man. I therefore read it:

> The Night most Terrible
> Know you the night, which is on Earth descending,
> With hollow wind and heavy fall of rain,
> This is the night no star winks down from heaven,
> No eye does penetrate the weather's heavy veil?
> But gloomy as this night may be, another morn' will dawn,
> So go to rest, and sleep without concern!
> Know you the night, which is on life descending,
> When death will put you to your final rest,
> And closing in on you, eternity comes calling,
> And terror pulses through your veins and chest?
> But gloomy as this night may be, another morn' will dawn,
> So go to rest, and sleep without concern!
> Know you the night, which on your spirit is descending,
> That for redemption does it scream in vain,
> Around your soul it twists in snakelike windings,
> And spits a thousand devils in your brain?
> Oh, keep from it awake and caring,
> For this night only does not have a morn'!
>
>   W.O.

I must admit that reading this poem touched me profoundly. Even if one thought it to be of little literary value, it held the horrified scream of a talented man trying in vain to fight the gloomy powers of insanity, while sensing that he was hopelessly falling under their spell. But I quickly overcame my emotion, since action was called for. I was convinced that William Ohlert was the author of the poem. In a directory I looked up the address of the publisher and went there.

Printing and editorial work were done at the same place. First, I purchased a copy of the newspaper at the printers, then had myself announced to the editor, from whom I learned that my guess had been correct. A certain William Ohlert had delivered the poem personally the day before and had asked for its immediate publishing. Since the editor was disinclined, the poet had paid ten dollars with the condition that it was to appear in today's edition and that he would receive a galley print. His manners had been impeccable, but he appeared to look somewhat disturbed and had explained repeatedly that the poem had been written with his heart's blood – this being an expression talented and untalented poets and writers alike used to banter with. He had to leave his address for the galley proof to be sent to and it was, of course, given to me. He was staying at a private lodging facility, fancy and expensive, on a street in a newer section of the city.

After changing my appearance in my room, at which I thought I succeeded very well, I left for this address. But first I called on two policemen, who were to post themselves at the door of the lodging place, while I went inside.

I was very much convinced that I would succeed in the arrest of the scoundrel I was after and of finding his victim, which is why, with some elation, I pulled the bell of the establishment, above which one read on a brass plate: "First Class Pension for Ladies and Gentlemen." It had to be the right place. The house as well as the business were the property of a lady. The doorman opened, asked for my wish, with which I requested to see the lady of the house. I handed him also my business card, showing a different name than my real one. I was taken to the parlor and did not have to wait long for the lady to appear.

She was a very nicely dressed, portly lady of about fifty years of age. It looked as if she carried a tiny portion of black blood in her veins, as her frizzy hair and a slight coloration of her finger nails let me guess. She gave the impression of being a woman with heart and received me very politely.

To my disgrace, I must admit that I put her on quite a bit by introducing myself as the feature editor of the 'German Newspaper,' showed her the respective issue, and asked to speak to the author of the poem. Supposedly, it had found good reception. I was bringing him his royalty and some new orders.

She listened quietly to me, observed me carefully, then said:

"So, this gentleman had a poem printed in your publication? How nice! It's too bad that I don't understand German, or I would ask you to read it to me. Is it nice?"

"Excellent! It was already my honor to tell you that it found great appeal."

"That is of great interest to me. This gentleman gave the impression of a fine, educated man, a real gentleman. Unfortunately, he did not say much and did not socialize with anyone. He went outside only once, it must have been to deliver the poem to you."

14

"Really? From the brief conversation I had with him I thought he had drawn some money here in town. He must have left your establishment several times."

"Then this must have been during my absence; maybe his secretary took care of these business activities."

"Oh, he had a secretary? He didn't mention him. He must therefor be a very well-off gentleman."

"Certainly! He paid well and ate only the best. His secretary, Mister Clinton, took care of money matters."

"Clinton! Ah, if this secretary's name is Clinton, I must have met him at the Club. He's from New York and is excellent company. We met yesterday at noon . . ."

"That is correct," she interrupted. "That's when he went out."

". . . and liked each other so much," I continued, "that he gave me a photo of himself. I did not carry one of myself, which is why I promised him one and to meet him today. Here's his photo." I now showed her Gibson's photo which I carried on me.

"Right, that's the secretary," she said after she looked at it. "Unfortunately, you will not be able to see him, and you won't receive another poem from Mister Ohlert. They both left."

I was shocked, but quickly caught myself to say:

"I'm very sorry to hear this. The idea to leave must have occurred suddenly to them?"

"Indeed. It's a very touching story. Of course, Mister Ohlert did not talk about it, but his secretary told me of the reason in the strictest confidence. You must know that I enjoy the special trust of those folks lodging with me for some time."

"I'm certain of it. Your gracious behavior and fine manners make this obvious," I exaggerated unabashedly.

"Oh, please!" she responded, flattered despite my awkward flattery. "The story almost moved me to tears, and I'm glad the unhappy young man succeeded in escaping at the right time."

"Escape? That sounds as if he's being pursued!"

"That is truly the case."

"Ah! How interesting! Such a talented, even brilliant poet, and being pursued! In my capacity as editor, in a sense a colleague of the unfortunate man, I'm burning with desire to hear more. Newspapers have substantial power. I may be able to support his position with an article. How unfortunate that this story was entrusted to you in strictest confidence!"

She blushed and pulled out a not quite clean handkerchief to have it handy if needed, and said:

"This discretion, sir, I no longer feel obligated to maintain, since the gentlemen have left. I am aware that the newspaper business is a major force and would be happy, if you could assist the poor poet with his rights."

"Whatever is in my power, I'll gladly do, but I should know at least something about his situation," making an effort to hide my excitement.

"You shall get to know it, for my heart commands me to tell you everything. It is about a faithful, but just as unhappy love."

"I thought so. An unhappy love is the greatest, heart-rending and overpowering suffering I know of."

Of course, at the time, I did not have the faintest idea of love.

"How simpatico you are, saying this, sir! Have you already experienced this pain?"

"Not yet."

"Then you are a fortunate man. I tasted it almost to my death. My mother was a mulatto. I became engaged to the son of a French planter, a Creole. Our happiness was destroyed, because the groom's father would not accept a colored lady into his family. How much I therefore sympathize with the pitiable poet, because he's so unhappy for the same reason!"

"Then he loves a colored woman?"

"Yes, a mulatto. His father forbade this love, and cleverly obtained a written resignation of the lady with which she abstained from a happy union with William Ohlert."

"What a cruel father!" I exclaimed with apparent fury, which gained me a kindly look from the lady.

The good lady had taken mightily to heart whatever Gibson had told her. One could assume that the talkative lady had told him of her once unhappy love, enabling him to come up with a fable that aroused her sympathy and explained his sudden departure. The information that he now called himself Clinton was, of course, of great importance to me.

"Yes, a truly cruel father!" she agreed.

"But William remained faithful and fled here with her. He, somewhere, put her up at a boarding house."

"But that still doesn't explain why he left New Orleans."

"Because his pursuer arrived."

"The father has him pursued?"

"Yes, by a German. Oh, those Germans! I hate them. They are called a people of thinkers, but they don't know how to love. This miserable German chased them from city to city all the way here with the resignation in hand. (I had to laugh inside about the lady's indignation for a gentleman she was presently happily engaged in conversation with.) He is a policeman and empowered to apprehend William and return him to New York."

16

"Did the secretary describe this terrible fellow?" I asked, curious of further information about myself.

"Exactly, since it must be assumed that this barbarian will discover William's residence and will come here. But I shall give him quite a reception! I've considered already every word I'm going to tell him. He is not going to learn of William's destination. I shall send him in the opposite direction."

She now described this 'barbarian', even gave his name – which was mine, and the description was very good, although it was presented in a rather unflattering way.

"I expect him to show up any minute," she continued. When you were announced, I thought it already to be him. But, fortunately, I was mistaken. You are not a persecutor of the lovers, a robber of sweetest fortune, an abyss of injustice and betrayal. One can see from your guileless eyes that you will publish an article in your newspaper that will crush the German and protect the party he's hunting."

"If I am to do this, which I will be happy to do, then it is however necessary for me to learn where William Ohlert is now. I must write to him. I hope you know his current address?"

"Of course, I know where he traveled to, but I cannot say whether he'd still be there, when your letter arrives. I would have sent this German to the northwest. But you, I will tell that he traveled west, to Texas. He intended to go to Mexico and land in Veracruz. But there was no ship that would weigh anchor right away. Danger forced him to hurry, which is why he took the 'Dolphin', headed for Quintana."

"Do you know this for sure?"

"Absolutely. He had to hurry. There was just enough time to get the luggage on board. My doorman took care of this and went on board with them. He spoke with some of the sailors and learned that the 'Dolphin' is going to Quintana, but before that will land at Galveston. Mister Ohlert truly left with this steamer; my doorman waited until the ship left."

"And his secretary and the miss joined him?"

"Of course. However, my man did not see the lady, since she had retired to the lady's cabin. He didn't ask for her anyway, since my employees are used to being discreet and considerate. But isn't it obvious that William wouldn't leave his fiancée back here and expose her to the danger of getting caught by this terrible German fellow. I'm actually looking forward to his arrival. It's going to make for a very interesting scene. First, I will try to touch his heart, and then, if I don't succeed, I shall throw some ugly words to his face and speak to him in a way that he will literally double up from my contempt."

The good woman was now truly excited, having taken the situation very much to heart. By now she had risen from her armchair, balled her small, fleshy fists towards the door and exclaimed threateningly:

17

"Yes, come, just come, you diabolical Dutchman! My looks shall pierce you and my words crush you!"

I had heard enough now and could leave. Someone else would have done that and simply left the lady with her misunderstanding. But I thought it my duty to explain the situation to her; she shouldn't take a scoundrel like Gibson for an honest person. Not that I would gain any advantage from it. Once more, the greenhorn showed itself, when I tried to tell myself that I was morally obligated to open the lady's eyes. The real reason to reveal myself was, that I wanted the pleasure of departing with a theatric effect. This is why I asked her:

"I don't think you will get the opportunity to throw your looks and crushing words at him."

"Why not?"

"Because he will approach the situation totally differently than you think. You'll also not succeed in sending him to the northwest, but he will head directly for Quintana, in order to capture William and his so-called secretary."

"But he doesn't know where they are!"

"Oh yes, you yourself told him."

"I? Impossible! I would know that! When should that have happened?"

"Just now."

"Sir, I do not understand!" the lady exclaimed much surprised.

"I shall help you understand. Permit me to make a small change in my appearance."

With these words I removed my dark wig, the full beard and my glasses. The lady took a frightened step back.

"In God's name!" she exclaimed. "You aren't an editor, but this German! You deceived me!"

"I had to do this, since you were previously misled. The story with the mulatto lady this Mr. Clinton told you about was a lie from the beginning to the end. They made fun of you and misused your good heart. Clinton is not a secretary of William's. His real name is Gibson and he is a most dangerous swindler, who I intend to render harmless."

As if fainting, she sank back to her armchair and exclaimed:

"No, no! That's impossible! This dear, friendly, handsome man cannot be a swindler. I don't believe you."

"You will believe me once you have heard what I have to say. Let me tell you!"

I informed her about the true state of affairs with the result, that her previous sympathy for the dear, friendly, handsome secretary turned into passionate anger. She realized that she had been disgracefully lied to, and finally even acknowledged her acceptance of me having approached her in disguise.

"Had you not done so," she said, "you would not have learned the truth from me and would have followed my information to travel north to Nebraska or

Dakota. The behavior of this Gibson/Clinton calls for the most serious punishment. I hope that you will leave immediately for your pursuit, and I ask you to write to me from Quintana, whether you succeeded in apprehending him. On his transport to New York you must bring him here so that I can tell him how much I despise him."

"That will likely be impossible. It isn't easy to apprehend a man in Texas and to bring him to New York. I would be greatly satisfied if I could free William Ohlert from the clutches of his seducer, and to retrieve at least part of the money the two have drawn in the course of their escape. But last-not-least, I would be mightily pleased to hear from you that you will no longer think Germans to be barbarians, who don't know how to love. It hurt me to see my fellow-countrymen so misjudged, especially by you."

She apologized and assured me that she felt converted from her misjudgment. We parted most cordially and when I slowly walked down the stairs, I had the pleasant feeling of having done a brilliant job, unlikely to find its equal in the annals of my boss, mister Josy Taylor.

That is why I may have sounded somewhat superior when I told the two waiting policemen that the issue had been taken care of. I gave them a tip and, in a very upright posture, walked away. There is nothing exceeding the pleasant image of being a man others cannot compare themselves with!

Of course, I had to get to Quintana as quickly as possible, which made finding a ship going there my first task. I wasn't in luck. There was a steamer going to Tampico, but it would not stop anywhere in between. Other ships would have taken me to Quintana, but were scheduled to leave only in several days. At last, I found a fast-sailing clipper ship with cargo for Galveston leaving this afternoon. I could take it. In Galveston I hoped to catch a fast connection to Quintana. I speedily closed my affairs and went on board.

Unfortunately, my hope of finding a ship in Galveston going to Quintana did not materialize. There was an opportunity that would take me past my desired destination to Matagorda, at the outlet of the eastern Colorado River. I was assured that from there I would find it easy to backtrack to Quintana. This caused me to use this transportation and I did not have reason to regret what followed.

Karl May – translated by Herbert Windolf

2. On the Colorado

This is how matters stood when we approached the long, flat spit separating Matagorda Bay from the Mexican Gulf. We entered through Paso Caballo, but had to drop anchor quickly, since the bay was so shallow that ships with a deeper draft would run the danger of running aground.

Behind the spit smaller vessels lay at anchor, while in front several larger ships, a three-master and a steamer, were anchored. Of course, I had myself rowed right away to Matagorda to inquire whether an early connection to Quintana was available, but, unfortunately, was told that a schooner would leave there only several days from now. This meant that I was stuck and it angered me, since Gibson now gained a head start of four days, which he could use to disappear without a trace. I only had the single comfort of knowing that I had tried everything, considering the existing possibilities.

Since there was nothing else but to wait patiently, I looked up a guest house and had my luggage delivered there.

At the time, Matagorda was a smaller place than it is today. It is located at the northern end of the bay and, as a port, is of lesser importance than, for instance, Galveston. As everywhere in Texas, the coast here consists of unhealthy lowlands, which, although it cannot be called swampy, is nevertheless rather watery. One can easily catch the fever here, which I did not care to at all, during my long wait.

My 'hotel' resembled a German one of third or forth class, my room that of a ship's cabin, and the bed was so short that either my head hung out at the top or my feet at the bottom.

Once I had stowed my belongings, I went outside for a look at the town. Stepping from my room to get to the stairs, I passed the open door of another room. Giving it a look I noticed that it was furnished just like mine. There was a saddle resting against a wall, above which hung the bridle gear. In a corner, not far from the window, leaned a long Kentucky rifle. Automatically, I thought of Old Death, but these items could easily belong to someone else.

After I stepped outside, I ambled down the lane. Just when I wanted to turn around a corner, a man, who had not seen me, bumped into me coming from the other side.

"Thunder and lightning!" he hollered at me. "Why don't you pay attention before storming around corners!"

"If you think my snail's pace to be storming, then an oyster must be a Mississippi steamer," I replied with a laugh.

The other backed up a pace, looked at me, and exclaimed:

"If it isn't that German greenfinch who didn't want to admit to being a detective! What are you doing here in Texas, even in Matagorda, sir?"

"Not looking for you, Mister Death!"

"I believe you! You seem to be one of these folks who never find what they are looking for and, in its place, run into the people they have no business with. In any case, you must be hungry and thirsty. Come, let's throw anchor where we can find some good beer. Your German Lager seems to be spreading everywhere. It can even be found in this miserable one-horse town, and I figure that this beer is the best to come from your country. Have you found a room yet?"

"Yes, down at 'Uncle Sam's.'"

"Nice. That's where I've set up my wigwam."

"By chance in the room upstairs, where I saw some riding gear and a rifle?"

"Yes. You must know, I like to hold onto this stuff. Come to cherish it. One can get a horse anywhere, but not a good saddle. But let's go, sir! I've just been in a joint where they serve some cool beer, a real delight on a June day like this. I'm ready to have another, or even several."

He took me to a small pub, where bottled beer at a rather high price was being served. We were the only patrons. I offered him a cigar, which he refused. Instead, he pulled some chewing tobacco from a pocket and cut himself a slug, large enough to satisfy five able-bodied seamen. He put it in his mouth, stowed it lovingly in one of his cheeks, then said:

"So, now I'm at your service. I'm curious to learn what kind of wind blew you so rapidly after me. Was it a favorable one?"

"On the contrary, it was a very adverse one."

"Then you didn't want to get here at all?"

"No, rather to Quintana. But since there was no fast connection, I came here after I was told that I would easily find a ship going from here to Quintana. But now I must wait for two days."

"Have patience, mister, and find comfort by the sweet conviction that you simply are an unlucky chap!"

"Nice consolation! You think I should send you a letter of appreciation for it?"

"Please," Old Death laughed. "I always give my advice at no cost. But then, I'm in the same pickle you are in. I also sit here uselessly, because I was too slow. I wanted to head up to Austin and on from there, a bit across the Río Grande del Norte. It's a good time of the year. It rained, so the local Colorado carries enough water to take shallow-draft steamers to Austin. For most of the year the river carries too little water."

"I understand a sandbar prevents ships from going upstream."

"No, it's not a sandbar but a mighty jumble of driftwood that's been washed up. About eight miles from here it splits the river into several arms. Behind the barrier there's clear water to Austin and farther upstream. Since travel is interrupted by the barrier, one will do well to get from here to behind the barrier, and then board a ship there. That had been my plan, but your German Lager did me in. I drank and drank, hung around for too long in Matagorda, and when I arrived at the barrier, the steamer had just blown its whistle. I had to carry my saddle back, and now must wait until tomorrow morning when the next boat leaves."

"Then we are brothers in misery, and you can extend to yourself the same consolation you earlier gave me. You are just as much an out-of-luck fellow as me."

"No, I'm not. I don't pursue anyone, and whether I arrive in Austin today or a week from now, won't matter. But it's nevertheless annoying, especially with this stupid tree frog ridiculing me. He had been faster then I and whistled at me, when I stood there with my saddle by the riverbank. Should I meet this fellow again, he'll get a bigger slap on his ears than the one he got on board the steamer we arrived in."

"You were in a brawl, sir?"

"A brawl? What do you mean, sir? Old Death never gets into a scrap. But there was this fellow who kidded about my figure and laughed whenever he saw me. When I asked him what he found so funny, and he replied that my skeleton cheered him so much, I gave him a slap in the face that made him sit down. After that he wanted to go after me with his revolver, but the cap'n walked up and told him to get lost, telling him that he deserved the slap for having insulted me. That is why the joker ridiculed me, when I arrived too late. It's a pity for the companion who's traveling with him! He seemed to be a veritable gentleman, only that he was always sad and gloomy and kept staring ahead as if mentally disturbed."

His last words really caught my attention.

"He was mentally disturbed?" I asked. "Might you have heard his name?"

"He was called Mister Ohlert by the cap'n."

Now it was as if I had received a slap in my face. I hastily kept asking:

"Ah! And his companion?"

"His name was Clinton, if I recall correctly."

"Is it possible; is it really possible?" I shouted, jumping off my chair. "These two traveled on the same ship with you?"

He looked at me in surprise and asked:

"Are you having a rapture, sir? You are going up like a rocket! Are these two men a concern of yours?"

"Much, very much so. They are the ones I'm trying to locate!"

Again, the friendly grin crossed his face, which I had seen repeatedly on him.

"All right!" he nodded. "You are finally admitting that you are looking for two men? And precisely these two? Hmm! You truly are a greenhorn, sir! You caused it yourself to miss this nice catch!"

"How so?"

"Because you weren't frank with me in New Orleans."

"But I couldn't," I replied sheepishly.

"A man can do everything that takes him to his desired goal. Had you disclosed your situation, the two would now be in your hands. I would have recognized them the moment they came on board the steamer, and would have fetched you or had someone get you. Don't you realize this?"

"But who could have known that you would meet them on board! By the way, they didn't want to go to Matagorda but to Quintana."

"They only said so. When we stopped there, they didn't even get off board. If you are smart, you'll tell me your story. Maybe I'll be able to help you in catching the fellows."

The man truly meant well. He wouldn't dream of hurting my feelings, and yet I felt embarrassed. Yesterday, I had refused him information, but today I was forced by circumstances to reveal it to him. Reason kept the upper hand. I pulled out the two photographs, handed them to him, and said:

"Before I give you the information, have a look at these two pictures. Are these the men you are referring to?"

"Yes, yes, they are," he nodded, after he had given them a look. "There's no mistake."

Now, I candidly explained the circumstances to him. He listened carefully, then, when I was finished, shook his head and said pensively:

"What you told me there is all very clear. There's only one thing that doesn't make sense to me. Is this William Ohlert truly insane?"

"No. Although I'm not familiar with mental disease, I'd rather speak of monomania in his case, since he is, aside from this one point, totally master of his mental faculties."

"What's more incomprehensible to me is that he allows this Gibson such unlimited influence. He seems to follow and obey this character in everything. At any rate, Gibson deals smartly with the patient's monomania and makes use of it for his purposes. Well, let's hope we'll learn all of his tricks."

"Then you are sure they are on their way to Austin? Or might they plan to get off board before?"

"No, Ohlert told the cap'n that he wants to go to Austin."

"I'm surprised he would reveal where he intends to go."

"Why not? Ohlert may not even know that he's pursued, that he's on a wrong track. He's likely of the opinion that he needs to act properly and to live only for his idea, while everything else is Gibson's affair. The lunatic didn't think it unwise to give Austin as his destination, as the cap'n told me. What do you intend to do?"

"I must go after him, of course, and that as fast as possible."

"Despite your impatience you'll need to wait until tomorrow; no ship leaves earlier."

"And when would we arrive?"

"Considering the present water level, only the day after tomorrow."

"What a long, long time!"

"Just think that the two will also be delayed by the low water level. It's unavoidable for the ship to run aground from time to time, which always takes a while to come free again."

"If we only knew what Gibson is actually planning and where he wants to take Ohlert?"

"Yes, that is obviously a riddle. He must have some kind of plan. The moneys drawn so far make him a rich man. He only needs to pocket them and simply abandon Ohlert. That he's not doing this, is a sure sign that he's intent on exploiting him further. I'm greatly interested in this matter and since we, at least for some time, travel in the same direction, I'm at your service. If you can use me, I'm yours."

I now accepted the help of Old Death, which I had spurned a few days earlier.

"I accept your offer with thanks, sir. You instill sincere trust and I appreciate your goodwill. You called me a greenhorn, which angered me, but I subsequently realized that you weren't far off the mark, which is why your help will be of a great advantage to me."

We shook hands and emptied our glasses. Had I only trusted this man earlier!

Just when we refilled our glasses, a big ruckus erupted outside. Bawling human voices and the bark of dogs came closer. The door to the pub was torn open and six men, who seemed to have already consumed a good quantity of alcohol entered, with none of them sober any more. Their coarse faces and figures, their light southern outfits and excellent weapons were conspicuous. Each of them was equipped with a rifle, knife, revolver or pistol, and all of them had a heavy 'nigger' whip hanging from their belts. In addition, each led a dog on a strong leash. These dogs were of great size and of the breed used in the South for catching escaped Negroes. They are called bloodhounds or 'people catchers'.

Without a greeting, these rogues stared at us insolently, threw themselves onto chairs that they croaked, put their feet on the tables, and banged with their heels in a most courteous request for service by the innkeeper.

"Man, do you have beer?" one of them hollered. "German beer?"

The frightened innkeeper confirmed it.

"That's what we want. But are you German yourself?"

"No."

"You are lucky. We want to drink the Germans' beer, but they themselves should fry in hell, these abolitionists, who helped the North and are to blame that we lost our jobs!"

The innkeeper quickly withdrew to serve his guests as fast as possible. I had involuntarily turned around to look at the speaker. He noticed it. I am convinced that my expression did not show anything to insult him, but he simply did not care to have himself looked at. Maybe he had a desire to brawl, and screamed:

"Why are you staring at me! Didn't I speak the truth?"

I turned around without answering.

"Watch out!" Old Death whispered to me. "These are rowdies of the worst kind. In any case, they are fired slave guards whose masters were driven to bankruptcy by the repeal of slavery. They've gathered to cause some trouble. It's better we don't pay any attention to them. Let's drink up and leave."

But the whispers did not please this man. He screamed at us:

"What secrets have you got to talk about, you old skeleton? If you talk about us, then do it openly, or we'll open your mouth!"

Old Death put his glass to his mouth and drank, but said nothing. The fellows received their beer and tried it. The brew was truly good, however these guests were in a real rowdyish mood and some poured it on the floor. The man who had spoken earlier, still holding his full glass, exclaimed:

"Not on the floor! Over there sit two, who seem to like the stuff. Let them have it."

He reached out and dumped his beer from across onto the two of us. Old Death calmly wiped his sleeve across his wet face, but I was unable to stomach this miserable insult as calmly as he had. My hat, my collar, my coat, everything was dripping, since most of the glasses' content had hit me. I turned around and said:

"Sir, I'm asking you not to do this a second time! We don't mind if you fool around with your companions, but leave us in peace."

"So! What would you do, if I would enjoy dumping some more on you?"

"We would see."

"See? Well, that means we must see right away what that means. Innkeeper, fill the glasses again!"

The others laughed and hollered applause to their leader. It was obvious that he would repeat his impertinence.

"In God's name, sir, don't fight with these characters!" Old Death warned.

"Are you afraid?" I asked haughtily.

"Not at all! But these men are quick with their weapons, and against a malicious bullet even the most courageous man is helpless. Bear in mind also that they have dogs!"

The rogues had their dogs tied to table legs. So that I would not be hit again from behind, I left my seat and took a chair turning my right side to the rowdies.

"Ah! He's getting ready!" their speaker laughed. "He's planning to defend himself, but the moment he makes a move, I'll sick Tiger on him. He's trained to get people."

He untied the dog, but kept it on its leash next to him. The innkeeper had not brought the beer yet, and there was still time for us to put some money on the table and leave. But I did not think that the gang would allow us to do this. Furthermore, it went against my grain to flee from these contemptible people, knowing that such braggarts are basically cowards.

I reached into my pocket and cocked my revolver. In wrestling I could hold my own; I knew that. But I doubted whether I would be able to take care of the dogs. However, I had dealt with animals trained on people, and did not need to be afraid, at least of a single attacker.

Now, the innkeeper came. He put the glasses on the fellows' table and asked his quarrelsome guests in an almost begging voice:

"Gentlemen, I truly appreciate your patronage, but ask to leave these two men in peace. They are also my guests."

"You scoundrel!" one of them yelled. "You want to give us advice? Just wait and we'll cool your zeal." With that the content of three glasses was poured over the poor chap, who thought it wise to quickly leave the room.

"And now to the big mouth over there!" my adversary shouted. "He's going to get it!"

Holding the dog with his left hand, he tossed the content of his glass, the only full one left, with his right hand at me. I shot up from my chair and to the side, so that I wouldn't be hit. I raised my fist, ready to leap at him and put him in his place, but he beat me to it.

"Tiger, sic'm!" he shouted, while he let go of the dog, pointing at me.

I had just enough time to step to a wall, when the mighty animal took a truly tiger-like leap at me. The dog had stood about five paces away, but crossed this space in a single leap. If I stayed put, he was sure to get me by my throat. But just when he intended to bite, I stepped aside, causing his muzzle to hit the wall. The leap had been so forceful that the bloodhound was nearly stunned by the impact. He collapsed to the floor. Lightning-fast, I grabbed him by his hind legs, swung the body and slammed it with the head against the wall so hard that the skull cracked.

Now, a wild ruckus ensued. The dogs howled and pulled the tables from their positions. The men cursed and the dead dog's owner made ready to throw himself on me. But by then Old Death had risen and shouted to the gang, pointing his two revolvers at them:

"Stop! That's enough now, boys. One more step or trying to reach for a weapon, and I'll shoot. You mistook us by a bit. I am Old Death, the Scout. I hope you've heard of me. And this young sir, my friend, is just as little afraid of you as I am. Sit down, and drink your beer in peace! And not a hand goes to your belts, or by my soul, I'm going to shoot!"

This last warning had been directed at one of the slave guards, whose hand had crept to his belt, likely to reach for his revolver. I, too, had pulled mine. Together we had eighteen shots. Before any of the fellows would get to his weapon, he would be hit by our bullets. The old scout seemed to have totally changed. His usually bent posture was now tall and erect, his eyes shone, and his face displayed such superior energy that it would not permit any resistance. It was funny to observe how meek the previously impudent fellows had become. Although they mumbled a few comments, they sat down, and even the dead dog's master did not dare step towards the animal, since that would have taken him right close to me.

We were both still standing, our revolvers threatening in our hands, when another guest entered – an Indian.

There are people who, right on first sight, before they have even spoken a word, make a profound, indelible impression. Without such a person acting friendly or hostile, one clearly feels whether one will hate or love them. This Indian was one of those.

He wore a white-tanned hunting shirt, decorated with red Indian embroidery. His leggings were of the same material and their seams were trimmed with thick tassels of scalp hair. There wasn't the least spot on his shirt or pants. His small feet were shod in pearl-embroidered moccasins, decorated with porcupine quills. Around his neck he wore a medicine bag, an artfully carved peace pipe and a threefold necklace of the claws of the gray bear, which he must have taken from this most-feared carnivore of the Rockies under great threat to his life. A broad belt, consisting of a precious Saltillo blanket, was slung around his waist. From it peered the handles of a knife and two revolvers. In his right hand he carried a double-barreled rifle whose stock was densely studded with silver nails. His head was bare. His long, dense, blue-black hair was tied to a high, helm-like bun, woven together by rattlesnake skin. No eagle feather and no other distinguishing mark decorated this hairdo, and yet, upon first sight, one could tell that this still young man had to be a chief, a famous warrior. The cut of his serious, manly face could be called Roman, his cheekbones protruded only imperceptibly; the lips of the totally beardless face were full but delicate, and his complexion was of a faint light brown with a touch of bronze.

He stopped for a moment at the entrance. A sharp, questioning look from his dark eyes covered the room. His eyes contracted a little in disdain, when he gave our adversaries a second glance. As we sat down again, putting the revolvers away, an almost unnoticeable, and as it seemed, well-meaning smile crossed his lips.

The effect of his personality was so great that a church-like silence ensued upon his entry. This silence seemed to convince the innkeeper that danger had passed. He stuck his head from the half-open door, and when he saw that he no longer needed to fear anything, stepped fully out.

"May I ask for a glass of beer, German beer?" the Indian said with a well-sounding, sonorous voice and in the most beautiful English.

This seemed to be as strange to the rowdies as it was to me. They put their heads together and began to whisper. The covert looks they gave the Indian let one guess that they were not saying anything positive about him.

He received his beer, lifted the glass against the light coming from the window, checked it with the contented look of a connoisseur, and drank.

"Well!" he said to the innkeeper while he smacked his tongue. "Your beer is good. The Great Manitou of the white men has taught them many arts, with beer brewing being not the least of them."

He spoke so fluently and with such good pronunciation that I turned to Old Death, saying softly:

"Should one believe this man to be an Indian?"

"He is, and what a one!" the oldster replied just as softly, but emphatically.

"Do you know him? Did you meet him before or have you seen him?"

"I've never seen him, but recognize him from his figure, his outfit, his age, but mostly by his rifle. It is the famous Silver Rifle, whose bullets never miss. You are fortunate enough to be seeing the most famous Indian chief in all of North America, Winnetou, the Chief of the Apache. He's the most distinguished of all Indians. His name is known in palaces, in every log cabin and at every camp fire. He's smart, honest, faithful, proud and courageous to the point of being reckless, a master in the use of all kinds of weapons; he's without guile, a friend and protector of all those in need, whether red or white, and he is known across the entire length and width of the United States and far beyond her borders as the most upright and famous hero of the far West."

"But how did he pick up his excellent English and the manners of a white gentleman?"

"He frequently travels to the East, and it is told that a European scholar, captured by the Apache, was treated so well that he decided to stay with them, took a daughter of the tribe for his wife and tried to teach peace to these Indians. He was Winnetou's teacher, but it doesn't look like as if his philanthropic views penetrated the Apaches' mindset and, eventually, he may have gone to seed."

This had been spoken very, very softly, so that I had barely understood it. Nevertheless, the Indian, who was sitting more than fifteen feet distant, turned to my new friend to say:

"Old Death is mistaken. The white scholar came to the Indians and was kindly accepted. He loved the sister of Winnetou's father, she who was called the Dove of the West and took her for his wife. He became the teacher of her nephew, Winnetou, and instructed him how to be good and to differentiate between sin and justice, between truth and lies. He did not go to seed, but was most honored and never desired to return to the white men. When he died, a tombstone was erected for him more magnificent than for any chief before, and it was planted with live oak and snow-white blooming magnolias. He went to the eternally green savanna country, where the blessed do not tear each other to pieces but drink happy delight from Manitou's face. There, Winnetou will meet him again to forget all hate he sees here on Earth."

What a sharp ear this man must have! Now I believed what I had previously doubted, that an Indian, hidden in the grass, would be able to hear an ant climbing a blade of grass.

Old Death found no time for surprise; he was enormously happy that he had been recognized by this man. He beamed with pleasure, when he asked:

"What, sir, you know me? Really?"

"I have not previously seen you, but recognized you the moment I entered. You are a scout, whose name carries all the way to the Las Animas River."

This said, he turned away. During his speech, not a feature of his face had moved; now he sat there silently and as if totally self-absorbed, only his earlobes twitched at times as if they busied themselves with something going on around him.

All the while the rowdies kept talking among themselves, looked at each other questioningly, nodded to each other, and at last appeared to have arrived at a decision. They did not know the Indian, had also not concluded from his speech who he was, and now probably wanted to compensate for their defeat by us by letting him feel their contempt for a red-skinned man. They might have been of the opinion that neither Old Death nor I would come to the aid of the red man, for, since we would not be insulted, then, according to common rule, we had to stay out of it and simply observe how a harmless man was mistreated. Thus, one of them got up, the same who had earlier tangled with me, and walked slowly and challengingly towards the Indian.

I quickly decided to support the Indian, should it become necessary, and pulled my revolver from my pocket, putting it before me on the table so that I could comfortably reach it.

"That's not necessary," Old Death whispered to me. "A man like Winnetou can take care of twice as many of this kind of boys."

The rowdy planted himself bumptiously before the Apache, pressed his hands to his hips, and said:

"What's your business here in Matagorda, redskin? We don't tolerate savages as company."

Winnetou did not acknowledge the man with even a look, brought his glass to his mouth, took a sip, then put it back on the table, smacking his tongue.

"Didn't you hear what I said, you cursed redskin?" the rowdy asked. "I want to know what you are doing here. You are hanging around to spy on us. The redskins support the scoundrel Juarez, whose hide is also red. But we are on the side of Emperor Max and shall string up every Indian we come across. If you do not right away join in the shout: "Long live Emperor Max," we'll put a rope around your neck!"

Again, the Apache did not respond. Not a feature of his face moved.

"Dog, don't you understand me. I want an answer!" the rowdy screamed openly angry now, while he put his fist on the Apache's shoulder.

Upon this touch the lithe figure of the Indian rose lightning-fast.

"Back!" he said commandingly. "I do not allow a coyote to howl at me."

Coyote, as the cowardly prairie wolf is called, is generally seen as being a contemptuous animal. Indians use this swear word when they want to express great contempt for someone.

"A coyote?" the rowdy exclaimed. "That's an insult calling for blood!"

He pulled his revolver. But now something happened that neither he nor I had expected. The Apache slapped the weapon from his hand, grabbed him by his hips, lifted him up and tossed him through the window which, of course, broke into shards flying outside together with the man.

This had happened much faster than can be told. The shattering of the window, the howl of the dogs, the angry uproar of the man's companions, all this caused such a dreadful racket, which was however drowned by Winnetou's voice. He walked over to the fellows, pointed with his hand to the window, and said:

"Does anyone else want to go through there? Let him say so!"

He had come too close to one of the dogs, which snapped at him, but received such a kick from the Apache that it crept whimpering under a table. The slave guards stepped timidly back and remained silent. Winnetou did not hold any weapon in his hand; his personality alone was what impressed all. None of the attackers said anything. The Indian resembled an animal trainer when entering a cage who controls the cats' wildness with his eyes.

Then the door opened and the thrown-out man came in again, his face slightly injured by glass shards. He had pulled his knife and with an angry shout leaped at Winnetou, who only made a slight sideways turn, then quickly grabbed the knife-wielding hand. Just like before, he lifted the man up by his hips, then slammed him onto the floor, where he remained lying unconscious. None of his companions made an attempt to lay hands on the victor, who, quietly, as if nothing had happened, reached for his beer and finished it. Then he waved to the innkeeper, who had fearfully retreated to the next room from where he had peered, to come and took a leather bag from his belt and put a small yellow object into his hand, saying:

"Take this for the beer and the window, mister landlord! You can see that the savage has paid his dues. I hope you will also get payment from those civilized folks over there. They do not tolerate a redskin with them. But Winnetou, the Chief of the Apache, does not leave because he is afraid of them, but because he recognizes that only the skin, but not the soul of these palefaces is of light color. He is not pleased being in their company."

He left the pub after picking up his Silver Rifle, without deigning to give a look to anyone else.

Now, life returned to the rowdies, but their curiosity seemed to be greater than their anger, their humiliation and concern for their unconscious companion. First of all, they asked the innkeeper what he had received.

"A nugget," the man replied, showing them the hazelnut-size piece of solid gold. "This nugget is worth at least twelve dollars. That pays well for the window, which was old and decrepit and had several cracks. His bag seemed to be full of more."

Now the rowdies expressed their displeasure that a redskin possessed such a store of gold. The nugget went from hand to hand to guess its worth. We used the opportunity to pay for our beer and leave.

"Well, what do you say of the Apache, mister?" Old Death asked me, when we were happily out on the street. "Can there be another Indian like him?"

"Hardly. Of course, I imagined the famous Apache quite differently."

"I believe you. But don't forget that he's the only one of his kind, an exception searching in vain for its like. These rogues retreated from him like sparrows from the sight of a falcon. It's too bad we don't see him any more. We could have followed him a bit. I'd love to know very much what he's doing here, whether he's camping outside of town or stays at a lodging place. He must have stabled his horse somewhere, for no Apache is ever without a mount, and neither is Winnetou. By the way, sir, you didn't do badly yourself. I almost became concerned, since it's always dangerous to tangle with such characters. But the courageous and agile way in which you handled that beastly dog, lets me guess that you won't remain a greenhorn for long. But we've arrived at our guest house. Shall we go in? I don't care to. An old trapper like myself doesn't like to confine himself between walls; I prefer free sky above myself. Let's walk a bit through this beautiful Matagorda. I wouldn't know how to kill time otherwise. Or would you prefer a game?"

"No. I'm no gamester and don't intend to become one."

"Right on, young man! But here, almost everyone gambles, and when you enter Mexico it gets worse. There, men and women, and cats and mice play, and knives sit quite loose. So let's enjoy a walk! Then we'll eat and hit the sack early. In this blessed land one never knows whether, how, or where one will find rest the next evening."

"It can't be that bad!"

"Don't forget, sir, that, so far, you've been only in the eastern States. But now, we're in Texas, which must be included with the West, and whose conditions are by far not ordered yet. We, for instance, intend to go to Austin. But it is questionable whether we'll get there. Events in Mexico have made waves across the Río Grande. Many a thing happens now, which, otherwise, wouldn't. Then, we must remember this Gibson's ideas. If it occurs to him to get off the ship somewhere, we'll need to do the same."

"But how will we learn, whether he disembarked somewhere?"

"By inquiring. The steamer takes its good time on the Colorado. No one hurries here as they do on the Mississippi and other places. We have at least a quarter of an hour at every stop for making inquiries. We must also brace ourselves to go on land where there's neither a town nor a hotel, where we can find sustenance."

"But what, in this case, is going to happen with my suitcase?"

He laughed out aloud, hearing my question.

"Suitcase, suitcase!" he exclaimed. "Taking a suitcase along; that's a pre-Deluge habit. What reasonable person lugs such a piece of luggage along? If I'd take along everything I need on my travels and wanderings, I'd never have made it very far. Take along that which you need for the moment and buy everything else when the time comes. What important things are you carrying in your old box?"

"Clothing, underwear, toiletry, and so on."

"These are all nice things one can get everywhere. And where they can't be had, there will be no need for them. One wears a shirt until it's no longer required, then buys a new one. Toiletry items? Don't take me wrong, sir, but hair and nail brushes, pomade, beard wax, and the like only defile a man. Clothing? That may have been of service where you've been, but not here any more. Here, you needn't hide behind a hairpiece. Such romantic nonsense won't take you to your goal. Here, it calls for a quick grab, as soon as you find Gibson. And . . ."

He stopped, looked me over, made a funny face, then continued:

"The way you stand before me, you could make your appearance in the rooms of a most demanding lady or on the *parquet* of some theater. Texas, however, does not in the least resemble a *boudoir* or a theater box. It could easily happen that your fine outfit will hang on you in tatters and your beautiful top hat look like an accordion. Do you have any idea where Gibson is going to turn? It can't be his intention to stay in Texas; he wants to disappear, which is why he must get the border of the United States behind him. Since he came here, that means, without doubt, that he is headed for Mexico. He can disappear in the chaos that's rampant in that country, and no one, not even police, will help you find him."

"You may be right. But my thought is, that if he truly wanted to go to Mexico, he would have gone directly to one of its harbors."

"Nonsense! He had to leave New Orleans so quickly that he had to take the next best ship leaving. Furthermore, the Mexican ports are in the hands of the French. He may not want to have anything to do with them. He has no choice, but must take the land route and is smart enough not to let himself be seen in larger towns. So it's possible that he's going to avoid Austin and disembark before. He'll head for the Río Grande on horseback, of course, which takes him through thinly settled country. Do you intend to follow him there with your suitcase, your top hat, and your elegant outfit? If that's what you want, I'll laugh at you."

33

Of course, I realized that he was correct. After I looked myself up and down and found it a bit pitiful, he once more erupted in a good laugh, slapped my shoulder, and said:

"Don't feel bad; simply part from this impractical outfit. See a trader here to sell all your useless odds and ends to and buy new clothing. You absolutely need a sturdy, lasting trapper outfit. I figure you were provided with sufficient money?"

I nodded.

"Well, then it's all right. So, get rid of the junk! I suppose you can ride and shoot?"

I emphatically confirmed this.

"You also need a horse; but don't buy one here on the coast where the animals are expensive and not worth much. In the country any farmer will sell you one, but not with a saddle. This you must purchase here."

"Oh my! Am I to run around like you with a saddle on my back?"

"Yes. Why not? Are you embarrassed in front of people? Whose business is it minding me carrying a saddle? Not anyone's! If I like, I'll carry even a sofa around so that, at times, I can rest comfortably on the prairie or in the forest. If anybody there laughs at me, I'll give him a punch in the nose so that he'll see plenty of stars twinkle before his eyes. The only time one ought to be ashamed is when one has committed some injustice or foolishness. Assuming Gibson disembarked with William at some place, bought horses and rode off, you'll see how advantageous it will be for you to have a saddle on hand. Do as you wish. But if you really want me to stay with you, then follow my advice. Decide quickly!"

Having said this, he did not wait for my decision, but took me by my arm, turned me around, and pointed to a house with a large store, where it said in yard-size letters 'Store for all Things', and, at the same time, pulled me towards its entrance. There, he gave me such a push that I shot into the store, banging against a herring barrel, and then followed me with a smile.

The store's name was no lie. It was very large and truly offered everything one would need here, even saddles and rifles.

The scene following was unique. I resembled a school boy standing with his father in front of a fairground stall, expressing my wishes only hesitantly, but, nevertheless, having to take that which the experienced father selects for him. Right at the beginning, Old Death stipulated to the store's owner that he would have to accept the entire content of my suitcase as part of my payment. The man was happy to oblige and immediately sent one of his helpers to fetch the suitcase. When it was delivered, the value of its contents was assessed, after which Old Death began to select for me. I received black leather pants, a red, woolen shirt, a like-colored vest with plenty of pockets, a black, woolen necktie, a rawhide deer leather hunting coat, a leather belt of two hand widths and hollow inside, a bullet bag, tobacco bladder, tobacco pipe, compass and twenty other necessary small items, foot rags instead of socks, a giant sombrero, a woolen blanket with a slit in the middle to put one's head through, a lasso, powder horn, lighter, Bowie knife, and a saddle with bridle and saddle bags. Then we went to the rifles. Old Death was no friend of newfangled things; he pushed everything that was of newer date aside, and picked an old rifle I wouldn't have paid attention to. After he had checked it with the expression of a connoisseur, he loaded it, stepped outside the store, and fired at the gable ornament of a right distant house. The bullet hit home.

"Well!" he nodded satisfied. "That will do. This gun's been in good hands, and I like it better than all the knickknacks called rifle these days. I figure this rifle's been made by a very knowledgeable gunsmith, and I hope you'll do it honor. Let's get now a bullet mold, then we're done. We'll also get lead here, then go home and cast us a supply of bullets, which should scare the devil out of those characters in Mexico."

After I had purchased a few more little things like handkerchiefs and so on, which Old Death, of course, thought totally superfluous, I stepped into a small adjoining room to change. When I returned, the oldster looked at me with satisfaction.

Silently, I had had the hope that he would carry the saddle; but no way he would think of doing it. He piled the stuff on me and pushed me out the store.

"So!" he grinned. "Now, you'll see whether you must really be ashamed! Every reasonable person will think you to be a sensible gentleman, and whatever the unreasonable world will say, matters the devil to you."

No longer did I now have an advantage over Old Death and had to carry my yoke patiently to our lodging place, while he walked proudly beside me. It obviously pleased him to see me being my own pack animal.

The next morning we rented two mules which we rode to the barrier where the steamer was waiting for passengers. The mules had been rigged with our saddles, which spared us from having to carry them.

The steamer was a shallow-draft boat, built the American way. A number of passengers were already on board. When we came across the gangway, carrying our saddles, a loud voice rose:

"By Jove! Here come a couple of two-legged saddled pack mules! Did you ever see something like that? Make room, men, so that they can get below deck! Such blasted animals mustn't stay with gentlemen!"

We knew this voice. The best places, covered by a glass roof, had been taken by the rowdies we had become acquainted with the day before. Yesterday's loudmouth, who seemed to be their leader, received us with this new insult. I now followed Old Death's lead. Since he let the words quietly slide off him, I did so too, as if I had not heard them. We took places opposite them and shoved the saddles under our seats.

The oldster made himself comfortable, took out his revolver, cocked it, and put it next to him. I followed his example, also putting my revolver beside me. The fellows stuck their heads together, hissed among themselves, but did not dare voice another insult. Of course, their dogs, minus one, were with them. However, the gang's speaker gave us hostile looks. He looked bad, no doubt as a result from his yesterday's flight through the window and the subsequent, not-very-soft treatment by Winnetou. His face showed the marks made by window shards.

When the conductor came asking how far we wanted to come along, Old Death specified Columbus, for which we paid. If required, we could continue passage from there. The old man was of the opinion that Gibson would not go all the way to Austin.

The bell had rung already twice, when one more passenger arrived – Winnetou. He rode an Indian-bridled, magnificent black stallion. Only when he was on board did he dismount and led his horse to the front of the deck, where there was a shoulder-high board shack for horses. Then he sat next to it on the railing, without seemingly paying attention to anyone. The rowdies kept their eyes on him. They loudly cleared their throats and coughed to cause him to look at them, but in vain. He sat, partly turned away, leaning on the Silver Rifle's muzzle, and did not seem to have an ear for them.

Now, the bell rung for the last time; a few more minutes of wait, in case more passengers might arrive, then the wheels started to turn and the ship began its journey, which looked as if it might pass peacefully. There was total silence on board all the way to Wharton, where a single man disembarked but, in his place, numerous other passengers came on board. Taking only a few minutes, Old Death went on land to the commissioner to inquire with him about Gibson, and learned that two men fitting his description had not disembarked here. Checking at Columbus brought the same result, which is why we paid for the next leg to La Grange. From Matagorda to Columbus the ship covered a distance of about fifty walking hours. It was therefore no longer early afternoon, when we arrived at Columbus. During this entire time Winnetou had left his place only a single time to water his horse and to feed it some corn.

It looked as if the rowdies had forgotten their anger against him and us. They had approached newly boarded passengers, but most had not wanted anything to do with them. Bragging about their anti-abolitionist viewpoint, they asked everyone for their own and cursed all not sharing their opinion. Expressions like 'damn Republicans,' 'Nigger uncle,' 'Yankee servant,' and worse flowed from their lips, which is why people withdrew, not wanting anything to do with them. This must have been also the reason why they refrained from tangling with us. If they had, they could not hope for others to support them. However, had there been more secessionists on board, surely peace on board would have been done for.

In Columbus many of the peaceful-minded people went off board with many others entering whose mindset appeared to be of the opposite position. Among them was a gang of maybe fifteen to twenty drunks, which gave us a bad feeling. The rowdies greeted them most joyously. Other new passengers joined them, and one could soon see that the unruly element now had the upper hand. The rogues sprawled on their seats without caring whether they became irksome to others, pushed each other back and forth through the quiet passengers, and did everything to demonstrate that they were the lords of the place. The captain let them make their noise, maybe thinking it the best not to take notice of them. For as long as they did not disturb control of the ship, he left it to the other travelers to protect themselves from infringements. His face did not have a single Yankee feature, his figure was stout, as one rarely sees in an American, and his red-cheeked face wore a continuous, good-natured smile, which, if I had wanted to bet, had to be of true Germanic origin.

Most of the secessionists had gone to the ship's restaurant, from where a terrible noise now sounded. Bottles were smashed, then a Negro came running out screaming, likely the waiter, and climbed up to the captain to wail to him his, to us, almost incomprehensible complaints. I only understood that he had been whipped and had been threatened to be hanged later from the smoke stack.

Now the captain's face became worried. He made sure that the ship was on the right course, then climbed from the bridge to go to the restaurant. That's when the conductor approached him. The two met close to us, and we were able to hear what they were talking about.

"Cap'n," the conductor reported, "we must no longer just watch. These people are planning worse. Let the Indian go on land over there! They want to hang him. Yesterday, he laid hands on one of them. Then there are two other Whites on board, I just don't know who they are, who are to be lynched, because they were also involved yesterday. Supposedly they are spies for Juarez."

"By the devil! That's getting serious. Who might the two be?" He looked searchingly across the deck.

"It's us, sir," I replied, while I got up and stepped up to them.

"You? Well, if you are a spy for Juarez, I'll eat my steamboat for breakfast!" he opined, while looking me up and down.

"It's not my idea at all! I am a German and don't get the least involved in your politics."

"A German? Then we are fellow-countrymen! The first running water I saw was at the Neckar River. I can't let anything happen to you. I'll land right away so that you can get to safety."

"I won't go along with that. I must get on with this ship and can't lose any time."

"Really? That's awkward. But wait!"

He walked over to Winnetou to tell him something. The Apache listened to what he had to say, then shook his head disdainfully and turned away. The captain returned, telling us annoyed:

"I thought so! These Reds have heads like iron. He, too, doesn't want to get on land here."

"Then he, together with these two gentlemen, is lost, for these fellows will get serious. And us few men of the steamer can't do anything against such superior strength."

The captain gazed ahead, pondering the situation. Then his good-natured face brightened happily when a good idea occurred to him, and he turned to us:

"I shall play a trick on these secessionists, they will remember for a long time. But you must follow my instructions exactly, especially by not using your weapons. Put your rifles underneath the benches with your saddles. Defending yourself would only worsen the situation."

"By the devil! Are we to have ourselves quietly lynched, mister?" Old Death exclaimed annoyed.

"No. Stay passive! My plan will take effect at the right moment. We will cool these fellows' heads with a nice bath. Trust me! There's no time to explain it; the fellows are coming."

And truly, the entire gang was now coming from the restaurant. The captain quickly turned away from us and issued some whispered instructions to the conductor, who hurried to the helmsman, who had been joined by the two deck hands. Shortly thereafter, I saw him busily whispering some secret instructions to the quieter passengers. However, I was unable to keep observing him, since I and Old Death were now kept busy by the secessionists. During the next ten minutes, I noticed only that the peaceful passengers were gathering on the fore deck.

Shortly after the drunken secessionists had left the restaurant, we were surrounded by them. Following the captain's instructions, we had stowed our rifles.

"That's him!" yesterday's speaker said, pointing at me. "He's a spy from the northern States, which support Juarez. Yesterday, he was still walking around like a fine gentleman, but today he's wearing a trapper outfit. Why is he disguising himself? He killed my dog, and they both threatened me with their revolvers."

"He's a spy, yes, a spy!" the others yelled wildly. "His outfit proves it. And he's a German. Form a jury! He must hang from his neck! Down with the northern States, with the Yankees and their creatures!"

"What's going on down there, gentlemen?" the captain now shouted from the bridge. "I'm asking for quiet and order on board. Leave the passengers be!"

"Shut up, sir!" one of the gang roared. "We, too, want order and will establish it now. Is it one of your duties to take spies on board?"

"My obligation is to transport people who pay for their passage. If secessionist fellows board, they can come along, provided they pay and behave properly. That's as far as my loyalty goes. If you and your kind spoil my business, I'll put you on land, and you can swim to Austin."

A disdainful bray of laughter was his response. Old Death and I were pushed so close together that we were unable to move. Of course, we protested, but our words were drowned out by the almost animal-like screams of this coarse gang. We were pushed from our place close to the smokestack, from which we were to be hanged. Iron eyelets were attached at its top through which ropes fed, all together a wonderful and practical arrangement to hang someone. All that was required now was to slacken the ropes and to attach us by our sensitive necks, then to raise us leisurely. Now a circle was formed around us with a tribunal over us, the latter being laughable. I believe the scoundrels never wondered why we did not defend ourselves, when they could see that we had knives and revolvers, but made no use of them. This had to have a reason.

Old Death had mighty troubles remaining quiet. His hand twitched frequently for his belt, but as soon as his look went to the captain, the man waved a surreptitious "no" to him.

"Well," he said to me in German, so that he would not be understood, "I'll go along for a bit, but if it gets too much, it will take only a minute to get our twenty-four bullets into their bellies. Start shooting right away when I begin!"

"Do you hear?" the rowdies' leader shouted. "They speak German. That proves that they are damned Dutchmen and belong with the scum bags doing the most ill to the southern States. What do they want here in Texas? They are spies and traitors. Let's make short shrift of them!"

His suggestion was agreed to with a roar. The captain, once again, shouted a serious warning to them, but was again drowned out by laughter. Then, one of them raised the question whether they should first hang the Indian, or to hang us first. They decided on the former. Their leader sent two men to fetch the redskin.

Since we were surrounded by people, we were unable to see Winnetou. Then we heard a loud scream. Winnetou had knocked down one of the delegates and tossed the other over board. After this he had slipped into the conductor's sheet metal cabin near the wheel box. The cabin had a small window from which now peered the muzzle of his double-barreled rifle. Of course, the altercation raised a terrible ruckus. Everyone ran for the railing and screamed for the captain to launch a boat to fish out the dumped man. He followed this request and signaled to one of the deck hands. The man jumped into the boat being towed at the stern, undid the rope, and rowed towards the rowdy, who knew how to swim a little, but had trouble staying above water.

I stood alone with Old Death. For the time being, the hanging had been suspended. We saw the helmsman's eyes and the rest of the crew focused on their captain, who called us to come closer and told us in a soft voice:

"Watch out, gentlemen! I'll give them the bath now. What ever happens now, stay on board. But make as much noise as possible!"

He had stopped the ship, which now drifted slowly downstream towards the

39

right bank, towards a spot where water broke, indicating a sand bank. From there to the bank, the river wasn't deep at all. A signal from the captain, and the helmsman, smiling and nodding, let the ship drift onto the sand bank. There was a brief crunch under us, a bump so that everyone reeled, with some falling down, and we had run aground. This directed everyone's attention from the rescue boat back to the ship. The peaceful passengers had all received instructions from the conductor; they now screamed as instructed as if they had been exposed to deathly danger. Others, believing a real accident had happened, of course, joined in. Now, one of the deck hands came running and, seemingly terrified, shouted to the captain:

"Water's coming in, Cap'n! The obstacle cut the keel in two. The ship's going to sink in two minutes."

"Then we are lost!" the captain exclaimed. "Everyone save yourselves! The water is shallow to the bank. Get over there!"

He came hurrying down from the bridge, tore off his coat, vest and cap, pulled off his boots, and jumped overboard. The water reached only to his neck.

"Down, down!" he shouted. "There's still time. Once the ship sinks, its whirlpool will pull everyone down who's still on board!"

He had taken off his clothes so that they wouldn't get wet. None of the secessionists considered that the captain was the first to save himself and that he even partly undressed before.

All were gripped by terror. They jumped overboard to work themselves quickly to the bank, without paying attention that the captain was swimming to the ship's opposite side, there to climb on board on the quickly lowered Jacob's ladder. The ship had been cleaned of the rabble. Where terror had ruled a minute ago, loud, happy laughter now sounded.

Just when the first of the rabble-rousers climbed on land, the captain gave orders to steam ahead. The shallow-draft, broad and strongly built vessel had not suffered the least damage and obeyed the wheel's pull. Swinging his coat like a flag, the captain shouted to the bank:

"Farewell, gentlemen! Should you enjoy forming a jury once more, then hang yourselves. Your stuff that's still on board I'll drop off in La Grange. You can pick it up there."

One can image the impression the disdainful words made on the fooled men. They raised an angry howl, demanded of the captain to pick them up that very moment, threatened to bring charges, death and other terrors, even fired their rifles, at least those had not been soaked, but all without causing any damage. At last, one of them screamed in helpless anger to the captain:

"You dog. We will wait here for your return, then hang you from your smoke stack!"

"Well, sir! For that you need to come aboard. In the meantime, our greeting to generals Mejia and Marquez!"

By then we had gained full steam and traveled upstream to make up for the lost time.

Karl May – translated by Herbert Windolf

3. The Klansmen

Even today, the above name is a linguistic riddle with several different explanations as to its origin. The name of the infamous Ku-Klux-Klan is, according to some sources, only the imitation of the noise made when cocking a rifle. Others assemble it from *cuc*, warning, *cluck*, and *Klan*, the Scottish word for tribe, family, or lineage. May it be as it is, the members of the Ku-Klux-Klan probably did not know either where the name originated from and what its meaning was, and likely didn't give a hoot about it. Someone might have come up with this word, with others picking it up without bothering about the sense or nonsense of this name.

Not as vague was the purpose this organization pursued. It first appeared in counties of North Carolina, then spread quickly to South Carolina, Georgia, Alabama, Mississippi, Kentucky and Tennessee, finally sending members also to Texas to work there for its purposes. The Klan included a number of grim enemies of the northern States, their task being to fight the order established following the end of the Civil War, by any means, even the most forbidden and most criminal ones. And indeed, the Klansmen kept the South in continuous upheaval for a number of years, made ownership insecure, held back industry and trade, and even the most severe measures did not succeed in stopping their scandalous activities.

The members of this secret organization, which originated as a consequence of the reconstruction measures the government was forced to apply to the defeated South, consisted of supporters of slavery and members of the Republican party, both enemies of the Union. Strong oaths required the Klan's members to obey its secret statutes, and, under threat of death, forced them to maintain the secrecy of the organization. They did not shy from any kind of violence, not even arson and murder; they kept regular meetings and appeared for the execution of their unlawful acts always on horseback and heavily disguised. They killed pastors in their pulpits and judges on the bench, attacked good family men and left them, their backs torn to the bones, amidst their families. All the ruffians and murderous arsonists together were not feared as the Ku-Klux-Klan, which acted so terribly that, for instance, the governor of South Carolina requested President Grant to send him military assistance, since this secret society, having already assumed such alarming dimensions, could not be reined in by other means. Grant presented the request to Congress, which issued an anti-Ku-Klux-Klan law, giving the President dictatorial powers to destroy the gang. That the government was forced to issue such a draconian law is proof of the danger the Klansmen's' actions posed to individuals as well as to the entire nation. The Klan became an infernal abyss wherein all kinds of subversive, reactionary and violent elements found each other. A clerical gentlemen, killed in his pulpit, had prayed for the salvation of a family whose members had been murdered by the Klan in broad daylight. In his pious zeal, but also according to the story, he had described the Klan's activities as "a fight of the children of the Devil against the children of God." That's when, from the opposite gallery, a disguised figure rose and shot him through the head. Before the terrified congregation had recovered from its horror, this devil had disappeared. –

When our steamboat arrived in La Grange, evening had settled in, and the captain explained to us that he would not continue to steam upriver today because of the dangerous conditions of the riverbed. We were forced to disembark here. Winnetou rode before us across the gangway and disappeared between the houses into the dark of night. We expected to see him again on board the next morning and therefore did not bother about him, particularly since he did not pay attention to us, and only once, after the secessionists had been expelled from the ship, had given us a longer look. But this look had not been very appreciative, just the opposite, it had been rather disdainful, likely because we had let ourselves be held in check by the secessionist rogues. He might not have known that the captain had asked us to act this way, and I must admit openly that this contemptuous look kept irritating me for a long time.

In La Grange, too, the commissioner stood ready to represent the interests of the ship owner. Old Death quickly addressed him:

"Sir, when did the last ship from Matagorda arrive and did all passengers disembark?"

"The last ship arrived here the day before yesterday about this time and everyone went off board, with the steamer continuing on the next morning."

"And you were here when people boarded again the next morning?"

"Of course, sir."

"Maybe you are able to provide me with some information then. We are looking for two friends, who traveled with that steamer and must, therefore, also have stayed here overnight. We would like to know whether they continued their travel the next morning."

"Hmm, that's not easy to say. It was so dark, with the passengers pushing to get on board, that one couldn't pay attention to particular individuals. Most likely, these folks traveled on that morning, except for a certain Mr. Clinton."

"Clinton? Aha, he's the one. Please, come on over to the light! My friend will show you a photo to see if it is Mr. Clinton's."

And truly, the commissioner confirmed that this was the man he was referring to.

"Do you know where he stayed?" Old Death asked.

"Not exactly, but most likely with *Señor* Cortesio, for his people picked up his suitcases. *Señor* Cortesio is an agent for just about everything, a Spaniard by birth. I believe he's busy now with covert weapons' shipments to Mexico."

"I hope we can find him to be a gentleman?"

"Sir, these days everyone wants to be a gentleman, even if he carries a saddle on his back."

Of course, this referred to us, who were standing before him with our saddles, but his tease wasn't spiteful, which is why Old Death continued in a friendly voice:

"Does your blessed place have a guest house where, except for your lantern, no light is burning and one can sleep without being bothered by people and other bugs?"

"There's a single one, and with you having stayed with me for so long, the other passengers likely beat you to the few rooms it has."

"That's certainly unpleasant," Old Death replied, overlooking also this tease. "Is it unlikely to find hospitality in private homes?"

"Hmm, sir, I don't know you. I can't take you in myself since my place is very small. But I know someone, who will probably not send you away, provided you are honest folks. He's a German, a blacksmith, who moved here from Missouri."

"Well, then," my friend replied, "my companion here is German, and I, too, am familiar with German. We are no scoundrels, and can pay. I figure your acquaintance could try us for once. Would you please describe where he lives?"

"That's not necessary. I would take you there, but I'm still busy with the ship. Mister Lange isn't yet home anyway. At this time, he's usually sitting in the pub. That's the German custom here. You only need to ask for him, Mr. Lange from Missouri. Tell him that the commissioner sent you! Walk straight ahead, then turn left after the second house, after that you will recognize the pub by its lights. Its shutters are likely still open."

I gave the man a tip for his information, then we walked off with our riding gear. The pub's location could be identified not only by its lights, but also from the noise coming through the open windows. Above its entrance an animal figure resembling a giant turtle was attached, but with wings and two legs. Below, it read 'Hawk's Inn'. Obviously, the turtle was to represent a raptor, but it looked more like a 'vulture'.

When we opened the door a thick cloud of nasty smelling tobacco smoke assaulted us. The guests had to be equipped with excellent lungs in order not to suffocate in this atmosphere, but evidently seemed to be doing well. The excellent condition of their lungs was also demonstrated by the extremely powerful activity of their talking faculties. No one spoke, but everyone yelled, so that it seemed that no one was quiet for even a second to hear what another hollered at him. Seeing this pleasant company, we stopped for several minutes at the door to accustom our eyes to the smoke and to differentiate the individuals and items in the room. Then we noticed that there were two rooms, a larger one for 'common' folk, and a smaller one for finer guests, as it seemed, for America a peculiar, even dangerous arrangement, since no resident of the free States recognizes a social or even moral difference between himself and others.

Since no seat was available any more in the front room, we went to the room in the back, which we reached unnoticed. There, two chairs were available, of which we took possession after we had put the saddles in a corner. Several men sat at a table, drinking beer, and talking in German. They had given us only a brief look, and when we came closer, seemed to quickly change the subject of their conversation as their searching talk let me guess. Two of them looked similar and were probably father and son. They were tall, strong men with sharply marked features and strong fists, proof of hard work. Their faces gave an expression of uprightness, but were presently flushed from their animated conversation, as if they had talked about an unpleasant subject.

When we sat down, they moved together, so that an open space formed between them and us, a gentle hint that they did not want to have anything to do with us.

"Keep sitting where you are, gentlemen!" Old Death told them. "We won't be any trouble to you, even if we haven't eaten anything since this morning. Maybe you can tell us if we can get something edible here, something that doesn't upset one's digestion?"

The one I thought to be the father of the similar-looking pair, pinched his right eye, and answered with a laugh:

"As to making a meal of us, sir, we sure would defend ourselves a bit. You happen to look like the real Old Death, and I don't think you must shy from a comparison with him."

"Old Death? Who's that?" my friend asked making a silly face.

"He's likely a more famous character than you, a frontiersman and scout, who has done more in every month of his ramblings than a thousand others in their entire life. My boy, Will, has seen him."

This 'boy' was maybe twenty-six years old, had a deeply tanned face, and gave the impression that he could easily take on half a dozen others. Old Death looked at him from aside and asked:

"He saw him? Where?"

"In 1862, up in Arkansas, just prior to the battle at Pea Ridge. But you likely don't know anything of these events."

"Why not? I wandered about old Arkansas quite often and believe that I wasn't far from there at that time."

"So? Who did you associate with at the time, if I may ask? These days, conditions in our area are such that one must learn the political colors of a man before one sits at the same table with him."

"Not to worry, mister! I guess you aren't keeping with the vanquished slave holders and I'm entirely of your opinion. And that I don't belong to this kind of people you can see from my speaking German!"

"Be welcome then. But don't be mistaken, sir! The German language is a deceptive means of recognition. There are also people in the other camp, who passably speak our language and use it to worm themselves into our confidence. I learned that well enough. But we talked of Arkansas and Old Death. You may know that this state intended to declare for the Union prior to the start of the Civil War. But then it turned out differently. Many good men, opposed to slavery and to whom especially the behavior of the southern barons was an outrage, came together and declared themselves against secession. But the mob, to which I, of course, also include these barons, quickly seized the public powers; reasonable people were intimidated, and thus Arkansas fell to the South. It was obvious that this raised great bitterness among the residents of German descent. Unable to do anything against it, they then experienced how, particularly, the northern half of the beautiful state suffered extensively from the ravages of the war. I lived in Missouri, in Poplar Bluff, near the border to Arkansas. My boy, who's sitting here in front of you, had joined one of the German regiments of the Missourians, of course. Wanting to come to the assistance of the Unionists in Arkansas, a detachment was sent over the border to reconnoiter. Will was among these men. They suddenly encountered a superior force and were eventually overcome after some fierce fighting."

"So he became a prisoner of war? That was terrible at the time. It is well known how the Southern States treated their prisoners; of a hundred at least eighty died from maltreatment. But they weren't after their lives right away?"

"Oho! There you are mightily mistaken. The good boys had fought well, had used up all of their ammunition, then kept working with rifle butts and knives. This caused heavy losses to the secessionists, who were mighty angry and decided to dispose of their prisoners. Will is my only son, and I was close to becoming an 'orphaned' father. That I did not, I have Old Death to thank for."

"How so, mister? You make me curious. Did this scout bring in a corps of soldiers to free the prisoners?"

"To do this he would have been too late. Before such help could have arrived, the murder would have been done already. No, he did it like a true, right and daring frontiersman. He got the prisoners out himself."

"Thunder and lightning! That must have been a feat!"

"And what a feat it was! He stole into camp, on his belly like one approaches Indians, a ploy made easier by a good rain that had fallen that evening and had extinguished the camp fires. That a few guards got to feel his knife is obvious. The secessionists, an entire battalion, were camped on a farm. Of course, the officers had taken over the living quarters, their troops accommodated as well as was possible. Watched by four guards, one on each side of the building, the prisoners, about twenty of them, had been locked up in the sugar press. The poor devils were to be shot the next morning. In the night, just prior to a change of the guards, they heard a peculiar noise on the roof which wasn't from the pouring rain. They listened. Suddenly there was a bang. The roof, consisting of long softwood shingles, had been broken open. Someone continued widening the hole until rain started falling into the sugar press. Then, for about ten minutes, it became quiet again. Thereafter a small tree trunk, its branch stubs still attached and strong enough to support a man, was lowered. On it, the prisoners climbed up onto the roof and from there to the ground. Below, they found the four guards lying motionless, not just asleep, and right away took their weapons. Their rescuer smartly led the freed men away from the camp and to the trail leading to the border they were familiar with. Only there did they learn that it was Old Death, the Scout, who had risked his life to save theirs."

"Did he join them?" Old Death asked.

"No. He told them that he had other important things to take care of, and hurried off into the rainy night, without allowing them time to thank him and to have a closer look at him. The night was so dark that one couldn't make out a face. Will didn't see more than the tall, lean figure of the man. But he talked with him, and still recalls every word the courageous fellow said to him. Should we meet Old Death some day, he would learn that we Germans are grateful people."

"He'll know that anyway. I figure your son isn't the first German who's met this man. But, sir, might you know a Mr. Lange from Missouri living here?"

The other's ears pricked up.

"Lange?" he asked. "Why do you ask?"

"I'm afraid that we won't find accommodation here at this 'Vulture Inn' any more. That is why I checked with the commissioner by the river for a man who might provide us with a place to sleep. He named Mr. Lange and advised us to tell him that the commissioner was sending us to him, suggesting that we would likely find the man here."

The elderly man once more gave us a searching look, then said: "He was right, sir, I am Lange. Since the commissioner sent you, and I figure you to be honest folk, you are welcome. I hope I will not be mistaken. But who's your companion who hasn't uttered a single word yet?"

"He's a fellow-countryman of yours, a Saxon, even a studied one, who's come over here to make his fortune."

"Oh my! The good people over there in the Old Country believe that roasted doves simply fly into one's mouth here. I'm telling you, sir, that over here one must work much, much more to make it than over there. But no hard feelings! I wish you success and welcome you."

He also shook my hand. Old Death shook his once more and said:

"And should you still have some doubts whether we deserve your trust or not, I shall turn to your son, who will prove that we don't deserve any doubt."

"My son. Will?" Lange asked surprised.

"Yes. He and no other. You said that he had talked with Old Death and would still recall every word. Would you care to tell me, young man, what was said? I'm extremely interested."

Will now responded very animatedly:

"When Old Death led us away, he walked ahead. I had received a grazing shot in an arm which hurt very much, and because I had not received any dressing, my sleeve had become attached to the wound. We walked through some bushes. Old Death let go of a branch which hit my wound. It hurt so much that I voiced a shout of pain, and . . ."

"And that's when the scout called you an ass!" Old Death completed the sentence.

"How do you know this?" Will asked surprised.

Without answering, the oldster continued:

"Responding to this, you told him that you had been shot and that the wound was inflamed, after which he suggested to you to soak the sleeve in water, then to cool the wound with, *plantain*, an herb, which would prevent further inflammation."

"Yes, that's how it was! But how can you know this, sir?" the young Lange exclaimed in surprise.

"You are still asking? Because it was me who gave you this good advice. Your father said earlier that I resemble Old Death quite a bit. Well, he's correct, for I resemble this old fellow exactly like a wife resembles a female spouse."

"Then – then – it is you yourself?" Will exclaimed joyfully, jumping from his chair and stepping over to Old Death with arms outstretched. But his father held him back and pulled him back onto his chair.

"Hold it, boy! If there's to be an embrace, then the father has prior rights and the duty to put his paws around your rescuer's neck. But let's avoid that, knowing where we are and how we might be watched. So, keep sitting quietly!"

Turning to Old Death, he continued: "Don't misinterpret my objection, sir! I've good reasons for it. The devil's loose around here. You can believe me that I'm grateful to you, but precisely because of this you must trust me in trying to avoid anything that could endanger you. As I know and have often heard, you are known as a supporter of the Abolitionists. You led some soldier corps during the war which made you famous, and who did great damage to the Southerners. You were attached to Northern army forces as guide and scout and took them into the rear of the enemy on trails no other would have dared. We honored you highly for it, but Southerners called you a spy, and still do so today. You know how things stand these days. Should you come across some Secessionists, you run the danger of being hanged."

"I know this very well, Mr. Lange, but don't worry about it," Old Death replied coolly. "While I don't care to be hanged, I can only say that I've often been threatened with it without anyone having succeeding yet. Just today, a gang of rowdies wanted to hang us from the smoke stack of the steamer, though they didn't make it."

Now Old Death recounted the events on the steamer. When he had finished, Lange responded pensively:

"That was very courageous of the captain, but also very dangerous for him. He's staying in La Grange until tomorrow morning, and the rowdies may yet get here this night. In that case he must expect their revenge. And you may fare even worse."

"Bah! I'm not afraid of these few men; I've dealt with worse already."

"Don't be so sure, sir! These rowdies will gain some important help here. For a few days already, something's fishy here in La Grange. From everywhere strangers are arriving; they linger at corners and behave suspiciously. They've nothing to do, simply hang around, which let's one conclude that they have something up their sleeves. Just now, they sit in the front room and open their mouths so wide that a grizzly could make its bed inside. They discovered that we are Germans and tried to provoke us. If we had answered them, there would have been murder and mayhem. By the way, I don't care to stay here for long, and you, too, will likely want to rest. However, it doesn't look too good for dinner here. Since I'm a widower, we take it easy and come here for lunch. And since the ground in La Grange became a bit too hot for me, I sold my house a few days ago. With that I don't want to say that I don't like the folks here. They are no worse than anywhere. But the murderous Civil War has barely been concluded and its aftermath lies still heavy on the land. And across the border in Mexico they still butcher each other. Texas is right between these two areas. It festers wherever one looks, and all kinds of rabble spoil living here. That's why I decided to sell and move to my daughter's, who is happily married. I can find a position with her husband. Added to this was that I found a buyer here in town who liked my property and was able to pay me in cash just yesterday. Now I can leave whenever I want to. I will go to Mexico."

"Are you the devil's, sir?" Old Death exclaimed.

"I? Why so?"

"Because you complained earlier about Mexico. You said that people butcher each other over there. And now you want to go there yourself!"

"It won't work any other way, sir. Then, not all areas of Mexico are the same. Where I want to go, a bit past Chihuahua, the war's ended. Although Juarez had to flee all the way to El Paso, he soon recovered and drove the Frenchmen back south. Their days are numbered; they will be chased out of the country and poor Maximilian will pay for it. I feel sorry for him, because I'm German and wish him well. They will fight it out by the capital city, while the northern provinces will be spared. That is where my son-in-law lives, and Will and I want to move to. There, everything we can hope for is awaiting us, because, sir, this good man is very wealthy, being the owner of a silver mine. He's now lived for over one-and-one-half years in Mexico and wrote us in his last letter that a little baby, his silver mine king arrived, crying mightily for his grandfather. By the devil; can I then stay here? I, as well as my son, have been promised good positions at the mine. In addition, I can teach the little one his first evening prayer, the German alphabet, and the multiplication tables. You see, gentlemen, nothing's holding me. A grandfather must be with his grandson, or he's not at the right place. That is why I want to head for Mexico, and should you care to ride with me, I'd like that."

"Hmm!" Old Death mumbled. "Don't jest, sir! It could be that we'll take you by your word."

"What, you, too, want to go there? That would be magnificent. Let's shake hands on it, sir, and ride together."

He held out his hand.

"Slowly, slowly!" Old Death laughed. "I meant to say that it is likely that we will ride to Mexico, but it's not certain yet. And should it come to it, we still don't know what direction we must take."

"If it's only that, sir, I'll ride with you wherever you'll go. From here, all trails lead to Chihuahua, and I don't mind if I arrive there today or tomorrow. I am a selfish fellow and like to watch out for any advantage I can gain. You are an experienced frontiersman and scout. If I can join you, I'm certain to arrive safely, which is very valuable in these unruly times. Where do you expect to learn more?"

"From a certain *Señor* Cortesio. Might you know the man?"

"And how! La Grange is so small that all cats are on personal terms, and it is precisely this *señor* who bought my house."

"Most of all, I'd love to learn whether he's a scoundrel or a man of honor," Old Death put in.

"The latter, the latter. Of course, his political colors are none of my business. Whether someone prefers to be ruled by an emperor or the republican way is all the same to me, provided he does his duty in all other respects. He's in constant contact across the border. I've observed that at night mules are loaded with heavy crates, and that men gather secretly at his place, who then head for the Río del Norte. That's why I believe my guess is correct that he's supplying the supporters of Juarez with weapons and ammunition and also sends people across to fight against the French. Taking the local conditions into account, this is a risk one takes only if one is certain that even if one takes a loss, it still remains good business."

"Where does he live? I must still talk to him tonight."

"You'll be able to talk to him by ten o'clock. I was supposed to have a conversation with him today, but the subject's been taken care of in the meantime, so that I need not see him any more. He told me to see him at ten o'clock, and that he'd arrive just prior to this time."

"Did he have visitors when you saw him earlier?"

"He did. Two men sat with him, a younger and an older one."

"Were their names mentioned?" I asked excitedly.

"Yes. We sat together for almost an hour. During such a long time one gets to hear the names of those one talks with. The younger one's name was Ohlert and the older went by the name of *Señor* Gavilano. The latter seemed to be an acquaintance of Cortesio's. They talked about having met in Mexico City several years ago."

"Gavilano? That name doesn't ring a bell. Might your man Gibson now go by this name?" Old Death asked.

I pulled out the photos and showed them to the blacksmith. He recognized the two immediately and confirmed it by saying:

"It's them, sir. The one with the lean, yellow Creole face is *Señor* Gavilano; the other is Mr. Ohlert, who embarrassed me quite a bit. He kept asking me about people I'd never heard of in my life, for example a Negro by the name of Othello, a young miss from Orleans, Johanna by name, who had earlier herded sheep, then went to war alongside her king. Then there was a certain mister Fridolin, who, supposedly had taken a walk for the Eisenhammer; an unhappy Lady Maria Stuart, whose head they chopped off in England, and a bell which had sung a song of Schiller's. Then he asked for a poetic gentleman, by the name of Ludwig Uhland, who had cursed two singers, for which some queen had tossed him the rose from her bosom. He was happy to have found a German in me and pulled out a whole slew of names, poems, and theater stories, of which I recall only what I just told you. All that went through my mind that it felt like a water wheel. This Mr. Ohlert appeared to be a good and harmless man, but I'd bet he had a loose screw. At the end he retrieved a piece of paper with some verses, which he read to me. In them, he talked of a terrible night, which twice had a morning, but not the third time. Then there was rainy weather, stars, fog, eternity, blood in the veins, a ghost screaming for salvation, a devil in the brain and a dozen snakes in the brain, in short, all of it rather confused stuff, nothing that's possible and really fitting together. I wasn't sure whether I should laugh or cry."

Without doubt, he had spoken with William Ohlert. His companion, Gibson, had now changed his name for the second time. Gibson was likely only an assumed one. That the seducer and kidnapper had a yellow Creole complexion I was also aware of; I had seen him. Maybe he really was from Mexico and his name was originally Gavilano, the name by which *Señor* Cortesio got to know him. Gavilano in English means sparrow hawk, a name doing honor to this character. For the most part, I was eager to learn the pretext he used for traveling with Ohlert. This pretext had to be a very attractive one for the mentally disturbed Ohlert, and had to be closely connected with his *idée fixe* of having to write a tragedy about an insane poet. Maybe Ohlert had also talked about this to the blacksmith, which is why I asked him:

"What language did the young man use in your conversation?"

"He spoke German and very often mentioned a tragedy he was going to write, but claimed that before he could write it, he had to experience everything himself, which the play was going to include."

"Unbelievable!"

"No? There, I'm of a different opinion, sir! Insanity manifests itself precisely in undertaking things a normal person would never think of doing. Every third word he said was of having to abduct a *Señorita* Perilla, with the help of his friend."

"That's truly insanity! Should this man transfer the personalities and events of his tragedy to the real world, then this must be prevented. I hope he's still in La Grange?"

"No. He's gone. Left yesterday. With Cortesio's assistance he traveled to Hopkins' farm, from there to head for the Río Grande."

"That's unfortunate, really unfortunate! We must follow him as quickly as possible, maybe even today. Do you know where one can buy a couple of good horses here?"

"Yes, from this *Señor* Cortesio. He always keeps animals for men he's recruiting for Juarez. But I would advise against a night ride. You don't know the way and therefore will need a guide, which you won't find any more tonight."

"Maybe we will. We will try everything to still get away tonight. But, most of all, we must talk with Cortesio. It is past ten o'clock, the time he expected to be home. Would you be so kind to show us where he lives?"

"Gladly. Let's go then, if you wish, sir!"

When we rose to leave we heard hoof beats in front of the building, and a few minutes later new guests entered the pub. To my surprise, but not to my reassurance, I recognized these people to be the Secessionists our captain had safely put ashore. They seemed to be known to several of the guests present since they were enthusiastically greeted by them. From the questions flying back and forth we heard that their arrival had been expected. At first, they were kept busy so that they found no time to pay attention to us. This pleased us, since it wasn't our wish to attract their attention. We therefore sat down again. Had we left now, we would have needed to pass by them, and they would certainly have used the opportunity to start a fight with us. When Lange heard who they were, he pushed the connecting door closer, so that they were unable to see us, but we could understand everything they said. In addition, he and his companions traded their seats with us, so that Old Death and I now sat with our backs towards the door to the front room, and our faces could not be seen.

"It isn't necessary for them to see you," the blacksmith said. "Already, there is an unfavorable mood out there towards us. If they spot you, a riot would start, since they think you to be spies and had wanted to hang you earlier."

"That's fine as it is," Old Death replied. "But do we care to keep sitting here until they've left? We haven't got the time, since we must get to Cortesio."

"You can, sir! We'll take a way where they can't see us."

Old Death looked around the room, then said: "And where would that be? The only exit is through the front room."

53

"No. Out there it's much easier," he said while pointing to the window.

"Are you serious?" Old Death asked. "It sounds as if you are afraid! Are we to leave the French way, like mice crawling into holes being afraid of the cat? We would be laughed at."

"I don't know fear. But there's a good old German saying that the smarter man yields. I'm totally satisfied saying that I'm not doing it from fear but only from caution, not to mention that, out there, we're outnumbered by ten. These tramps are in high spirits but angry, too. They wouldn't let us pass without causing trouble, and since I'm not the man to take that quietly, it would result in a big fight. I don't shy away from a fight with fists, punches and torn-off chair legs against such a superior force, for I'm a blacksmith and know how to flatten heads. But a revolver is a devilishly stupid weapon. The most cowardly midget can down the most courageous giant with a bullet the size of a pea. Simple shrewdness tells us to outwit these fellows by secretly leaving this room by the window. Should they find out about it, they would be the angrier for it. But if we face them and bash in some heads, we'll also fetch ourselves some bloody noses or worse."

Silently, I agreed with the sensible man, and also Old Death said a moment later:

"Your opinion isn't so imprudent after all. I'll go along with your suggestion, and shove my body and legs with everything else that's attached to it out the window. Just listen how they roar! I believe they are talking of the adventure on the steamer."

He was correct. The newcomers told about what had happened on the ship, then of Old Death, the Indian and myself, and the cunning of the captain. They were not agreed on how to avenge themselves. The six rowdies and their followers wanted to wait for the steamer, with the others neither wanting to nor having the time.

"Of course, we didn't care to sit for an eternity by the river bank," the narrator said, "since we wanted to get here, where we were expected. It was fortunate we found a nearby farm, where we borrowed some horses."

"Borrowed?" one of them asked, laughing.

"Yes, borrowed, done our way. But there weren't enough, so we had to double up. Later, things improved. We passed by other farms, so that finally every one of us had a horse." A wild laughter followed this thieving story.

Then the narrator continued: "Is everything in order here? And have the people in question been found?"

"Yes, we've got them figured."

"And the outfits?"

"We brought two boxes; that should be enough."

"Then we'll have some fun. But the spies and the captain will get their share. The steamer stops in La Grange overnight, which means we will find the captain, and for the Indian and the two spies we won't need to search for long either. They are easy to recognize. One of them wore a new trapper outfit, and both carried saddles, but had no horses."

"Saddles?" it now sounded almost joyously. "Didn't the two who entered earlier, and who sit back there . . ."

The rest was said in a low voice since, of course, it meant us.

"Gentlemen," the blacksmith said, "it's time we take our leave. In a moment they will come in here. You two go ahead! We'll hand you the saddles."

He was right, which is why, without any qualms, I quickly exited through the window. Old Death followed, after which the blacksmiths handed us our belongings and rifles, then jumped out, too.

We found ourselves at the gable end of the house on a small fenced yard, apparently a small grassy garden. When we jumped the fence, we noticed that the other guests that had been in the room with us, were also coming out the window. They, too, could not expect to be treated cordially by the Secessionists and thought it best to follow our lead.

"Well," Lange laughed, "these characters will be surprised when they find out the birds have flown the coop. But it's best that way."

"But a devilish shame at the moment!" Old Death cursed. "It's as if I'm hearing their disdainful laughter."

"Let them laugh! We'll laugh later, which, as everyone knows, is better. I will prove to you that I'm not afraid of them, but I'm just not going for a pub brawl."

The two blacksmiths took our saddles, assuring us that they couldn't permit their guests to lug such a load. Soon we arrived between two buildings. The one to our left lay darkly hidden, from the other light shone through a shutter slit.

"*Señor* Cortesio is home," Lange said. "Where the light shines through is his home. Just knock on the door, and he will open. When you are done, come over to the left where we live, and knock on the shutter next to the door! In the meantime we'll fix something to eat."

They left for their house, with us two turning right. Our knocking resulted in the door being opened by a small gap, with a voice asking:

"Who are you?"

"Two friends," Old Death answered. "Is *Señor* Cortesio home?"

"What want from *Señor*?"

From his expression, it was a Negro asking these questions.

"We want to do some business with him."

"What kind of business? Say first, or not allowed to come in."

"Tell him only that Mr. Lange sent us!"

"Massa Lange? He good. Then allowed to come in. Wait a moment!"

He shut the door, but momentarily opened it again to tell us:

"Come in! *Señor* said will talk with strangers."

Walking through a narrow hallway, we entered a small room, obviously an office, with a desk, a table and several chairs being the only simple furnishings. A tall, lean man stood behind the desk, facing the entrance. We were sure that he was a Spaniard.

"*Buenas tardes!*" he responded to our polite greeting. "*Señor* Lange is sending you? May I ask what brings you to me, *Señores?*"

I was curious what Old Death would say. Before we entered, he had told me to remain silent.

"Maybe it will be some business, maybe only a quest for some information, *Señor*. We don't quite know yet ourselves," the oldster replied.

"We shall see. Sit down and have a *cigarillo*."

He held a cigarette case and lighter out to us, an offer we could not refuse. Mexicans cannot imagine a negotiation, and least of all a conversation, without smoking. For Old Death, to whom a slug of chewing tobacco was preferred ten times over the best cigarette, took one of these small, thin things, lit it, took a few mighty draws, and – the cigarette was reduced to a stub. I smoked mine more economically.

"What brings us to you," Old Death began, "isn't of great importance. We are only so late, because you weren't available earlier. And we didn't want to wait until tomorrow for our visit, since the local conditions aren't inviting for a longer stay. We intend to go to Mexico to offer our services to Juarez. Of course, something like this isn't done on the spur of the moment. One would appreciate a certain assurance to be welcome and to be accepted. This is why we inquired covertly and, in the process, learned that one can find recruitment here in La Grange. Your name was mentioned, *Señor*, which is why we came to see you. Maybe you are kind enough to tell us whether we have come to the right man."

The Mexican did not reply immediately, but looked at us searchingly. Satisfied, his eyes came to rest on me; I was young and looked in good shape. He cared less for Old Death. The lean, forward-bent figure of the oldster did not appear as if it could endure great strain. He then asked:

"Who gave you my name, *Señor?*"

"A man we met on the steamer," Old Death lied. "By chance, we then met Mr. Lange, who told us that you would not be home before ten o'clock. We are Northerners of German descent and fought against the Southern States. Having military experience, we would be of some use to Mexico's president."

"Hmm! This sounds very well, *Señor*, but I want to tell you honestly that you don't give the impression to be up to the exertions and deprivations that would be demanded of you."

"This is, of course, said sincerely, *Señor*," the oldster smiled. "But I need only give you my name to convince you that I would surely be of use. I am commonly called Old Death."

"Old Death!" Cortesio exclaimed in surprise. "Is it possible? Are you then the famous scout who did such great damage to the South?"

"It's me. My figure should legitimize me."

"Indeed, indeed, *Señor*. I must be very cautious. It must not become known that I work for Juarez, especially now that I'm forced to watch out. But you being Old Death, there's no longer any reason to hold back, and I can tell you that you came to the right address. I would be happy to recruit you immediately, and can even assure you a good position, for a man like Old Death would certainly be of great value; he would not be engaged as a common soldier."

"That I hope indeed, *Señor*. And concerning my companion, he too, even if he were to start as a soldier, would quickly move to something better. Among the Abolitionists he made it to captain, despite his youth. Although he has the common name of Müller, you most likely heard of him after all. He served under Sheridan, and as a Lieutenant commanded the *avant garde* in the famous flanking operation across Missionary Ridge. You surely must have heard of the daring raids made at the time. Müller was a favorite of Sheridan's, and because of it had the advantage of always being put in command of these daring ventures. He was also the much-celebrated cavalry officer who, in the bloody but successful battle at Five Forks freed General Sheridan, who had been captured there. That's why I think that he wouldn't be a bad acquisition for you, *Señor*."

The oldster was lying through his teeth! But, could I expose him as a liar? I felt blood rushing to my cheeks, but the good Cortesio thought my blushing came from modesty, for he offered me his hand and said, lying just as much as a newspaper writer:

"This well-earned praise must not embarrass you, *Señor* Müller. Indeed, I've heard of your accomplishments and bid you a hearty welcome. Of course, you, too, will right away be appointed officer, and I'm prepared to provide you with sufficient cash to acquire everything necessary."

Old Death was ready to agree, I noticed, which is why I quickly broke in:

"That's not necessary, *Señor*. It isn't our intention to have you equip us. We need nothing more than two horses, which we hope to obtain here. We have saddles."

"That is well. I can leave you a couple of good animals, and if you truly intend to pay for them, I shall let you have them at cost. We can go to the stable tomorrow morning to look at the horses. They are the best I have. Have you already found accommodation for the night?"

"Yes. Mister Lange invited us."

"Excellent. If that were not the case, I would have invited you, although my place is rather cramped. What do you think? Shall we arrange for everything now or tomorrow morning?"

"Right away," Old Death answered. "What formalities do we need to take care of?"

"None, right now. Since you will pay for everything yourself, you will be taken under oath only upon your arrival with the corps. The only thing necessary is to provide you with a letter of recommendation and legitimization to secure the positions you desire, based on your experience. It is, of course, best to issue these papers right away. One can never know what is going to happen the next moment. Please be patient for a quarter of an hour. I shall hurry. There lie the *cigarillos*, and I'll offer you also a good sip, which I usually don't do for others. That is why I have only a single glass."

He pushed the cigarettes over and fetched a bottle of wine. Then he sat by the desk to write. Behind the Mexican's back, Old Death grimaced at me, which I took as him being highly satisfied. He then poured himself a glass, toasted to Cortesio's health, and downed it in one gulp. I was by far not as satisfied as he, for the two men I was after had not even been mentioned. I whispered this to the oldster. He responded with a gesture, telling me, that he would take care of it yet.

A quarter of an hour later, when Cortesio was finished, Old Death had emptied the bottle all by himself. Before sealing the letters, the Mexican read their content to us, which met with our satisfaction. Then he completed four forms, two for each of us. I was surprised to find them to be passports, one in French, signed by General Bazaine, the other printed in Spanish and signed by Juarez. Cortesio noticed my surprise and said with a smile of cunning satisfaction:

"You notice, *Señor*, that we are able to protect you from whatever events you may encounter. How I obtained the French papers is my business. You don't know who you may come across, which is why it's best to make sure you are safe in any case. I would resist giving others these duplicate passports. They are issued only for exceptional cases, and the groups leaving from here under guidance do not receive any legitimization at all."

Finally, Old Death posed my so long-desired question:

"When did the last of these men leave?"

"Just yesterday. I had a crew of more than thirty recruits, whom I accompanied to Hopkins Farm. There were also two privately traveling *señores*."

"Then you also provide transport to private parties?" Old Death asked with a surprised voice.

"No, that would have a detrimental effect. However, I made an exception, since one of these gentlemen was a friend of mine. Come to think of it, with you being well-mounted, and if you leave early tomorrow morning, you would be able to catch the detachment before it reaches the Río Grande."

"Where does the group want to cross the Río Grande?"

"They are headed in the direction of Eagle Pass. But since they cannot let themselves be seen there, they will keep a bit farther north. Between the Río Nueces and the Río Grande they will cut across the mule trail coming from Fort Inge, which they must also avoid. They will cross the Río Grande between its two little tributaries, the Las Moras and Morales, where there is an easily

58

passable ford, known only to our guides. From there, they will keep to the west to reach Chihuahua via Baya, Cruces, San Vincente, Tabal and San Carlos.

Every single one of these places was like Greek to me. But Old Death nodded, repeating every name aloud, as if he were very much familiar with the area.

"We shall surely catch up with them, if our horses aren't too bad, and theirs aren't too good," he said. "But are you permitting us to join them?"

Cortesio confirmed it vigorously, after which my friend kept asking:

"Will the two private gentlemen you mentioned agree to it?"

"Absolutely. They have nothing to say in this matter, but must be glad to be able to ride under the detachment's protection. Since you are going to meet them, I can tell you that they are gentlemen. One of them, a native Mexican by the name of Gavilano, is an acquaintance of mine. I have spent some pleasant hours with him in the capital city. He has a younger sister, who turns every *señor's* head."

"Then he must also be a handsome-looking man?"

"No. They do not resemble each other, being step-siblings. Her name is Felisa Perillo. Being an attractive singer and dancer, she was very well-introduced into upper society. Later, she disappeared, and only now did I learn from her brother that she's still alive and resides in the area of Chihuahua. He could not give me details on her whereabouts, since he must yet inquire about where she lives once he gets there."

"May I ask what this *señor* actually was or is?"

"A poet."

Old Death made a very astounded and condescending face, causing Cortesio to add:

"Señor Gavilano wrote poems for free, being of considerable wealth, which is why he had no need for payment to publish them."

"Then he must be envied!"

"Yes, he was envied, and following a cabal that was hatched against him because of that, he had to leave the city, even the country. He is now returning with a Yankee, who wants to get to know Mexico and who requested to be introduced to the world of poetry. They intend to build a theater in Mexico City."

"I wish them luck! Did Mr. Gavilano know that you are presently in La Grange?"

"Oh no. I happened to be at the river when the steamer arrived for the passengers to spend the night here. I recognized the *Señor* right away and invited him and his companion to spend the night at my place. It turned out that the two were on their way to Austin, in order to cross the border from there. Hearing this, I offered them the opportunity to cross the border faster and more safely. It is not advisable for a stranger, especially if he isn't oriented towards secessionism, to stay here for long. There are now men in Texas who like to fish in troubled waters, all kinds of useless, even dangerous rabble, whose origin and purpose in life is unknown. From everywhere one hears of acts of violence, muggings and atrocities, no one knows a reason for. The perpetrators disappear without a trace, just as they arrived, and the police are totally helpless."

"Might this be the Ku-Klux-Klan?" Old Death asked.

"Many asked this, and in recent days some discoveries were made, which make it likely that it is this secret society we are dealing with. Yesterday, two bodies were found in Halletsville which had notes attached saying 'Yankee hounds'. In Shelby a family was almost whipped to death, because the father had served under General Grant. And today I learned that down by Lyons a black hood was found, onto which two white, lizard-like patches were sewn."

"Thunder and lightning! Klansmen wear such masks!"

"Yes, they hang black hoods, decorated with white figures, over their faces. Each individual is to use a specific figure by which he can be recognized, since they are not supposed to even know their names."

"Then one can assume that this secret society will start its evil doings also here. Watch out, *Señor* Cortesio. They will surely come here. First, they showed up in Halletsville, then the hood was found in Lyons. Isn't the latter place considerably closer than the former?"

"Indeed, *Señor*, you are correct. Beginning today, I shall secure doors and windows twice as carefully and keep my rifles at the ready."

"You will do well doing this. These fellows must not be spared, for they don't spare either. Whoever surrenders to them without a fight, relying on their leniency, is mistaken. I would only talk to them with powder and lead. By the way, something seems to be fishy at the pub. We saw some men there we don't expect anything good to come from. You would be smart to hide everything that would prove you are allied with Juarez. Do this still today! It's better to be cautious when it's not necessary, than to have yourself whipped or even gunned down for some small neglect. But I think we are done now. We shall see you again tomorrow morning. Or do you have something more to tell us?"

"No, *Señores*. We are finished for now. I am glad I got to know you and hope to hear good things from you yet. I am certain that you will make your fortune with Juarez and advance quickly."

With that we were discharged. Cortesio shook hands with us, and we left. When the door had closed behind us and we were walking to Lange's house, I couldn't help giving the oldster a punch in the ribs, while telling him:

"But, mister, what came to your mind that you told such tall stories to the *señor*! Your lies were sky-high!"

"So! Hmm! You don't understand this, sir! It was possible that we would be rejected. That is why I aroused as great an appetite as possible for us in the *señor*."

"And you were even going to accept money! That would have been fraud!"

"Well, evidently not, with him not knowing about it. Why should I not have accepted what he offered us freely?"

"Because it isn't our intention to earn this money."

"So! Well, at this moment we, of course, do not have this intention. But how do you know so precisely that we won't find occasion to serve Juarez? We might be forced to do so in our self-interest. But I can't disagree with you. It is well that we did not accept any money, for only in this way did we likely get the passports and the letters of recommendation. But the best now is that we know where Gibson went. I know this trail very well. We will leave very early, and I'm convinced that we will catch up with him. Once we present our papers, the detachment's commander will not hesitate for a second to hand the two over to us."

There was no need for us to knock at Lange's door. The blacksmith was leaning in the open door and took us inside. The room had three windows which were covered by blankets.

"Don't be surprised by these curtains, gentlemen!" he said. "There's a purpose for them. Altogether, let's speak softly as much as possible. The Klansmen needn't know that you are with me."

"Did you see any of the miscreants?"

"At least some of their scouts. I got bored while you were so long with *Señor* Cortesio and went outside to wait for you, so that you did not need to knock. That's when I heard someone stealing up on the pub's side. I closed my door except for a small gap from which I peered out. Three men walked up and stopped close to the door. Despite the darkness, I saw that they were wearing very long, wide pants, just as broad jackets and hoods, which they had pulled over their faces. Their disguise was of dark cloth and trimmed with bright figures."

"Ah, as is the case with Klansmen!"

"Right. Two of the three stayed by the door. The third stole to the window and tried to look through the shutter. When he returned, he reported only a young man being in the room, my son, and that the old one wasn't in, but food was on the table. They talked about going around the house to find out how best to enter it. Then they disappeared around the corner. When you arrived, we had just finished covering up the windows. But I mustn't forget that you are my guests, in spite of these rogues. Have a seat, eat and drink! Today, you'll find only the food of a backwoodsman with me, but what I have, I'm glad to share. We can talk of the danger threatening me, while you eat."

"A danger from which we won't leave you alone, of course," Old Death replied. "But where's your son?"

"When you came out of Cortesio's house, he stole away. I have a few good German friends I can rely on. He is to get them secretly. You met two of them already. They sat with us at the table in the pub."

"I hope they will sneak covertly into your house? It's to your advantage to make the Klansmen think they are only dealing with you and your son."

"Not to worry! These men know what to do, and I also told my Will what he's to do."

Our dinner consisted of ham, bread and beer. We had barely started when we heard the whimper of a dog, apparently just a few houses away.

"That's the signal," Lange said, as he rose. "The people have arrived."

He went to the door to open it and returned with his son accompanied by five men, armed with rifles, revolvers and knives. They sat down wherever they found something to sit on. None of them spoke a word, but every one of them looked at the windows to see if they had been properly covered. These were the right kind of men, not speaking many words, but ready for action. Among them was an old, gray-haired and gray-bearded man, whose eyes did not leave Old Death. He was the first to speak, and that to my companion:

"Pardon me, mister! Will told me who I would meet here. I was glad, for I think we've met before."

"Possible!" the scout replied. "But I've seen many people's children."

"Do you really not remember me?"

Old Death looked closely at the speaker, then said:

"Indeed, I figure we once met, but I cannot recall where that was."

"Over in California, about twenty years ago in the Chinese Quarter. Give it a try! There was hard gambling with opium being smoked. I had gambled away all my money, close to a thousand dollars. I had a single coin left, which I did not want to put on a card, instead, have a smoke, then put a bullet through my head. I had been a passionate gambler, and was at the end of my rope. Then . . ."

"That's good enough! I remember!" Old Death interrupted him. "It's not necessary for you to go on."

"Oh, yes, sir, for it was you who saved me. You had won half of my losses. You took me aside, returned the money to me and, in its place, demanded my holy promise never to gamble again, and to give up my acquaintance with the opium devil. I made you this promise and kept it, even though it became very hard for me. You are my savior. Since then, I have become a wealthy man, and should you be willing to make me happy, you would permit me to return that money to you."

"I'm not that silly!" Old Death laughed. "For a long time, I was proud to have done something good, and will beware of selling this feeling for money. The day I die, there'll be nothing good I can claim except for this one deed, which I won't give away for anything! Let's talk of other more important things now. Long ago, I warned you of two devils, which I, unfortunately, knew very well myself. You must thank your will power alone for your being saved. Let's forget it!"

Hearing these words made me think of something. In New Orleans he had told me that his mother had put him on his way to fortune; he, however, had taken his own direction. Now, it seemed, he had become familiar with the two worst vices, gambling and smoking opium. Could he have acquired this knowledge only by the observation of others? Hardly so. I guessed that he himself had been a passionate gambler and maybe still was. And concerning the opium, his scraggy, skeleton-like figure pointed to its destructive indulgence. Might he still smoke opium covertly? Likely not, for the smoking of this poison requires time, which was not available during our ride. Maybe he was an opium eater. In any case, he must still depend on the consumption of this dangerous substance. Had he given it up, his body would have recovered little by little from the effects. I began to see the oldster with different eyes. A good portion of pity was now added to the respect I had had for him until now. How much might he have fought these two devils? What healthy body, and what a highly gifted mind he must have possessed, since, even to this day, the poison had not succeeded in totally destroying both. What were all the adventures he had experienced, all the efforts and deprivations of his life in the wilderness compared to the scenes which must have played out inside of him. He might fight just as strongly against the relentless, overpowering passions as does the Indian suffering extinction in his struggle against the superior paleface. He learned that every phase of this battle ended with his defeat, and yet he kept fighting while still on the ground. Old Death, from now on this name carried a horrible overtone for me. The famous scout was doomed to ruin, against which mere physical death was an indescribable relief!

Old Death's final words: "Let's not talk about it any more," had been spoken in a voice, causing the old German to abstain from talking any more about the subject. He answered:

"Well, sir! We are now dealing with an enemy who is just as fierce and relentless as is gambling and opium, but fortunately, it will be easier to get a hold of it than those two vices, and getting a hold of it, we certainly want. The Ku-Klux-Klan is surely a clear opposite of who we Germans are, and all of us must fight the Klan, not just the solitary individual who is directly attacked by its participants. It is a monster, consisting of thousands and thousands of members. Every leniency would be a mistake which will come back to haunt us. Upon the first attack, we must demonstrate that we are merciless. Should the Klansmen succeed in gaining a foothold here, we would be lost. They would tear into us and throttle us, one after the other. That is why I am of the opinion of giving them a reception that would scare them so much that they won't dare come back. I hope this is also your opinion."

Everyone agreed.

"Fine!" the old man continued, since being the oldest made him the speaker. "Then we must make our preparations, so that not only their intentions fail, but they themselves will get to feel the dirty end of the stick. Does anyone have a suggestion? Whoever has a good idea, let's have it."

He, as well as the others, now looked at Old Death. Being an experienced frontiersman, he would know better than anyone else how to deal with such foes. He noticed the expectant looks and silent request expressed by them, made a face, nodded, and said softly:

"If you want to remain silent, I shall say a few words, gentlemen. We can expect that they will come only after Mr. Lange has gone to bed. How is your back door locked? By a bolt?"

"No, by a lock, like all of my doors."

"Fine! That, too, they will know, and I figure, they will bring lock picks. It would be unforgivable if they didn't. The organization will have members who are locksmiths or who know how to handle a lock pick. We can be sure that they will get in, and it is up to us to decide how to receive them."

"Of course, with our rifles. We will fire at them right away," the old German suggested.

"And they will shoot at you, sir! The muzzle flash from your rifles will give away your position. No, we won't shoot. I figure it would be great fun to take them prisoner, without being endangered by their weapons."

"You think this to be possible?"

"Relatively easy, even. We'll hide in the house and let them enter. Once they are in the room, we'll shut the doors and lock them in. Some of us will guard the doors and some the windows. This way, they can't get out and must surrender."

The old German shook his head slowly, then strongly voiced his opinion to gun the intruders down. Upon the old man's comment, Old Death pinched one of his eyes and made such a face that everyone would have erupted into loud laughter, had the situation not been so serious.

"Why do you make such a face, sir?" Lange asked. "Are you not agreed?"

"Not at all, mister. Our friend's suggestion appears to be very practical and easy to accomplish, but I am of the opinion that it would turn out quite different from what he expects. These crooks deserve to be raked over coals, if they come as he thinks. He expects them to enter together and to line up in front of our rifles. If they did, they wouldn't have any brains. I am convinced they will quietly open the backdoor to send at first only one or two men in to reconnoiter. These one or two fellows we could, of course, gun down, but the others would quickly run away, only to come back to finish what they started. No, sir, this plan's no good. We must let them all come in to catch them. I have another, important reason for doing so."

"Even if we would follow your plan, I don't care sending such a number of men with a single fusillade to their death, without them having a moment to recall their sins. We are human and Christians, gentlemen. Of course, we intend to defend ourselves against these people and spoil their return, but we can accomplish this in a less bloody way. If you insist on gunning them down like a herd of wild animals, then go ahead, but I and my companion will not participate in it. We shall leave and look for another place to spend the night, so that we need not think back later with horror and self-reproach!"

These were exactly my sentiments, and his words had the intended effect. The men nodded to each other and the old man said:

"What you said last, sir, is obviously very true. I thought that such a reception would drive them once and for all from La Grange. But I forgot the responsibility we put on ourselves. This is why I'd love to agree to your plan, if only I could see it succeeding."

"Even the best plan can misfire, sir. It's not only humane, but also smart, to let the people enter and fall into our hands alive by locking them up. Believe me, this is much, much better than shooting them. Imagine saddling yourself with the prospect of the Klan's revenge, should you kill so many of its members. You could not keep the Klansmen away from La Grange; just the opposite, they would call in more to avenge their members. Hence, I ask you to accept my plan. It's the best you can do. So as not to miss anything which could spoil the success of our plan, I will now have a look around the house. Maybe I can discover something favorable for us."

"Is it not better if you refrain from this, sir?" Lange asked. "Didn't you say yourself that they likely posted a guard. That man could spot you."

"See me?" Old Death laughed. "No one ever told me that! Old Death is supposed to be so stupid as to let himself be spotted when he steals up on a man or scouts around a house? Mister, that's ludicrous! Should you have a piece of chalk, draw the outline of your house and your yard onto the table, so that I can gain some overview. Then, let me out the back door and wait there for my return. I will not knock, but scratch on the door with my fingernails. So if someone knocks, it is someone else and you mustn't let him in."

Lange picked up a piece of chalk from the door ledge and drew the asked-for outline. Old Death had a good look at it and expressed his satisfaction. When the two men were in the process of leaving, Old Death turned at the door and asked me:

"Did you ever steal up on another person, sir?"

"No," I replied truthfully.

"Then you now have an excellent opportunity to learn how it's done. If you want to come along, let's go!"

"Hold it, sir!" Lange broke in. "That would be too much of a risk. Your companion admitted himself that he's inexperienced in these matters. If he makes the least mistake, the guard will notice you, and all is lost."

"Nonsense! Although I know this young gentleman for only a short time, I know that he's eager to acquire the qualities of a good frontiersman. He will make every effort to avoid mistakes. Yes, if it were to steal up on an Indian, I would beware of taking him along. But let me assure you that no good prairie man would join the Ku-Klux-Klan. That is why we need not expect the guard to possess much experience and the agility to catch us. And even should he spot us, then Old Death would be right there to compensate for the mistake. I want to take this young man along, which is why he will. Come then, sir! But leave your sombrero here, just as I do mine. Their light weave is too shiny and could give us away. Pull your hair down over your forehead and your collar up to your chin, so that the face is mostly covered. You must always stay behind me and do exactly what I'm doing. Then I want to see the Klansman who will spot us!"

No one dared to object, after which we went through the hallway to the back door, for Lange to let us out. He opened it quietly and locked it again after us. As soon as we were outside, Old Death crouched down, with me following suit. It was as if he wanted to penetrate the darkness with his eyes, and I heard how he sucked in air in great draws through his nose. Did he think he could smell our enemies? The thought caused me to smile, which he fortunately did not see. Later, however, he indeed succeed in differentiating a White from an Indian just by his odor.

"I figure there's no one in front of us," the oldster whispered to me, while he pointed across the yard to the stables. "Nevertheless, I want to convince myself. We must be cautious. Did you perhaps learn as a boy to imitate the chirping of a cricket by using a blade of grass holding it between both thumbs?"

I softly affirmed his question.

"There, before the door is some grass. Take a blade and wait for my return, and don't move. Should something happen, chirp, and I shall come immediately."

He lay down on the ground and disappeared into the dark, crawling on all fours. It took about ten minutes for him to return. And, truly, I did not see him coming, but an odor told me of his approach. For the first time I became aware what a sense can do when every organ is strained to the utmost.

"It is as I thought," he whispered. "No one's in the yard or around the corner at the gable end. But behind the other corner, where the window to the bedroom is, there's one standing. Lie down, too, and crawl after me! But not on the belly like a snake, but like a lizard on finger tips and toes. Do not put your soles onto the ground, but only the tips of your shoes. Check the ground with your hands so that you don't break a twig, and tie up your hunting coat so that it will not drag on the earth! Let's go!"

Yes, it was easy for him to give commands. He was experienced, but not I! It worked all right for me for several yards, but it took significant strength to support the weight of the stretched-out body by finger tips and toes. Soon, my arms and legs began to shake, and I needed to lie down from time to time to relieve the strain temporarily. But everything must be learned; when one reads of an Indian or trapper who crawls for half an hour through the grass to attack his foes, then one has no idea of the exertion he experiences. Thus we reached the corner. Old Death halted there; I therefore did, too. After a while he turned his head back to me and whispered:

"There are two. Better be careful!"

I had strained my eyes, nose and ears, but had not noticed anything. I only saw the deep darkness before us, and was barely able to see the scout's head if I forced my eyes to their utmost. He pushed himself farther ahead with me following. Moving away from the wall of the house, he crawled towards a vine-covered fence enclosing the garden. We crept along the fence parallel to the gable side of the house, maybe ten paces distant. Soon, a dark heap, looking almost like a tent, appeared in the space between house and fence. As I later learned, these were stacked bean and hop poles. At their base someone spoke softly. Old Death reached back to me, grabbed me by the collar, pulled me close to him, so that my head was right next to his, and whispered:

"There they sit. We must learn what they are talking about. I should actually go there by myself, since you are still a greenhorn who could spoil the fun. But two hear better than one. Do you trust yourself to get so close that you can understand them?"

"Yes," I whispered, shaking from excitement.

"Then let's go for it. You approach them from this side, I from the other. Once you are close, lower your face to the ground, so that they don't spot the sparkle of your eyes. Should they become aware of you after all, maybe because you are breathing too loudly, then we must immediately render them harmless."

"Kill them?" I whispered fearfully, for the thought to send a man to eternity did not appeal to me.

"No. That would have to be done silently, in which you aren't experienced. We can't dare use our revolvers. As soon as they discover you or me, I'll throw myself on one, you on the other, then put both your hands around his neck and squeeze his throat so that he cannot make a sound. Simultaneously, you must pull him to the ground. After that I'll tell you what to do. Just be sure there's no noise! I saw that you are a strong fellow, but are you sure of being able to silently do in such a scoundrel?"

"Absolutely," I answered, although I didn't quite feel the way he must assume from my reply.

"Then let's do it!"

He crawled around the poles, with me creeping along the other side. I hardly dared to breathe, but precisely because of this, I heard my breathing that much more. I therefore lay down to calm myself and resumed my forward movement only when I was convinced that my lungs would obey me. Then I reached the pyramid of poles. The two scoundrels sat close together facing the house. I was able to approach them so silently that my head was barely three feet distant from the body of the fellow closest to me. Now I rested on my belly and put my face down onto my hands. This had two advantages, as I soon noticed. First, my bright face could not give me away, then I was able to hear much better in this position than with my head raised. The two spoke in this hasty kind of whisper which made their words audible across a few paces.

"We spare the captain," the one closest to me was just saying. "Even though he put you high and dry, he has done his duty, if we look at it seriously. You know, 'Locksmith', although he's one of these damn Germans, it wouldn't be of any use, even hurt us, if we go after him. If we want to settle in here in Texas and also hold our position, we mustn't spoil it with the steamer people."

"Fine! As you wish, Cap'n. I guess the redskin got away. No Indian heads for La Grange, then waits an entire night for the boat to continue. But those two others are still around, those German dogs we wanted to hang. They are spies and must be lynched. If we could only find out where they are. They disappeared into thin air from the pub, out the window, those cowards!"

"We will find them. For that reason, the 'Snail' stayed in the pub, and won't rest until he's found out where they are. He's a smart fellow. We have to thank him also for finding out that this Lange here received payment for his house from the Mexican. It will make for some nice business with lots of fun. The young one, Lange's son, fought us as an officer and must be strung up. His father stuck him into this uniform and must be punished for it; but we are not going to hang him for this. He'll get such a heap of blows that his flesh will leap off his back. Then we'll toss him outside and put fire to the joint."

"That won't hurt him, because it's no longer his," the other replied.

"All the more reason to anger the Mexican, who will no longer send men across the Río Grande to serve Juarez. We are going to clean up and teach him a lesson. Our men got their orders. But are you sure, Locksmith, that your keys will fit?"

"Don't insult me, Cap'n! I know my business. The doors on this house won't be able to resist my lock-pick."

"That should work then. If only these fellows would go to bed soon. Our men will be impatient; they sit devilishly uncomfortable in those elder bushes behind the stable. The Langes tossed all their broken glass in there. I wish you could soon leave to give our comrades a signal. I'm going to listen one more time whether these German night owls are still not in bed."

The Cap'n, got up and walked softly to the shuttered window of the living room. He had been called 'Cap'n', and from this title and the conversation I had overheard, he had to be the leader. The other had been called 'Locksmith'. Maybe that was his name, but more likely this was his profession, since he had said he was proficient in the use of a lock-pick. Just then he made a move from which I heard a soft jingle. He carried keys. I was interrupted in my thoughts by a slight pull on one of my legs. I crept back. Old Death lay behind the poles. I pushed my face close to his, after which he asked whether I had heard and understood everything. I confirmed it.

"Then we know where we are at. We shall play a trick on these characters, from which they'll shake their heads for a long time to come! If I could only rely on you!"

"Give it a try! What am I to do?" I replied, annoyed about Old Death's constant doubts.

"Take one of the fellows by his throat."

"Well, sir, I shall!"

"Fine! But to make sure, I'll explain to you how to do it. Listen! I hope he isn't coming here behind the poles!"

"The Cap'n was returning from the window. Fortunately, he sat down right away.

Old Death did not think it necessary to continue eavesdropping on them. He whispered to me:

"So, let me tell you how you must grab the fellow. You creep up on him from behind. As soon as I emit a subdued call, you put both your hands around his neck, but properly; do you understand? Your thumbs must be on his neck with their tips touching each other, with the other four fingers around each side pressing against the throat. With these eight fingertips you press his larynx inward as hard as possible!"

"That will cause him to suffocate!"

"Nonsense! Suffocating doesn't happen so fast. Rogues, scoundrels and other such characters belong to a class of carnivores with an immensely tough life. Once you've got him, you push him down, because then you can apply much more force. But make no mistake! As I've said, you'll be behind him, so you mustn't pull him towards you, but push him down sideways to your left, so that he comes to lie first on his side, then on his belly, with you on top of him. That's the safest way to hold him. Since you aren't familiar with such tricks, it's possible he'll make a sound. But that will be at most a brief, desperate "bah". Then he'll be quiet and you'll hold him down until I come. You think you can do it?"

"Sure. When I was younger I scuffled quite a bit."

"Scuffled!" the oldster sneered. "That doesn't mean a thing! Take also into account that the Cap'n is taller than the other. Make your teacher proud and don't have yourself laughed at by our men in the house! Let's go! But wait for my call!"

He pushed away from me again, while I crept back to where I had lain earlier. I now approached the Cap'n even closer and pulled my knees up to my body in order to be able to rise momentarily. I must admit that my feeling was not one I could call 'happy'. For the first time in my life I was to attack another man in a truly hostile manner, and was to take him by his throat, which could easily cause his death. And if the attack failed, it was very likely that a small revolver bullet would have dire consequences for me. I felt like a schoolboy facing a test, not certain whether he will stumble or not. But then, I thought of the seven men who had advised Old Death against taking me along, and decided not to give them a reason to laugh at me. The two Klansmen were continuing their conversation which no longer provided anything of value to us, both expressing their annoyance that they, and their companions, had to wait so long. Just when they mentioned the two of us, and that the Snail was going to find our whereabouts, I heard Old Death's subdued call:

"Here we are, gents! Watch out!"

I quickly rose behind the Cap'n and put my hands around his neck the way the scout had told me. With my fingertips hard on his larynx, I pushed him sideways to the ground, then, with my knee pressed him farther to the side, then knelt on his back. He had not made a sound, only jerked convulsively with arms and legs, after which he lay still. Now Old Death crouched down before us and knocked the Cap'n with his revolver handle on the head, then said:

"Let go, or he'll truly suffocate! For a beginner you didn't do too badly. You've got talent, and I figure that at some time in the future you'll make a capital villain or a competent frontiersman. Put the fellow on your back and come along!"

He took one, while I slung the other over my shoulder; then we returned to the back door, on which Old Death scratched as had been agreed earlier. Lange let us enter.

"What are you bringing there?" he asked softly, when he noticed, despite the darkness, that we were carrying loads.

"You'll see," Old Death replied amused. "Lock behind us and come along!"

The men were very much surprised when we put our catch onto the floor. "Thunder and lightning!" the old German said startled. "These are two Klansmen! Are they dead?"

"Hope not," the scout replied. "Do you see how right I was to take this young man along. He kept himself well, even took down the leader of the gang."

"The leader? Ah, that's wonderful! But where are his men, and why are you bringing these two here?"

"Must I explain that to you? It's easy to guess. I and this young man here, will put on the outfits of these two scoundrels, then bring the entire gang here that's hiding by the stable."

"Are you the devil's? You are risking your lives. What if they discover that you are Klansmen in disguise?"

"They won't," the oldster replied in a superior voice. "Old Death is a crafty devil, and this young man isn't quite as thick as he looks."

This ambiguous praise was no insult to me, for I felt an immense satisfaction for what I had accomplished. When, as a boy, I had to translate 'old father Homer', I had at times lamented not having lived at that time, not to have besieged Troy and to have conquered it with the help of the well-known hollow horse. How magnificent must it have been to challenge the enemy hero with a proud address, then to ram the spear through his shining armor! Although I had only taken a common Klansman by his neck, I figured that it still held a trace of classic Greek heroism, which made my heart beat faster. That it was very sad having to pounce on a fellow man I did not contemplate. Old Death recounted what we had overheard and when done, explained his plan. I was to go behind the stable to bring the Klansmen in, disguised as the Locksmith. He was to put on the Captain's outfit, which happened to fit him, and play the leader. "It's obvious," the scout added, "that we'll speak only softly, because when whispering all voices sound alike."

"Well, if you care to risk it, go ahead!" Lange said. "You aren't risking our necks, but your own. But what are we to do in the meantime?"

"First, go outside and bring several strong poles in, which we'll brace against the bedroom door, so that it can't be opened from inside. Then you'll extinguish all lights and hide in the house. That's all you need to do. What's going to happen then, I can't say yet."

The Langes went out into the yard to get the poles. In the meantime we relieved the two prisoners of their outfits, which were black with a white sewn-on insignia. The Captain's outfit showed a dagger on the hood, chest and thighs, while that of the Locksmith's had keys attached at the same locations. So the dagger was the leader's symbol. The one in the pub, trying to find our whereabouts, had been called 'Snail.' He, therefore, would carry an outfit with snail symbols. Just when we were removing the Captain's pants, cut like a Swiss game-keeper's trousers worn over the actual pants, he awoke. Confused and surprised, he looked around, then made a move to jump up, at the same time reaching for his side where he had kept his revolver. Old Death pushed him quickly down again, held his Bowie knife's tip to his chest, and threatened:

"Quiet, my boy! A sound or a move I haven't allowed you, and this nice piece of steel is going into your body!"

The Klansman was a fellow in his early thirties with a militarily-trimmed beard. His sharply cut, dark-complexed face made one guess him to be of Mediterranean extraction. He reached with both hands to his hurting head, where he had been struck by the blow, and asked: "Where am I? Who are you?"

"This is Lange's house, the one you wanted to attack, boy. And I and this young man here are the Germans, whose whereabouts the Snail was to find out. You see that your intentions drove you right to where you wanted to be."

The man pinched his lips and threw a wild and scared look around. At that moment Lange and his son returned, bringing several poles and a saw. "There's enough rope, sufficient to tie up twenty men," Lange senior said.

"Let's have some for these two first."

"No, I won't have myself tied up!" the Captain exclaimed, again trying to get up. But Old Death once more put his knife to him, saying:

"Don't dare to move! In any case, they forgot to tell you who I am. I'm called Old Death, and you may know what that means. Or do you think me to be a friend of slave breeders and Klansmen?"

"You are Old . . . Old Death!" the Captain stammered, fearfully.

"Yes, my boy, that's me. And now, don't entertain any useless illusions. I know that you wanted to hang young Lange and whip his father to the bone, after which you intended to burn down the house. If you still hope for any leniency, you can get it only if you resign yourself to your fate."

"Old Death, Old Death!" the pale-as-death looking man repeated. "Then I'm lost!"

"Not yet. We aren't wicked murderers like you, but shall spare your lives, provided you surrender without a fight. If you don't, your bodies will be tossed into the river. I'll tell you now what I want. If you act accordingly, you and your fellows can leave the county, even Texas, but without coming back. If you scorn my advice, it's the end for you. I'm now going to get your men in here. They will become our prisoners, same as you. Command them to surrender. If you don't, we'll gun you down like a bunch of wild pigeons in a tree!"

The Klansman was tied up and gagged. The other had also come to, but preferred not to say anything. Now the two were carried to Lange's and his son's beds, where they were tied up so thoroughly that they were unable to move, after which they had the covers pulled up to their necks.

"So!" Old Death laughed. "Now, the comedy can begin. These fellows will be mightily surprised when they recognize their own in these cozy sleepers. They will be very happy! But tell me, mister Lange, how it might be possible to talk with these fellows, once we've got them, and to watch them simultaneously?"

"Hmm!" Lange responded, while he pointed to the ceiling, "from up there. The ceiling consists only of a layer of boards. We could loosen one of them."

"Then come along, all of you, and bring your weapons. You climb up the stairs and stay up there until it's time. But let's first take care of suitable bracing poles."

Several poles were shortened with the saw, so that they fit properly, then were put aside. I put on the pants and blouse of the Locksmith, while Old Death dressed up in the Captain's outfit. In the wide pocket of my borrowed pants I found an iron ring with a lot of false keys.

"You won't need them," Old Death said. "You are no locksmith and no burglar and would give yourself away by some clumsiness. You must remove the proper keys and take only those along. Then you act as if you were using the lock pick. We will carry our knives and revolvers. But we'll leave our rifles here with the men who, while we accomplish our task outside, will loosen a board upstairs. After that all the lights must be extinguished."

Now we readied ourselves to step outside. We were let out, after which I locked the door from outside. I carried only the keys to the front door, the living room and the bedroom. Now, Old Death instructed me in greater detail than he had earlier. When we heard the bang, caused by the forcing off of the board, we separated. He walked to the gable side of the house where the poles stood, while I crossed the yard to fetch my 'dear comrades'. At that moment I felt like a man who's walking to the river, convinced that he will be tossed into the water to learn how to swim. If the bandits discovered my disguise, I could find rescue only by a quick escape. I turned for the stable. In doing so, I did not step too softly, for I wanted to be heard and be addressed by them, and talk to them as little as possible. Just when I was turning a corner, a figure I almost stumbled over, rose before me. "Stop!" I was told. "Is it you, Locksmith?"

"Yes. Come now, but very quietly."

"I'll tell the Lieutenant. Wait here!"

He walked away. So, there was also a Lieutenant! The Ku-Klux-Klan seemed to be like a military organization. Not a minute later, someone else came and softly said:

"That took long. Are the damned Germans finally asleep?"

"At last! But now the better news. They finished a whole crock of brandy together."

"Then it will be an easy game. How's it with the doors?"

"All's going well."

"Then let's go. It's past midnight already, and soon the ruckus will start at Cortesio's for which we set an hour past midnight. Lead us!"

Behind him, a number of disguised figures appeared, who now followed me. When we got to the house, Old Death, whose figure could not be differentiated in the darkness from that of the Captain, quietly stepped up.

"Do you have any special orders, Cap'n," asked the second officer.

"No," the oldster replied with his self-assured voice. "It'll all depend on what we find inside. All right, Locksmith, let's give the door a try."

I stepped to the door, holding the proper key, but acted as if I had to try out a few others first. When I had the door open, Old Death and I stood outside to let the others pass. The Lieutenant remained also with us. When all had entered, he asked us:

"Lights on now?"

"Only yours for the time being."

We walked in, too. I closed the door, but without locking it. The Lieutenant lit a shielded lantern, which he pulled from a pocket of his wide pants. His outfit was marked with the white symbols of a Bowie knife. We had counted fifteen men, with everyone having different symbols. There were balls, half-moons, crosses, snakes, stars, frogs, wheels, hearts, scissors, birds, quadruped animals and many other figures. The Lieutenant, apparently, loved to give orders. While the others stood motionless, he shone the light around, then asked:

"Shall we post a guard by the door?"

"What for?" answered Old Death. "It's not necessary. Locksmith can lock it; then no one can enter."

I locked it right away, so as not to afford the Lieutenant time for concern, but left the key in the lock.

"We must all enter," Old Death told them now. "These blacksmiths are mighty strong fellows."

"Today, you are quite different, Cap'n!"

"Because the situation is different. Let's go ahead now!"

He pushed me towards the living room door where the same procedure ensued. I fumbled, acting as if I couldn't find the proper key right away. Then we all entered. Old Death took the lantern from the Lieutenant and shone the light at the bedroom door.

"In there!" he said. "But quietly, quietly!"

"Shall we pull out our other lanterns now?"

"Not yet, only when we are inside the room."

By asking this, Old Death wanted to prevent our captive sleepers from being recognized right away. It was important to get all fifteen men into the room, so that the siege would not extend into the living room. I now proceeded even more slowly and seemingly careful. At last, the door opened. Old Death let light fall into the room, looked in, and whispered:

"They are asleep. Get inside, but quietly! The Lieutenant first!"

He did not leave the man any time to object, but pushed him forward, the others tiptoed after him. The last had barely entered, when I closed the door and locked it.

"Quickly! Get the poles!" Old Death commanded.

We picked them up. They were of just the right length to wedge them at an incline between window frame and the edge of the door. It would take the strength of an elephant to break the door open. I now hurried to the stairs.

"Are you ready?" I asked. "We've got them in the trap. Come on down!"

They quickly came down.

"They are all in the bedroom. Three of you hurry out in front of the window and wedge poles against it. Whoever tries to climb out will get a bullet!"

I opened the back door again, and three of the men hurried outside, the others followed me to the living room. In the meantime a terrible ruckus had started in the bedroom. The tricked gang had discovered that they had been locked in, taken their lanterns out and had found out who lay in the beds. They now cursed and screamed wildly and were hitting the door with their fists.

"Open up, open up, or we'll wreck everything!" they shouted. When they found their threats to be of no use, they tried to break the door open, which, however, did not give, as the poles were doing their job. Then we heard them open the window, trying to push open the shutters.

"It doesn't work!" we heard an angry voice shouting. "They wedged something against it from outside."

Then we heard the threatening response from outside:

"Get away from the shutters! You've been captured. Whoever pushes the shutters open will get a bullet!"

"Yes," Old Death added from the living room, "the door's also guarded. There are enough people here to send you all to hell. Check with your captain what to do."

And more quietly he said to me:

"Come with me up to the attic. Bring the lantern and your rifle! The others should light a lantern here."

We went up to the attic above the bedroom, where we quickly found the loosened board. After we had covered up the lantern light and had taken our hoods off, we lifted the board out and were now able to look down into the bedroom, which was illuminated by several lamps.

There they stood, tightly packed. The two prisoners had been freed of their bonds and gags. The Captain was speaking softly and urgently to his men. "Oho," the Lieutenant said louder. "We are to surrender! With how many opponents are we actually dealing?"

"With more than enough to gun you down in less than five seconds!" Old Death shouted down.

All eyes now looked up. That same moment we heard a shot being fired, then another. Old Death immediately understood the meaning and how he could make use of it.

"Did you hear it?" he continued. "Cortesio is also receiving your buddies with bullets. All of La Grange is against you. Everyone knew of your coming and was ready to welcome you, a bit differently from what you expected. We need no Ku-Klux-Klan here. In the living room next to you stand twelve, outside, in front of the window six, and up here are another six men. My name's Old Death, you understand? I give you ten minutes. If by then you put your weapons down, we'll treat you mildly. If you don't, we'll gun you down. I've nothing more to tell you; this is my last word. Think about it!"

He retuned the board to its place and said softly to me:

"Let's get down quickly to help Cortesio!"

We took two men along from the living room, with Lange and his son remaining, and from outside another two. One guard was enough for the time being. Now we were five. Just then another shot cracked. We darted over and saw four or five disguised figures standing there. Just then, as many came running from behind Cortesio's house, with one of them shouting louder than he probably intended:

"They are also firing back there. We can't get in!"

I lay down on the ground and crept closer, from where I heard one of them standing in the front of the house, answering:

"By the devil! Who would have thought that? The Mexican smelled a rat and is waking everyone with his shots. Lights are coming on everywhere. Back there we can already hear steps approaching. They will be after us in a few minutes; let's hurry, and bash in the door with our rifle butts! Shall we?"

I did not wait to hear the reply, but darted back to my companions, asking them:

"Quickly, gents, let's hit the gang with our rifle butts! They want to break through Cortesio's door."

"Well, well! Let them have it then!" was the answer, and instantly blows fell onto the desperate fellows as if coming from a blue sky. They ran off, leaving four of their cronies behind, who had been struck so well that they were unable to flee. They were disarmed, after which Old Death walked to Cortesio's door and knocked.

"Who's there," it came from inside.

"Old Death, *Señor*. We got rid of the scoundrels. They are gone. Open up!"

The door was cautiously opened. The Mexican recognized the scout, although Old Death still wore the Captain's pants and blouse, and said:

"Are they truly gone?"

"Yes. It was fortunate you warned me, or I would have been done in. I was shooting up front and my Negro from the back of the house, so that they couldn't come in. But then I saw that you attacked them."

"Yes, we relieved you. But now come to our assistance! They won't come back for you, but we still have fifteen fellows caught over there that we don't want to get away. In the meantime, have your Negro run from house to house and make some noise. All of La Grange must be woken up, so that these scoundrels can be told what's what."

"Then he should, first of all, run for the sheriff. Listen, people are coming! I'll be over there in a minute, *Señor*."

He stepped back into the house. From the right came two men, rifles in hand, and asked for the reason of the shots. When we told them, they were right away ready to join us. Even those residents of La Grange who held secessionist sentiments, were still not allied with the Klansmen, whose activities should be an outrage to adherents of every political orientation. We grabbed the four impaired crooks by their scruffs and took them over to Lange's living room. Lange told us that the Klansmen had kept quiet until now. *Señor* Cortesio joined us, and soon so many residents of La Grange drifted in that Lange's living room became too small and many had to stay outside. This caused a confusion of voices, and from the noise of people running back and forth the Klansmen could figure how things stood. Old Death once more took me along to the attic. Once we removed the board, an image of silent, but angry desperation presented itself. Our captives leaned against the walls, sat on the beds, or lay on the floor and, in the truest sense of the word, were hanging their covered heads.

"Well," Old Death called down, "the ten minutes are over. What did you decide?"

He received no response. Only one uttered a curse.

"You are staying silent. Well, then I assume that you don't intend to surrender. Let's start shooting then."

He aimed his rifle with me following suit. Strangely enough, none of them thought of using their revolvers against us. These crooks were simply cowards and their courage consisted only in committing atrocities on defenseless people.

"An answer then, or I'm going to shoot!" the oldster threatened. "This is my last word."

None replied. Now Old Death whispered to me:

"You shoot too. We must hit them or they won't respect us. Aim for the Lieutenant's hand, I for the Captain's."

Our shots cracked simultaneously, the bullets hitting home. The two 'officers' screamed, followed by the repulsive concert of the entire gang. Our shots had been heard outside. The men thought us to be in a fight with the Klansmen, which is why shots were fired from the living room and from outside the window. Bullets whizzed through the door and through the shutters into the bedroom. Several men were hit. All threw themselves on the floor, where they felt safer, and screamed as if they were being roasted at the stake. The Captain knelt before the bed where he had wrapped his bleeding hand in some linen cloth, and called up to us:

"Stop! We surrender!"

"Fine!" Old Death replied. "All of you: step away from the beds! Throw your weapons on them, then you will be let out. But if we still find a weapon on any one of you, he will get a bullet. You can hear that there are several hundred people outside. Only total surrender will save you."

The Klansmen's' situation was such that they could not even think of fleeing, and they were aware of it. If they surrendered, what could then happen to them? Their intentions had not come to pass, which is why they could not be accused of a crime. In any case, it was better to submit to Old Death's demand than to try for a futile attempt to break out, which would have serious consequences. So we watched them tossing their knives and revolvers onto the beds.

"Fine, gents!" the oldster told them. "Now, let me tell you that I'll shoot anyone trying to pick up his weapon when the door is opened. Wait a moment now."

He sent me down to the living room to tell Lange to let the Klansmen out and to take them prisoner. But to carry out his order was not as easy as we had thought. Illuminated by several lamps, the downstairs was completely filled with people. I was still wearing the Klansmen' outfit, so that I was thought to be a member of this secret society, and I was immediately apprehended. My objections were not listened to; I was pushed and bumped aplenty, so that the spots where I was hit still hurt a few days later. The people wanted to get me outside the house to lynch me on the spot.

I sure was in a tight spot, since my attackers did not know me. Particularly, a tall, rawboned fellow kept punching his fists into my side, while he roared:

"Out with him, out! The trees have branches, beautiful branches, magnificent branches, strong branches, which are sure not to crack when we hang such a character from one." In the process he was pushing me towards the backdoor.

"But, sir," I shouted at him, "I'm no Klansman. Ask Mr. Lange!"

"Beautiful branches, magnificent ones!" was his answer with a renewed punch to my ribs.

"I demand to be taken to Mr. Lange in the living room! I put on this disguise only to . . ."

"Veritably pretty branches! And a rope will also be found in La Grange, a fine, really elegant rope made of good hemp!"

He kept pushing me, and when he punched me again on my side, I finally lost patience. The fellow might be able to incite the people to the point of lynching me. Once outside, I couldn't expect anything good.

"Mister," I now roared at him, "I won't stand for more of your coarseness! I want to see Mr. Lange. Understood!"

"Magnificent branches! Incomparable ropes!" he shouted even louder than I, and at the same time, gave me a mighty blow to the ribs. Now my pot boiled over. I punched him full force in his face, so that he surely would have tumbled backwards onto the floor, had there been sufficient space and people not been standing so tightly packed. But I gained a bit of room nevertheless. I used the opportunity to push forward with all my strength, shouted with all my might and beat about me, dishing out punches, pushes and blows, from which people moved away far enough, so that I was able to win a narrow passage through which I gained the living room. However, while I used my fists aggressively on my way forward, the opening behind me closed right away again, and every arm that could reach me resulted in a hail of fists landing on me. Woe to the real Klansmen, with an imitation already beaten in this way! The rawboned fellow had followed me quickly. He screamed like a stuck pig and arrived almost at the same time as me in the living room. When Lange saw him, he asked:

"Heavens, good sir, what's that. Why are you screaming like this? And what are you bleeding from?"

"Onto a tree with this Klansman!" the angry man shouted. "He smashed my nose and broke two, three or four of my teeth! Wonderful teeth! The only ones I still had up front! Hang him!"

His anger was now more justified than before, for he was bleeding quite a bit.

"This one?" Lange asked, pointing at me. "But good man, he is no Klansman! He's our friend, and we have to thank him most of all for catching the fellows. Without him, neither we, nor *Señor* Cortesio would still be alive and our houses would be on fire!"

The rawboned man opened his eyes and with his bleeding mouth opened wide, pointed at me, and asked:

"With – out – this one?"

Everyone broke into laughter about the wonderful scene. With his handkerchief he dried sweat from his forehead and the blood from his mouth and nose, while I rubbed the various spots where still later the impacts from his bony fingers were visible.

"Now you hear it, man!" I thundered at him. "You were so wild to see me dangle! And from your devilish punches I now feel every little bone in my body. I am an abused make-believe Klan's-fellow, sir!"

The man looked helpless as he silently held out his left open hand and showed us the two incisors now removed from their earlier safe domicile. I now had to laugh too, for he looked simply too pitiful. Then I was, at last, able to complete my mission.

Thoughtfully, every available rope had been gathered. Together with cords, strings and straps they lay ready in a corner.

"Let them come out then!" I said. "But singly, and every one of them must be tied up as soon as he comes out. Old Death won't know what took so long. The sheriff should actually be here. Wasn't Cortesio's Negro going to get him?"

"The sheriff?" Lange asked surprised. "But he's here. Then you don't even know who you have to thank for all the punches. There he stands!"

With that, he pointed at the rawboned man.

"By the devil, sir!" I snapped at him. "You yourself are the sheriff? And you are the foremost executive of this beautiful county? You are the one who must maintain order and the proper observance of the law, yet you personally led the attempted lynching. That's just too much! It's no wonder that the Klansmen dare spread so nicely in your county!"

This caused him an indescribable embarrassment. About all he could do was to hold his two teeth once more out to me, and stammer: "

"Pardon, sir! I was mistaken, but you simply looked too criminal!"

"Thanks a million! You look a lot more pitiful. Better do your duty now, if you don't want to come under suspicion of wanting to lynch good people because you are secretly in cahoots with the Klan!"

This returned his awareness to his official position.

"Oho!" he exclaimed, strutting about. "I, the sheriff of this honorable county Fayette, am to be a Klansman? I shall right away demonstrate the opposite. We will judge these scoundrels still tonight. Step back, gents, so that we'll make room for them to come out. Step out into the hallway, but have your rifles pointed through the door, so that they see who's lord of the premises. Pick up some ropes and open the door!"

His command was followed and half a dozen double-barreled muzzles pointed from the door into the room. There were now the sheriff, the two Langes, Cortesio, two of our German allies from earlier, and myself left in the room. Outside, the crowd hollered to speed up the action. We therefore opened the shutters, so that the people could look in to see that we were not idle. We removed the braces and I unlocked the door. None of the Klansmen wanted to be the first to come out. I asked the Captain and the Lieutenant to come. Both had their hands wrapped in handkerchiefs. In addition to them, three or four members of the gang had been wounded. Up, where the board had been removed from the ceiling, sat Old Death aiming down his rifle. The Klansmen, outsmarted by Old Death, had their hands tied to their backs, then had to step outside to join the four bound companions whom we had captured at Cortesio's. Seeing this, the folks outside rose to cheers and hurrahs. For the time being, we left the prisoners their hoods, except for the Captain and the Lieutenant, whose faces we exposed. Upon my questioning and efforts, a man was fetched who was said to be a healer and claimed to be able to quickly dress, operate and heal all kinds of injuries. He checked the injured men, then rushed half a dozen of the La Grange people through the house to find cotton wool, oakum, rags, tape, fat, soap and other items he needed to carry out his humanitarian efforts.

When, at last, we had all Klansmen secured, the question arose of where to put them, for there were no prison facilities for nineteen men in La Grange.

"Put them into the pub's saloon!" the sheriff ordered. "It's best to clean up the situation as quickly as possible. Let's form a jury and execute the judgment right away. We are dealing here with an exceptional situation, which calls for exceptional rules."

This information spread quickly and the crowd hurried to the pub to find a good place there. Many who did not succeed at that, stood on the stairs, the hallway and in front of the place. They welcomed the Klansmen with terrible threats, requiring their escort to stay on guard against any violence. It took some effort for us to make it into the so-called saloon, a large but very low-ceilinged room, frequently used for dances. The musicians were cleared out, and the captives were put in their place. When their hoods were removed, it turned out that not a single one was from the area.

Now a jury was formed, with the sheriff as chairman. The jury consisted of the prosecutor, an attorney for the defense, a secretary and the jurors. The tribunal was composed in a way that caused me to shudder, but it could be excused somewhat by the present conditions and the nature of the case.

Witnesses were the two Langes, Cortesio, the five Germans, Old Death and myself. For evidence, the accused's weapons were deposited on a table, including their rifles. Old Death had taken care to have them fetched from their hiding place behind the horse stable. It turned out that every barrel was loaded. The sheriff declared the hearing opened, remarking that swearing-in the witnesses could be omitted, since the ethical condition of the accused was insufficient to trouble such moral and honorable gentlemen like us with an oath. Except for the Klansmen, there were supposedly only men in the saloon whose moral mindset was beyond all doubt, something he wanted to state to his delight and satisfaction. A multi-voiced bravo rewarded this flattery, which he acknowledged with an appreciative bow. But I spied several faces which made me doubt the law-abiding character of these men.

First, the witnesses were heard, and Old Death recounted the events broadly. The rest of us were limited to confirming his narrative. Then the prosecutor stepped forward, asserting that the accused belonged to an outlawed organization pursuing the ruinous purpose of undermining lawful order, of destroying the foundation of the state, and were spreading those damnable crimes, which could only be punished by many years of imprisonment or even with death. Even their membership was sufficient to justify ten or twenty years of imprisonment. Furthermore, it was shown that the accused intended the killing of a former officer of the republic, the cruel whipping of two honorable gentlemen, and the burning-down of a house in this blessed city. And, finally, it had been their intention to hang two exceptionally peaceful and honorable men – upon these words he bowed towards Old Death and me – which, in all likelihood would have led to our death, and this needed to be punished most severely, especially since the residents of La Grange had to be most grateful to us for having prevented this misfortune. He was therefore calling for strict punishment and asked for several of the Klansmen, whom the honorable jurors would very well know how to select, to hang by their neck, and to heartily whip the others for their moral education, and afterwards to put them behind bars for life, so that they would be unable to further endanger the state and the recognized honorable citizens.

The prosecutor, too, received bravos and also acknowledged them with a dignified bow. He was followed by the attorney, who remarked in his opening statement that the chairman had made the inexcusable omission of not having asked the accused for their names and other circumstances, which he, herewith, humbly requested to be done, since one ought to know who was to be hanged and who locked away, thus simplifying the issuing of death certificates and other required recordings. It was a valid statement, which received my full but silent agreement. He fully admitted to the said intentions of the Klansmen, accepting their veracity. However, since none of their intentions had come to pass, and all of them had remained in a state of attempt only, there could not be any talk of hanging or imprisoning them. Hence, he was questioning whether the mere attempt had done any damage or could further endanger anyone. Certainly not! Therefore, since no one had incurred any losses, he insisted on a full acquittal, by which the members of this high court would attest to being humanitarian gentlemen and peaceful Christians. He, too, received applause from a few voices. Then he did a semicircle bow, as if all the world had cheered him.

Now the chairman rose for a second time. His first remark was that it had been his intention to avoid asking for the names and 'other habits' of the accused, since he was entirely convinced that they would have lied to him anyway. Should hanging be decided on, he suggested, in order to shorten things, to issue a single, summary death certificate which could read as follows: "Nineteen Klansmen hanged, it being their own fault." He admitted that this was only a proposal, following which he was going to pose the question of responsibility. "But we can thank only the two visitors that their attempts did not turn into actual deeds. Attempts by themselves are dangerous and must be punished." He went on that he did not care, nor had the time, to accept the back and forth between the prosecutor and the defense; that he was also not prepared to occupy himself with a gang, who, nineteen men strong, had let themselves be caught by two men. Such heroes were not worth the attention of even a canary or sparrow. He had already been accused of possibly being a friend of the Klan, which he could not let rest, and would make sure that these people would be shamed and quickly moved out, never to think of returning. He, therefore, put the question to the gentlemen-jurors, whether the accused were thought guilty of attempted murder, robbery, bodily harm and arson, asking them not to delay their decision to December of next year.

His sarcastic exposition was rewarded by loud applause. The gentlemen-jurors gathered in a corner, discussed the situation for not much longer than two minutes, then their spokesman reported the decision to the chairman, who made it public. It was 'guilty.' A soft-spoken conversation now ensued between the sheriff and his committee members. It was highly conspicuous that the sheriff issued an order during this consultation to relieve the captives of everything they carried in their pockets, especially money. When the order was completed, the money was counted. The sheriff nodded satisfied, then rose to announce the verdict.

"Gentlemen," he began, "the accused have been found guilty. I believe it will be according to your wishes when I tell you without many words what the punishment will be and on whose imposition and efficient execution we have agreed upon. The suggested crimes did not come to be committed. For this reason we followed the attorney's suggestion, who appealed to our humanity and Christian persuasion, and decided to refrain from lethal punishment . . ."

The accused breathed easier, as one could see, but among the listeners individual shouts of dissatisfaction arose. The sheriff continued:

"As I said already, attempted crime nevertheless implies danger. If we do not punish these Klan fellows, we must at least take care that they will not become a danger to us in the future. That is why we decided to remove them from the State of Texas, and this in such a shameful way that they will not entertain the thought of ever coming back. Therefore, it has been decided that they will have their head hair and beards shorn down to the skin. Some of the gentlemen present will surely enjoy doing this. Whoever lives close by may leave to get some scissors; those scissors which don't cut too well, will get preference from the honored jury."

General laughter followed this comment. One of the men opened a window and shouted:

"Get some scissors! The Klan fellows will be shorn. Whoever brings a pair of scissors will be admitted inside."

I was convinced that just about everyone waiting outside was running off that very moment to fetch some scissors and, truly, I heard that I had guessed correctly. There ensued a general commotion of running and shouting for shears and scissors. One voice could be heard roaring even about shears for clipping trees and sheep.

"It has further been decided," the sheriff continued, "to take the convicts to the steamer which arrives after 11 PM from Austin and will leave at daybreak for Matagorda. When it arrives here, the convicts will be put on board ship, which will not land at any Texan port again. They will be put on deck of this vessel, no matter who they are, or where they came from, and where the ship is headed to. From now until their boarding in Matagorda, they will not be permitted to take off their outfits, so that every passenger can see how we Texans deal with Klansmen. Their bonds will also not be removed, and they will receive water and bread only when they arrive in Matagorda. The expenses we incurred will be paid for from their own money, about three thousand dollars, most likely robbed from others. In addition, we will confiscate their property, especially the weapons, to be immediately auctioned-off. The jury decided that the proceeds from the auction are to be used for the purchase of beer and brandy. These libations are intended for the honorable witnesses of this hearing, together with their ladies, as a sip during the reel, which we'll dance here upon the conclusion of the court procedures. Then, at daybreak, we will accompany the Klansmen under the sounds of some dignified music and the singing of a tragic song to the steamer. The convicts will watch our dance and remain standing right where they presently are. Should their defense attorney have any objections against this judgment, we will be glad to listen, provided he will make it short. We must yet shear the fellows and auction off their belongings, which is quite a bit to take care of prior to the dance."

The shouts of acclaim that now arose should actually have been called more of a roar. The chairman and the defense attorney had to make a real effort to return silence for the latter to be able to speak:

"I must say the following for the benefit of my clients," he said. "I find the judgment of the highly respected court somewhat hard, however, its severity is compensated sufficiently by the last part of the judgment concerning beer, brandy, dance, music and song. Therefore, in the name of the party whose interests I am representing, I declare myself in full agreement with the judgment and hope that it will serve them as a call for a better and more useful way of life. I warn them also never to come back to us since, in that case, I would refuse to assume their defense again, following which they would not find such excellent legal advice. On the business side, I would like to note that I am asking for two dollars per client for my defense, which for nineteen men amounts to thirty-eight dollars. If this amount is paid to me right away in front of these many witnesses, I see no need for me to sign a receipt. In that case I shall take only eighteen for myself and donate the remaining twenty for lighting and rent of the saloon. The musicians can be compensated by an entry charge which I suggest to amount to fifteen cents per gentleman. Of course, the ladies need not pay anything."

He sat down with the sheriff, who voiced his complete agreement.

I sat there like in a dream. Was this real? I could not doubt it, for the defense attorney received his money, and many ran off to get their women for the dance. Others returned with all kinds of scissors. I felt like getting angry, but did not succeed, and thus joined Old Death in his laughter; he found the outcome of the adventure hilarious. Then the Klansmen were truly shorn bare, followed by the auction. The rifles went quickly and were well paid for, and the rest of the items soon disappeared, too. The noise caused in the process, the coming and going, the pushing and pulling, were indescribable. Everyone wanted to get into the saloon, although its capacity would hold only a tenth of those present. Then the musicians arrived, a clarinetist, a violinist, a trumpeter and one with an old bassoon. This fantastic band found a place in a corner and began to tune their pre-Deluge instruments, giving me a not quite pleasant foretaste of their forthcoming performance. I wanted to leave, especially since the ladies were now arriving on the scene, but this did not go down well with Old Death. He declared that the two of us, being the main characters, now, after the effort and the danger, must also enjoy the forthcoming pleasure. The sheriff happened to hear this and quickly agreed, even insisted energetically that it would be an insult to the citizenry of La Grange if both of us refused to lead the first round of dances. For this he offered Old Death his wife and me his daughter, supposedly excellent dancers. Claiming that since I had knocked out two of his teeth, with him having punched my ribs a number of times, we ought to see ourselves as kindred spirits, and it would, therefore, insult his soul profoundly if I would not agree to his request to remain. He offered to reserve a special table for the two of us. What could I do? Unfortunately, his two ladies arrived at this very moment to whom we were introduced. In for a dime, in for a dollar! I realized that I had to risk the famous round dance and maybe a few Rutschers[4] and Hopsers[5], I, one of today's

---

[4] Black Forest folk dance

heroes and – private detective in disguise.

The good sheriff was extraordinarily happy to have engaged us with his home's goddesses. He arranged for our table which, however, had the shortcoming of accommodating only four people, which is why we were at the mercy of these two absolutely precious ladies. The position of the husband and father demanded that they displayed dignity at its best. Mama was over fifty years old. She was knitting a woolen vest and once spoke of the Code Napoleon, after which she shut her mouth for the rest of the evening. The little daughter was past thirty and had brought along a volume of poetry in which she seemed to read constantly despite the hellish spectacle surrounding us. She honored Old Death with a profound remark about Pierre Jean de Beranger, and when the old scout sincerely assured her that he had never spoken with this individual, she too retreated into deep silence. When beer was offered, the ladies did not accept any, but when the sheriff brought them a couple of glasses of brandy, their harsh, misanthropic features came alive.

Then the dignified official used the opportunity to give me one of his rib punches and whispered to me:

"The round dance is coming up. Make a quick grab!"

"Will we not be rejected?" I asked with a voice in which not much pleasure was obvious.

"No. The ladies know what to do."

I rose and bowed before the daughter, while I mumbled something about honor, pleasure and appreciation – and was handed the poetry volume to which the miss seemed to be attached. Old Death approached the issue more pragmatically. He called to the mama:

"Well, come along missus! To the right or the left, just as you like. I'm jumping with both legs."

How we both danced, what disaster my old friend caused when he fell with his dance partner, how the gentlemen got into more and more drinking – I shall refrain from telling. Enough! When morning dawned, the innkeeper's stores had been drawn down. However, the sheriff assured the guests that the money made from the auction had not been used up, so that, maybe, tomorrow or even tonight another little reel could be danced. In the two downstairs rooms, in the garden and in front of the house sat or lay the intoxicated participants, some obviously with heavy heads. But as soon as the procession to the steamer's mooring place was getting under way, everyone got on their legs again. In the lead were the musicians, followed by the members of the court who, in turn, were followed by the Klansmen in their strange disguise, then came we two witnesses, and after us the various gentlemen as it pleased them.

The American is a wonderful fellow. Whatever he needs is quickly

[5] Polka-like German folk dance

procured. Where from the people had obtained everything so quickly we were unable to deduce, but the many who joined the procession, and this seemed to be the entire citizenry, the dignified preachers and ladies excluded, each and everyone was carrying some kind of suitable instrument to join in the caterwauling. When everyone had lined up, the sheriff gave the signal to move off. The procession began with the virtuosos in the lead starting to mistreat 'Yankee-doodle,' the entourage in the rear entering in the caterwauling. What else was whistled, roared and sung is impossible to say. It all seemed as if I was among crazies. And so, in a slow funeral walk we headed for the river where the prisoners were handed over to the captain, who made sure to put them into secure custody, and guaranteed that escape would be impossible. In addition, they were sharply guarded by other passengers.

When the steamer took off, the musicians played their best fanfare, a renewed caterwauling. While everyone's eyes followed the departing steamer, I took Old Death by his arm and together with Lange and his son headed for home. We decided on a nap only; however, it turned out longer than intended. When I awoke, Old Death was already up. He had been unable to sleep because of pain in his hip and, to my shock, explained to me that he would be unable to start our ride today. This was the bad result of a round dance. We called for the doctor, who, when he arrived, checked the patient and claimed that the leg had snapped from its socket and would need to be snapped back. I would have loved to box his ears. For an eternity, he yanked at the leg, assuring us that we would hear it snap in. We listened but, of course, in vain. The yanking caused the scout almost no pain, which is why I pushed the incompetent fellow aside to look at the hip. There was a blue mark with a yellow border, which is why I was certain that it was a contusion.

"We must rub it with mustard or some kind of spirit. That will get you going again," I told Old Death. "Of course, you will have to rest today. Too bad that Gibson will get away in the meantime!"

"He?" the oldster replied. "Don't worry, sir! Once the nose of an old hunting dog like me has been put on some tracks, he won't let go until the game's been caught. Rest assured of this."

"I do, but he and William Ohlert will gain a big lead!"

"We'll catch up. I figure it doesn't matter whether we'll find them a day sooner or later, as long as we find them. Keep your head up! The very honorable sheriff wrecked our plan a bit with his reel and his two ladies, but rest assured that I'll make amends for it. I'm called Old Death. You understand?"

This sounded rather comforting, and since I trusted the oldster to keep his word, I made an effort not to worry. I could not have left alone anyway. More and more I realized that I was a greenhorn and had to rely on Old Death. It was therefore welcome news to hear that Mr. Lange over lunch said that he wanted to join us, his way being the same as ours, at least for some distance.

"You won't find poor companions in me and my son," he assured us. "I know how to ride a horse and to handle a rifle. And should we on the way come across some white or red rabble, we won't think of running away. Will you take us along? Let's shake hands on it!"

Of course, we did. Some time later, Cortesio, who had slept even longer than us, arrived to show us the two horses. Despite his pain, Old Death limped to the yard, wanting to see the horses himself.

"This young sir claims to know how to ride," he said, "but someone like me knows what to think of it. And I don't trust him to know horses. When I buy a horse, I select maybe the one looking the worst, but knowing that it is the best after all. It's happened more than once."

I had to ride every single horse from the stable, while he observed with expert eyes every move, after having asked for the animal's price. And it truly happened as he had said: he did not take the two intended for us.

"They look better than they are," he said, "but after a few days they'd be ailing already. No, we are going to take the two old chestnuts which happen to be so cheap."

"But they are just jalopy hinnies!" Cortesio said.

"Permit me to say, *Señor*, you don't know. These two chestnuts are prairie horses that happened to fall into bad hands. They won't run out of air and I figure that they won't faint from a bit of stress. We'll take them! That's that!"

4. Across the Border

A week later, five horsemen, four Whites and a Negro, passed the point where the southern corners of today's Texas counties Medina and Uvalde meet. The Whites rode in pairs, with the Negro bringing up the rear. The two Whites riding in front were dressed alike in leather, except that the younger man's outfit was newer than that of the older, who was very lean. Their two chestnut steeds trotted happily along and, from time to time, snorted as if they felt well up to the strenuous ride through this remote area. The pair of horsemen following were obviously father and son, who were also dressed alike but in wool, not leather. They wore broad-brimmed felt hats, and were armed with double-barreled rifles, knives and revolvers. The wiry Negro was dressed in lightweight, dark calico, and wore a shiny, almost-new top hat. He held a long, double-barreled rifle in his hand with a machete stuck in his belt, one of the long, bent, saber-like knives used in Mexico.

Old Death had taken three full days to recover from the injury he acquired in such a ridiculous way, and I felt that he was ashamed of it. To be injured in battle is honorable, but to fall in a dance and to have his body trampled is most annoying to a frontiersman. It was just too much for the old scout. The contusion seemed to be much more painful than he let on, or he would not have had us wait three days for our departure. From the frequent and sudden twitching of his face I noticed that he was still feeling some pain.

Cortesio had learned that the two Langes were going to join us. The day before our departure he had come over and asked whether we would do him the favor of taking his Negro, Sam, along. Of course, we were much surprised about his request, but did not let on to it. It isn't everyone's idea to ride for weeks with a Black, one has no connection with. Cortesio explained the reason: he had received an important message from Washington, requiring him to get a corresponding letter to Chihuahua. He could have asked us to carry the letter, but he needed a reply back, which we would be unable to undertake. This made it necessary to send a messenger, a task for which none was better suited than his Negro, Sam. Although he was a Black, his talents were much greater than was common among people of his color. Having served Cortesio for many years he was very loyal to him. He had made the trip across the border many times already and had every time comported himself well. Cortesio assured us that Sam would not be the least trouble to us, just the opposite, that he would be an attentive and obliging servant. Hearing this, we agreed, and have had no reason to regret it. Sam wasn't only a good but even an excellent horseman. He had learned this skill when he still lived with his master in Mexico, herding cattle on horseback. He was quick and helpful and always kept respectfully behind us. Of the four of us, he seemed to like me the most, demonstrated by the frequent tokens of kindness he extended me, which could only be construed as an expression of personal affection.

Old Death had found it not only unnecessary, but also a waste of time to look for Gibson's tracks and to follow them from place to place. We knew exactly the direction the detachment he was a member of was going to take, which is why the scout thought it advisable to ride straight for the Río Nueces and from there to Eagle Pass. It was very likely that between this river and the pass, but maybe even earlier, we would come across the troop's tracks. Of course, we had to hurry with these men having such a great lead. I did not believe that we would be able to catch up with them, but Old Death explained that the Mexican escorts of these recruits could not let themselves be seen and were thus forced to take substantial detours, sometimes to the left, then to the right. We, though, could ride in a straight line, a fact which would compensate for their lead of several days. In the six days of our ride we had covered almost two hundred miles, a feat no one except Old Death would have thought our chestnuts to be capable of. It seemed the two old horses literally revived here in the West. The open fields' pasture, the fresh air, and the fast movement did them good; from day to day they became more venturesome, livelier and seemingly younger, something the scout enjoyed very much, for this proved that he possessed excellent horse sense.

By now we had San Antonio and Castroville behind us, had crossed Medina county, so rich in water, but were now approaching the area where water becomes ever scarcer, and where the miserable Texan 'sand box' begins, which reaches its greatest dreariness between the Nueces and the Río Grande. We wanted to get first to the Río Leona, a main arm of the Río Frío, then to the confluence of Turkey Creek with the Río Nueces. To the northwest of us was the Leona Mountain, with Fort Inge nearby. That is where the detachment had to pass, yet had to beware of being spotted by the fort's garrison. We could therefore expect to soon find signs of life of Gibson and his group.

The ground we were riding across was well-suited to a fast ride. It was flat, short-grass prairie, easy to cover by our horses. The air was so pure that the horizon lay clearly before us. Riding southwest, we obviously were looking mostly in this direction and did not pay much attention to other directions. For this reason, it was no wonder that we noticed the approach of another group of horsemen rather late, which Old Death made us aware of. He pointed to the right, saying:

"Have a look over there, gentlemen! What do you think this is that can be seen over there?"

We saw a dark spot that appeared to close on us very slowly.

"Hmm!" was Lange's reply, while he shaded his eyes, "it looks like an animal grazing over there."

"You think so!" Old Death smiled. "An animal! One that's grazing there. Excellent! Your eyes don't seem to have adjusted to the perspective. This spot is about two miles away from us. Across such a distance an object of the size of this point isn't a single animal. It would have to be a buffalo, five times the size of a grown elephant, and there are no buffalo hereabouts. One such fellow may get lost down here, but assuredly not at this time of the year, only in spring or fall. Furthermore, someone not experienced is easily mistaken by the movement of such an object at such a distance. When grazing, a buffalo or horse moves very slowly, step by step. But I bet that the spot over there is moving at a fast gallop."

"Impossible," said Lange.

I, too, was of this erroneous opinion, since the said point, the size of a small four-footed animal, maybe a hare or fox, did not seem to move.

"Well, if the Whites are so wrong," Old Death said, "let's hear what the Black has to say. Sam, what do you think of the spot out there?"

Modestly, the Negro had remained silent until now. But after he had been asked, he said:

"Be horsemen; four, five or six."

"I think so, too. Maybe they are Indians?"

"Oh no, sir! Indians not come directly towards Whites. Indians hide to secretly observe Whites before talk with them. Horsemen come straight toward us; must be Whites."

"That is absolutely correct, my dear Sam. I'm very satisfied to learn that your mind is brighter than the color of your skin."

"Oh, sir, oh!" the good fellow said with a smile, while he showed all his teeth. To be praised by Old Death was an exceptional honor for him.

"If these people are really intent on meeting us," Lange said, "we must wait for them."

"Not at all!" the scout replied. "Don't you see that they aren't heading straight for us, but more to the south. They see that we are moving and are riding at a diagonal to meet us. Let's go then! We've got no time to wait here. Maybe they are soldiers from Fort Inge, out to reconnoiter. If that's the case, we won't be pleased meeting them."

"Why not?"

"Because we will learn something unpleasant, mister. Fort Inge is located rather far from here to the northwest. If its commander dispatches patrols over such a distance, something unpleasant must be in the air. We can be sure of it."

We continued our ride at our regular speed. The spot came noticeably closer now, and finally separated into six smaller points which quickly became larger. Soon, we clearly saw them to be horsemen, and five minutes later recognized their military uniforms. Then they were close enough that we heard their shout to stop. It was a cavalry sergeant with five men.

"Why do you travel at such a speed?" he asked, pulling up his horse. "Didn't you see us coming?"

"Sure," the scout replied cold-bloodedly, "but there was no reason why we should wait for you."

"But we need to know who you are."

"Well then; we are Whites traveling in a southerly direction. That should be sufficient for you."

"The devil you think!" the sergeant exclaimed. "Don't think you can play jokes with us!"

"Pshaw!" was Old Death's smiling response. "I'm not at all inclined to jest. We are here on the open prairie, and not in a classroom where you can play teacher and we must obediently answer to your questions if we don't want to run the danger of getting to feel the cane."

"I must follow my instructions and demand that you tell us your names!"

"And if we don't care to obey?"

"You can see that we are armed and can make sure to gain your obedience."

"Ah! Can you really? I'm glad for you then, but I don't advise trying it. We are free men, mister sergeant! We'd like to see the man who dares tell us that we must obey him; are you listening – must? I would simply gun down this scoundrel!"

With eyes flashing, he pulled the reins of his horse so that it rose up and, following his legs' pressure, made a threatening leap towards the sergeant. The man quickly pulled his animal back and was going to shout, but Old Death didn't let him get there, but quickly continued:

"I don't want to count that I'm twice as old than you and have most likely experienced more than you ever will. I only want to respond to your mentioning of your weapons. Do you think then that our knives are made of marzipan, our rifle barrels of sugar and their balls of chocolate? These sweets would agree very poorly with you! You say that you must follow your instructions. That's fine by me. But have you also been ordered to snarl at experienced frontiersmen and talk to them in a voice a general uses with his recruits? We are willing to talk with you, but haven't called for you to come here and, most of all, demand courtesy!"

The sergeant became embarrassed. Old Death had changed, and his manner had its effect.

"Don't talk yourself into such anger!" the sergeant responded. "It's not my intention to be rude."

"Well, I didn't find much tact in your voice nor expressions."

"That's because we aren't here in a lady's salon. There's all kinds of rabble roaming about, about which we must keep our eyes open, being in a forward position."

"Rabble? Are you including us with such doubtful gents?" the oldster responded angrily.

"I can say neither yes or no. But a man with a clean conscience would not refuse giving his name. Presently, there are plenty of these darn characters in this area on their way to Juarez. One can't trust these rogues."

"Then you side with the Secessionists, with the southern States?"

"Yes. I hope you do, too?"

"I side with every good man against any rogue. Concerning our names and where we come from, there's no reason to keep them secret. We come from La Grange."

"Then you are Texans. Well, Texas sided with the South. I must be dealing with kindred spirits."

"Kindred spirits! By the devil! That's quite an expression I wouldn't have trusted a sergeant to voice. But instead of telling you our five names you would soon forget again, I will tell you only mine to satisfy you. I'm an old prairie runner and those who know me call me Old Death."

"You are Old Death? The spy from the Northern States!"

"Mister!" the oldster threatened. "Watch out! If you've heard of me, you'll know that I won't let an insult stick. I risked my property, my blood and even my life for the Union, because I cared to do so, and because I thought the North's intentions to be right, and still think so. I see a spy as something different from what I've been, and if an overgrown child like you uses a word like this towards me, I do not drop him immediately with my fist simply because I pity him. Old Death isn't afraid of six cavalry men, neither of ten nor even more. It's fortunate that your companions are more reasonable than you. You can tell the commander of Fort Inge that you've met Old Death, and talked to him as if he were a boy. I'm convinced he'll then stick a nose into your face, long enough that you cannot recognize its tip with a telescope!"

His last words had their effect. The fort commander was likely a more reasonable man than his subordinate. Of course, the sergeant had to report his meeting with us and its result. If the leader of a patrol meets a famous hunter like Old Death, it is to his advantage to exchange thoughts and observations and to receive advice, often to good use. Frontiersmen of Old Death's kind are treated with consideration and respect by officers, that is, as equals. But what would the sergeant be able to report, having dealt with us in this way? He now seemed to be telling this silently to himself, for his face flushed from embarrassment. To increase the impact, Old Death continued: "Your military coat in all honor, but mine is worth at least as much as yours. With your age, it wouldn't hurt to get some advice from Old Death. Who's presently the commander at Fort Inge?"

"Major Webster."

"The one who was still captain at Fort Ripley two years ago?" Old Death continued.

"He's the one."

"Well, then say hello to him from me. He knows me quite well. I often did target shooting with him and drove the nail into the black with my bullet. Hand me your note book that I can enter a few lines you may show him! I figure he will be much pleased to hear that one of his subordinates called Old Death a spy."

In his embarrassment, the sergeant did not know how to react. He kept swallowing until, finally, he exclaimed, visibly strained:

"But, sir, I can assure you that it wasn't meant that way! We don't have a holiday every day, but have our troubles, which makes it no wonder that one sometimes uses a tone that hadn't really been intended!"

"Well! That sounds more polite than earlier. Let me therefore assume that our conversation begins only now. Are you provided with cigars at Fort Inge?"

"No more. To everyone's regret tobacco ran out."

"That's very bad. A soldier without tobacco is only half a man. My companion here took half a saddlebag-full along. Maybe, he will give you some."

The group's eyes looked expectantly at me. I pulled out a handful of cigars, shared them out and lit them. Once the sergeant had taken the first puffs, his features erupted in the purest delight. He nodded gratefully to me and said:

"A cigar like this is like the best peace pipe. I think I could no longer be angry at the worst enemy if he handed me such a thing here on the prairie, with us having been unable to smoke for weeks."

"If a cigar has greater power on you than the worst enmity, you can't be a real villain," Old Death laughed.

"No, of course I'm not one. But, sir, we must get on, which is why it's advisable to ask and say what's necessary. Did you see any Indians or other tracks, by chance?"

Old Death denied this, but asked whether he was of the opinion that Indians were around here?"

"Very much so! And we have every reason to inquire, because these rogues have taken up the war tomahawk again."

"By the devil! That's bad! Which are the tribes?"

"The Comanche and Apache."

"Then it's the two most dangerous ones! And we are right between their territories. If scissors snap closed, then whoever is in between experiences the worst."

"Yes, watch out. We have made various preparations and sent several messengers for reinforcement and additional provisions, and we patrol a large area almost every day and night. Everyone we come across is suspect until we've convinced ourselves that he isn't a scoundrel. I hope that you will therefore excuse my earlier approach!"

"All's forgotten. But what's the reason for the redskins moving against each other?"

"Because of this devilish – pardon me, sir! Maybe you think differently of him than I do – this President Juarez. You must have heard that he had to flee all the way to El Paso. Of course, the French pursued him and came as far as Chihuahua and Cohahuela. He had to hide from them like a raccoon from the dogs. They chased him to the Río Grande and would have pursued him farther and have captured him, had our president in Washington not been so silly to disallow it. Everyone was against Juarez and all had renounced him, even the Indians no longer wanted anything to do with him, although, being born a redskin, he's one of them."

"Also not the Apache?"

"No. But it means only that they were neither for nor against him. They didn't take sides but simply remained in their hiding places. The better did the French General Bazaine's agents succeed in stirring the Comanche up against Juarez. They came in droves, but, of course, surreptitiously, as is their way, across the border into Mexico to finish off Juarez's followers."

"Hmm! You meant to say, to plunder, murder and to burn! The Comanche have no business in Mexico; their territory and hunting area does not extend beyond the Río Grande. It makes no difference to them who rules Mexico, whether it is Juarez, Maximilian, or Napoleon. But the attempts by the French to set them against peaceful people, this one cannot hold against the Comanche, being savages, if they quickly use this sudden opportunity to enrich themselves. Whose responsibility it is, I don't want to enter into."

"Well, it's also none of my business. Anyway, they crossed over and, of course, did everything they had been asked. In the process they encountered the Apache. The Comanche have always been sworn enemies of the Apache. This is why they attacked their camp and gunned down everyone who did not surrender, then took the remainder captive and moved on, taking their tents and horses along."

"And then?"

"What then, sir? As is the Indian custom, the males were put to the stake."

"I figure this custom isn't very pleasant for those who are knifed and roasted alive. That's on the conscience of the French! Of course, the Apache immediately went on the war path to avenge themselves?"

"No, because they are cowards!"

"That's the first time I've heard this being claimed. In any case, they didn't accept this lying down."

"They sent a few warriors to negotiate with the oldest chiefs of the Comanche. These negotiations took place at the fort."

"At Fort Inge? Why there?"

"Because it's neutral ground."

"Fine. I understand. So the chiefs of the Comanche came?"

"Five chiefs with twenty warriors."

"And how many Apache arrived?"

"Three."

"With how many escorts?"

"Without any."

95

"Hmm! And you call them cowards. Three men dare cross enemy lands to meet twenty-five opponents! Mister, if you know Indians only a bit, you must admit that this is heroic. What was the result of the negotiations?"

"It wasn't peaceful; the conflict got worse. Eventually, the Comanche attacked the Apache. Two of them were stabbed to death. The third, although wounded, made it to his horse and jumped the nine foot high palisade. The Comanche pursued, but were unable to catch him."

"And that happened on neutral ground, under the fort's protection and the supervision of a major of Union troops? What a betrayal by the Comanche! Is it any wonder then that the Apache have now also raised the war tomahawk? The escaped warrior will bring them the message, after which they will take off en masse to avenge themselves. And since the murder of their delegates was committed in a fort of the Whites, their weapons will also be used against palefaces. How will the Comanche act towards us?"

"Friendly, as the chiefs assured us before leaving the fort. They told us that they were only fighting Apache, this being their only purpose, with the palefaces being their friends."

"When did these negotiations, which came to such a bloody result take place?"

"On Monday."

"And today is Friday; so it happened four days ago. How long did the Comanche stay at the fort after the Apache's escape?"

"Only briefly. They left an hour later."

"And you let them go? They had violated the law and should have been held to be punished. They acted against the United States on whose territory the betrayal, the murders took place. The major should have taken them prisoner and reported to Washington. I don't understand him."

"He had left on a hunt that day and returned only in the evening."

"So that he did not have to witness the negotiations and the betrayal! I knew it! If the Apache learn that the Comanche were allowed to leave the fort, then woe to every White falling into their hands! They won't spare any."

"Sir, don't get too much excited. It was also good for the Apache that the Comanche were permitted to leave, since, only an hour later, another one of their chiefs would have been lost, had the Comanche not left already."

"Old Death, with a gesture of surprise, said:

"Another chief, you say? Ah, I think, I know! It was four days ago. He had an excellent horse and rode faster than we. It was him, I'm certain!"

"Who do you think it was?" the sergeant asked, surprised.

"Winnetou."

"Yes, it was him. The Comanche had barely disappeared to the west, when we saw a horseman appear from the east, the Río Frío. He came to the fort to purchase powder, lead and revolver cartridges. Not wearing any tribal markings, we did not recognize him. During the purchase he learned what had happened. By chance, the acting officer was present, whom the Indian now addressed.

"That's highly interesting," Old Death exclaimed. "I would have loved to be present. What did he tell the officer?"

"Only the words: 'Many Whites will pay for the deed which happened at your place without you preventing it or, at least, punishing the perpetrators!'" Then he walked out of the store and jumped on his saddle. The officer followed him to admire the magnificent black horse the redskin was riding. That's when the Indian said to him: 'I want to be straight with you and tell you, that from this day, there will be fighting between the warriors of the Apache and the palefaces. The warriors of the Apache sat peacefully in their tents when the Comanche treacherously attacked them, took their women, children, horses and tents, killed many of our people, and led the others away to have them die at the stake. Even then, the wise fathers of the Apache were still listening to the warning words of the Great Spirit. They did not right away raise the war tomahawk, but sent delegates to you to negotiate with the Comanche. But in your presence our delegates were attacked and killed. You let the murderers go free and with it demonstrated that you are the enemies of the Apache. All blood which is going to be spilled, beginning today, will be on your heads, not on ours!' "

"Yes, yes, that's how he is! It's as if I heard him speak!" Old Death commented. "And what did the officer respond?"

"He asked who he was, and only now did the Red say that he was Winnetou, the Chief of the Apache. The officer called right away to close the gate to take the Red prisoner. He had the right to do it, since war had been declared, with Winnetou not visiting us in the role of a delegate. But the chief only laughed, rode a few of us down, including the officer, then did not even turn for the gate but, like the other Apache before him, leaped the palisade. A detachment was immediately sent after him, but they never got to see him again."

"There you go! Now it's the devil's! Woe to the fort and its garrison if the Comanche aren't victorious! The Apache won't let any of you stay alive. Did you have any other visitors?"

"Only one other, the evening before yesterday. It was a single horseman on his way to Sabinal. His name was Clinton, as I recall; I had gate duty when he arrived."

"Clinton! Hmm. Let me describe this man to you, then you tell me whether it was him."

He described Gibson, who had already earlier used the false name Clinton. The sergeant confirmed that the description fit him perfectly. In addition, I showed him the photo, from which he positively identified the man.

"He lied to you," Old Death now said. "The man wasn't headed for Sabinal. He visited you only to learn how things stood at the fort. He belongs to the rabble you referred to earlier. After he left, he returned to the group waiting for him. Did anything else of importance happen?"

"Not that I know."

"Then we are done. Tell the major that you met me. You are his subordinate, but must not tell him my thoughts about what happened. But you could have prevented much harm and bloodshed had you not been so lax in the execution of your duty. Good bye, boys!"

He turned his horse aside and rode off. Following a brief farewell with the cavalry men, we followed Old Death, while the soldiers headed north. For some time, we silently covered a great distance in a gallop. Old Death, his head low, contemplated what he had learned. Sunset was close, with at most an hour's daylight left. Still, we saw the southern horizon sharp as a knife blade ahead of us. It had been our intention to reach the Río Leona today, where we would find trees, a fact which would have shown the horizon to be less sharp. We had to assume that we still were not close to today's destination. This must have also been on Old Death's mind, for he kept driving his horse on whenever it fell to a slower pace. Our hurry brought success, for, just when the gibbous disc of the sun touched the horizon, we saw a dark line in the south that became more distinct as we approached. Towards the end of our ride, the ground had been sandy. Now, it bore grass again and we soon noticed that the dark line was trees, whose crowns looked very inviting after the tough ride we had had. While Old Death permitted his horse to fall into a trot, he pointed to the trees, saying:

"Where there are trees hereabouts there must also be water nearby. This is the Leona River ahead of us on whose banks we will camp."

We soon reached the trees, which formed a narrow copse along both river banks. Below their crowns grew dense brush. The river's bed was very broad, but it carried a low volume of water. However, when we got closer, we found the bank there unsuited for crossing, which is why we slowly rode upstream. After a brief search we found a spot where shallow water flowed over shiny pebbles. This is where we were going to ford the river, with Old Death in the lead. Just when his horse was going to enter, he stopped, dismounted, and bent down to examine the river bottom.

"Well!" he nodded. "I thought so! There are some tracks we couldn't make out earlier because the bank here is made up of large pebbles, which do not keep tracks. Have a look at the river bottom!"

We, too, dismounted and saw some round, palm-size impressions leading into the river.

"Those are tracks?" Lange asked. "You must be right, sir. Maybe they are from a horse."

"Well, let Sam have a look. Let's see what he thinks."

The Negro had kept behind us. He now stepped forward, looked into the water, and said:

"This be two horsemen that crossed river."

"Why do you think these tracks were made by horsemen, not wild horses?"

"Because horse with shoes is not wild mustang but tame horse, always carrying rider. Tracks are also deep. Horses carried load, which must be horsemen. Wild horses not go side-by-side but behind each other. Also stop at water to drink before crossing. But here, they not halt, but cross right away. They so do only when must obey reins. And where reins, there are saddles with riders."

"You did very well!" the oldster praised him. "I couldn't have done better. There you see, gents, that there are situations where a White can learn from a Black. But the two horsemen were in a hurry and didn't even allow their horses to drink. But they must have been thirsty and since every frontiersman looks after his horse, I figure that they were only allowed to drink at the opposite bank. These two men must have had a reason to cross first. I hope we will find the reason for it."

During this conversation about the tracks our horses had had their fill of water. We mounted up once more and reached the opposite banks without getting wet. The river was so shallow that our stirrups didn't even touch the water's surface. Barely were we on dry land, when Old Death, whose eyes didn't miss anything, said:

"Here's the reason. Have a look at this linden tree, whose bark's been peeled off to the height of a man! And here, what's that sticking there from the ground?"

He pointed down to two rows of thin pegs, the length and diameter of pencils.

"What's the purpose of these pegs?" Old Death continued. "What's their relationship to the peeled bark? Don't you notice the small, dried-up fiber pieces lying all about here? These pegs were used as holders. Might you, at some time, have seen a board for knotting and tying nets, cloth, and the like? No? Well, that's what we have here, only that it isn't made of wood and iron pins. These two horsemen knotted a long and wide sheet, about sixty inches long and six inches wide, as one can deduce from the arrangement of the pegs. It looks like a belt. Indians like to use such belts made of fresh fiber for the dressing of wounds. Fresh fiber cools the wound, and when it dries it contracts firmly so that it even keeps injured bones in place. I figure that at least one of the two was injured. Now take a look into the water. Do you see the two shallow indentations in the sand? That's where the two horses rolled in the water. Only Indian horses do this. Their saddles had been taken off, so that they could roll and refresh themselves. The Indians permitted the animals to do this only because they had a tough ride ahead. We can be certain that the two men did not linger for longer than it took them to fashion the fiber belt, and then rode off.

The result of our investigation is thus: two men on Indian horses, with at least one of them injured. They were in such a hurry that they didn't allow their horses to drink upon their approach to the river because they noticed the linden on the opposite bank whose bark they needed for the dressing. After they put on the dressing, they quickly resumed their ride. What to you conclude from this, gentlemen? Put your brains to good use!" the oldster asked me.

"I'll try," I replied, "but don't laugh at me should I not hit on the right answer!"

"I wouldn't do that, since I consider you my student, and from an apprentice one cannot ask the judgment of a full-grown."

"Since these were Indian horses, I'd guess that their owners are members of a red tribe. I recall now the events at Fort Inge. One of the Apache escaped, but was wounded. Winnetou quickly followed him and, since he rides an excellent horse, he soon caught up with the injured."

"Not bad!" Old Death nodded. "You know some more?"

"Yes. It was important for the two Apache to reach their tribal members as quickly as possible to tell them of the outrage they suffered at the fort, and to warn them of the arrival of hostile Comanche, which is why they were in such a hurry. That's why they took only the time to dress the wound, knowing that they might find fiber here by the river, and why they allowed their horses the necessary refreshment, then resumed their ride right away."

"That's how it was. I'm satisfied with you. I don't doubt that it was Winnetou with the escaped delegate. It's too bad we arrived too late to still find their tracks in the grass away from the river, but I can imagine the direction they took. They must cross the Río Grande, just like us, and take the most direct route. We'll do this, too, which is why I expect to find some signs of theirs along the way. Let's have a look for a good camp site now. We must leave early tomorrow morning."

His trained eyes soon spotted a suitable place surrounded by dense shrubbery with plenty of juicy grass for our horses. We took off their saddles and staked them to our lassoes. Then we settled down and had a modest meal from the rest of our provisions. Upon my question whether we could light a fire, Old Death answered with a mocking, crafty smile:

"I expected this question from you, sir. You probably read many a nice Indian story of Cooper's and others, and liked these cute stories?"

"I did."

"Hmm, yeah! They read very well with everything working out nicely. One lights a pipe or a cigar, sits on the sofa, raises one's legs and immerses oneself in such a good book from the library. But walk out into the forest in the Wild West! There, things happen a bit differently from the lines told in such books. Cooper was a good novel writer and I, too, enjoyed his 'Leather Stocking Stories,' but he didn't travel the West. He knew very well how to combine prose with reality, however, here in the West one is dealing only with the latter, and I, at least, haven't yet been able to discover any trace of poetry. In these stories one reads about a nicely burning camp fire on which a juicy buffalo loin is roasting. But let me tell you: if we now start a fire, the smoke would bring every redskin here inside a radius of two miles."

"Almost an hour! Is it possible?"

"You will find out yet how good Indian noses are. And if they don't smell it, their horses will, and then tell them with that disastrous snorting, which they have been trained for, and which has cost many a White his life. This is why I think we shall desist from a poetic camp fire tonight."

"But we mustn't fear Indians to be nearby, since the Comanche cannot be under way already. Until their delegates return home and the warriors of the various tribes gathered, a goodly time must pass."

"Hmm! Amazing, the smart talk such a greenhorn can put forth! Unfortunately, you've missed three items. First, we are in Comanche territory. Second, their warriors have already swarmed all the way into Mexico. And third, those that stayed back must not be slowly gathering, but have long since come together and are ready for the war path. Or do you think the Comanche to be so stupid to kill the Apache delegates without being ready for an immediate departure? I tell you, the betrayal of the Apache delegates wasn't the result of momentary anger, but had been planned beforehand. I figure that the Comanche have posted themselves by the Río Grande already, and that Winnetou will find it difficult to get past them unnoticed."

"Then you hold with the Apache?"

"Secretly, yes. They have been wronged and were dastardly attacked. I'm also exceptionally sympathetic towards Winnetou. But shrewdness forbids us to take sides. We can congratulate ourselves if we reach our destination with our skins intact. So, let's not toy with the idea of siding with one or the other party. I've also no reason to fear the Comanche. They know me. I have never done them harm and often visited them and was well received. One of their best-known chiefs, Oyo-koltsa, meaning White Beaver, is even a good friend of mine. I once did him some service he promised never to forget. That happened up at the Red River, where he was attacked by a group of Chickasaw and would surely have lost scalp and life had I not happened to show up. This friendship is now very important to us. I shall appeal to it when we meet Comanche and they should act hostilely towards us. We are also five men, and I hope each of us can handle a rifle. Before a Red gets my scalp, a dozen of his companions will purchase a ticket to the Eternal Hunting grounds. We must be prepared and act as if we are in enemy territory. This is why, from now on, all five of us will not sleep at the same time, but one will take guard duty to be relieved every hour. We shall draw lots using grass blades of different length to determine the sequence of guard duty. That will give each of us five hours of sleep, which should be sufficient."

He cut five grass blades. I got the last watch. In the meantime night had fallen. As long as we weren't asleep, no guard was necessary, and none of us was ready for sleep yet. We lit cigars and enjoyed a lively conversation made more interesting by Old Death telling us of some of his experiences. I noticed that he picked them in such a way that we would learn something while we listened. I was just checking my watch, which showed eleven o'clock, when Old Death stopped to listen attentively. One of our horses had snorted and that so peculiarly as if it were from excitement and fear that even I noticed it.

"Hmm!" he grumbled. "What was that? Wasn't I right when I told Cortesio that our two steeds had seen the prairie already? Only an animal that has carried a frontiersman snorts like that. There must be something suspicious nearby. Gents, do not turn around. It is pitch dark in the bushes, and if one opens one's eyes wide to spot something in such darkness, they acquire a reflection an enemy is able to see. Keep looking down. I will have a look myself, but pull my hat lower onto my face so that my eyes are not so easily noticed. Listen! Again! Don't move!"

There had been a second snort. One of the horses – seemingly mine – pounded with its hooves as if it wanted to tear free from its lasso. We kept silent, which I thought to be the obvious tactic. But Old Death whispered:

"What's occurred to you that you are so quiet suddenly! Should someone really be nearby listening to us, then he heard us talk and will now know from our silence that we noticed the snorting of one of our horses and have become suspicious. Keep talking! Tell yourself something, no matter what."

That's when the Negro said quietly:

"Sam know where man is. Sam has seen two eyes."

"Fine! But don't look there any more, or he'll see also your eyes. Where was it?"

"Where Sam tied up his horse, to right by plum bushes. Very low to ground and very faint. I saw sparkle two points."

"Good! I will steal to the rear of the man and take him by his neck. It's unlikely that there are more. In that case our horses would have reacted differently. Keep talking aloud. This will have two advantages: first, the man will think that we are no longer suspicious, and second, your talk will cover the noise I can hardly avoid making in this darkness."

Aloud, Lange asked me a question to which I replied just as noisily. This triggered a colorful exchange with which I tried to get us to laugh. Loud laughter seemed to be best suited to convince the listener of our nonchalance and cause him to miss Old Death's approach. Will and Sam, too, joined in, which is why we were rather loud for about ten minutes. Then we heard Old Death's voice:

"Hey! Quit roaring like a pride of lions! It's no longer necessary. I've got him and will bring him in."

We heard a rustle where Sam had staked down his horse; then the oldster stepped forth to drop the load he was carrying before us.

"So!" he said. "This was an easy fight. The noise you made was so great that this redskin wouldn't have noticed even an earthquake and everything with it."

"An Indian? That means there are more in the vicinity?"

"Possible, but not likely. But let's have a bit more light now that we can have a look at our man. I saw some dry leaves and a small withered tree. I'm going to get this material. Watch this fellow meanwhile!"

"He doesn't move. Is he dead?"

"No, but he lost a bit of his consciousness. I used his own belt to tie his hands behind his back. I'll be back before he comes to again."

He left to cut down the little tree. When he returned with it, we used our knives to cut it to splinters, lit it, and soon we had a little fire going by whose light we were able to have a look at our captive. The wood was so dry that its fire barely produced smoke.

Now we had a look at the Red. He wore Indian-type leather pants with tassels, a matching hunting shirt and simple moccasins without any adornment. His head was shorn bare, with only a scalp lock left in the middle, and his face was painted with diagonal, black stripes on a yellow background. Old Death had taken everything that had hung from his belt, including his weapons, consisting of knife, bow and a leather arrow quiver. The last two items were strapped together. The man kept lying motionless with his eyes closed, as if dead.

"A simple warrior," Old Death said, "who doesn't even carry any proof that he has killed an enemy. He neither had a scalp hanging from his belt, nor are his leggings dressed with human hair. And he doesn't even carry a medicine bag. This means he either doesn't have a name yet, or lost it, since he lost his medicine. He was sent out as a scout, this being a dangerous task at which he can excel, provided he can kill an enemy and thus gain a name again. Look, he's moving. In a moment, he'll come to. Be quiet!"

The prisoner stretched his legs and caught a deep breath. When he felt his hands tied, a shock traveled through his body. He opened his eyes and made an attempt to jump up, only to collapse again. Then he stared at us with glowing eyes. When his look fell on Old Death, some words escaped him:

"Kosha-pehve!"

This is a Comanche word meaning the same as 'Old Death.'

"Yes, it's me," the oldster nodded. "Does the red warrior know me?"

"The sons of the Comanche know the man of this name, for he has visited them."

"You are a Comanche. I saw it from the war colors on your face. What is your name?"

"This son of the Comanche has lost his name and will never again bear one. He left to get himself a new one, but now fell into the hands of palefaces and shamed himself. He asks the white warriors to kill him. He will begin singing the war song, and they will not hear a sound of lament when they burn him on the stake."

"We cannot fulfill your request, for we are Christians and your friends. I took you prisoner only because it was so dark, and I was unable to see that you were a son of the Comanche who live in peace with us. You will stay alive and commit many great deeds yet, and find a name for yourself from which your enemies will tremble. You are free."

He untied his hands. I expected the Comanche to happily jump up, but he did not, rather kept lying there as if still bound, and said:

"The son of the Comanche is not free after all. He wants to die. Stab your knife into his heart!"

"There's no reason for it, nor do I feel like it. Why should I kill you?"

"Because you outwitted me and took me prisoner. When the warriors of the Comanche learn of it, they will chase me away and say: First, he lost his medicine, then his name, only to fall into the hands of a paleface. His eyes are blind and his ears are deaf. He will never be worthy to carry the symbols of a warrior."

He spoke this with such a sad voice that I couldn't help feeling pity for him. Although, I was unable to understand every word he was saying, since he spoke English interspersed with many Indian terms, I tried to guess what I could not understand.

"Our red brother does not carry any shame," I said quickly, before Old Death was able to answer. "To be outwitted by a famous paleface like Kosha-pehve is not shameful. Then, the warriors of the Comanche will never learn that you were captured. We will keep silent about it."

"Will Kosha-pehve confirm this?" the Indian asked.

"I do," the oldster agreed. "We shall act as if we met in a friendly way. I am your friend, and you made no mistake when you approached me openly, after you recognized me."

"My famous white brother speaks words of joy to me. I trust what you are saying and can rise, for I will not return with shame to the warriors of the Comanche. But I shall be grateful to the palefaces for as long as my eyes will see the sun."

He rose to a sitting position and took a deep breath. One could not see any emotion on his heavily painted face, but we observed right away that we had brought joy to his heart. Of course, we left it to the experienced scout to continue the conversation, which the oldster did not hesitate to do:

"Our red friend saw that we meant well with him. We hope he will see us also as his friends and will answer my questions honestly."

"Kosha-pehve may ask. I will speak only truth."

"Did my red brother venture out alone, maybe only to kill an enemy or a dangerous, wild animal, so that he could return with a new name to his wigwam, or are there other warriors with him?"

"As many as there are drops in the water."

"Is my red brother saying that all warriors of the Comanche have left their tents?"

"They left to get the scalps of their enemies."

"Which enemies?"

"The dogs of Apache. A stink arose from the Apache that penetrated all the way to the tents of the Comanche. This is why they mounted their horses to eradicate these coyotes from the face of the earth."

"Did they listen to the advice of their old, wise chiefs before?"

"The elder warriors gathered and decided on war. This is why the medicine men asked the Great Spirit, and his answer was satisfactory. Our warriors swarm already from the camps of the Comanche to the great river the palefaces call Río Grande del Norte. The sun has sunk four times since the war tomahawk was carried from tent to tent."

"And my red brother belongs to one of these war parties?"

"Yes. We are camped upstream. Scouts were sent out to check if the area is secure. I went downstream when I smelled the palefaces' horses. I crept through the bushes to learn how many they were. That's when Kosha-pehve came over me to kill me for awhile."

"That's forgotten now, and no one will talk of it. How many warriors of the Comanche are camped upriver?"

"They are just ten times ten."

"And who is their leader?"

"Avat-vila, Big Bear, the young chief."

"I do not know him, and never before heard his name."

"He received this name just a few months ago, after he killed a gray bear in the mountains and brought back his hide and claws. He is the son of Oyo-koltsa, whom the palefaces call White Beaver."

"Oh, him I know. He is my friend."

"I know, since I saw you with him, when you were the guest of his tent. His son, Big Bear, will greet you most friendly."

"How far is it from here to where he is camped with his warriors?"

"My white brother need not ride more than what he calls one hour."

"Then we shall ask him to become his guests. My red brother may lead us there."

Five minutes later we were in our saddles and rode off, with the Indian up front. He first led us from the trees to open terrain, then upstream.

I was to enter an Indian camp for the first time in my life, at that a war camp. I felt curiosity, yet also a certain worry, which was no wonder. To me, it looked as if Old Death had acted a bit incautious not knowing whether the Comanche would receive us hospitably. When I expressed my concern, he gave me short shrift.

On our short ride, I found confirmed what I had heard earlier, this being that Indians were very good runners. Our horses had to pick up a sharp trot to keep up with the Red. Then, suddenly, several dark figures appeared before us, the camp's guards. Our guide exchanged a few words with them, then left us to wait. He returned shortly to get us. It was pitch-dark; the sky had clouded over and not a star was visible. I looked hard to the left and right, but was unable to make out anything. Then we had to stop again. Our guide said:

"My white brothers should not advance any farther. The sons of the Comanche do not light any fires when on the war path. But since they are convinced now that no enemy is nearby, they will start a fire."

He hurried away. A few moments later, I saw a glowing point, not much larger than the head of a pin.

"That's a punk," Old Death explained.

"What's a punk?" I asked.

"It's the prairie lighter, consisting of two pieces of wood, a wide one and a thin, round one. The wide one has a small depression which is filled with punk, that is dry mold from tree hollows. This is the best tinder there is. Then the thin, round stick is placed onto the mold and is rotated rapidly with both hands like a quill. The friction produces heat and lights the tinder. See!"

A small flame flickered up and quickly grew into a fire, nourished by dry leaves being thrown on. But the flames soon died lower again, since the Indians would not permit far-reaching fire light. Branches were now added in a circle, their ends pointing to the fire's center. An easily controlled fire burned now, achieved by moving the branches closer to the center or away from it. When the leaves had flamed up, I saw where we were, that is under trees and surrounded by Indians, all holding weapons. Only a few carried rifles, most were armed with spears, bows and arrows. But all carried tomahawks, the terrible war ax of Indians which, in the hand of an experienced warrior, is a more dangerous weapon than is commonly thought. Once the fire was under control, we were told to dismount. Our horses were taken away, after which we were in the power of the Reds, for, without horses, nothing could be done hereabouts. Although we had not been asked for our weapons, one can imagine that five against one hundred was not a comfortable relationship.

We were allowed to step to the fire, where a single warrior was seated. One could not make out whether he was young or old, since his face was totally covered by the same colors and patterns as those of the scout. His hair was tied in a tall bun, from which rose the white feather of a war eagle. From his belt hung two scalps, and on a string around his neck the medicine bag and a calumet, the peace pipe, were fastened. Across his legs lay a rifle, seemingly dating back to the 1820s or 30s. He was looking us over carefully, one after another, paying no attention to the Black, for the red man despises Negroes. These were some unpleasant moments, for, should he not care for us, we would be done for. At least that's what I thought and expressed myself in this way to our old friend.

"Nonsense!" Old Death replied in German, so as not to be understood by the Red. "Let's show him that we are also chiefs. Sit down, too, but let me do the talking!"

He sat down opposite the chief with us joining him. Only Sam remained standing, knowing that he would risk his life if he were to assume the right to face the chief seated by the fire.

"Uff!" the Indian exclaimed angrily, followed by a few more words I did not understand.

"Do you speak the palefaces' language?" Old Death asked.

"This chief understands it, but will not speak it, since he does not care to," he replied, which Old Death translated right away to us.

"I ask you, though, to speak it now."

"Why so?"

"Because my companions do not understand Comanche, but must know what is being said."

"They are among Comanche now and must use their language. Courtesy request this."

"You are mistaken. They cannot use a language they do not know. You must see this. They are also guests of the Comanche, which is why they can demand the courtesy you ask of them. You can speak English; if you don't, they will not believe that you can."

"Uff!" he exclaimed once more, after which he continued in broken English. "I did say that I can speak it; I do not lie. If they do not believe it, they are insulting me, and I shall have them killed! How come you dared to sit down with me?"

"Because, being chiefs, we have the right to do so."

"Whose chief are you?"

"The Chief of Scouts."

"And he?" with that he pointed at Lange.

"He is the Chief of Blacksmiths, who makes weapons."

"And he?" meaning Will.

"He is the blacksmith's son and makes swords and tomahawks, with which heads are split."

This seemed to impress the redskin, for he now said:

"If he can do this, then he is a very skillful chief. And what is he?" nodding towards me.

"This famous man has come across the ocean from a distant country to get to know the warriors of the Comanche. He is a Chief of Wisdom and knowledge of all things. After his return, he will tell thousands of people what kind of men the Comanche are."

This seemed to exceed the Reds understanding. He looked me over very closely, then said:

"Then he belongs among the smart and experienced men? But his hair is not white."

"In his country sons are born smart right away, like old ones here."

"Then the Great Spirit must love this country very much. But the sons of the Comanche have no need for his wisdom, for they are smart themselves to know what they need for their fortune. Wisdom has not accompanied him by coming to this country, since he dares crossing our war path. Once the warriors of the Comanche have taken up their tomahawks they do not tolerate white men among them."

"Then you don't appear to know what your delegates said at Fort Inge. They assured us that they wage war only against the Apache, but shall remain friendly towards the palefaces."

"They may hold what they promised, but I was not present."

Until now, he had talked in a very hostile tone, which did not reduce my concerns. Old Death had replied in a friendly voice. He now thought it advisable to change his tone by raising his voice angrily:

"Is this how you talk? Who are you that you dare say such words to Kosha-pehve? Why did you not tell me your name? Do you have one? If not, then tell me that of your father!"

The chief seemed to stiffen in surprise about this boldness. He gazed at the speaker for a long time, then answered:

"Man! Shall I have you tortured to death?"

"You shall refrain from it!"

"I am Avat-vila, Chief of the Comanche!"

"Avat-vila, the Big Bear? When I killed my first bear, I was still a boy, and since then I have killed so many grizzlies that I could hang their claws over my entire body. Killing a bear does not make a hero in my eyes!"

"Then look at the scalps on my belt!"

"Pshaw! Had I taken the scalps of all those I conquered, I could adorn your entire band of warriors with them. That's nothing, either!"

"I am the son of Oyo-koltsa, the great Chief!"

"That I count more as a recommendation. I smoked the peace pipe with White Beaver. We swore to each other that his enemies would also be mine, and my friends would be his. And we always kept our word. I hope his son is of the same mind as his father!"

"You speak boldly. Do you think the warriors of the Comanche to be mice, a dog dares to bark at any way he likes?"

"What did you say? Dog? Do you think Old Death to be a dog one can whip anytime one likes? Then I send you instantly to the Eternal Hunting Grounds!"

"Uff! Here stand a hundred men!" Saying this, he pointed around.

"Fine!" the oldster replied. "But here we sit, and we count as much as your hundred Comanche. All of them cannot prevent me from sending a bullet into your body, and after that we would have a word with them. Look here! I have two revolvers, each with six bullets. My companions are armed alike, which makes it sixty bullets. Then we have our rifles and knives. Before we would be overcome, half of your warriors would be dead."

No one had spoken like this to the chief before. Five men against a hundred! And yet the oldster spoke like this. It appeared incomprehensible to the Red, which is why he said: "You must possess strong medicine!"

"Yes, I do have a medicine, an amulet, which, until now, has sent every enemy to his death. And it will stay that way. I ask you whether you will acknowledge us as friends or not!"

"I will consult with my warriors."

"A chief of the Comanche must ask his men for advice? I have not heard that before! But since you say so, I must believe it. We are chiefs who do what we want. This gives us greater esteem and more power than you and we can therefore not sit with you by a fire. We shall mount our horses and ride off."

He rose, still pointing his two revolvers. We, too, got up. Big Bear shot up from his sitting position as if bitten by a rattlesnake. His eyes flashed and his mouth opened so that one could see his white teeth. Inside himself, he was obviously fighting a mighty battle. Had it come to a fight, the oldster's boldness would have cost us our lives, but just as certain, many Comanche would have been wounded or killed by us. The young chief was aware what a terrible weapon a revolving pistol was, and that he would be the first to be hit by a bullet. He would have to answer to his father for everything that happened, and although among Indians no man is forced into what resembles military discipline, once he has joined the war path, he is subject to iron-discipline and unrelenting rules. Situations may arise, where a father may kill his own son. If one has displayed cowardice in battle, or incompetence, or shown a lack of forcefulness, the ability to control himself, and to put care for the general welfare below his personal motivations, he is subject to general disdain or may be expelled, with no other tribe, even a hostile one, accepting him. Exiled, he will roam the wilderness and can only partially recoup a good name by returning to the proximity of his tribe and give himself the slowest, most painful death to prove, at least, that he can endure pain. This is the only means to keep his path to the Eternal Hunting Grounds open. It is the idea of these hunting grounds that drives the Indian to do all that someone else would be incapable of doing.

These considerations might presently be crossing the Red's mind. Was he going to kill us, then tell his father, or, should he be killed, have survivors report to his father that he had been incapable of controlling himself, that he, in order to play the chief, had refused hospitality to his father's friend and addressed him and his companions as coyotes? Old Death must have calculated these considerations would arise. His face did not display the least concern as he now stood before the Red, his fingers on the revolvers' triggers, while facing him with angry eyes.

"You want to leave!" the Indian exclaimed. "Where are your horses? You will not get them back! You are surrounded!"

"And you are too, together with us! Think of White Beaver's face. Once my bullet has hit you, he will not cover his head and start singing the lament for the dead, but will rather say: 'I have had no son. He, who was killed by Old Death, was an inexperienced boy, who did not show respect to my friends and listened only to the voice of his ignorance.'"

"The shadows of those we will kill together with you, will refuse you entry to the Eternal Hunting Grounds, and old women will open their toothless mouths to deride the leader who did not spare the lives of the warriors entrusted to him, because he was unable to control himself. Look, how I stand here! Do I appear afraid? I do not speak like this to you from fear, but because you are the son of my red brother.

"Decide now! A wrong word to your men or a wrong move of yours and the fight begins!"

For a full minute the chief stood motionless. One could not see what was going on inside of him, since his face was so thickly covered by paint. Suddenly, he lowered himself, fingered the calumet from the string, and said:

"Big Bear will smoke the peace pipe with the palefaces."

"It is well that you do this. Whoever wants to fight the swarms of the Apache, ought not to make also enemies of the Whites."

We, too, sat down again.

Big Bear pulled his little bag from his belt and stuffed the pipe with kinnikinnik, tobacco mixed with wild hemp leaves. He lit it, rose once more, gave a short speech, whose content I forgot, in which the terms of peace, friendship, and white brothers came up frequently, took six individual puffs, blew the smoke towards the sky, the earth, and the four directions of the wind, then handed the pipe to Old Death. The scout, too, now held a very friendly speech, took the same draws, then handed it to me, saying that he had spoken for all of us, and that we only had to copy the six draws. I then passed the calumet on to Lange and his son. Sam was passed over, since the pipe would never again have touched the mouth of an Indian once a Black had smoked from it. But the Negro was, of course, included in our peace alliance. When this ceremony was finished, the Comanche warriors, who had remained standing, sat down in a wide circle around us. Their scout was now asked to tell how he had found us. He gave his report, but left out that he had been captured by Old Death. When he had stepped aside, I had Sam take me to the horses to fetch cigars. Of course, aside from my companions, only the chief received one. It would have damaged my position as a chief had I shared cigars also with common warriors. Big Bear seemed to know what a cigar was. His face contorted with delight, and once he had lit it, his first draws elicited a grunt resembling that of those well-known, lovely animals – the source of Prague and Westfalian hams – when they contentedly rub themselves on a corner of their sty. Thereafter, he inquired in most friendly fashion about the reasons for our ride. Old Death did not feel it necessary to tell him the truth, but explained only that we wanted to catch up with some white men riding towards the Río Grande for Mexico.

"Then my white brothers can ride with us," the Red offered. "We will leave as soon as we have found the tracks of a particular Apache."

"From which direction was this man supposed to have come?"

"He was at the place where the warriors of the Comanche spoke with the vultures of Apache. Whites call it Fort Inge. He was to be killed, but escaped. But he was hit by some bullets, so that he should not be able to remain in his saddle for long. He must be somewhere in this area. Might my white brothers have seen his tracks?"

It was obvious that he was referring to the Apache Winnetou had taken across the river to dress him there. Big Bear did not seem to know anything of Winnetou, though.

"No," Old Death told him. In so doing, he did not really tell a lie, since we had not seen tracks, but only some impressions in the river. It would have been a big mistake had we given Winnetou away.

"Then this dog must be somewhere downstream. He could not have gotten farther because of his wounds, and with the warriors of the Comanche standing ready on the river's opposite side to catch the Apache, had they all escaped from Fort Inge."

That sounded rather dangerous for Winnetou. I was, however, convinced that the Comanche would not find the impressions in the river, since our horses had destroyed them when we rode across. But if other bands of Comanche had positioned themselves already four days ago in the area, one could assume that the two Apache had fallen into their hands. That Big Bear did not know anything about it, was no proof that it had not happened. The cunning scout, thinking of everything, remarked:

"If my red brothers look, they will find the spot where we crossed the river, and where we peeled a tree. I have an old wound that opened up again, and had to dress it with its fibers. It is an excellent means, my red brother may want to remember."

"The warriors of the Comanche know of this way and always use it when in a forest. My white brother is not telling me anything new."

"Then I wish that the brave warriors of the Comanche will not find reason to apply this method very often. I wish them to find victory and fame, for I am their friend. But I am sorry to say that I cannot stay with them. You must search for these tracks, while we must hurry to catch these white men."

"Then my white brothers will surely meet White Beaver, who will be glad to see them. I shall assign a warrior to lead you there."

"Where is your father, the famous chief?"

"If I am to answer Old Death's question, I must name the places the way the palefaces do. When my brothers ride downstream from here, they will reach the tributary of the Nueces, called Turkey Creek. Then they must cross Chico Creek, from where a large desert extends all the way to Elm Creek. The warriors of White Beaver roam through this desert, so as not to let anyone pass the ford on the Río del Norte, upstream from Eagle Pass."

"By the devil!" it escaped Old Death, but he quickly added: "That's precisely the way we must take! My red brother gladdened me mightily with this information, and I'm most happy to see White Beaver again. But now we must sleep, so that we can rise again very early."

"Then I will show my white brothers the place where they can sleep."

He rose and took us to a big tree with dense foliage where we were to sleep, after which he had our saddles and blankets brought over. He had totally changed since he had smoked the calumet with us. After he had left, we checked our saddle bags. Nothing was amiss, which we found commendable. Using the saddles as pillows, we lay down next to each other and wrapped ourselves in our blankets. Soon, the Comanche came, too, and despite the darkness, we noticed that they formed a circle around us when they settled down.

"This is no cause for suspicion," Old Death told us. "They are doing it to protect us, not to prevent us from escaping. Once one has smoked the peace pipe with a Red, one can rely on him. But let's see that we can get away from them after all. I took him for a ride about Winnetou, trying to get them away from his tracks. I figure, though, that it would be very, very difficult to make it across the Río Grande. None other but him could do it; only him do I trust to accomplish this feat. But it is twice as doubtful with him having an injured man along. Usually, the most experienced people are sent to councils like the one this man participated in, which makes me think that the man was old. If we figure the wound fever he must have gotten on a hard ride like theirs, then I'm mightily worried for him and Winnetou. Well, let's catch some sleep. Good night!"

While he wished us good night, I did not find it. To me, sleep was out of the question. Whoever has rubbed his thighs sore on a ride, so that his leather pants stick to the torn flesh, and who faces the beautiful prospect of a fifty-mile ride the next day through burning hot desert, would not fall into a dream of sitting in a rocking chair with a glass of champagne and an issue of a German magazine in his hands. This caused me to be awake, or rather, to still be awake, when dawn came. I woke my companions by a process likely accompanied by a bit of malice. Since I had been unable to sleep, they could also wake up now. Although they rose noiselessly, the entire group of Indians stood also immediately around us. Now, in daylight, the redskins could be observed better than the night before in the light of the low fire. I was overcome by the creepiness of the awfully painted faces and the wildly dressed figures. Few had their nakedness fully covered. Many were covered only in miserable rags, which seemed to be brimming with vermin. But all were of strong build, as the tribe of the Comanche is known to have some of the most handsome men. Of course, one cannot speak about their squaws in this respect. The squaw is the despised slave of the Red. She is not even permitted to eat with him, but must make do with that which he leaves. All work, even the hardest, rests on her. The man lives only for hunting and war.

The chief asked whether we wanted to eat something, and truly had several pieces of sinewy horse meat brought that had been ridden soft. We thanked him and declined with the excuse that we were still well provided, although our remaining provisions consisted only of a small piece of ham. He also introduced the man who was to accompany us, and it took quite a diplomatic effort by the scout to talk him out of it. At last, he desisted, after the oldster explained to him that it was an insult for white warriors like us to be assigned a guide; this was done only for boys or inexperienced men. He assured the chief that we were sure to find White Beaver's group. After we had filled our goat hides with water and had packed a few bundles of grass for our horses, we took our leave with a few words of farewell. Our watches showed four o'clock in the morning.

At first, we rode slowly to let our horses find their pace. While we still covered grassy ground, it became ever thinner and unsightly to finally end and be replaced by sand. Once we were unable to see the trees along the river behind us, it was as if we had entered the Sahara: a wide open plain without the least rise, and everywhere sand, nothing but sand. And above us stood the sun, which, despite the early morning hour burned piercingly down on us.

"We will soon fall into a sharper trot," Old Death suggested. "We must make haste in the morning hours while we have the sun behind us, since our way takes us straight west. In the afternoon, the sun will strike us in the face, which makes for a harder ride."

"Isn't it possible to lose one's way on this monotonous plain, which does not provide any features by which one can orient oneself?" I asked Old Death, being the true greenhorn. Old Death let go of a pitying laugh and replied:

"That's another one of your famous questions, sir. The sun's the most secure guide there can be. Our next destination is Turkey Creek, about sixteen miles from here. If it's all right with you, we shall reach it in a bit over two hours."

I wasn't quite pleased to make sixteen miles in two hours, but what could I do about it? First, the scout had his horse fall into a trot, then to a gallop, in which we followed him. From now on, we no longer talked. Everyone was intent in lightening the load on his horse and not to stress it by unnecessary movements. An hour passed, and another, in between we let the animals walk for some distance to catch their breath. Then, Old Death pointed ahead and said to me:

"Have a look at your watch, sir! We rode for two hours and five minutes, and there's the Nueces before us. Right?" To my surprise his statement matched the time on my watch almost exactly.

"As you can see, I've a built-in watch. I'd tell you even in the dark of night what time it is, being at most a few minutes off. You'll learn that, too, over time."

A dark strip indicated the river's course, not composed of trees, but only of bushes. We easily found a ford, then reached Turkey Creek, emptying here into the Río Nueces. It carried almost no water. From there, we headed towards Chico Creek, where we arrived shortly after nine o'clock. Its bed was also almost dry, only here and there did we find a dirty puddle from where a pitiful little trickle ran downstream. There were no trees nor any bushes, and the sparse grass was dried up. We stopped on the creek's opposite bank and watered the horses from our goat skins, with Will Lange's hat serving as a bucket. The grass we had taken along was quickly devoured by the animals, then, following half an hour's rest, we left for Elm Creek, our next destination. Now it showed that the horses were tired. The brief rest had refreshed them little and we had to ride slowly.

Noon arrived. The sun burned down, almost incinerating us, and the sand was hot and so deep that the horses had to literally wade through it, slowing our advance. Around two o'clock, we once more dismounted to give the horses the rest of our water. We did not drink ourselves. Old Death would not allow it, being of the opinion that we could endure thirst much better than the animals, who had to carry us through this sand.

"By the way," he added smilingly, "you carried yourself well. You aren't aware what kind of distance we have covered. I had said that we would reach Elm Creek only by evening, but we will get there already in two hours. That's an accomplishment no one will easily copy with horses like ours, especially, since there's one among us who sits on his horse like a clothes pin on a clothesline."

He was referring to me and was correct. My posture was neither elegant nor artistic. I kept my legs far from my horse and felt a desperate resignation, eventually becoming totally indifferent. I was fully aware that Old Death had been correct when he had claimed yesterday that there was no poetry to be found in the West. Eventually, the oldster turned a bit southward from our westerly heading.

"It's a real wonder," he said, "that we haven't come across the tracks of Comanche. They must have kept more to the river. How stupid can they be to search that long for the Apache. Had they crossed the Río Grande right away, they would have surprised the Apache."

"They may think that they can still do this," Lange commented, "provided Winnetou and his injured comrade haven't crossed it yet, the Apache have no idea that the treacherous Comanche are so close to them."

"Hmm! That's not far off the mark, sir. Precisely the fact that we aren't seeing any Comanche worries me for Winnetou. They don't seem to roam any longer, but have concentrated someplace. This is not to the Apache's advantage.

The two may have been captured."

"What would be Winnetou's fate in this case?"

"The worst imaginable. He would not be killed or tortured while on the war path. Not at all. To have captured the most famous Chief of the Apache would be an historic event, calling for a dignified celebration, meaning a most gruesome one. He would be taken to the Comanche's pastures under safe cover, where only women, boys and the old remained. There, he would be well taken care of, so that he would not be amiss of anything, except his freedom. The women would read any fulfillable wish from his lips. But if you think it to be very kind to attend so well to the captive, you are very much mistaken. The intent is to strengthen the prisoner, so that he can endure the pains of torture for as long as possible and not die right away from the first injuries inflicted on him. Once the warriors returned, they would, little by little, tear his body with a literally scientific attention to pieces, so that many days would pass before death would release him from his suffering. This is death worthy of a chief, and I'm convinced that, even with these select torments, he would not flinch, but would rather deride and laugh at his executioners. I am truly concerned for him and tell you honestly that, were he captured, I would risk my life to save him from their hands. In any case, the Comanche must be ahead, to the west of us. We are going to veer a bit south to get to my old friend, from whom we may learn about the situation at the Río Grande. We'll stay with him over night."

"Will we be welcome?"

"Of course, or I wouldn't call him a friend. He is a *ranchero*, a rancher, a real Mexican of pure Spanish descent. One of his ancestors was knighted, which is why he calls himself a *caballero*, a knight. For this reason, he gave his *rancho* the well-sounding name *Estancia del Caballero,* Estate of the Knight. You must call him *Señor* Atanasio."

Silently, we rode on following this explanation. It was impossible to get our horses to gallop; they sank almost to their knees into the sand. But over time their tiredness lessened, and by about four o'clock in the afternoon we were greeted by the first blades of grass. A while later, we entered a prairie, where mounted *vaqueros*[6] guarded horses, cattle and sheep. Our animals revived visibly and assumed a faster pace on their own. Trees rose ahead, and at last we saw something white shimmer through the greenery before us.

"That is the *Estancia del Caballero*," Old Death said. "It is a very peculiar building, constructed in the Moqui and Zuni style. It is a real fort, as is required in this area."

When we came closer to the building, we were able to make out details. A wall, twice a man's height, surrounded it. A high and wide gate provided access via a bridge crossing a deep but now dry ditch. The body was of a cubic design,

---

[6] Cowboys

with the ground floor invisible, since it was entirely hidden by the perimeter wall. The next higher story was set back, leaving space for a platform covered by white tent cloth. There was no sign of windows. From this cube story rose another of like shape, it again being smaller than the one below, so that, again, a platform, a gallery, was created, also protected by canvas. Thus, the first floor and the second and third story consisted of three masonry cubes, of which the next higher was always smaller than the lower one. The walls were painted white, and with the canvas being of the same color, the building gleamed far into the distance. When we came closer, we noticed that each story was surrounded by narrow, embrasures, which might also serve as windows.

"A nice palace, isn't it?" Old Death smiled. "You'll wonder about its design. I'd like to see the Indian chief who thinks of storming this house!"

We now rode across the bridge to the gate, which had a small opening. On the gate's side, a bell as large as a man's head was suspended. Old Death rang. Likely one could hear its sound far and wide. Soon, something that looked like an Indian's nose appeared in the small opening, together with a pair of thick lips, which asked in Spanish:

"Who's there?"

"Friends of the master of the house," the scout replied. "Is *Señor* Atanasio home?"

Nose and mouth dropped lower and two dark eyes peered from the hole. Then we heard:

"What joy! *Señor* Death! Of course, I will let you enter right away. Come in, *Señores*! I shall announce you."

We heard the sliding of a bolt, then the gate opened and we rode in. The man who had opened it was a fat Indian, clad entirely in white. He was one of these *Indios Fideles,* Christianized Indians, who, in contrast to the wild *Indios Bravos*, found peaceful accommodation with civilization. He locked the gate, made a deep bow, strode solemnly across the yard, then pulled a wire dangling from the building's wall.

"We have time to ride around the building," Old Death suggested. "Come along to have a look at it."

Only now were we able to observe the ground floor of the house. It, too, had a series of small embrasures surrounding it. The building stood within a wide, grassy yard. Except for the embrasures, there were no windows and, to our surprise, neither was there a door. We rode around the entire structure and arrived back at its front without spotting a door. The Indian was still waiting there for us.

"But how does one get inside?" I asked.

"You'll see in a moment!" Old Death replied.

Now, a man bent down from the platform above the ground floor to see who had arrived. When he saw the Indian, his head withdrew again. A narrow ladder was lowered for us to climb up. Whoever might now be of the opinion that, up there, at least one door would be found, was mistaken. Above us stood another servant, again dressed in white, who lowered one more ladder, by which we reached the top level. This platform, or what could be called the roof, consisted of zinc sheeting, covered with sand. At its center was a square hole, a laddered entry to the inside of the house.

"This is how Indian pueblos were built for hundreds of years," Old Death explained. "No one can enter the yard. And should an intruder succeed to make it over the wall, the ladder will be pulled up, and he faces a wall without any entry. In peaceful times one can also enter without coming through the gate, by standing on one's horse and climbing over the wall. But in times of war I wouldn't advise anyone to try this, for the building's occupants can cover the yard, the perimeter wall, and also the terrain outside with their bullets. *Señor* Atanasio likely has about twenty *vaqueros*, *peones* and servants, each armed with a rifle. If these twenty men are positioned up there, hundreds of Indians would die before the first would make it across the perimeter wall. This style of construction has many advantages here at the border. The *hacendado*, the rancher, did put up with more than one siege and repulsed them all."

From the top of the building one could see far in every direction. I noticed that behind and not far from the house Elm Creek, also called Saus Creek, flowed past. It carried beautifully clear water, and not surprisingly, provided fertility to both its sides.

Led by a servant, we climbed down the ladder, arriving in a long, narrow hallway, illuminated by two embrasures at its front and back. Doors opened to both sides of the hallway, and stairs led down at its end. This meant that to reach the inside of the ground floor required climbing two ladders on the building's outside, then descending two stairs inside. This appeared very cumbersome to me; however, it seemed justified considering the area's insecure conditions. The servant disappeared through a door to return a short while later, telling us that *Señor Capitán de Caballería,* Captain of the Cavalry, was expecting us. While we waited, Old Death instructed us:

"Don't hold it against my old friend *Señor* Atanasio if he receives you somewhat formally. The Spaniard loves etiquette, and the Mexican, descended from him, has maintained the custom. Had I come by myself, he would long since have welcomed me. But since there are others with me, it will turn out to be a state reception. Don't smile should he appear in uniform! He had the rank of a Mexican cavalry captain when he was young, and, even today, still likes to present himself in his old, but now antique uniform. In all other matters, he's a fine fellow."

The servant returned and we entered a soothingly cool room, whose once likely precious furnishings were now totally bleached. Three partially veiled embrasures provided a soft light. In the midst of the room stood a tall, lean

117

gentleman with snow-white hair and a mustache. He wore red trousers, trimmed with shining gold, high riding boots with spurs, whose wheels had the diameter of a five Mark silver piece. His uniform jacket was blue and richly adorned with golden stripes across his breast. The golden epaulettes did not display the rank of a cavalry captain, but that of a general. From his hips hung a saber in a steel sheath, its buckles also golden. He held a three-cornered hat, whose tips bristled with golden whirls, and, fastened to its side, was a sparkling clasp supporting a colorful feather bush. Altogether, it looked like he was coming from a masquerade. But if one saw the old, serious face and the still fresh, kindly looking eyes, one could not bring oneself to smile even secretly. Once we had entered, he clicked his heels making his spurs clink, straightened up, and said in Spanish:

"Good day, gentlemen! You are very welcome!"

This sounded very stiff. We responded by bowing silently. Old Death replied in English:

"We thank *Señor Capitán de Caballería*! Since we were in the neighborhood, I wanted to offer my companions the honor and opportunity to make your acquaintance, the brave fighter for Mexico's independence. Allow me to introduce them!"

Hearing these flattering words a satisfied smile crossed the *hacendado's* face. He nodded agreeably and said:

"Do so, *Señor* Death! It is my great pleasure to get to know these *Señores* you have brought."

Old Death gave our names and the *Caballero* shook hands with every one of us, even with the Negro, then invited us to sit down. The scout asked about the *Señora* and the *Señorita*, whereupon the *hacendado* opened a door, asking the two ladies, who had been waiting behind it to enter. The *Señora* was a very pretty, friendly-looking matron, the *Señorita* a lovely girl – her granddaughter, as we later learned. Both were dressed entirely in black silk, as if ready to appear at any moment in court. Old Death appeared to display respect only for uniforms. He rushed for the ladies and shook their hands so heartily that I became afraid for them. The two Langes' tried to produce a bow. Sam grinned broadly and exclaimed:

"Oh, missus, missus, you so nice, like silk!"

But I shone far beyond everyone else. Dismounting, I had already had difficulty making it to the ground. My legs had become stiff, making it difficult for me to get up the ladders. Every movement of my leather pants caused me pain, and now I was to greet two ladies dressed in rustling silk! I decided to suppress all pain by imitating a real, full-blooded Indian: I stepped towards the *Señora*, took her hand onto my fingertips, bowed with what I thought was overwhelming elegance, and raised them to my lips. The lady wasn't aware that I gritted my teeth while I executed this performance. She accepted my courtesy very kindly, even offering me her cheek to receive the *Beso de Cortesia*, the kiss of honor, a great honor for me. The same was repeated with the *Señorita*. Thereafter we sat down. Of course, talk immediately centered on the purpose of our ride. We said that which we thought necessary, also of our meeting with the Comanche. The ladies and the *Caballero* listened with great attention, and I noticed them giving each other significant looks. When we were finished, *Señor* Atanasio asked for a description of the two men we were looking for. I pulled out the two photos to show them to our hosts. They had barely seen them, when the *Señora* exclaimed:

"It is them, it certainly is! Is it not so, dear Atanasio?"

"Yes," the *Caballero* agreed, "it is truly them. *Señores*, these men were here last night."

"When did they come and when did they leave?"

"They arrived late at night and were very tired. One of my *vaqueros* had come across them and brought them here. They slept for quite awhile to wake up only in the afternoon. They left three hours ago."

"Fine! Then we'll catch up with them by tomorrow. We'll find their tracks."

"Surely, *Señor*, you will. They were headed for the Río Grande to cross it somewhere upstream of Eagle Pass between the Río Moral and the Río las Moras. We will hear about them yet, since I sent some vaqueros after them who will be able to tell you exactly where they rode."

"Why did you send men after them?"

"Because these two returned my hospitality with ingratitude. After they left, they sent a *vaquero*, who was tending a group of horses, with a fictitious message to me, and while he was away, stole six horses, with which they left in a hurry."

"Miserable! Then the two men were not alone?"

"No. They were accompanied by a group of disguised troopers, taking newly hired recruits to Mexico."

"I don't think your men will be able to retrieve these animals. They are not strong enough against these thieves."

"Oh, my *vaqueros* know how to use their weapons. I chose the most experienced men."

"Did Gibson and William Ohlert talk about their plans, what they were up to?"

"Not a word. The former was very funny, and the latter rather taciturn. I fully trusted them. They asked me to show them my house, where they also saw the injured Indian, whom I'm hiding from everyone."

"A wounded redskin? Who is it, and how did he get to you?"

The *Caballero* put on a superior mien and replied:

"Yes, this must be very interesting to you, *Señores*! I have taken in the delegate of the Apache, whom you mentioned earlier, and whom Winnetou bandaged at the Río Leona. He is the old Chief Inda-nisho."

"Inda-nisho, Good Man, a name he rightfully carries! He is the smartest and most peace-loving chief of the Apache! I must see him."

"I shall take you to him. He arrived in very bad condition. You must know that I am known to Winnetou. He visits me every time he comes to this area, knowing that he can trust me. Coming from Fort Inge, he caught up with the wounded chief, who had received a bullet into his arm and a second one into his thigh. After Winnetou dressed him at the Río Leona, they continued their ride immediately but wound fever mightily attacked the old man, with the Comanche swarming the desert to catch him. How Winnetou managed to get him past these obstacles to my *Estancia del Caballero* is still a riddle to me. Only Winnetou could accomplish it. But once here, they were unable to continue. Inda-nisho could not keep himself in the saddle, so weak had he become from fever. He lost much blood and is more than seventy years old."

"Unbelievable! To stay in the saddle from Fort Inge all the way here! The distance they rode is more than one-hundred-sixty miles. Only a Red can do this at this age. Please continue!"

"They arrived in the evening and Winnetou rang the bell. I went down myself and recognized him, of course. He told me everything and asked for protection of his red brother until he could be picked up. He, himself, had to cross the Río Grande as fast as possible to inform his tribes of the betrayal and the approach of the Comanche. He said that having succeeded in escaping their enemies with the injured chief, his cunning would also suffice to reach his Apache brothers. I sent my two best *vaqueros* along, so that I might learn whether he made it through."

"Well," Old Death asked expectantly. "Did he make it?"

"Yes. It took my worries away. He was smart enough not to cross the Río Grande upstream of the Río Moral, where the Comanche were positioned, but downstream of it. Of course, there is no ford; the river is very fast there, and it is life-threatening to swim it. Nevertheless, my *vaqueros* crossed with him to accompany him far enough to be certain he would no longer meet any Comanche. By now he must have informed his Apache and they will receive the Comanche appropriately. But now, come along to the old chief, if that's all right with you, *Señores*."

We all rose. I, too, – regretfully – had to leave my chair. I rose with a single, desperate jerk and a brief bow, said my good-byes to the ladies, all accompanied by a painful twitch of my face. Downstairs, we found ourselves in a hallway similar to the one upstairs, and at its end stepped through a door.

Inside a very cool room lay the old chief. The fever had lessened, but he was so weak that he could barely speak. His eyes lay deep in their sockets, and his cheeks were hollow. No doctor was available, but the *Caballero* explained that Winnetou was a master in the treatment of injuries. He had applied healing herbs and had strongly forbidden to remove the dressings. As soon as the wound fever had passed, there would be no further concern necessary for the life of the ill man, endangered only by the loss of blood and the fever. Once outside the room and facing the stairs again, I involuntarily let go of a loud sigh. The *hacendado* stopped and asked:

"Is something wrong, *Señor*? This was a deep breath you took."

I felt myself blushing. Without intending to, my look nevertheless went to the stairs. Old Death gave away what had troubled me so deeply. Laughing, he said:

"My young friend is afraid of the stairs. He isn't used to these long rides, and we just covered more than four hundred miles. It's no wonder that climbing stairs causes him pain."

"Have courage!" the *hacendado* responded. "You will get some help in a minute, my friend. Let's forget about climbing these stairs and rather have a bath."

This was very kind of him, for my thighs hurt very much. He led us through two hidden doors to the yard, after which he and Old Death climbed the outside stairs. I had no idea how important it would shortly become that the *hacendado* had taken me through these two doors to take a bath. When the two men had reached the first platform, the *Caballero* shouted, then came quickly climbing down again. He must have seen someone outside and went to open the gate. When I looked, I saw five horsemen approaching at a gallop, who were now crossing the bridge into the yard. They were magnificent-looking characters – the men he had sent after the horse thieves.

"Well," he asked. "You didn't get the horses, did you?"

"No," one of them replied. "We were close to them. They had crossed our river and from their tracks we figured to catch up with them in a quarter of an hour. But we suddenly came across the tracks of many horses, coming from the right to join theirs. The two parties must have met. We followed the tracks and soon saw them ahead of us. They were more than five hundred Comanche, and we wouldn't dare tackling such a superior force."

"Quite so. You ought not to risk your lives for a few horses. Did the Comanche interact peacefully with the Whites?"

"We were too far away to see this."

"In which direction did they ride?"

"Towards the Río Grande."

"That's away from here, and we need not be concerned about anything. That's fine, you can return to your herds."

The good *Caballero* was mightily mistaken. He had to worry much, for the Comanche heard from Gibson, as we later learned, that the injured Apache chief was at the *Hacienda del Caballero*. The result was that a number of red warriors had been dispatched to the *hacienda* in a hard gallop, where they were to capture the chief and to punish *Señor* Atanasio for his friendly disposition towards the

Apache.

The *Caballero* quietly climbed the stairs again, then a *peon* came down and asked me to follow him. He led me out through the gate to the river. Upstream of the *hacienda* was a ford, as one could see from the swirling waves. Downstream of the ford, the water was very deep. There the *peon* stopped. He had carried a white linen outfit together with a bottle.

"Here, *Señor*," he said. "This will do you good. When you are finished bathing, pull on this linen outfit instead of your leather pants. If you take them off now, I can take them back with me. When you are done, ring the bell and someone will open the gate."

He left with my old outfit, while I jumped into the water. After the day's heat and the exertion of the ride, it was a real pleasure to dive into and swim in the river. I must have spent half an hour in the water. When I finally climbed out, I followed the *peon's* advice to take a sip from the bottle and put my interim outfit on. Just when I was done, my look fell across the opposite bank. From where I stood, I could see upstream through the trees to where the river made a bend. There, I saw a long line of horsemen, one behind the other, as Indians prefer to ride. I, quickly ran for the gate and rang. The *peon*, who had waited for me, opened.

"Quick! Let's get the *Caballero*!" I said. "Indians are coming from across the river towards the *hacienda*."

"How many?"

"It looks like more than fifty."

Upon my saying this, the man was at first visibly shaken, but when I then told him the number, his expression calmed."

"No more?" he asked. "Well, that means we need not fear anything. We can handle fifty or even more Reds, *Señor*. We are ready for such a visit at any time. I cannot go up to the Caballero, but must inform the *vaqueros* right away. Here, take your things, which I can't take up after all. Lock the gate after me and hurry to *Señor* Atanasio. But make sure to pull the ladders up after you."

"What about our horses? Are they safe?"

"Yes, *Señor*. The *vaqueros* took them out to graze. The leather gear was taken into the house."

He now hurried off. I bolted the gate behind him and climbed up the ladders, which I pulled up after me, of course. Just when I reached the upper platform, I saw *Señor* Atanasio and Old Death appear from inside. The *hacendado* was not troubled at all when I told him of the approaching Indians and their number. He asked me very quietly:

"To which tribe do they belong?"

"That I don't know. I was unable to recognize their face paintings."

"Well, we will soon find out. They are either Apache, Winnetou met and sent here to pick up the wounded chief, or they are Comanche. In that case, we are likely dealing only with a reconnoitering group, coming to ask whether we might have seen any Apache. They will leave again, once they receive our answer."

"But they seem to have some hostile intentions," Old Death said. "I'd advise you to take all necessary means for defense as quickly as possible."

"That has been done already. Every one of my people knows what to do in such a situation. Look, the *peon* out there is running for the nearby horses to inform the *vaqueros*. In at most ten minutes they will have gathered the herds. Two of them will remain with the animals to guard them; the others will come to face the Reds. Their lassos are dangerous weapons, in whose use a *vaquero* is much more experienced than an Indian, and their rifles carry farther than the bows or old rifles of the savages. They need not fear fifty Indians. And inside the *estancia*, we are protected anyway. No redskin will make it across the outer wall. I hope I can also count on you . Together with the Black, you are five well-armed men. To this we can add the eight *peones*, who are presently inside the building, which makes us fourteen men. I would like to see the *Indios* who succeed in breaking open the gate. No, *Señor*, the Reds will peacefully ring the bell, voice their request, then leave again. If their leader sees fourteen well-armed men standing up here, he will respect this. The situation is totally without danger."

Old Death looked doubtful. He shook his head and said:

"A worrying thought crossed my mind. I am convinced we are dealing with Comanche, not with Apache. What do they want here? It cannot be a simple reconnoiter, for, if there were a group of hostile Apache here, their tracks would show this. There would be no need for them to inquire with us. No, this group has a very specific reason to come here to you, *Señor*, which is the injured chief you are hosting."

"But they don't know about him! Who would have told them?"

"Gibson, the man we are pursuing and who visited you, would have told them. You showed him the Apache. He betrayed him to the Comanche to gain their favor. If that isn't right I will, not for a moment, be called Old Death any longer, *Señor*. Or do you doubt me?"

"It is possible. In that case the Comanche will attempt to force us to hand over the wounded chief."

"Indeed. Would you do it?"

"No way! Winnetou is my friend. He entrusted Good Man to me, and I must and will honor this trust. The Comanche will not get the injured man. We shall defend ourselves!"

"That will endanger you very much. Although we will succeed in repulsing the fifty, they will return with a tenfold force, after which you will be lost."

"That will be in God's hands. In any case, I will keep my word, which I gave Winnetou."

That's when Old Death offered the *Señor* his hand, saying:

"You are a man of honor and can count on our support. The leader of the Comanche is a friend of mine. Maybe, this will make it possible for me to prevent the attack on you. Might you have also shown Gibson the secret doorways in the walls?"

"No, *Señor*."

"That is very well. For as long as the Reds do not know of these entries, we will be able to fend them off. Let's go in now to get our weapons."

During my absence my companions had been assigned rooms to where their belongings, as well as mine, had been taken. I went to my room, which was located at the front of the house, getting its light through two embrasures. When I wanted to take my rifle from the wall next one of the openings, I happened to look outside to see the Indians appear from under the trees where the ford was located. They had crossed it, and were now galloping towards the building, not with a howl, as is their custom, but in malicious silence, which appeared highly dangerous to me. They were Comanche, as I was now able to determine from their facial colors. They were armed with spears, bows and arrows. Only their leader carried a rifle. Some of them were pulling some long objects behind their horses. In my inexperience, I thought them to be tent poles, but soon realized that I was mistaken. Presently, they stopped in front of the perimeter wall, so high that one could no longer see the horsemen. Obviously, I right away left my room to inform the others. When I entered the hallway, Old Death was stepping out of an adjacent room.

"Watch out," he hollered. "They are coming over the wall. They brought some young tree trunks along to serve as ladders. Quickly, let's get up on the platform!"

But that did not work as fast as he wished. The *peones* were on the lower, servants' floor, and the two of us were also held up from quickly ascending the stairs, for, together with the *Caballero*, his two ladies were stepping into the hallway and assailed us with fearful questions about the attack. Two minutes passed likely before we made it up the stairs, precious time in such a situation. The negative effect of this loss of time showed right away when we reached the platform. The first Indian was just coming over the wall, quickly followed by a second, third and fourth. Although we had our weapons at the ready, we could no longer prevent their entry if we did not want to gun them down.

"Aim your rifles at them! Don't let them get closer!" Old Death ordered. "Of all things, we must gain some time."

I counted fifty-two Reds, none of whom had uttered a single sound. We had been caught unawares by them. However, they did not dare get closer, but kept standing at the edge of the platform with bows and arrows in hand. They had left their spears below, which would have only been a hindrance in climbing. The *Caballero* walked a few paces towards them and asked in the mishmash of Spanish, English and Indian lingo used in the border areas for communication:

"What do the red men want from me? Why do they enter my house without asking permission?"

Their leader, who had carried his rifle on his shoulder, had now taken it to his hand, stepped several paces forward, and replied:

"The warriors of the Comanche have come because the paleface is their enemy. Today's sun is the last he is going to see."

"I am no enemy of the Comanche, but love all red men without asking to which tribe they belong."

"The paleface is saying a great lie. A chief of the Apache is hidden in this house. The dogs of Apache are the enemies of the Comanche. Whoever takes in an Apache is our enemy and must die."

"*Carajo*! (damn) Are you forbidding me to take anyone in I like? Who has the say here, you or I?"

"The warriors of the Comanche have climbed up this house and are therefore its masters. Turn the Apache over to us! Or do you deny that he is here?"

"I don't deny anything. Only someone afraid tells lies; but I am unafraid of the Comanche and shall openly . . ."

"Hold it!" Old Death interrupted softly. "Don't commit a foolishness, *Señor*!"

"Are you saying I should deny it?" the Mexican asked.

"Of course. Lying is a sin – I admit – but telling the truth in a situation like this is simply suicide, which is why I ask you: What is more sinful? To tell an untruth or to kill oneself?"

"Suicide? What can these people accomplish against our fourteen rifles?"

"Much, since they are already up here. The majority of them would certainly be killed, but we, too, would get a few arrows and knives in our bodies, *Señor*. Even if we won, the survivors would bring the other five hundred here. Let me give it a try by talking with them."

He now turned to the Reds' leader:

"My brother's words surprise me. How did the Comanche arrive at the idea that an Apache is in this house?"

"They do know," the Red replied curtly.

"Then you know more than we do."

"Are you saying that we are mistaken? Then you are telling a lie."

"And you are using a word for which you will pay with your life, should you repeat it. I won't have myself called a liar. You see our rifles aimed at you. It takes only my signal to our men and as many of your warriors will die."

"But others would follow them. Some place not far from here are many more warriors of the Comanche, more than ten times ten times five. They would come and destroy this house to the ground."

"They would not make it across the wall, for we are warned now. From up

125

here we would greet them with so many bullets that none of them would remain alive."

"My white brother has a big mouth. Why is he talking to me? Is he the owner of this house? Who is he, and what does he call himself that he dares to speak to a leader of the Comanche?"

With a dismissive hand movement, Old Death said:

"Who is this leader of the Comanche? Is he a famous warrior; does he sit in the council of wise men? He does not wear an eagle or raven feather in his hair, and I see no other symbols of a chief on him. But I am a chief of the palefaces. To which tribe of the Comanche do you belong that you must ask who I am? My name is Kosha-pehve, and I smoked the peace pipe with Oyo-koltsa, the Chief of the Comanche. I also spoke with his son Avat-vila yesterday and for a night slept with his warriors. I am a friend of the Comanche, but if they call me a liar, I shall answer them with a bullet."

A murmur passed through the group of Reds. Their leader turned to speak softly to them. From the looks they now gave Old Death, one could see that his name had made an impression. After a brief council, their leader turned back to the scout:

"The warriors of the Comanche know that Old Death is a friend of White Beaver, but his words are not those of a friend. Why does he keep secret the presence of the Apache?"

"I do not keep anything secret, but simply tell you that he is not here."

"Yet we learned very well that Inda-nisho is here. This from a paleface who has entered the protection of the Comanche. His name sounds like Ta-hi-ha-ho."

"Might it be Gavilano?"

"Yes, that is it."

"Then the Comanche made a big mistake. I know this man. He is a scoundrel with lies on his tongue. The warriors of the Comanche will regret having offered him protection."

"My brother is very much mistaken. The paleface told the truth. We know that Winnetou brought Good Man, then escaped by way of Avat-bono. But we will go after him to catch him for the stake. We know that Good Man is injured in an arm and a leg. We even know exactly the place where he is kept."

"If that is true, tell me where it is."

"One climbs from here twice into the depth of the house to where there are many doors to the right and left of a narrow passage. Then one opens the last door on the left. There, the Apache lies on a bed, which he cannot leave, being too weak."

"The paleface lied to you. You would not find an Apache at the place you described."

"Then let us climb down to look, who speaks the truth, you or the paleface."

"That I will not do. This house is only for those people to enter with the permission of its owner, but not for those who attack it."

"According to your words we must think that the Apache is here. White Beaver commanded us to get him, and we shall obey him."

"Once again, you are mistaken. I do not refuse your wish because the Apache is here, but because your demand is an insult. When Old Death says that you have been lied to, then you must believe him. If you, nevertheless, want to force entry, then give it a try! Aren't you comprehending that a single man is enough to defend the entrance? If he stands inside by the stairs, he can kill every one of you trying to climb down. You came here with hostile intent, which is why we refuse you entry. Go back behind the gate and request to be let in, as is proper, then we may receive you perhaps as friends!"

"Old Death is giving us advice, which serves him very well, but not us. If he has a clean conscience, he will let us enter the house. If not, we shall remain here at this spot and dispatch a messenger to bring all the Comanche here."

"Surely not! Even if a thousand Comanche would come, then, still only one would be able to climb down here, and would instantly pay with his life for it. Also, you would not be able to send a messenger, for, as soon as your messenger would leave the protection of the perimeter wall, I would shoot him down from up here. I am a friend of the Comanche, but you came as enemies and will be treated as such."

During this back and forth talk we kept our rifles aimed at the Indians. Although they had succeeded in climbing up onto the first platform, they were still at a disadvantage. Their leader realized this, which is why he talked again with his men. However, neither was our position enviable. Old Death scratched himself worryingly behind an ear, and said:

"This situation is very bad. Good sense forbids us to treat the Comanche with hostility. If they bring in their main force, we are done for. Yes, if we could hide the Apache so that they would not be able to find him! But I know the house only too well and am aware that there is no such hiding place available."

"Let's get him outside then!" I suggested.

"Outside?" the oldster laughed. "Are you the devil's, sir? How would you accomplish this?"

"Did you forget the two secret doors? They are in the back of the house; while the Comanche are standing in front and cannot see what's going on back there, I will carry Good Man outside into the bushes by the river until the Comanche have left."

"That's not a bad thought," Old Death said. "I didn't think of those doors. You could get him outside, but what if the Comanche have posted guards there?"

"I don't believe so. They are not many more than fifty. Some must stay with their horses, which are up front by the wall. We can expect that they did not also post anyone in the back."

"All right, let's try it, you and a *peon*. We will arrange it so that the Indians

127

cannot observe you climbing down now. Afterwards, we will position ourselves closely so that they cannot count us to notice that two are missing. The ladies can help you and, once you are outside, push the small closet again in front of the door."

"One more suggestion. Couldn't the ladies stay in the sick room? If the Reds see that women live there, they will be twice as likely to believe that no Indian was kept there."

"Quite right!" *Señor* Atanasio commented. "You need only place a few blankets in the room and bring the hammocks from my wife's and granddaughter's rooms down. There are hooks for them in just about every room of the house. Then the ladies can lie down in them. For you, sir, the best hiding place is right below the spot where you were bathing earlier. There you will find dense, blooming petunias hanging way down to the water. Underneath, we have hidden our boat. If you put the Apache in it, no Comanche will find him. Pedro should accompany you. Only after you have come back will we allow the Indians to enter the house."

Together with Pedro, I climbed covertly down the stairs into the house where the two ladies were waiting, very much concerned about the developments outside. Once we had explained to them what we intended to do, they quickly helped us in the execution of our task, bringing the blankets and hammocks down themselves. We wrapped the Apache in one of the blankets. When he heard that Comanche were outside, looking for him, he said in his weak voice:

"Inda-nisho has seen many winters and his days are numbered. Why should the good palefaces be murdered because of him? Turn me over to the Comanche, but kill me first, I ask of you."

He had spoken in the earlier mentioned mishmash, which I readily understood. My only response was a forceful shake of my head. After that, we carried him from the room. The small closet was moved aside, after which we were able to carry the injured man out behind the perimeter wall. No one had seen us so far. Outside, next to the wall, grew bushes providing cover, but between them and the river was an open area we had to cross. I cautiously peered out and was disappointed to spot a Comanche sitting a short distance away, his spear, quiver and bow lying next to him. He was guarding the rear wall, a fact that seemed to make the execution of our plan impossible.

"We must get back, *Señor*," the *peon* said, when I pointed the Red out to him. "We could kill him, but that would bring the revenge of the others upon us."

"In no case shall we kill him. But it must be possible to remove him, to lure him away."

"I don't think so. He will not abandon his post until he is relieved."

"I have an idea. Maybe I will be able to pull it off. You remain hidden here, but I will let myself be seen. Once he sees me, I will act as if I became frightened, and flee. He will pursue me."

"Or send an arrow after you."

"I must risk this."

"Don't do it, *Señor*. It is too dangerous. The Comanche shoot their arrows as well as we do our rifles. When you run away, you will turn your back to him, and can therefore not see the arrow to avoid it."

"I shall flee across the river. If I swim on my back, I will see him shoot and can dive right away. He will think that I plan something against his people and likely follow me into the water. Once, being on the other bank, I shall render him harmless with a blow against his temple. You will not leave your place until I return. Earlier, I noticed the petunia creepers and know where the boat is hidden. I will get it and bring it directly opposite from here."

The *peon* tried to talk me out of it, but I would not listen to his objections, since I knew how we could finish the task that had been assigned us. I now left the place where we were, so as not to give it away, stole some distance through the bushes along the wall, then stepped away from it, as if I had apparently come around the corner. The Comanche did not spot me right away, but it did not take long for him to turn towards me, after which he immediately jumped up. I partially turned my face away, so that he would be unable to identify me. He shouted for me to stop, and when I did not listen, picked up his bow and an arrow from his quiver, getting ready to shoot. A few quick leaps and I had reached the bushes along the river bank before he was able to shoot. I leaped into the water and used back strokes to reach the opposite bank. Moments later he broke through the bushes, saw me, and let his arrow fly. I dove, unhurt. When I surfaced again, I saw him stand at the bank, expectantly bent forward. He saw that I had not been hit. Not carrying a second arrow, since he had left his quiver behind, he dropped his bow and jumped into the water. That was what I had wanted. To lure him on, I acted as if I were a poor swimmer, letting him approach closely. Then I dove again and swam quickly downstream. When I surfaced again, I was close to the bank. He was waiting far upstream from me, looking where I would come up. I now had the intended lead, swam to the bank, climbed up, and ran upstream under the trees. Then I spotted a very big, moss-covered live oak, just right for my purpose. I passed it about five paces away, ran on a bit, then returned to hide behind its trunk. Hugging the trunk, I waited for the arrival of the Red, who had to follow my very visible tracks. I had been running like I would have thought impossible only one-and-one-half hours ago. Then the man came rushing up, panting heavily, and dripping wet like myself, his eyes on my tracks. He passed me, I obviously now followed him. His loud panting prevented him from hearing my steps, especially since I ran on the tips of my toes. I had to take great leaps to catch up. Then, with a final big leap, fully hitting his body, I caused him to hit the ground full force. Quickly, I knelt on him and took him by his throat. Two blows with my fists against his head, and he no longer moved. Not far from us a sycamore had fallen over. It was hanging over the river so that the water flowed perhaps six yards below its desiccated branches. This setting provided an excellent opportunity to enter the river without leaving tracks. I climbed on the trunk and walked along it until I was above the water and I jumped in. Almost directly opposite from where I was, I saw the blooming petunias. I swam there, untied the boat, climbed in and rowed to the spot on the bank where we wanted to board the Apache. Once there, I tied the boat to an exposed root and climbed out. We had to hurry to finish before the felled Comanche revived again. We carried the Apache to the boat and made him a passable bed with the blanket and his clothing. Then the *peon* returned right away to the wall. I rowed the boat back below the petunias, tied it up, swam back and took off my linen outfit to wring it out. Dressed again, I searched the opposite bank to see whether the Comanche had revived to observe our actions, but despite my best effort was unable to see anything of my foe. Now I made it back to the house. Barely a quarter of an hour had passed.

The *Señora* handed me a dry outfit and, properly dressed again, I could laugh at any Comanche's face who would claim that I had been outside the house, or even swam the river.

The ladies now lay down in the hammocks, after which the *peon* and I went back up to the platform, taking our weapons along. Both parties were still negotiating. Old Death had stuck to his claim that the search of the house would constitute an insult to him and the *hacendado*. When I told him that the Apache was safe, he slowly relented and finally said that five Comanche would be permitted to enter to convince themselves that the Apache was not here.

"Why only five?" their leader asked. "Isn't one of us like any other? What one does, all should be able to do. Old Death can trust us. We shall not touch anything. None of us will steal."

"Fine! You are to see that we are magnanimous. You will all be allowed to enter the house, so that everyone of you can convince yourselves that I told the truth. But I demand that all of you put down your weapons before entering, and that we can hold anyone for punishment who touches a thing or person without our permission."

The Reds discussed this demand, then agreed. They put down their bows, quivers and knives, then climbed in one after the other. Already before I had gone outside with Pedro, the *vaqueros* had gathered out on the plain. They were well armed and mounted, and kept looking towards us. Waiting for a signal of their master, they had remained quiet after none had been given.

Of us fourteen men, Old Death and the *hacendado* were the ones to open the rooms to the Comanche. Two of us remained on the platform, and five each posted themselves in the corridors, ready to oppose any stepping-out of the Reds. I was one of the men standing in the lower hallway and positioned myself next to the door of the room the Apache had occupied. The Comanche came straight for this entrance. Old Death opened it. One could see that the Indians were expecting to see Good Man lying in there. Instead, they found the two ladies, who lay reading in the hammocks.

"Uff!" the leader exclaimed disappointed. "Squaws are here!"

"Yes," Old Death laughed. "This is where the chief of the Apache is supposed to be, like this paleface lied. Why don't you step inside to look for him!"

The leader's looks crossed the room, after which he replied:

"A warrior does not enter the wigwam of women. There is no Apache here. I would see him."

"Search the other rooms then!"

It took more than an hour before the Indians had completed their search. When they did not find a trace of the man they sought, they once more returned to the room the ladies occupied, who now had to leave it, after which the Comanche searched it in great detail. The Reds even lifted the blankets and mattresses from the floor, checking whether some cavity might be hidden below. At last, they were convinced that their quarry was not on the *hacienda*. When the leader admitted to it, Old Death told him:

"I told you, but you didn't believe me. You trusted a liar more than me, who is a friend of the Comanche. When I meet White Beaver, I shall complain to him."

"Does my white brother intend to see him? Then he can ride with us."

"That will not be possible. My horse is tired. I can continue my ride only tomorrow, while the warriors of the Comanche will leave here already today."

"No. We will stay. The sun is going to rest, and we will not ride by night. We shall leave at daybreak; therefore my white brother can ride with us."

"All right! But I am not alone; I have four companions with me."

"They, too, will be welcome to White Beaver. My white brothers may permit us to camp this night in the vicinity of the house."

"We don't mind," the Mexican replied. "I told you already that I am the friend of all red men, provided they come peacefully. To prove this, I will make you the gift of a steer. You can butcher it, make a fire, and roast it."

This promise impressed the Comanche. They were convinced to have done us an injustice, and now behaved most peacefully. Of course, it was most likely the high esteem they had for Old Death which contributed to it. Truly, they had not touched anything inside the house and now left without being asked. The ladders were lowered and the gate left open. Several armed *peones* remained on the platform as guards. Despite the Indians' changed behavior, caution could not be abandoned. We, too, climbed down, and the *vaqueros*, who received orders to corral a steer, approached. All the Comanche's horses stood in front by the perimeter wall. Three guards had been assigned to them. Guards had been posted on the other sides. These men were now called back. Among them was the one I had lured across the river. His rather simple covers were still wet. He had returned to his post and had not had the opportunity to report to the leader what had happened. He now walked to him and told him so softly that we Whites were unable to understand anything. When he was finished with his report, he happened to see me. Because of his face paint I was unable to notice a change in his expression. With an angry hand movement he pointed at me and shouted several Indian words to his leader, whose meaning remained unclear to me. The leader now walked up to me, gave me a questioning and threatening look, and said:

"The young paleface swam earlier across the river! Did you knock down this red warrior?"

Stepping closer, Old Death took over and asked the Indian leader what he meant. The man now told him what supposedly had happened. Amused, the scout laughed, and said:

"The red warriors seem to have difficulties differentiating between the faces of Whites. It is even a question whether it was a paleface, this son of the Comanche saw."

"It was a White," the man said firmly. "And no other than him. I saw his face when he swam on his back. He also wore the same white outfit."

"Really! He swam the river wearing this outfit? Your loincloth is still wet. His outfit would also need to be wet. Touch it to convince yourself that it is totally dry."

"He took off the wet one and put a dry one on in the house."

"How would he have gotten in? Did your warriors not stand here by the gate? No one can get in or out of the house without climbing these ladders, next to which stood the warriors of the Comanche. Would it then be possible for my young companion to have been outside the house?"

They had to admit to Old Death's logic, and the outsmarted guard, at last, said that he must have been mistaken. When the *hacendado* remarked that a group of horse thieves was roaming the area lately, to which the unknown man likely belonged, the case was closed. Only the riddle remained as to why the guard had not found any tracks from which he could have identified the direction in which his assailant had escaped. To resolve the question, the leader, together with the guard and a few other warriors, rode through the ford to the respective spot. Fortunately, it was getting dark, so that a close inspection of the place was no longer possible. Smart Old Death took me along for a walk along the river. Seemingly looking only at what the horsemen on the other side of the river were doing, we kept on going until we stopped by the petunias. There, the scout said so softly that only I and the Apache in the boat were able to understand him:

"Old Death is standing here with the young paleface who hid Good Man down there. Might the Chief of the Apache perhaps recognize me from my voice?"

"Yes," it came back just as softly.

"The Comanche believe now that Good Man is not here. They will leave at daybreak. Will my brother be able to stay for that long in the boat?"

"The Apache will be able to take it, for the scent of the water is refreshing and the fever will not return. But the Chief of the Apache would like to know for how long Old Death will remain here with his companions."

"We will ride off tomorrow together with the Comanche."

"Uff! Why is my friend joining our enemies?"

"Because we are looking for some men who are with their main group."

"Will the white men also meet warriors of the Apache?"

"That is likely."

"Then I would like to give the young warrior, who dared his life to hide me, a totem which he can show the sons of the Apache so that they will always make him welcome. Old Death is an astute and experienced hunter. The dogs of Comanche will not catch him once it is dark, when he brings me a piece of leather and a knife. Before daybreak he can then pick up the totem, which I will inscribe during the night."

"I shall bring both, the leather and a knife. Do you want anything else?"

"No. The Apache is content. May good Manitou always watch over the trails of Old Death and the young paleface."

We returned to the house. No one had noticed that we had stood by the river for a few minutes. The oldster explained to me:

"It is rare for a White to be given a totem by an Indian chief. You are very lucky, sir. Good Man's writing may come to be of great use to you yet."

"And you will dare bring him the leather and knife? If the Comanche catch you at it, you will both be lost!"

"Nonsense! Do you think me to be a schoolboy? I always know precisely what I can dare and what not."

By now the leader of the Comanche had returned without having achieved anything. The tracks had no longer been clearly visible.

I was awakened early in the morning. Old Death handed me a squarish piece of white-tanned leather. I looked at it, but could not identify anything, except for a few cuts in the smooth side of the leather, which seemed inconsequential to me.

"This is the totem?" I asked. "I cannot discover anything exceptional on it."

"It's not necessary. Show it to the first Apache you come across, and he will enlighten you as to the treasure you own. The writing on this totem is not yet visible, since Good Man had no paint available. But when you hand it to an Apache, he will color in the cuts, after which the respective figures will appear. But, for God's sake, let no Comanche see it; he will think you to be a friend of the Apache. Change now and come down. The Comanche will be ready to leave shortly."

The Indians were occupied with their morning meal, consisting of the remains of last night's steer. They then gathered their horses to water them at the river. Fortunately, this took place upstream from the spot where the Apache remained hidden. The *hacendado* with his two ladies joined us now, with the two women not showing the least concern about the Reds. When the *Caballero* saw our horses that were brought in by the *vaqueros*, he said to Old Death, shaking his head:

"These are no horses for you, *Señor*. You know the value of a good horse. *Señor* Lange and his son are none of my business, just as little is the Negro. But you are an old friend of mine, and with you having taken this young gentleman into your heart, I have done the same. You are both to get better horses."

We happily accepted the *hacendado's* offer. Upon his order the *vaqueros* corralled two half-wild horses, which we accepted in place of ours. My old one had been used to riders, the new one, however, caused me quite some trouble during the first few days, and I had to make every effort not to make a fool of myself before the Comanche, or Old Death, on whose face showed a faint, ironic grin whenever the spirited and reluctant animal discomforted me for a moment by displacing me from my proper manly posture.

The sun had not yet risen above the horizon when we crossed Elm Creek to then move westward at a gallop. Our small group of five rode ahead, followed by the Comanche's leader and his men. It gave me a feeling of insecurity, for I expected at any moment to get an arrow or a spear in my back. The Indians, riding their small, unkempt and lean yet persevering horses, together with their weaponry, painted faces, and the way they acted, did not give the impression that we should trust them. However, Old Death reassured me when I remarked about this. It had not been discussed yet when and where we were to meet the main force of the Comanche. Now we learned that this group had not stopped to await the return of our group of fifty, but that their leader had been given orders to take Good Man prisoner at the *hacienda*, then to send him under cover of ten warriors to the Comanche's camp where the stake waited for him. The remaining forty were to hasten for the Río Grande, there to follow and catch up to the main force. Since White Beaver had been told by Gibson that Winnetou had escaped across the river and would be able to warn his people, the Comanche thought it necessary to maintain the greatest possible speed in order to be able to surprise their enemies before they would be ready to defend themselves. To us, it was most important to find Gibson still with the Comanche. Once I had caught this man and William Ohlert, I could turn back and need no longer to be concerned about the Indians' enmity.

After approximately two hours we arrived at the place where our Indian companions had yesterday split from the main group. South from us, by the Río Grande, Eagle Pass and Fort Duncan were located, which the Reds had to avoid. After another two hours, some sparse grass appeared, telling us that we were past the Nueces Desert. The tracks we were following led straight ahead and had nowhere been crossed by others, telling us that the Comanche had remained unobserved. Little by the little, the earth came alive: there was intensely green grass and we finally saw a forest appear in the west. This told us the proximity of the Río Grande del Norte.

"Uff!" exclaimed the leader of our Comanche troop with a sound of relief. "We did not meet any palefaces, and no one will prevent us from crossing the river. The Apache dogs will soon see us and will howl from fright when they face our brave warriors."

For some time we passed slowly among sycamores, elms, ashes, and hackberries, until we arrived at last at the river. White Beaver was a good leader of his troops. The mile-wide tracks we had followed led straight to the ford. Here, the Río Grande was very wide, but shallow. Sand banks rose from the water, some likely with quicksand in which one could easily get stuck. Here, by the bank, the Comanche's main group had camped last night, as could be seen from the tracks. We could assume that they had broken camp just as early as we had, but that they were not able to ride as fast as we, since they had now entered the foray areas of the Apache, requiring them to be cautious, thus slowing them down. One could see that the crossing of the ford had been done very carefully. Numerous foot impressions showed that some men had dismounted to check for the deceiving quicksand accumulations. Passable areas had been marked by twigs stuck in the sand. This simplified our crossing, since we only had to follow their tracks. The sand banks divided the river into several arms which our horses had to pass by swimming. On the opposite side, we again passed through a narrow tree and brush region, followed by grass, then sand. We now entered the area between the Río Grande and Bolson de Mapimi, well-suited to the roaming of wild Indian groups. It was a far-flung sand plain, broken only by larger and smaller stretches of cacti. The clear tracks led in an almost westerly direction, only slightly veering south. I had been of the opinion that we would still catch up with the Comanche today, but was mistaken. The sand kicked far back by the hooves of their horses told us that they had hurried. Towards noon we crossed a narrow range of low and bare hillside, followed again by another sandy plain.

I had to admire the staying power of the Indian horses. By now it was late afternoon, yet they still showed not a trace of tiredness. The three horses of the Langes and the Negro had difficulties following, but Old Death's and my horse demonstrated that we had made a very good exchange. Darkness threatened, when we found, to our surprise, that the tracks changed direction. A quarter of an hour earlier we had crossed the trail from San Fernando to Baya, but now the tracks led southwest. Why so? There had to be a reason. Old Death explained it to us. From the hoof impressions one could see that the Comanche had stopped here. Coming from straight north, the tracks of two horsemen met those of the Reds. The oldster dismounted, checked the new tracks, then said:

"Two Indians met the Comanche. They brought a message which caused White Beaver's warriors to change direction. We cannot but follow them."

The leader of our Comanche group also got off his horse, checked the tracks, then confirmed the scout's assumption. Thus, we now also headed south. For as long as it was possible to follow the tracks, we kept on riding, since we still wanted to cover an as great as possible distance. Even when dusk fell, the tracks could still be differentiated in the smooth sand. But then, everything turned black on black. We were going to halt. Suddenly, my horse puffed up its nostrils, neighed loudly, and took off with me. I was not a good enough horseman to quickly regain control of it. Neither hard pulling of the reins, nor command, nor pressure of my thighs helped. It simply bolted away with me, and following in full gallop came the Comanche. Behind, I heard Old Death's laughing voice:

"Hello, sir, stay in the saddle! The animal is thirsty and the devil got into its belly. It knows that it is ridden by a greenhorn and has given up its respect for you. I figure it will take us to some water source."

In this way we covered a good distance in a hurry, then a dark shadow rose in front of me. Branches or whatever hit my face. One more leap of the horse – I was thrown from the saddle, somersaulted, and landed in the water. Desperately holding onto my rifle, I worked myself to the surface. I was unable to see whether I was in running or standing water and where the bank was. There was nothing else to do but try to stay on the surface. Then hoof beats sounded, and shouts of joy made it clear that the Comanche were glad to have found water. Above the brouhaha I heard Old Death's voice:

"Hello, sir, where are you? There's water with a horse standing in the middle, but the rider can't be seen."

"Here I am; I'll be right there," I replied.

"Well, let yourself be fished out."

Someone got me by an arm and I heard the Negro say:

"Massa have no fear of water! Negro Sam is good swimmer, very good. He saved his massa from big river."

The good fellow had jumped in the water to retrieve me, although, by now, there was no need anymore. My horse stood close to the bank, up to its belly in water. I, though, had been tossed a bit farther, where the water was deeper. It took only two strokes to find bottom, showing that I had been in no danger for my life, but only that I had embarrassed myself. To let a horse bolt, then even be thrown, is an enormous disgrace for Reds.

After today's hot and strenuous ride the water was a real refreshment for men and animals. Quickly, a campsite was selected, the Reds posted guards, and let the animals graze under their supervision. We Whites sat together, but because of being ashamed, I kept rather quiet. Old Death tried to figure out what the water course was, which we had so unexpectanctly found, and at last arrived at the conviction that it had to be the Morelos which enters the Río Grande near Fort Duncan. I spent the night in a somewhat moist condition, which is why I felt more than refreshed in the morning. Some checking established that this was a substantial watercourse, which, not too far from where we camped, had been crossed by the main force of the Comanche. We did likewise and kept following their tracks again. By noon, the tracks veered west, and we saw bare mountains rise ahead. Old Death showed concern. When I asked him for the reason, he answered:

"I don't like this. I can't understand White Beaver entering this area. Might you know what kind of nice area lies ahead of us?"

"Yes, the Bolson de Mapimi."

"And you know this desert?"

"No. I haven't heard much of it."

"Because nothing much is known. The Mapimi is a real crock of worms from which wild tribes have erupted many times to plunder the adjoining lands. But don't think this is a fertile area since it appears to breed people in such numbers. It has been shown again and again that desolate areas are the point of origin for the migration of peoples. It is impossible to get the better of the tribes living on this plateau and in the canyons and valleys. I know very well that several bands of Apache have established themselves there. If it is the intention of the Comanche to attack these, then I feel terribly sorry for them, not for the Apache, but for the Comanche. To the north, the Apache roam between the Río Grande del Norte and the Río Pecos, and they literally own the entire northwest far beyond the Gila. This is why the Comanche are entering a trap, which can easily snap closed behind them."

"Oh my! We, too, are then inside!"

"Yes, but I'm not much afraid. We haven't done anything to the Apache, which is why I hope they won't show us any hostility. In an emergency, your totem will be to good effect."

"Isn't it our duty to warn the Comanche?"

"Go, try it, sir! Tell a fool ten times that he's stupid, and he'll still not believe you. I earlier gave my opinion to their leader. He dressed me down and said that he had to follow White Beaver's tracks. He told me, that if we didn't want to do this, we were free to ride to wherever we wanted."

"That was coarse!"

"Yes, the Comanche haven't taken lessons in manners and decent conversation. I wouldn't be surprised if something isn't brewing up there for us. We are past the border; whether and how we get back has been printed in a book I haven't read yet."

5. Crossing the Mapimi

The old scout's words had made quite an impression on me. I had been certain that I would catch Gibson while he was still in the United States. Now, I had to pursue him into Mexico and enter the most dangerous area of this country.

The direction we had intended to follow to reach Chihuahua would have merely touched the north of the wild Mapimi and have crossed mostly open countryside. But now we had to keep farther south where dangers might lie in wait which we might not be up to dealing with. Adding to these downbeat thoughts was my physical tiredness, a tiredness that even the Comanche had difficulty fighting. We had galloped most of the time since leaving the *Hacienda del Caballero*. The Reds had run out of their dried meat provisions and we, too, had little of the food left which had been packed for us at the *hacienda*.

The terrain ahead gradually rose. We arrived at the mountains we had seen at noon, rocky rises without any vegetation, and now wound our way through them, always in a southerly direction. Between the steep hillsides the heat was even worse than on the plain, causing the horses to slow down more and more. The main force of the Comanche had also moved very slowly here, as we saw from their tracks. Above us swooped several vultures, which had followed us for hours, as if expecting that our exhaustion would result in some prey for them. Suddenly, we spotted a dark strip in the south. There seemed to be forested mountains and immediately the horses fell to a faster pace, as if being aware of them. Old Death's face lightened up.

"I think I know where we are headed," he said. "I figure we are in the vicinity of the Río Sabinas, coming from the Mapimi. If the Comanche decided to ride the *río* upstream, our plight will soon end. Where there's water, there's also forest and grass and some game, even in this miserable area. Let's give our horses the spurs. The more they exert themselves now, the longer they can rest later."

The tracks had veered more to the east. We entered a long, narrow canyon, and when it opened a green valley lay ahead of us, well watered by a creek. In the blink of an eye, we hurried for this creek and jumped from our saddles. Even had the Comanche wanted to maintain control, they would have had to let their horses have their wills. But once the animals had their fill, we right away mounted up to ride on. Not much later the creek emptied into a larger one which we followed upstream. It led into a canyon whose steep walls were partly covered by bushes. Once it was behind us we rode past green mountain slopes, whose color felt good to our dazzled eyes. By now dusk was approaching, and we had to be on the lookout for a campsite. The leader of the Comanche insisted on riding on for some distance until we would find some trees, and we had to agree. But now our horses were stumbling over rocks. Night had almost come, when we were suddenly hailed. Our leader answered joyously, for the call had been in the Comanche language. We stopped. Old Death and the leader rode ahead, and the scout soon returned to report:

"The Comanche are camped ahead of us. From the condition of their tracks, this wasn't expected. But they didn't dare advance farther without first reconnoitering the area. This is why they camped here and sent scouts out this afternoon, who, as yet, have not returned. Come on! You will see their camp fires in a moment."

"I thought that no fires are lit when the Reds are on the war path," I said.

"The terrain is such that it is possible. Since they sent scouts ahead, they are certain that no enemy is close to see the fires."

We rode on. The canyon ended, and we now saw at least ten low-burning fires ahead, as is customary with Indians. The place appeared to be a round, treeless, and steep-sided valley, a condition the Comanche seemed to consider favorable for their security.

The Reds we had arrived with rode straight for the camp; we were asked to wait until called. It took a while before a warrior came to lead us to the chief, who had taken his place at a fire in the center which was surrounded by other fires. He was joined by two men, likely accomplished warriors. His hair was gray and long, but tied into a bun in which three eagle feathers were attached. He wore moccasins, black cloth pants, a vest and jacket of a brighter material, and had a double-barreled rifle lying next to him. Peering from his belt was an old pistol. He held a piece of meat and a knife in his hands, but seeing us, put them aside. The scent of roasted horse meat suffused the air. Close to where he sat, a spring bubbled from the ground. We had not yet dismounted, when a wide circle of warriors, standing close together, formed around us, among which we spotted several white faces. Our horses were taken from us to be led away. Since Old Death let this happen without objecting to it, I did not consider it dangerous either. Now the chief rose, joined by the two others. He stepped towards Old Death, offered him his hand in the manner of Whites, and said in a friendly but serious voice:

"My brother, Old Death, surprises the warriors of the Comanche. How could they have expected him here. He is welcome and will fight with us against the Apache dogs."

He had spoken in the typical mishmash, likely wanting to make sure that we, too, would understand him. Old Death responded likewise:

"Wise Manitou leads his red and white children in wonderful ways. Happy is the man, who meets a friend in this way, and on whose words he can rely. Is White Beaver going to smoke the pipe of peace also with my companions?"

"Your enemies are my enemies, and whoever you love, I love. Your companions may sit by my side and drink from the calumet of the Chief of the Comanche."

Old Death sat down, with us following his example. Only Sam stepped aside, to find a place to sit. The Reds stood motionless and silently around us. I was unable to recognize the faces of the Whites, the light of the fires being insufficient. Oyo-Koltsa untied his calumet from his neck, stuffed it with tobacco from a bag hanging from his belt, and lit it. What followed now was almost the same ceremony as when we had met his son. Only now were we safe from any hostility by the Comanche.

While we had to wait before entering the camp, the leader of our group of fifty had reported to the chief, as we now learned. He asked Old Death to tell him himself how the events had taken place. The oldster did it in such a way that distrust would fall neither on us nor on *Señor* Atanasio.

White Beaver gazed ahead for some time, then said:

"I must believe my brother. Even were I to doubt, I don't see anything in his story from which I could conclude that he would want to deceive me. But I must also trust the other paleface, for he had no reason to lie to the warriors of the Comanche, for a lie would cost him his life. He is staying with us and would long since have left, had he told us an untruth. I can therefore only think that one of you was mistaken."

This was incisive thinking. Old Death had to be careful. The chief could easily think of dispatching another group to surprise the *hacendado*[7] at night! It would be best to admit to a believable explanation of the assumed error. This was also the scout's idea, which is why he said:

"Yes, a delusion happened, but it was not I, but rather the paleface who was mistaken. Where is the man who could mislead Old Death? My red brother knows that."

"Then my brother may tell me how the affair happened!"

"Let me say first that the Chief of the Comanche himself was misled."

"By whom?" White Beaver asked, becoming serious.

"I suppose by the palefaces staying with you."

"I must not listen to an assumption. Give me proof! If they, with whom we smoked the pipe of peace, have deceived me, they must die!"

"So, you not only offered them the hand of peace, but even smoked the calumet with them? Had I been with you at the time, I would have prevented you from doing so. I shall give you the proof you asked for. Tell me whose friend you are, by chance that of President Juarez?"

The chief gestured disparagingly, and answered:

"Juarez fell from being a redskin. He, like others, lives in houses and lives the lives of palefaces. I despise him. The warriors of the Comanche lent their courage to the great Napoleon, who presents them with weapons, horses and blankets, and will deliver the Apache to them. The palefaces are also friends of Napoleon's."

---

[7] Rancher

"But this, precisely, is the lie with which they deceived you. They came to Mexico to serve Juarez. My companions sit here as witnesses to what I am telling. You are aware whom the Great White Father in Washington has taken into his protection?"

"Juarez."

"And that on the U.S. border adjoining Mexico soldiers are hired to be sent on secret routes to Juarez. Well, in La Grange lives a Mexican by the name of *Señor* Cortesio. We visited him ourselves. These two men here were his neighbors and friends. He told us himself that he hires many men for Juarez, and the day before we came to him, he made some of the Whites here soldiers for Juarez. Some others are troops to accompany the hirelings. You are an enemy of Juarez, yet have smoked the pipe of peace with them, although they lied to you."

The chief's eyes flared angrily. He was going to speak, but Old Death prevented him from doing so, saying:

"Let me speak before you do! So, these palefaces are soldiers of Juarez. They came to the *hacienda* of *Señor* Atanasio, a friend of Napoleon's. He was hosting an old, highly esteemed leader of the French, whom the palefaces would have killed had they recognized him. This is why he faked being sick and lay in bed. His face was painted with a dark color to give him the appearance of an Indian. When the palefaces saw him and asked who he was, they were told that he was Good Man, a chief of the Apache."

The chief raised his eyebrows. He believed the scout, but was cautious enough to ask:

"Why was this name given?"

"Because the Apache hold to Juarez. For this reason, the palefaces thought this man to be a friend. He was also old and had gray hair, which could not be hidden. The palefaces knew that Good Man had also gray hair. This is why he was given the name of this Apache."

"Uff! Now I understand. This *señor* must be a very astute man, that he came up with such an explanation. But where was this leader of Napoleon's when my warriors arrived? They did not see him any more."

"He had left already. You can see that it had only been an excuse claiming that Winnetou had brought Good Man. The palefaces believed this. Afterwards, they met you and your warriors, and knowing the Comanche to be friends with the French they passed themselves off as Napoleon's men."

"I believe you, but I need proof that they are truly followers of Juarez, or I cannot punish them, since they smoked the calumet with us."

"I repeat that I will provide this proof. But I must tell you that there are two men among them, whom I want to take prisoner."

"Why?"

"They are enemies of ours. For many days, we have kept our horses on their tracks."

This was the best explanation. Had Old Death made a long speech about Gibson and Ohlert, he would not have accomplished any more than with the brief explanation: "They are our enemies." This became apparent when the chief said:

"If they are your enemies, they are also ours, as soon as we have again taken away the smoke of peace from them. I will make the two a gift to you."

"Fine! Then have the leader of the palefaces come here! Once I speak with him, you will soon realize how right I am when I claim them to be followers of Juarez."

The chief gave a signal. One of his warriors stepped up and received the respective order. He walked to one of the Whites, said a few words to him, after which the man, a tall, strong and bearded figure with a military appearance came to us.

"What do you want?" he asked, taking our measure with a grim, hostile look. Gibson must have recognized me and told the man not to expect anything good from us. I was curious to hear how Old Death was going to wriggle out of it. The old, crafty scout faced the man with a kindly look and replied most courteously:

"I have a greeting to you from *Señor* Cortesio in La Grange, *Señor*."

"Do you know him?" the man asked too quickly, not figuring that he had taken a most dangerous bait.

"Of course, I know him," the oldster continued. "We are friends from way back. Unfortunately, I came too late to meet you at his place, but he gave me directions to follow and meet you."

"Really? Then you must be a good friend of his. What direction did he give you?"

"The ford between Las Moras and Río Moral, then via Baya and Tabal to Chihuahua. You actually diverged a bit from this route."

"Because we met our friends, the Comanche."

"Your friends? I thought the warriors of the Comanche are your enemies!"

The man became visibly embarrassed. He coughed, trying to give Old Death a signal, which the scout did not seem to notice and continued:

"You are holding with Juarez, while the Comanche fight on the side of the French."

Now, the man tried to recover, and explained:

"*Señor*, there you are quite mistaken. We, too, are on the side of the French."

"And take hirelings from the United States to Mexico?"

"Yes, but for Napoleon."

"Oh! Then *Señor* Cortesio recruits for Napoleon?"

"Of course! Who else?"

"I thought for Juarez."

"He wouldn't think of it!"

"All right! Thank you for your clarification, *Señor*! You can return to your place now."

The man's face contorted angrily. Was he to have himself sent away like a subordinate by this nondescript man?

"*Señor*," he said, "who gives you the right to send me off like this?"

"Only chiefs and outstanding men sit by this fire."

"I am an officer!"

"Of Juarez?" Old Death quickly asked, rising again.

"Yes – no, no, of Napoleon's, as I said already."

"Well, you just misspoke splendidly. An officer, especially in situations like this, ought to be better able to control his tongue. I'm finished with you; you can go."

The officer wanted to say some more, but the chief made a preemptory move with his arm to send him away, which he had to obey.

"Well, what does my brother say now?" Old Death asked.

"His face indicts him," White Beaver replied, "but this is still no proof."

"But you are convinced that he is an officer and has been with this *Señor* Cortesio?"

"Yes."

"Which means that he belongs to the party Cortesio is recruiting for?"

"So it is. But prove to me that this man recruits for Juarez, then I will be satisfied!"

"Well, here's proof."

He reached into his pocket and pulled out the passport signed by Juarez. He opened it and continued:

"To convince ourselves that Cortesio works for Juarez, and that all palefaces coming to him are friends of Juarez, we acted as if we, too, wanted to be recruited. He accepted us and issued a passport to each of us, signed by Juarez. My companion can show you also his."

The chief took the passport and examined it closely. A grim smile crossed his face.

"White Beaver did not learn the palefaces' art to speak on paper," he said, "but he knows the symbol he sees here – the totem of Juarez. And among my warriors is a young man, a half-blood, who, as a boy, spent much time with the palefaces and learned the art of having paper speak. I shall call him."

He shouted a name. A young, light-skinned man walked up and, following a few words of the chief, took the passport, knelt by the fire and translated its text. I did not understand him, but Old Death's face brightened ever more. When the semi-savage was finished, he returned the passport, visibly proud of his knowledge, and left. Old Death put the document away again and asked:

"Do you want my companion to show you also his?"

The chief shook his head.

"Is my red brother now convinced that these palefaces have lied to him and are his enemies?"

"He knows it very well now, and will immediately call his most prominent warriors together to discuss what must be done."

"Am I to participate in this council?"

"No. My brother is wise in council and courageous in action, but we do not need him, for he demonstrated what he intended to prove. What must be done now, is a matter for the Comanche, who have been lied to."

"One more thing. It's not part of what we just discussed, but is, nevertheless, of great importance to us. Why did my red brother move so far south? Why dares he enter the heights of this desert?"

"At first, the Comanche intended to keep farther north, but learned that Winnetou with many warriors was headed for the Río Conchos, following which the Apache's camps are not guarded around here. We, therefore, quickly turned south and will gain so much booty, as we have never before taken home."

"Winnetou went to the Río Conchos? Hmm! Is this information reliable? Who gave it to you? It likely came from the two Indians you met north from here?"

"Yes. You saw their tracks?"

"We noticed them. What tribe do they belong to?"

"They are father and son of the Topia tribe."

"Are they still here, and may I talk to them?"

"My brother may do anything he likes."

"May I also talk to the two palefaces you are going to hand over to me?"

"Who is to prevent you?"

"Then I have only one more request: Permit me to walk around this camp! We are in enemy country, and I wish to convince myself that everything necessary for our security has been taken care of."

"Do so, although it is not really necessary. White Beaver has arranged for the camp and its guards. We have also sent out scouts. Everything is in order."

His friendship for Old Death had to be so great that he did not feel insulted by the scout's request to convince himself of the safety measures taken. The two distinguished Comanche, who had been sitting silently with us, now rose and solemnly walked away to call together the participants for the council. The other Comanche resumed their seats by the fires. The two Langes and Sam were assigned seats at one of the fires, and were handed three hefty pieces of roasted horse meat. Old Death took me by the arm and pulled me over to the fire where the Whites were sitting. When they saw us coming, the officer got up, approached us two paces, and with a hostile voice asked us in English:

"Mister, what was the point of the examination you cared to engage me in?"

The oldster grinned at him amicably and answered:

"That you will later tell the Comanche, which is why I can spare myself the

145

answer. There are also horse thieves among you, by the way. Do not speak in such a highfalutin' tone to Old Death! Every single one of the Comanche is on my side and against you. It would take only a slight signal of mine, and you are done for."

He proudly turned away, but stopped to give me the opportunity to speak to Gibson and Ohlert, who also sat with this group. The latter looked exceptionally ill and run down. His outfit was torn and his hair looked unruly and neglected. His cheeks were sunken and his eyes lay deeply in their sockets. He held a pencil in his hand and a piece of paper on his knee at which he kept staring, neither seeing nor hearing what was going on around him. It seemed useless to address him, as he appeared to be without willpower. I therefore turned to his seducer:

"We finally meet, mister Gibson! I hope we will stay together from now on."

He laughed at me and replied:

"Who are you talking to, sir?"

"To you, obviously!"

"Well, that isn't so obvious. Only from your looking at me do I take it you meant me. You called me Gibson, I believe?"

"Indeed."

"Well, that isn't my name."

"Did you not run away from me in New Orleans, you fake psychiatrist?"

"Mister, there seems to be something off under your hat! I'm neither a psychiatrist, nor is my name Gibson."

"Yes, whoever carries so many names as you can easily deny one. Didn't you call yourself Clinton in New Orleans? Then in La Grange you went by the name Gavilano?"

"That is, indeed my correct name. What do you actually want from me? I've nothing to do with you. Leave me be! I do not know you!"

"Sure! At times, a policeman gets into the position that he's not recognized. You won't get away with a denial; your role-playing has ended. I did not follow you all the way from New York, only to be laughed at by you. From now on, you will follow me to where I'm going."

"Oh! And if I won't?"

"Then I'll tie you to a horse, and I think the animal will obey me."

He jumped up, pulled his revolver, and screamed:

"Man, another word like this and the devil will . . ."

He did not get any further. Old Death had stepped behind him and with the butt of his rifle hit his arm so hard that he dropped the revolver.

"Quit the big words, Gibson!" the oldster told him. "There are people here who are happy to shut your mouth!"

Holding his arm, Gibson turned, shouting:

"Mister, do you want to get my knife in your ribs? Do you think that just because your name is Old Death I will be afraid?"

"No, my boy, you needn't be afraid, but simply obey. Another word and I'll answer you with a nice rifle bullet. I hope the gentlemen here will be grateful to us for relieving them from a rogue like you."

The scout's voice and posture had an effect on Gibson, who now replied meekly:

"But I don't even know what you want from me. You are mistaking me for someone else.!"

"That is highly improbable. You've got a scoundrel's face that can't be mistaken for another, and the chief witness against you sits right next to you."

With these words, he pointed at William Ohlert.

"He? A witness against me?" Gibson asked. "This is more proof that you are mistaken. Go ahead, ask him!"

I put my hand on William's shoulder and said his name. He slowly raised his head, stared at me without comprehension and without saying anything.

"Mister Ohlert, William, don't you hear me?" I repeated. "Your father sent me for you."

His empty gaze kept hanging on my face, yet he spoke not a word. Gibson now bellowed at him threateningly:

"They want to hear your name. Tell it immediately."

The ill man turned his head towards the speaker and answered in a faint, fearful voice, like an intimidated child:

"My name is Guillermo."

"What are you?"

"A poet."

Now I asked: "Is your name Ohlert? Are you from New York? Do you have a father?"

But he replied to all these questions in the negative, without giving them any thought. One could hear that he had been trained to reply in this way. With Ohlert so long now in the hands of this crafty crook, it was certain that his mind had become more and more benighted.

"There, you've got your witness!" Gibson laughed. "He proved you wrong. So, have the decency to leave us alone!"

"I want to ask him something special yet," I said. "Maybe his memory is still stronger than the lies you instilled in him."

I had an idea and pulled out my wallet, which had been tight enough that no water had penetrated during my last night's bath. I had kept the newspaper clipping with Ohlert's poem. Removing it, I now slowly but loudly read the first verse, thinking that the sound of his poem would pull him from his spiritual insensitivity. However, he continued to look down to his knees. I read the second verse, which also produced no reaction. Then came the third:

147

"Know you the night, which on your spirit is descending,
That for redemption does it scream in vain,
Around your soul it twists in snakelike windings,
And spits a thousand devils in your brain?"

The final two lines I read even louder than before. He raised his head, stood up and reached out with his hands. I continued:

"Oh, keep from it awake and caring,
For this night only does not have a morn'!"

He screamed, jumped towards me and reached for the piece of paper. I gave it to him. He now bent down to the fire to read it himself, aloud, from the beginning to the end. Then he straightened up and shouted triumphantly, so that it reverberated widely through the silent valley:

"A poem by Ohlert, by William Ohlert, mine, written by me! I am this William Ohlert, it's me. You are not called Ohlert, not you, but me!"

The last words had been directed at Gibson. A terrible suspicion arose in me. Gibson was in possession of William's documents . . . might he, despite being older, try to pass himself off as him? Might he . . .? But I was given no time to pursue my thought, for the chief came leaping up, totally forgetting the council and his dignity, pushed William to the ground, and demanded:

"Be quiet, dog! Are the Apache to hear that we are here? You are calling for fight and death!"

William Ohlert let out an incomprehensible shout of dismay while he stared up at the Indian. The brief flicker of his sanity had died again. I took the newspaper clipping from him and put it away. It might help me at a later time to return him to an awareness of his true self.

"Do not be angry with him!" Old Death asked the chief. "He is mentally deranged and will be quiet now. But tell me whether these two men are the Topia you mentioned earlier." He said this while he pointed at two men in Indian garb, who sat at the fire with the Whites.

"Yes, they are the ones," the chief confirmed. "They do not understand the language of the Comanche very well. You must use the language of the border with them. But take care that this White, whose soul is lost, will remain quiet, or I will have him gagged!"

He returned to the fire and the interrupted council. Old Death did not leave, but rather examined the two Indians carefully, after which he asked the older one:

"My red brothers came down from the Topia plateau? Are the warriors living up there friends of the Comanche?"

"Yes," the man replied. "We lend our tomahawks to the Comanche."

"How come, though, your tracks came from the north, where not your brothers dwell, but the enemies of the Comanche, the Llanero and Tracon Apache?"

This question seemed to embarrass the Indian, something easily visible, since neither he nor his son wore face paint. A bit later he answered:

"My white brother asks a question, he can easily answer himself. We raised the war tomahawk against the Apache, and rode north to reconnoiter their whereabouts."

"And what did you find there?"

"We saw Winnetou, the greatest chief of the Mapimi Apache. He had left with his warriors to carry the war across the Río Conchos. We returned to report this to our people to hurry to attack the camps of the Apache. In so doing we met the warriors of the Comanche and led them here, so that they, too, can bring ruin to our enemies."

"The Comanche will be grateful. But since when did the warriors of the Topia forget to be honest men?"

It was obvious the oldster thought the two suspect. While he spoke kindly, his voice carried a peculiar tone I had noticed before when he intended to outwit someone. The alleged Topia were obviously discomforted by his questions, causing the younger one to look at him with angrily flashing eyes. The older one made an effort to respond in a friendly manner, but one could hear that his words came across with difficulty.

"Why does my white brother question our honesty?" he asked. "Why does he doubt us?"

"It isn't my intention to hurt your feelings. But, how come, you have not joined the warriors of the Comanche at their fires, but are sitting with the palefaces?"

"Old Death asks more than he should. We sit here because it pleases us."

"But you raise the impression that the Comanche disdain the Topia. It looks as if they want to gain advantage from you, but will not allow you to sit with them."

This was an insult, causing the Red to fly off his handle:

"Do not speak like this or you will have to fight us. We sat with the Comanche and now came to the palefaces to hear what they have to say. Or is it forbidden to learn about what is happening in the lands and cities of the Whites?"

"No, it is not. But I, in your place, would be more cautious. Your eyes have seen the snows of many winters; you should understand what I mean."

"If I do not know it, then tell me!" he replied with a sneer. That's when Old Death stepped close, and bending down to him, told him in a serious voice:

"Did the warriors of the Comanche smoke the peace pipe with you, so that you blew the calumet's smoke through your noses?"

"Yes."

"Then you are obligated to act only to their advantage."

"Are you implying that we are not doing this?"

Both now faced each other sternly, their looks clawing at each other, ready to fight. Old Death replied:

"I see that you understood me, that you guessed my thoughts. If I were to speak them, you would both be lost."

"Uff!" the Red exclaimed, while he jumped up and reached for his knife. His son, too, stood up pulling his tomahawk from his belt. Old Death responded to their hostile moves only with a stern nod of his head and said:

"I am convinced that you will not be with the Comanche for long. Once you have returned to those who sent you, tell them that we are their friends. Old Death loves all red men, and does not ask to which tribe they belong."

That's when the older one hissed at him:

"Are you implying that we are not members of the Topia tribe?"

"My red brother may consider how incautious he is to voice this question. I kept my thoughts to myself, because I do not want to become your enemy. Why are you trying to give yourself away? Do you not stand amidst a five-hundred-fold death?"

The Red raised his knife as if he wanted to stab him. "Tell me then who you think we are!" he challenged the scout.

Old Death grabbed the Indian's knife arm and pulled him to where I stood and softly, but still loud enough for me to hear, said a few words in an Indian language to him. Of course, I did not understand their meaning. Later, Old Death explained to me that they had been: "You are Apache." The scout's words had their effect. The Indian stepped back apace, tore his arm from the oldster's grip, raised his knife ready to stab, and said:

"Dog, you lie!"

Old Death made no move to parry the stab. He, softly, whispered to the excited man:

"Do you want to kill Winnetou's friend?"

Whether it was the words or the stern, proud look of the oldster that brought about the intended effect, the Indian dropped his arm. He brought his mouth close to Old Death's ear, and said threateningly:

"Be quiet!"

Then he turned away and sat down again. His face was quiet and had assumed an impenetrable expression as if nothing had happened. He knew he was caught, yet he did not display the least trace of fear. Did he know Old Death so well that he did not expect him to betray him? Or did he know himself safe, for whatever reason? His son, too, sat quietly down next to him and stuck his tomahawk back into his belt. The two Apache had dared to engage themselves with their mortal enemies, an admirable audacity. If they succeeded in their intent, the Comanche were doomed. We were just ready to leave the Whites' groups, when a movement among the Comanche caused us to halt. We noticed that the council had come to an end. Its participants had risen, and the chief had obviously issued a command to everyone to leave their fires to form a tight circle around the Whites' fires, enclosing also us. In a dignified walk, White Beaver entered the circle and raised his arm as a signal that he was going to speak. Deep silence ensued. The Whites were not aware yet of what was to come. They stood up. Only the two supposed Topia remained sitting and looked quietly down as if the event did not concern them. William Ohlert, too, had remained seated and stared at the pencil he still held in his fingers.

Then the chief began speaking slowly and emphatically:

"The palefaces came to the warriors of the Comanche and told them that they were their friends. This is why they were accepted and we smoked the pipe of peace with them. But the Comanche have learned that they were lied to by the palefaces. White Beaver weighed everything speaking for and against them and consulted with his most experienced men as to what is to be done. He, together with them, agreed that the palefaces lied and no longer deserve our protection. This is why, from this moment on, our alliance with them is dissolved and enmity replaces friendship."

He halted for a moment. Quickly, the officer used the opportunity to ask:

"Who has slandered us? It must have been the four men with their Black who provoked this situation we do not deserve. We proved, and I repeat it once more, that we are friends of the Comanche. But it is the strangers who ought to prove that they are honest with our red brothers! Who are they? Who knows them? If they spoke evil of us, we demand to be heard so that we are able to defend ourselves. We will not permit ourselves to be judged without being heard! I am an officer, a chief of my people. I can and must demand to participate in every council discussing our fate!"

"Who gave you permission to speak?" the chief asked sternly. "When White Beaver speaks, everyone must wait when he is spoken to! You demand to be heard. You were heard when Old Death earlier talked to you. It was proven that you are Juarez's warriors. But we are friends of Napoleon, which makes you our enemies. You ask who these four palefaces are, and I tell you that they are brave and honest warriors. We knew Old Death many winters before we got to know you. You demand to participate in our council, but I tell you that even Old Death was not invited to it. The warriors of the Comanche are men who have no need for the wisdom of palefaces to know what is wise and unwise, what is right and what wrong. I have come here to tell you what we have decided. You must listen quietly and not say a word, for . . ."

"We smoked the calumet with you," the officer interrupted. "If you treat us with hostility, then we . . ."

"Silence, dog!" the chief thundered. "You were going to speak an insult. Consider that you are surrounded by five hundred warriors who are ready to avenge it instantaneously! You were handed the calumet only following deceit, a lie. However, the warriors of the Comanche are familiar with the will of the Great Spirit. They obey his laws and know that you are still under the protection of the calumet and that they must treat you as friends until such time as you have stepped beyond. Red is the sacred clay from which the calumet has been fashioned. Red is the color of the light and the flame with which the calumet is lit. Once it has died down, peace rules, until light reappears. When the light of day begins, our peace will be finished, and our union will have come to an end. Until then you are our guests, but thereafter, there will be enmity between us. You may sit here and sleep and no one will touch you. But as soon as the day will gray, you shall ride away in the direction you came. You will be allowed a lead of what you call five minutes; then we shall pursue you. You will be allowed to keep everything of yours to take along, but then we will kill you and take everything. The two among you, whom Old Death wants for himself, shall also remain our guests, since they, too, smoked the calumet with us, but they will not be allowed to ride with you, but stay here as prisoners of Old Death. He can do with them as he pleases. This is our decision. White Beaver, the Chief of the Comanche, has spoken!"

He turned away.

"What?" Gibson shouted. "I shall be the prisoner of this man? I shall . . ."

"Be quiet!" the officer interrupted him. "The chief's decision cannot be changed. I know these Reds. But I am convinced that the blow against us will fall back upon the slanderers. It isn't morning yet. Much can happen until then. Maybe revenge is closer than one thinks."

The Whites returned to where they had been sitting. However, the Comanche did not resume their original positions, but extinguished their fires and lay down to surround the Whites fourfold. Old Death led me from the circle. He wanted to reconnoiter.

"Do you think we finally got Gibson, sir?" I asked him.

"If nothing unexpected happens, he can't get away," was his reply.

"Wouldn't it be best, if we seized the two right away?"

"That's impossible. The devilish peace pipe prevents it. Prior to dawn the Comanche will not tolerate us laying hands on Gibson. Afterwards, we can cook or fry him, then eat him with or without forks, just as we like."

"You spoke of something unexpected. Are you concerned something might happen?"

"Unfortunately! I figure the Comanche let themselves be lured into a dangerous trap by the two Apache."

"Then you think them indeed to be Apache?"

"You can hang me if they aren't. I became suspicious when I heard that two Topia had come from the direction of the Río Conchos. They can fool a red Comanche, but not an old scout like me. When I then saw them, I right away knew that my suspicion was correct. The Topia are members of the semi-civilized Indians. They have a soft, somewhat indistinct facial expression. But look at the distinct and boldly-cut features of these two Reds! Once I heard them speak, they immediately gave themselves away by their pronunciation. And when I told the one to his face that he was an Apache, didn't his behavior tell me that I was right."

"Could you not be mistaken?"

"No. He called Winnetou the greatest chief of the Apache. Would an enemy of the Apache use such an honorable and distinctive expression? I bet my life that I'm not mistaken."

"Indeed, you have good reasons. But should you be correct, then these two men must be admired. Two Apache, daring to enter an army of more than five hundred Comanche. This is more than heroic!"

"Oh, Winnetou knows his people!"

"You think that he sent them?"

"In any case. We know from *Señor* Atanasio when and where Winnetou swam the Río Grande. It's impossible for him to be already at the Río Conchos, especially with all his warriors. No, the way I know him he rode straight for the Bolson de Mapimi to gather his Apache. He right away dispatched scouts to find the Comanche and to lure them into the Mapimi. While they think him to be at the Río Conchos and believe the Apache's camps to be undefended, he is waiting here to attack them and destroy them with one stroke."

"By the devil! Then we sit right in the middle with the two Apache considering us their enemies!"

"No. They know that I saw through them. I only need to tell White Beaver a single word after which they would die a gruesome death. That I am not doing it, is to them the surest proof that I carry no hostility towards them, but rather friendship."

"I still do not comprehend one thing, sir. Isn't it your duty to warn the Comanche?"

"Hmm! You are touching there on a devilishly sore point. The Comanche are traitors and are allied with Napoleon. They attacked innocent Apache in the midst of peace and murdered them miserably. This must be punished by the law of God and men. But we smoked the peace pipe with them and may not become traitors to them."

"You are, of course, correct. But my sympathy is for Winnetou."

"Mine, too. I wish him and his Apache the best. We may not betray his two men, yet this means that the Comanche will be lost, on whose side we must stand. What's to be done? This is a bad situation," Old Death said.

"Can we not prevent Winnetou's attack without sacrificing his two men?"

"I wouldn't know how to do it. Yes, had we Gibson and Ohlert, we could simply depart and leave the two enemy groups to their own."

"Well, that will be the case tomorrow morning."

"Or, maybe not. It is very well possible that about this time tomorrow evening we, together with a bunch of Apache and Comanche, will catch a few dozen beavers or even eat an old buffalo steer in the Eternal Hunting Grounds."

"Do you think danger to be that close?" I asked him.

"I do think so, for which I have two reasons. First, the closest settlements of the Apache aren't located too far from here, and Winnetou cannot allow the Comanche to approach them too closely. Then, this Mexican officer talks in a way that lets me guess at some kind of blow coming still tonight."

"Quite possible, you say. But we can rely on having smoked the calumet with the Comanche and my totem being good with the Apache; also that Winnetou knows you and has seen me already. But whoever gets between two mill stones will be ground to dust, even if he has nothing to fear from a single stone."

Old Death's comment now was:

"Then we must stay away from getting in between or try to prevent them from grinding. Let me do a bit of reconnoitering now. Maybe, despite the darkness, it is possible to see something to illuminate my mind a bit. Follow me slowly and quietly! If I'm not mistaken, I've been in this valley once before, which is why I figure to find my way easily."

It turned out as I had guessed. We were in a small, almost circular, steep-sided valley one could easily cross in about five minutes. Its entrance was just as narrow as its exit. Outside, scouts had been dispatched. The Comanche were camped in its middle. The valley's walls were pure rock, rising steeply, making it certain that no one could ascend nor descend them. Completing our round, we passed by the guards that had been posted at both entrances. Then we returned to the camp.

"Disastrous!" the oldster mumbled. "We are truly in a trap, and I don't have any idea how to get out of it. We'd have to act like the fox, who chewed off his leg after been caught in a snare."

"Could we not convince White Beaver to abandon this camp for another one?"

"That's the only thing we can try. But I don't think he will agree without us telling him that two Apache spies are in his camp. That we want to avoid."

"Maybe you view things too gloomily, sir. Maybe we are perfectly safe here. The two entrances are very well guarded."

"Yes, ten men on each side; that looks good. But let's not forget that we are dealing with Winnetou. It's a riddle to me how and why the otherwise so smart and cautious White Beaver arrived at the foolish idea to camp in this enclosed valley. The two Apache scouts must have painted an X for a U. I shall have a talk with him. Should he maintain his opinion and something happens, we shall remain neutral as far as that will be possible. We are friends with the Comanche, but must also beware of killing Apache. Well, we are back in camp, and over there stands the chief. Let's go over to him."

Against the light from the fire, one could recognize White Beaver by his eagle feathers. When we had walked up to him, he asked:

"Did my white brother convince himself that we are safe here?"

"No," the oldster replied.

"What does he find wrong with this place?"

"It looks to me like a trap in which we are caught."

"My brother is very much mistaken. This valley is no trap, but resembles a place the palefaces call a fort. No enemy can enter it."

"Yes, not by the entrances which are so narrow that they are easily defended by ten Comanche warriors. But can the enemy not also come down from the heights?"

"No. They are too steep."

"Did my red brother assure himself of this?"

"Very much so. The sons of the Comanche arrived here in broad daylight and checked everything. They tried to climb the rock walls, but were unsuccessful."

"Maybe it is easier to climb down then to get up. I know Winnetou can climb like a wild mountain sheep."

"Winnetou is not here; the two Topia told me so."

"Maybe they are mistaken; maybe they heard it from someone who wasn't sure himself."

"They said so, and, being enemies of Winnetou, I believe them."

"But if it is true that Winnetou was at Fort Inge, then he cannot already have been here to gather his warriors and be beyond the Río Conchos. My brother may compare the short time with the long distance."

The chief lowered his head in thought. His conclusion seemed to agree with the scout's opinion, for he said:

"Yes, the time was short and the distance far. Let's ask the Topia once more."

He walked to the campfire where the two were sitting, with us following. The Whites looked at us grimly. Aside from them sat Lange with his son and the Negro, Sam. William Ohlert was scribbling on his piece of paper, oblivious to everything. The supposed Topia looked up only after the chief addressed them:

"Are my brothers quite certain that . . ."

He stopped in mid sentence. From the ridge above sounded the fearful cry of a small bird, followed by the greedy scream of an owl. The chief listened, Old Death did, too. As if he wanted to play with it, Gibson picked up a branch lying next to him, pushing it into the fire so that it briefly flared. Almost every single White observed this with satisfaction. Gibson was going to do it for a second time, but Old Death leaped towards him, tore the branch from his hand, and told him threateningly:

"Leave that be! No more!"

"Why not?" Gibson asked angrily. "Isn't one permitted to stoke the fire?"

"No. When an owl screams up there, one does not reply down here with a previously agreed upon signal."

"A signal? Are you crazy?"

"Yes, I'm crazy enough to put a bullet into anyone's head, who dares to stoke the fire again!"

"Damn! You act as if you are master here!"

"That I am, and you are my prisoner, of whom I will make short process, should I not like your physiognomy any more. Don't imagine that Old Death can be deceived by you!"

"Something like this is one to stand for? Do we really, *Señores*?"

He had asked his companions. In a second, Old Death and I had our revolvers in hand, quickly joined by the two Langes and Sam armed the same way. We would have shot anyone incautious enough to reach for his weapon. And if that wasn't enough, the chief called on his men to put arrows to their bows.

Instantly, the Comanche were on their legs, and dozens of arrows pointed at the Whites, now sitting amidst a forest of arrows.

"There you see!" Old Death laughed. "You are still protected by the calumet, even your weapons were left you. But should one hand reach for a knife, your protection is void."

Once more, the bird's cry, followed by the owl's scream, sounded, as if coming from the sky. Gibson's hand jerked, as if he wanted to push the branch into the fire again, but he did not dare to follow through. The chief now repeated his earlier interrupted question to the Topia:

"Are my brothers truly certain that Winnetou is beyond the Río Conchos?"

"Yes, we are certain," the older man replied.

"They may think about it once more!"

"We are not mistaken. We were hiding in some bushes when he passed by."

The chief asked another question to which the Topia answered promptly. At last, White Beaver said:

"Your explanation has satisfied the Chief of the Comanche. My white brothers may come back with me!"

With that, he asked Old Death and me, but the scout waved to the Langes and Sam to come along.

"Why does my brother also call on his companions?" the chief asked.

"Because I think that I will soon have need for them. When danger threatens, we want to stand by each other."

"There is no danger."

"You err. Didn't the owl's scream catch your attention? It was made by a man."

"White Beaver knows the voices of all birds and animals. He knows how to distinguish them from the sounds made by the mouths of men. This was a real owl."

"And Old Death knows that Winnetou can perfectly imitate the voices of many animals, so that one cannot distinguish them from the real ones. I ask you to be cautious! Why did this paleface poke into the fire? It was an agreed-upon signal he had been asked to give."

"Then it would have had to be arranged with the Apache, who he cannot have met!"

"Then someone else arranged it with them, and this paleface received the order to give the signal, so that the actual traitor would not be given away by it."

"Do you think there are traitors among us? I do not think so. Even were this the case, we need not fear the Apache. They are unable to get past our guards and cannot come down the rocks."

"That may be possible, after all. They could use lassos to lower themselves point to point. It is . . . listen!"

The owl's screech sounded again, this time not from high above, but lower down.

"There is that bird again," the Comanche remarked without being alarmed. "Your concern is unwarranted."

"No. By the devil! The Apache are here, right in the valley. Do you hear?"

A loud, shrill, shocking scream, a death scream, sounded from the valley's exit. Then the quiet air of the valley trembled from the many-voiced war whoops of the Apache. Whoever has heard this for the first time will never forget it. Barely had these screams arisen, when the Whites jumped up from the fires.

"There the dogs stand," the officer shouted, pointing at us. "Onto them!"

"Yes, let's hit them!" screeched Gibson. "Beat them dead!"

We stood in darkness, making poor targets. This is why they preferred not to shoot, but to throw themselves onto us with their rifles raised high. This must have been previously agreed upon, for their movements were so fast and assured that they could not be the result of a momentary decision. We stood at most thirty paces away from them. However, this space gave Old Death time to say:

"Well, wasn't I right? Get your rifles ready! We'll receive them properly."

Six rifles were aimed at the rapidly approaching men, with the chief having joined us with his gun. Our shots cracked, twice from our double-barreled rifles. I had no time to count how many we dropped. The Comanche, too, had leaped up and sent their arrows at the Whites. I saw that Gibson, although he had been the one to call for the attack, had not been among the men approaching us. He still stood by the fire, trying to pull Ohlert up. I was able to observe the two for only a moment. Further observations became impossible, for the howls had quickly come closer, with the Apache now pressing onto the Comanche.

Since the firelight did not reach far, the Apache were unable to make out how many enemies they were facing. The Comanche still stood in a circle, which was however instantly ruptured by the attack and rolled up from a side. Shots cracked, spears and arrows whistled past, and knives flashed. Added to this were the howls of the hostile groups and the chaotic view of shadowy wrestling figures looking like angry devils. Ahead of the Apache, one man had penetrated the lines of the Comanche in mighty leaps, in his left hand a revolver, in his right the raised tomahawk. Every bullet from his revolver downed a Comanche, and his battle ax whipped like lightning from head to head. He wore no distinguishing mark on his head and his face was not painted, which is why we could clearly see it. Even had this not been the case, then the way he fought, and that he used a revolver, would have told us who he was. White Beaver recognized him as quickly as we did.

"Winnetou!" he shouted. "Finally, I have him. I will take him on."

He leaped away from us into the thick of the fight. Men closed behind him, so that we were no longer able to see him.

"What shall we do?" I asked Old Death. "The Comanche will expect us to participate in their battle against the enemy."

The scout did not reply right away. He first surveyed the ongoing battle, then answered:

"They don't need us. The Apache are in the minority; they will be annihilated if they do not quickly retreat. Let's hurry to the horses to prevent a stampede."

A stampede is when horses shy or are being purposely scared so that they take flight. We were forced to run in a wide arc, the others being faster than me, with me being unable to tear my looks away from the tumult of battle. Then I heard a shout. A number of Indians separated from the fighting crowd to flee. They were Apache. Not because of fear, but so as not to be in their way, I arced farther out, so that they would not see me or have to make a greater detour in their getaway. They were running for one of the valley's exits and escaped into the dark of night. Others followed. The Apache had realized that they could not cope with the Comanche's superior forces. I had reached the wall of the valley and walked along it, thinking that I could reach the horses that way. That's when a terrible din arose from the place of battle.

"After him, after him!" I heard White Beaver's voice. He must not get away!"

I stopped to look in that direction. The fire had been almost stomped out, but I was nevertheless able to see that the place had emptied, with everyone rushing for the valley's exit screaming at the top of their lungs to produce a truly hellish racket. Then I heard hurried steps. A shadowy figure surfaced before me, leaped, and threw me to the ground. The man knelt on me and put his hands around my neck so that I was unable to utter a sound. I noticed him to be an Indian, likely an Apache, who, in the process of fleeing had come across me. He was going to throttle me to prevent me from making a noise. He possessed enormous strength. His fingers lay like iron clamps around my throat. Only cunning could save me. I made some convulsive movements, stretched out and went limp, fooling him into believing that I had lost consciousness. Now his right hand let go of my throat, likely to reach for his knife to kill me, then to take my scalp. He still held on to me with his left hand, but I was able to take a breath. I had to use this very moment. I reared up and tossed him off. He fell aside, and I threw myself on him to take him now by his throat. That's when I received a stab against my jaw, so that my head was thrust backwards. I felt, what sounded like crunching and crackling in my left jaw, but I paid no attention to it. He had stabbed his knife into my jaw from below, as was clear later. The blade had penetrated into my mouth, fortunately without injuring my tongue. I had him by his throat, pressing so hard that he let go of his knife. It remained stuck in my wound. He grabbed for my hands to loosen them, tried to toss me off, but all in vain. I felt that I was fighting for my life and gathered all my strength to save myself.

Neither one of us had uttered a word or made a sound; each of us was only intent on not letting the enemy gain the upper hand. He made it terribly hard for me and displayed an agility that was probably even greater than his strength. With eel-like movements he tried to get away from me, but was unable to do so. Finally, his movements slowed and became weaker; then his hands fell away. He lay still.

This could be a ruse, like mine, earlier. I, therefore, removed my hands very cautiously from his throat, but it turned out that he was truly unconscious. I could now have killed him, or tied him up to drag him to the Comanche. But I wasn't willing to do either – he was to escape. First, I pulled the knife from my wound, which immediately began to bleed profusely. Then I patted him down, since it was too dark to really see him. And what a surprise – I had defeated Winnetou! To protect him from whatever action that would be to his disadvantage once he came to, I tied his hands and legs, pulled him to the next tree, righted him to a sitting position and tied him with my lasso to the trunk of the tree.

The battle was not finished. The Apache had noticed that Winnetou had not escaped yet. To allow him time, they had positioned themselves at the valley's narrow exit through which the Comanche could not readily follow. Although the Comanche sent their arrows into the darkness, it was without success, since the Apache were smart enough to have taken cover. I hurried to the horses where I found Old Death to tell him of my accomplishment.

"Winnetou!" escaped him in surprise. "You must be mistaken or you were unbelievably lucky. And you are injured. Come quickly to the fire!"

The abandoned fire was barely burning, but it was enough for the oldster to check my wound.

"A bit farther in, and he would have pierced your tongue," he determined.

"But as it is, the situation isn't that dangerous. The stab will prevent you from speaking and chewing for some time, but that will be all. Take me to the Apache now."

When we arrived there, he still sat by the tree the way I had left him, however, consciousness had returned, and he received us with the words:

"The white traitors may untie me. I shall not flee, and they can turn me over to the Comanche dogs, so that they can tear me apart. My death song will triumph over them."

"Yes, I shall untie Winnetou," I said.

I was going to add something, but he quickly fell in:

"The paleface recognized Winnetou despite the darkness? Why did he not kill me?"

"Why would I kill the famous Chief of the Apache, whose friend I am?"

"You claim to be my friend? Yet you or your white comrades gave us a wrong signal!"

"How do you mean?"

"You made the fire flare up only once, when I sounded the voice of the owl, yet you were to do it once for every one hundred of the Comanche. Our enemy was more than five hundred men, but I was made to believe that there were only one hundred."

"Ah, that's how it was! We did not know this."

"You did know!"

"No. You misjudge us," I responded and briefly explained how we had joined the Comanche, closing with the words: " Here's your knife. You are free."

While speaking, I had untied him, and now handed him his knife. He jumped up.

"Is it true?" he asked. "You are setting Winnetou free, although he stabbed you?"

"Yes. You can go wherever you wish. We shall lead you from the valley without the Comanche spotting you."

"Winnetou needs no guide; he knows this place very well. He hears his warriors' battle cry and must show himself to them. He will be grateful to the two palefaces for as long as he lives. They should part from the Comanche, for they are doomed. Howgh!"

Upon his last word he was no longer visible.

"Darn it! It wasn't to happen that quickly!" Old Death said. "I had a few things to talk to him. Who knows whether he'll succeed in getting away. You should not have untied him so quickly so that he would have been forced to answer some questions. Just think how much we would have learned! Come now! Let's get back to the horses. I have some dressing material in my saddle bag and want to try stuffing that hole in your chin."

When we got to the horses, the two Langes and Sam were no longer there.

They must have gone to the Comanche to learn of the outcome of the skirmish. It took a while in the darkness until the oldster had found his horse among the others. Then, because of the darkness, he was unable to properly dress my wound. We were therefore heading to the fire to stoke up its flames, so that the scout could see properly. We had not reached it yet when the Old Death held me back by an arm and pointed ahead where a burning branch still produced a small flame, and said:

"Do you see those busy figures there? By the devil! I think those are Apache!"

I forced my eyes and now noticed a number of shadowy figures moving busily about.

"Could those truly be Apache?" I asked. "This would really be daring."

"Trust them to do it, being under Winnetou's command. They want to carry their dead away so that they will not be scalped by the Comanche. A scalped man must serve his victor as a slave in the Eternal Hunting Grounds. This is the Indians' belief, which is why they dare everything to wrest their dead from the hands of their enemies. But how did these Apache get back into the valley they fled earlier? I'm becoming utterly afraid for the Comanche. They will pay dearly for their betrayal. We cannot go to the fire, but must turn back."

We retreated some distance and settled down in the grass. The scout assured me that with his trained eyesight, he was still able to make out the Apache from where we sat. I was unable to do so. At the exit, fighting still continued, as the screams of Indians following each arrow shot told us. We might have been sitting there for ten minutes when Old Death asked me to follow him to the fire. Stumbling over the many corpses lying about we reached the fire, where a branch was still flaming a bit. Old Death collected the wood remains lying about and blew the fire to life. We now saw that every one of the dead had been scalped, a terrible sight to me, seeing this for the first time. My wound was quickly dressed, after which we returned to the still fighting men. The Comanche had dispersed, so that they were not offering good targets to their enemies' arrows. We looked for the chief.

"Where were my white brothers?" he asked. "I did not see them fighting with us."

"The Chief of the Comanche had no time to look for us. We, too, fought bravely. My companion was even injured. I dressed him."

"Then my brother may forgive my words. The Apache escaped us, but early tomorrow morning we will pursue and destroy them."

"Do you really think you will succeed?"

"For sure! Does my brother think differently? Then he is mistaken."

"Did you not earlier say also, when I warned you, that I was mistaken? I called this valley a trap. You may be unable to leave this valley."

"Let only the day rise that we see the enemy, the few that are left, and we shall quickly exterminate them. Now, darkness protects them."

"Then it is not necessary to shoot at them! Once you have spent your arrows, there's enough wood in the valley, but what about iron points? Don't waste your means of defense! And how about the ten Comanche warriors, who guarded the entrance to the valley? Are they still there?"

"No, they are here. The fight drew them in."

"Send them right away back, so that you can at least retreat!"

"My brother's concern is totally unnecessary. The Apache fled; no one can get through."

"And yet I advise you to send them back. The ten men are of no use to you here; there they are needed more."

The chief followed this suggestion, although more from respect for Old Death than from conviction that this measure was truly called for. It soon turned out how right the oldster had been, for after the ten men had received their order and seemed to have arrived at the valley's entrance, two rifle shots cracked, followed by a wild howl. A few minutes later, two of the ten returned to report that they had been received with two bullets and a volley of arrows; the two were the only survivors.

"Was I mistaken again?" the scout asked. "The trap is now closed front and back, with us stuck in here."

White Beaver knew not how to respond. Stunned, he asked: "Uff! What shall I do?"

"Don't waste the strength and the arrows of your men! Post twenty to thirty each at each exit to guard these points and have the others retreat to rest, so that they gather strength for tomorrow morning. That's the only thing, and likely the best, I can suggest."

This time the chief followed the advice. Thirty warriors were kept at the exit here and thirty more were dispatched to the opposite one; the rest returned to the campsite. When they found many of their brothers scalped, they fell into terrible howls of rage. After we had walked back, we counted more than thirty Comanche corpses but not a single Apache. White Beaver found no explanation for this and thought it to be magic, while we knew. Now the chief walked away.

Old Death said to me: "Where might the palefaces have gone?"

Only now did I think of them. Only their dead lay about, the rest had disappeared. Also Gibson and William Ohlert were gone.

"That's bad!" I exclaimed. "These fellows found safety with the Apache."

"Yes, and they were, of course, happily accepted, since they kept it with the two Apache scouts, the supposed Topia."

"Then we've lost Gibson again!"

"No. We have Good Man's totem, and the Apache know me. Winnetou owes you his life and freedom. It's obvious that he will receive us as friends. Then I'll take care for Gibson and Ohlert to be handed over to us. We will lose a day, that's all."

"But what if the two leave?"

"I don't think they will. They would have to cross the Mapimi, which they can't dare on their own . . . But, what is that?"

There stood a group of Comanche. From their midst came a gut-wrenching groaning and whimpering. We walked there and found a White who was not dead and had now returned to consciousness. He had received a spear thrust from behind into his abdomen, which must have been from a Comanche, when the Whites attacked us earlier. The Apache had thought him dead and had scalped him.

Old Death knelt beside him to check his wound.

"Man," he said, "you may have perhaps another ten minutes to live. Ease your heart and do not enter eternity with a lie. You held it with the Apache, didn't you?"

"Yes," the man replied, whimpering.

"You knew that we were to be attacked this night?"

"Yes. This was the reason why the two Topia led the Comanche here."

"And Gibson was to signal with the fire?"

"Yes, sir. He was supposed to poke the fire once for each one hundred Comanche. Winnetou would then not have attacked tonight, but tomorrow at another place, because he had only a hundred warriors available. By tomorrow, though, many more will join him."

"I thought so. Preventing Gibson from poking the fire four more times caused the Apache to attack us tonight. But now they occupy the valley's exits. We cannot get out, and by tomorrow this valley will become an open grave wherein we will be slowly butchered."

"We shall defend ourselves!" the chief grated, who stood beside us. "But this traitor here shall enter the Eternal Hunting Grounds like a mangy dog, to be pursued there by wolves, so that he may drool for all eternity."

He pulled out his knife and stabbed it into the wounded man's heart.

"What folly!" Old Death exclaimed angrily. "There was no need for you to become his murderer. His punishment would have been worse, had he lived for a short while longer having been scalped."

"I killed him, so that his soul will be my slave. But let us gather for a war council. The warriors of the Comanche do not like to wait until the Apache dogs arrive here in large numbers. This night, we will still break through the exit."

Together with his other leaders he gathered by the fire. Old Death was also asked to participate. Together with the two Langes and Sam I sat so far from the fire that I was unable to understand anything of the subdued conversation; however, I recognized from the scout's expressions and his vivid hand movements that he did not agree with the Indians' opinion. He appeared to strongly defend his own, but in vain. At last, he angrily jumped up, and I heard him say:

"Well, then go run into ruin! I warned you repeatedly without you listening. My suggestions always turned out right and will be again this time. Do as you want. But I and my companions will remain here."

"Are you too cowardly to fight with us?" one of the sub-chiefs asked.

Old Death made ready for a stern response but reconsidered and said quietly:

"My brother must first demonstrate his own courage before he can ask about mine. My name is Old Death, which says enough."

He walked over to us and sat down while the Reds continued their discussion for a while. At last, they arrived at a decision and rose. Suddenly, from beyond where the Comanche were sitting around the campfire, a loud voice sounded:

"White Beaver may look over here. My rifle is hungry for him."

Everyone turned in this direction. There stood Winnetou, erect, his rifle aimed. Both barrels flashed simultaneously. White Beaver dropped together with one of his other leaders.

"This is how every single liar and traitor will die!" he called, then the Apache disappeared. It happened so quickly that the Comanche had not thought to react, had not even found the time to jump up. But now, everyone leaped up to dash for the spot where Winnetou had disappeared. Only the five of us stayed put. Old Death walked over to the two fallen men. They were dead.

"What risk he took!" Lange exclaimed. "This Winnetou is a real devil!"

"Bah!" Old Death laughed. "The worst is yet to come. Watch!"

He had barely spoken the words, when we heard a penetrating howl.

"There you go!" he commented. "Not only did he punish the two leaders for their betrayal, but lured the Comanche also into range of his warriors. The Apaches' arrows will find their victims. Listen!"

The sharp, thin crack of a revolver could be heard, sounding three, five, six times.

"That's Winnetou," Old Death said. "He uses his revolvers. I think the fellow stands amidst the Comanche, without them being able to do anything against him!"

Events like these were common to the old frontiersman. His face was calm, as if he were following a theater presentation whose sequence and ending he was familiar with. I, though, was shocked by the way human lives were being destroyed. Then the Comanche returned without having been able to shoot Winnetou. Instead they carried back several of their own, either dead or wounded. Civilized people would have kept quiet, if only from sympathy, but also from shrewdness. However, the Reds howled and screamed as if they were being impaled and danced around the bodies while they swung their tomahawks above their heads.

"In their place I would extinguish the fire and keep quiet," Old Death said. "They howl their own death song."

"What did the council actually decide?" Lange asked

"To break out towards the West, and that at once."

"What stupidity! They would head straight for the Apache coming here."

"Not quite, mister, for they won't be able to break out. However, even if they were to succeed, they would have Winnetou behind them, and the additional warriors he expects, in front of them. They would therefore find themselves in between and would be annihilated. But they believe the Apache to be in the minority and think they can destroy them. They are also aware that White Beaver's son with his warriors will come, which increases their confidence. This makes them burn twice as hot from the desire to avenge the death of their two leaders. I recommended to the Comanche to wait for daybreak, then try to break out at the opposite exit from where we came. In daylight one can see the enemy and the obstacles he has thrown up. But my viewpoint wasn't accepted. But to us it can all be the same. We will not participate."

"The Comanche will take offense of this."

"I don't mind. Old Death has no desire to futilely bash his head in. Listen! What was that?"

The Comanche were still howling, so that it was impossible to say from where the sound had come."

"These fools!" Old Death said angrily. "Winnetou is just the man to make use of this inopportune noise they produce. Maybe, he's dropping trees to close the exits. The crashing noise sounded quite like a tree was being dropped. I'd swear that none of the Comanche will escape. It will be a terrible but just punishment for their attack on the peaceful, unsuspecting Apache settlements and especially the murder of their delegates. If Winnetou succeeds in closing the exits, he can withdraw his men, then gather them in the valley and attack these incautious Comanche from behind. I trust him to do this."

Finally, the provisional death lament was finished. The Comanche fell quiet, gathered, and received instructions from a sub-chief, who had now assumed command. They picked up the dead, fallen in their pursuit of Winnetou, and carried them away. The scalped corpses were left lying, for their souls could no longer be saved for the Eternal Hunting Grounds.

"It looks like they want to try their breakout," Old Death said. "We must get to our horses so that they do not take them. Mister Lange, go there with your son and Sam to get them. The two of us will stay here, since I think their new chief will yet have a talk with us."

He was correct. When the three had left, the new leader slowly walked towards us and said:

"The palefaces sit quietly here, while the Comanche are going for their horses. Why do they not rise, too?"

"Because we were not told what the Comanche decided."

"We will leave the valley."

"You will not succeed in getting out."

"Old Death is like a crow whose voice sounds ugly. The Comanche will ride down whatever they find in their way."

"They will ride no one and nothing down, but only themselves. We shall stay here."

"Is Old Death not our friend? Did he not smoke the pipe of peace with us? Is he not obligated to fight with us? The palefaces are courageous and daring warriors. They shall accompany us and put themselves in the lead."

Now Old Death rose, stepped very close to the Comanche, laughed into his face, and said:

"My brother has a smart idea. The palefaces are to ride in front to open a way for you Reds, dying in the process. We are friends of the Comanche, but we need not obey their chiefs. We happened to meet them, but we did not commit ourselves to participate in their campaign. We are courageous and brave; my brother spoke truth with these words. We help our friends in every fight, which is conducted with sense and consideration, but we will not take part in plans of which we know in advance that they will fail."

"Then the Whites will not ride with us? I thought them to be courageous men!"

"We are. But we are also cautious. We are guests of the Comanche. When did they acquire the custom to place their guests, whom they are obligated to protect, in the lead of an attack, where death will be unavoidable? My brother is clever, but we are not stupid. My brother, too, is a very courageous warrior, which is why I am convinced that he will ride in the lead of his men, for this is the place where he belongs."

The Red became embarrassed. His intention to sacrifice us in order to save himself, was brazen. When he saw that he did not get anywhere, and recovered from his embarrassment, he became angry. His until then quiet voice became more stern, when he inquired:

"What will the palefaces do when the Comanche have left? Will they join the Apache?"

"How would that be possible when my brother intends to destroy them? There would be no Apache left for us to join."

"But some will follow. We cannot permit the palefaces to remain here. They must come with us."

"I told you already that we will stay."

"If the Whites will not come with us, we must consider them our enemies."

"And should the Reds see us as such, we must see them as our enemies."

"We will not let them have their horses," the Red retorted.

"We have taken them already. They are just being brought."

Indeed, our friends were just arriving with our horses. The chief grimly pinched his eyebrows and said:

"Then the Whites have made their preparations. I see that they are hostile towards us and I shall have them taken prisoner by my warriors."

The scout produced a brief, weird-sounding laugh and replied:

"The chief of the Comanche is very much mistaken. I had told White Beaver already that we would stay here. If we do this now, then it is only what I said previously, but it does not contain the least enmity towards the Comanche. You have therefore no reason to take us prisoner."

"We will do it nevertheless; if the Whites don't agree right away that they will ride with us and put themselves in the lead."

Old Death looked around. He grinned as usual when he got ready to deal someone a drubbing. The three of us were standing by the fire. Not a single Comanche had stayed around, all had gone for their horses. Old Death said in German, so that the Comanche was unable to understand what he was saying:

"When I knock him down, run quickly for your horses and follow me to the entrance of the valley. The Comanche have all gathered at the opposite end."

"My brother must not speak in this language. I want to know what he is saying to his companions."

"The chief will learn it right away. You disregarded my advice repeatedly today and did not learn anything from the resulting harm that befell you. You are facing certain death and want to force us to lead you and ourselves into it. It seems you still do not know Old Death. Do you think you can force me to do something I've decided not to do? Let me tell you that I neither fear you nor your Comanche. You want to take us prisoners? Aren't you aware that I have you in my hands? Look at this weapon! The least move from you and I'll shoot you down!"

He pointed the revolver at him. The Indian was going to reach for his knife, but instantly felt Old Death's weapon on his chest.

"Keep your hand off!" the oldster thundered at him, and the chief dropped it.

"So! As you can see, I'm not joking. You made yourself our enemy, and should you not instantly obey me, I'll give you a bullet!"

The painted features of the Red contorted. He looked around searchingly, but Old Death cautioned him:

"Don't look for help from your men. Even were they here, I would shoot you. Your mind is weak like that of an old woman whose brain has dried up. You are surrounded by enemies to whom you must succumb, yet you make yourself even more enemies in us, whom you must fear even more than the Apache. The way we are armed we would shoot down a hundred of you before a single arrow would reach us. If you want to drive your people to death, go ahead, but your orders do not apply to us."

167

The Indian stood silent for awhile. Then he said: "My brother should think that my words were not meant as such!"

"I took your words the way they sounded. What you really meant by them is of no concern to me."

"Take your weapon away, and we shall remain friends!"

"That we can. But before I remove the weapon from your chest, I must be sure that your friendship is serious."

"I said so, and my word is true."

"Yet, you just said that your words were meant differently from the way they sounded. One can therefore not rely on your words and promises."

"If you do not believe me, I cannot give you more assurance."

"Oh, yes. I demand that you give me your peace pipe and . . ."

"Uff!" the Indian broke in, startled. "One does not give the calumet away."

"That isn't all. I not only ask for your calumet, but also for your medicine."

"Uff, uff, uff! That is impossible!"

"You need not give both to me forever, not as a gift. The moment we part peacefully, you will get them back."

"No warrior will give away his medicine!"

"Yet I demand it. I know your customs. Once I have your calumet and your medicine, I am you, and any hostility towards us would cause you to lose the joys of the Eternal Hunting Grounds."

"But I will not hand them over!"

"Well, then we are done. I will shoot you now, then take your scalp, so that you will be my dog and slave once you are dead. I shall raise my left hand three times. On the third time, I will shoot, should you not obey."

He raised his hand once and a second time, while he kept his revolver pointed at the Red's heart with his right hand. The third movement of his hand was already halfway done, when the Indian said:

"Wait! Will you return both items to me?"

"Yes."

"Then you shall have them. I shall . . ."

He lifted both hands, as if he were going to reach for his medicine bag and the pipe, both suspended from his neck.

"Stop!" Old Death commanded, interrupting him. "Down with your hands, or I'll shoot! I trust you only once I have both items. My companion may take them from your neck and hang them on mine."

The Comanche dropped his arms again. I took the two objects from him and hung them on Old Death who now withdrew his revolver.

 "So, he said. "Now we are friends and my brother may do as he pleases. We shall stay here to wait and see how the battle will end!"

The chief must never have felt as angry as now. His hand went for his knife, but dared not draw it. But he went as far as hissing:

"The palefaces are certain now that nothing will happen to them, but as soon as they have returned the calumet and my medicine, there will be enmity between us until they have died at the stake."

He turned and ran off.

"We are now as safe as if we were in Abraham's lap," the scout said, "but let's not forget to take whatever precaution we can think of. We will not stay here by the fire, but withdraw to the back of the valley, where we'll wait for what's going to happen. Let's go, gents; take the horses!"

We took our horses by their reins, and walked to the spot the scout had indicated. There, we staked down the animals, then sat under the trees by the valley's wall. The fire still glowed at the abandoned camp site and deep silence ruled around us.

"Let's wait now," the scout said. "I figure the dance is going to start soon. The Comanche will try breaking out with satanic howls, but many of them will raise their voices for the last time. There . . . there it's started already!"

The howling he had mentioned now arose, sounding as if a horde of wild animals had been loosened.

"Listen! Do you hear a single Apache responding?" the oldster asked. "Certainly not. They are smarter, doing their thing silently."

The rock walls returned the war whoops much multiplied, just as the two shots we now heard.

"This is Winnetou's silver rifle again," the scout told us, "a sure sign that the Comanche are being stopped."

If flying arrows and thrown spears would make a sound, the valley would surely have been filled now by a wild din. As it was, we heard only the voices of the Comanche and Winnetou's repeated shots. This took about two minutes. Then we heard a marrow-penetrating "Jwiwiwiwiwiwi."

"This be Apache!" Sam rejoiced. "They won and beat back Comanche."

He was correct, for when this victorious howl had died down, a deep quiet ensued. At the same time, we saw the shadows of several horsemen appear by the fire, to which more and more gathered. They were Comanche. Their breakthrough had failed. At the fire, great confusion showed for awhile. We saw dead and wounded carried in, and a lament arose once more. Old Death wiggled angrily back and forth where he was sitting, cursing the stupidity of the Comanche. He mentioned that they had better dispatch a group of guards towards the two entries of the valley, a most necessary precaution. After a long time, when the lament had died down, the Comanche seemed to gather for another council. Close to half an hour might have passed, when we observed several warriors leave the fire to spread out through the back of the valley we had retreated to.

"They are looking for us," Old Death said. "They realize the folly they committed and won't be too proud any longer to listen to our advice."

One of the dispatched messengers came close to us. Old Death coughed softly. The man heard it and came closer.

"Are the palefaces here?" he asked. "They are to come to the fire."

"Who's sending you?"

"The chief."

"What for does he want us there?"

"A council will be held in which the palefaces are permitted to participate this time."

"Permitted? How nice of you! Are we finally worthy to be listened to by the smart warriors of the Comanche? We lie here to rest and want to sleep. Tell this to the chief! Your enmity with the Apache is now totally irrelevant to us."

The Red now reverted to almost begging. This had an effect on the kindhearted oldster, for he said:

"Well then, if you see no way out to save yourselves without our advice, then you shall get it. But we do not care to be ordered about by your chief. Tell him, he should come to us, if he wants to talk with us."

"He will not do so, since he is a chief."

"Listen, man, I am a much greater and more famous chief than he is. I don't even know his name. Tell him that!"

"Even if he wanted to, he is unable to walk, since he was wounded on an arm."

"Since when do the sons of the Comanche walk on their arms, and no longer on their legs? If he does not want to come to us, he may stay where he is. We do not need him, nor any one of you!"

This had been spoken in such a decisive voice that the Red resorted to saying:

"I shall tell him Old Death's words. Maybe he will come after all."

"Tell him to come alone. I don't care to hold a long council with many men. Go now!"

The man left. We saw him stepping to the fire into the circle of warriors. Some time passed before anything happened. Finally, we saw a figure rising from the midst of the seated men to leave the fire and walk towards us. The man now wore eagle feathers in his hair.

"Look, he took dead White Beaver's chiefly symbol and put it on himself. He's going to lower himself to us with the greatest grandeur."

When the chief came closer, we saw that his left arm was in a sling. Our location must have been very well described to him, since he came straight to where we were sitting, then halted before us. Seemingly, he expected to be addressed, for he did not speak, but Old Death remained lying down and stayed silent. Of course, we others acted likewise.

"My white brother asked for me to come to him?" the Red eventually asked.

"Old Death need not climb down to beg for it. You wanted to talk with me.

It is therefore you, who must ask, if there can be anything to be asked. First, I will politely ask for your name. I do not know it yet."

"It is known all across the prairies. I am called Agile Stag."

"I have been to all prairies, yet never heard this name. You must have kept it secret. But now that I've heard it, I allow you to join us sitting here."

The chief stepped back apace. To be allowed to sit was not his idea, but he sensed very well that the conditions forced him to accede. This is why he slowly and solemnly sat down across from Old Death, and only now did the rest of us rise to a sitting position. If the Comanche had expected that the scout would initiate the conversation, he was mistaken. Old Death maintained his assumed indifference, requiring the Red to begin:

The warriors of the Comanche want to hold a great council, and the palefaces should take part in it, so that we hear their advice."

"That is superfluous. You've heard my advice many times, yet never followed it. But since I am used to having my words heeded, I will keep them from now on to myself."

"Would my brother consider that we have need for his experience!"

"Ah! Finally! Did the Apache teach you that Old Death is smarter than five hundred Comanche? How did your attack turn out?"

"We were unable to break through. The Apache had blocked it with rocks, branches and trees."

"I thought so! The Apache felled the trees with their tomahawks, which you did not hear, because of your lament for your dead. Why did you not extinguish the fire? Don't you realize that this endangers you?"

"The warriors of the Comanche had to do what had been decided at the council. Now, something more sensible will be decided. Will you speak to us?"

"I'm convinced that you will not follow my advice again."

"But we shall."

"If you promise this, then I'm willing to give it to you."

"Come along to our fire then!"

"No, thank you. I will not go there. It is very incautious to maintain a fire by which the Apache can see what is happening. I'm also not willing to quarrel with your men. I will speak my thoughts, and you can do as you please."

"Say so, then!"

"The Apache are not only at both exits of the valley, but also inside the valley. They barricaded both ends and from there can move to the left and right, just as they wish. To drive them away will be impossible."

"But we are far superior to them."

"How many warriors have you lost already?"

"The Great Spirit has called many of us already, more than ten times ten. And we have also lost many horses."

"Then you must not attempt anything more during the night, because the same would happen to you. And by day the Apache will position themselves in such a way that their weapons will reach you, but yours not them. Then, the groups Winnetou sent for will arrive, after which there will be more Apache than Comanche. You are doomed."

"Is this truly my brother's opinion? We will follow his advice, if it will save us."

"Since you speak of saving you, I hope you realize that I was right when I called this valley a trap. Thinking about it, I see two ways you could try saving yourselves. But it is only a try, for whether it would succeed, I cannot know. First would be trying to climb the valley's walls, but for that you must await daybreak and the Apache would see you and await you at the rim. There, they will be superior to you, since you will not have your horses available. There is only one other means to save yourselves. Start negotiations with the Apache!"

"We will not do this!" the chief roared. "The Apache would ask for our death."

"I cannot blame them for it; you provided plenty of reasons. In the midst of peace you attacked their settlements, robbed them, dragged away their wives and daughters, and killed their warriors or put them to the stake. Then you broke your word to their delegates and murdered them. Such miserable deeds call for revenge, and it is no wonder if you cannot expect mercy from the Apache. You see and admit to yourself that your people acted totally irresponsibly and sinned against them."

This had been spoken most sincerely, so sincerely that the chief fell silent for a moment.

"Uff!" he then exclaimed. "You tell this to me, me, the Chief of the Comanche!"

"I would tell you this even if you were the Great Spirit. It was shameful of you to treat the Apache who had done nothing to you the way you did. What did their delegates do to you that you killed them? What was it the Apache did that you undertook your present campaign to carry death, ruin and shame to them? Answer me!"

Only after a long time did the Indian pronounce grimly:

"They are our enemies."

"No. They lived in peace with you, and no delegate of yours brought the message that you would take up the war tomahawk against them. You are very well aware of your guilt, which is why you are so certain not to be given any mercy. And yet, it might be possible to arrive at a passable peace. You are fortunate that Winnetou is their leader. He does not thirst for blood, and is the sole chief of the Apache, and could decide to make peace with you. Send a messenger to him to, hopefully, start some negotiation. I would be willing myself to go and try to make him relent."

"The Comanche will prefer to die, rather than ask for mercy."

172

"Well, that's up to you. This is my advice. Whether you follow it or not is unimportant to me."

"Does my brother not know of any other help? He speaks in favor of the Apache and is, therefore, their friend."

"I am well-meaning towards all red men, for as long as they aren't hostile to me. The Apache didn't cause me the least harm. Why should I be their enemy? But you displayed hostility towards us wanting to take us prisoners. Weigh now, who has a greater right for our friendship, you or they!"

"You carry my calumet and medicine, which means that your words are like my own. This is why I cannot give you the answer I wish to give. Your advice is no good. With it, you intend to deliver us into the hands of the Apache. We now know what we must do."

"Well, if you know that, why do you ask for my advice? We're done; there's nothing more to be discussed."

"Yes, we are finished," the Comanche agreed. "But keep in mind that, although you are still under our protective agreement, you are our enemy. You may not keep my calumet and my medicine, but must return it to me before we leave this place. Then, everything you have caused will come to haunt you."

"Well! I am agreed. Whatever is supposed to come over me, I await peacefully. You threatened Old Death, even with death at the stake. I repeat that we are done; you can go."

"Uff!" the chief exclaimed angrily, but then turned and walked solemnly back to his fire. We did not observe his return, since our attention was drawn to a place we had not thought about earlier. Barely had the Comanche left, when it rustled behind us and a shadowy figure, who had lain between us and the rock wall, rose. Instantly, Old Death, and the rest of us jumped up, too.

"My brothers may relax," the shadowy figure said. "I am a friend of the palefaces."

"Who are you?" Old Death asked.

"Do you not recognize me, the one whose life you spared earlier, although he was in your power?"

"Winnetou?" the oldster asked surprised. "By the devil! Only Winnetou could accomplish stealing up behind me without me noticing. This is a masterpiece I am incapable of copying."

"Winnetou has learned to move like a snake, which cannot be heard by even the sharpest ears."

"But you entered into great danger doing it! You crept past the Comanche guards and then, all the way here, and must also get back."

"No, I did not. The palefaces are my friends and I can trust them. This valley lies in the territory of the Apache. Winnetou arranged for it to become a trap for enemies penetrating here. The rock walls are not as impassable as they appear. The Apache built a small trail which encircles the valley at the height of several men. It is easy to get up and down with the help of a lasso. My scouts lured the Comanche into this trap to perish here."

"Has their death truly been decided?"

"Yes. Winnetou listened to your conversation with the chief, and concluded from it that you are on the side of the Apache. You described what the Comanche committed against us, and admit that we must avenge these multiple murders."

"But must rivers of blood flow?"

"You heard yourself that the Comanche neither admit to their crime, nor want to do that which you recommended and astuteness would call for. Therefore, may their blood come over them. The Apache will demonstrate how to punish their betrayal. We must do this to be save from repeats."

"This is ghastly! But I feel no commitment to ears who have heard my advice but do not believe that they need to hear it anyway."

"You would again not be heard. From what you said, I understand that you hold the Comanche chief's sacred items. How did you obtain them?"

Old Death told the story. When he was finished, Winnetou said:

"Since you promised to return them, you must keep your word. Return them right now, then come to us. You will be received as friends. Winnetou was vanquished for the first time in his entire life. His life and scalp belong to this young man, who took neither. You can ask anything from the Chief of the Apache. He will give it to you."

"Are we to join you right away?"

"Yes. Winnetou came only to tell you this and lead you to his men. In three hours more than six hundred warriors of the Apache will arrive. Many of them have rifles. Their bullets will cover the entire valley, after which your lives will no longer be safe."

"But how are we to get to you?"

"Old Death asks this question?"

"Hmm! Yes! We mount up and ride to the fire. There we hand the chief his sacred items, then gallop away towards the Apache and ride down the guards in-between. But how are we going to get across your barriers?"

"Easily. Wait about ten minutes to leave after I am gone. Then I will stand to the right of the valley's exit over there to meet you."

He slipped away. We just stood there, and despite the darkness looked at each other in surprise.

"Well, and what do you say now?" Old Death asked.

"An exceptional man!" Lange replied.

"No doubt about that. If this man were a White, a soldier, he could make it to general. And woe to the Whites if he would think of gathering the Reds to fight for their hereditary rights. But he loves peace and knows that the Reds, despite all their uprisings, are doomed, and holds this terrible knowledge close to his heart. Well, let's sit down then for another ten minutes."

It remained quiet in the valley, as it had for the past half-hour. The Comanche were still debating. Ten minutes later, Old Death rose and mounted up.

"Do exactly as I do!" he advised us.

We rode slowly to the fire. The Comanche's circle opened and we entered. Had their faces not been painted so heavily, we would surely have noticed their surprise.

"What do you want?" the chief asked, jumping up. "Why do you come on horseback?"

"We come as horsemen to honor the brave and wise warriors of the Comanche. So, what is it you are going to do?"

"Our council is not yet concluded. But dismount! You are enemies of ours and we cannot allow you to be on horseback. Or are you coming to return my sacred belongings?"

"Would this not be very unwise of me? You said, that from the moment you have your property returned, there will be enmity between us, and we are to die at the stake."

"It will be so. I did say this and will keep my word. The anger of the Comanche will destroy you."

"We fear this anger so little that I shall let enmity begin right now. Here, have your things! And now see what you can do to us!"

He tore both items from his neck and tossed them far away. At the same time, he gave his horse the spurs, crossing the fire in a mighty leap and, on the other side, broke an opening into the groups of Comanche. Sam was the first to follow, in the process riding down the chief. We followed instantly. Ten or fifteen of the Comanche were ridden down, in addition to one of the guards standing outside, blocking Old Death's path. Then we galloped across the flat, grassy ground, pursued by the indescribable howls of rage of our so unreliable friends.

"Uff!" a voice sounded in front of us. "Stop! Here stands Winnetou!"

We brought our horses to a halt. Before us stood a number of Apache, who took our animals by their reins after we had dismounted. Winnetou escorted us to the narrows leading from the valley. The Apache had opened the barricade so that we and the horses could pass through single-file.

Once past the barricade, the passage became wider, and soon we saw the faint light of a fire where two Reds sat preparing a roast. They left deferentially when we approached. The other men also withdrew after they had staked down our horses. At some distance we noticed a number of horses with their guards. Everything looked somewhat like a military enterprise. The Apache's movements were so exact and secure as if they had been trained.

"My brothers may sit by the fire," Winnetou offered. "I had the loin of a buffalo roasted for them. They can eat until I come back."

"Will you be away for long?" Old Death asked.

"No. I must get back to the valley. As angry as they are, the Comanche might get carried away and attack my warriors, in which case I will send them a few bullets."

He left. In Matagorda he had spoken perfect English. Here, he used the customary Indian mishmash. Seemingly, he dropped some traces of White culture once he was with his own people.

Old Death made himself comfortable by the fire, and pulled his knife to check whether the roast was done. It was excellent. The oldster and I had not eaten anything for a while, and our three companions had only had a taste of the Comanche's horse meat. The big piece of loin quickly shrank. Then, Winnetou returned. He had a look at Good Man's totem and completed it with a few cuts, after which he swore eternal friendship to me for not having killed him.

He now asked: "But why did my brothers act with such enmity against the Whites who were with the Comanche?"

"In general, we had nothing against them. We were only after one of them, a great scoundrel, whom I had been pursuing for some time already, but without success."

"Who was it? Was he killed or did he escape?"

"He escaped. We did not find him among the dead."

"The Whites came to me, and all gave me their names."

"Being a criminal, who must hide behind different ones, he uses several names. He calls himself Gibson, Clinton and Gavilano."

"Gavilano? Yes, he was one of them."

"Where are the Whites who escaped to you?" I asked.

"They are gone."

"Gone?" the oldster exclaimed startled. "Also this Gavilano?"

"Yes."

"And how about a young man with a very sad face?"

"His mind was sick. He, too, left."

"By the devil! Then he escaped us again! We must go after him right away!"

Eagerness caused the oldster to jump up, but Winnetou said:

"My brother may sit down again. Circumspection is often faster than the greatest rush.'

"That's true," the scout agreed. "But why did Winnetou let these people leave so quickly, even though it was still night time?"

"Having taken a large detour with the Comanche, they were in a hurry to get to Chihuahua, to the warriors of Juarez. Winnetou loves Juarez, which is why he supported them in their hurry to get on."

"But Gavilano has nothing to do with Juarez!"

"I had learned this, too. But Gavilano said that he had to bring his poor, sick friend to a house in Chihuahua where poor spirits can be healed. The young White had become more ill while with the Comanche, and if they would not hurry, he could not be healed again. I supplied all of them with fresh horses and provisions, also gave them two guides who know the trail across the Mapimi to Chihuahua very well."

"That's a setback for us. Fresh horses, provisions, and knowledgeable guides! Did Winnetou, by chance, smoke the peace pipe with them?"

"No, Winnetou is not as careless as the chief of he Comanche. He checks first very carefully before he lets his calumet touch the lips of another man."

"Then, there's still some fortune in misfortune to be found. I hope you will also support us, so that we might succeed in catching these jokers after all?"

"I can promise this only after I have learned of what you accuse this Gavilano."

"I shall tell you right away."

He now told him what needed to be told. When he had finished, Winnetou said:

"I am saddened that you want to leave so quickly. But you must, which is why I cannot hold you back."

"Yes, we will leave immediately."

"Wait! Old Death has lived for many years, but his blood is still quick like that of a youngster. What you need, I cannot give you right away, but only when the warriors I expect have arrived."

"According to what you have told us, this will still take two hours! That's too long."

"No. You shall make up for this delay. Several of my men will accompany you on another trail, enabling you to catch up with the Whites. My men will be available to you to Chihuahua, and even farther, for as long as you have need for them."

"We are very grateful to you for this help. I have entered the Mapimi for some distance, but have not come that far, and never crossed it entirely."

"Your horses are also not suited for this ride. They are more used to flat ground. I will give you some others in their place, horses that were born and ridden here in the Mapimi. Nothing unforeseen happening, you will catch up with the Whites by noon of the second day."

That's when an Apache came running from the valley to report:

"The Comanche dogs have extinguished their fire and left their camp. They must be preparing to attack."

"They will be repulsed, as they were before," came Winnetou's reply. "If my white brothers will join me, I shall post them somewhere from where they can see and hear everything."

Of course, we rose right away. He took us back towards the entrance, almost to the barricade. Upon arriving, he handed Old Death a lasso hanging from the rock wall, and said:

"Climb up the lasso by twice a man's height. Then you will find bushes and behind them the trail I told you about. I cannot accompany you, but must join my warriors."

He reached for something leaning against the wall. It was his rifle.

"Hmm!" the scout grumbled. "Climb up twelve feet on a thin lasso like this! I'm no ape who's learned to climb among lianas. Let's try it though."

He succeeded. I climbed after him, and the others followed, although with some difficulty. A tree had grown in the rocks from which the lasso was suspended. Bushes growing next to it hid the trail. It was so dark that instead of seeing we had to use our sense of touch. We hesitantly made our way a short distance forward until Old Death stopped. Leaning against the rock wall, we waited for what was to come. To me, it seemed as if the silence of death was hanging over the valley. As much as I strained my ears, I could not hear anything other than a soft snuffle from Old Death's nose. That the old man was able to observe much more than I, who neither heard nor smelled anything, he proved when he whispered to me:

"Stupid fellows, these Comanche! Don't you think so, too, sir?"

I did not understand why he had called them such.

Sensing my unspoken question, he asked. "Don't you smell anything?"

"No."

"Over there, to the right, it smells of horses, horses on the move, which is quite different from horses standing still. With horses at rest, their odor hangs over them thick and unmoving; one can, so to speak, push one's nose into it. But as soon as horses get moving, their odor also moves, it becomes diluted, more liquid, and is carried away. As unbelievable as it may sound, the frontiersman senses from the smell's density whether he's facing standing or moving horses. Of course, this assumes the air is at rest. Presently, there's some such airy horse smell coming from the right, and it appeared to my old ears as if I had heard a horse stumble in the grass. I figure the Comanche are on the way, stealing towards the entrance to try for their breakthrough."

Now, we heard a clear voice shouting: "Ntsa-ho!"

This means "now." A moment later, two shots cracked from Winnetou's Silver Rifle, followed by revolver shots. An indescribable howling arose. The Indians' wild screams shrilled across the valley and tomahawks clanked. The battle had started.

It did not last long. Through the snorting and neighing of the horses, the victorious "Jwiwiwiwiwi" of the Apache penetrated the din. We heard the Comanche withdrawing in a wild flight. The sounds of their footsteps and the stomping of their horses disappeared towards the center of the valley.

"Didn't I say it?" Old Death commented. "We should have actually participated in it. The Apache keep themselves wonderfully. They shoot their arrows and stab with their spears from protected places. The Comanche come in a dense bunch so that every arrow, every spear, and every bullet of Winnetou's rifle and revolver must hit home. And now that the enemy has retreated, the Apache are smart enough not to follow, but remain behind cover, knowing that the Comanche cannot escape. They know not to enter the valley!"

The Comanche were now following Old Death's advice by remaining quiet following their failure to break out. Their howls had stopped, and since their fire no longer burned, they left their enemies in the dark as to their moves. We waited for a while longer, but nothing more happened. Then we heard Winnetou's subdued voice coming from below:

"My white brothers may come down again. The fight is over and will not resume."

We used the lasso to let ourselves down. Below stood the chief with whom we went back to the fire.

"The Comanche tried it on the other side," he said. "They were just as unsuccessful. They are being observed and cannot do anything without Winnetou learning of it. The Apache followed them and are lying in a long line in the grass across the valley to observe closely what the Comanche may be planning."

While he said this, he inclined his head to the right side, as if listening for something. He now jumped up, so that the fire brightly illuminated his figure.

"Why did you do this?" I asked.

He pointed into the night and answered:

"Winnetou heard a horse stumble on rocky ground. A horseman is coming; one of my warriors."

The man appeared, halted his horse next to us and dismounted. The chief welcomed him with a not very friendly look, and reproached him about the noise the horse had made.

Standing straight and respectfully before his chief, a free Indian, he nevertheless gladly acknowledged the greater experience of his leader.

"They are coming," he replied.

"How many horses?"

"All of them; not a single warrior is missing. When Winnetou calls, no Apache stays with the women."

"How far are they?"

"They will be here by daybreak."

"That is good. Take your horse to the others, then sit with the guards to rest!"

The man obeyed instantly. Winnetou maintained discipline. It seemed to me that his warriors were allowed to talk to him only if addressed by him. He sat down again with us, and we had to tell him of the events at the *Hacienda del Caballero*, and subsequently of those that transpired at La Grange. Time passed with no thought of sleep. The chief listened to our account and only from time to time made a brief remark or asked a question. Thus the night passed and dawn came. That's when Winnetou pointed west, saying:

"My white brothers may see how punctual the warriors of the Apache are. There they come."

I looked in the direction he indicated, but saw nothing. Fog lay like a gray, wave-less lake to the west, pushing its impenetrable masses between the mountains. Except for a pair of vultures high up, I was unable to see even a trace of a single living being. Old Death noticed that I tried in vain to spot the approaching Apache, and said:

"Are you once more a greenhorn, sir? I guess you can't make out the Reds."

"That's true, mister, but do you see them?"

"No, because they are in the thick of the fog, but the flight of the vultures tells us that there's something alive over there, moving in our direction. The horsemen impart their movement to the fog. If you watch the fog closely, you will notice the narrow strip on its surface, an opening, beginning about a mile from here, leading between the two mountains before us. This is the long line of Apache, who, following their custom, ride one behind the other. You can see from it how easily an inexperienced man could become endangered. You, for example, would be totally surprised by the Apache with the fog being so dense that you would see them only when it would be too late to flee. The opening through the fog and the vultures tell me that the Apache will arrive here in, at most, five minutes."

He was correct. The opening visibly extended towards us, until it disappeared when the horsemen arrived at our elevation. Shortly thereafter, I noticed the smell of horses Old Death had mentioned last night, and, finally, we saw the first horseman appearing from the fog, followed in a long line by his comrades. When he saw us, he stopped for a moment, but once he recognized Winnetou, he quickly trotted towards us. He was a chief, which we recognized from two eagle feathers in his bun. None of the horsemen appearing now was using proper bridle gear; all guided their horses by the halter, yet their control, when they approached us in an elegant gallop to arrange themselves five deep, was so secure as one rarely finds even with European cavalry. Most of them were armed with rifles, only a few carried spears, bows and quivers. Their leader spoke briefly with Winnetou, but I was unable to understand a single word. When Winnetou then gave a signal, the group of warriors dismounted. Those not in possession of rifles now tended to the horses, while the others walked to the valley's entrance. The lasso we had used to climb up to the trail, was still hanging, and I observed that one after another used it to climb up to the trail. Everything happened precisely and noiselessly as if it had long before been agreed upon. Standing nearby, Winnetou observed his men's moves carefully. When the last had disappeared, he turned to us:

"My white brothers will realize now that the sons of the Comanche are lost, if I so command."

"We are certain," Old Death replied. "But does Winnetou really want to spill the blood of that many human beings?"

"Did they earn anything different? What do white men do when one of them has been murdered? Will they not search for the murderer? And when he is found, their chiefs will gather to confer about his judgment and then have him killed. Can you reproach the Apache when they do the same?"

"But you don't do the same!"

"Can my brother prove this?"

"Yes. We punish the murderer by killing him. But you will shoot also those who were not even present when your settlements were attacked."

"They carry the same guilt, for they agreed to it. They were also present when the captured Apache had to die at the stake. They became the husbands of our wives and daughters and the owners of our property, our horses, that were taken from us!"

"But you cannot call them murderers!"

"I do not understand what Old Death wants. Among his brothers there are also other deeds beyond murder that are punishable by death. Frontiersmen gun down a horse thief. If a White's wife or daughter is kidnapped, he kills all those connected with the deed. There, in the valley, are the owners of our captured wives, girls and horses. Are we, by chance, to give them what the Whites call a medal?"

"No, but you could forgive them and take back your property."

"One takes back horses, but not women. And to forgive? My brother speaks like a Christian, who demands from us something which he does the exact opposite of. Do Christians forgive us? Is there anything for them to forgive us? They came here and took our earth. If, amongst you, someone moves a boundary marker or kills an animal of the forest, he is put into a dark building you call penitentiary. But what do you do? Where are our prairies today, where are the herds of horses, buffalo and other animals that were ours? You came in large numbers with every boy even carrying a rifle to rob us of the meat we needed for living. One territory after another was taken from us without you having any right to it. And when the red man defended his property, he was called a murderer and he and his people were killed. You want me to forgive my enemies, whom we did not harm? Why don't you forgive us, you who do us all the harm without us having given you any reason for it? If we defend ourselves we do our duty, but you punish us for it by ruining us. What would you say if we came to you to force our ways upon you? Would we force it on you, as you did to us, you would kill us to the last man or even put us away in your insane asylums. But why are we not allowed to act likewise? But then it would be said everywhere that the red man is a savage, for whom one cannot have any mercy or compassion, that he could never be educated and would, therefore, have to disappear. Did you prove by your behavior that you are educated? You force your religion upon us. Demonstrate it to us! All red men honor the Great Spirit in the same way, but every one of you wants to be blessed in a different way. I know of a good Christian belief, taught by pious *padres*, priests, who came to our land without wanting to kill us or push us out. They built missions and taught our parents and children. They walked about in friendliness and taught us everything good and useful. Much of that has changed. These pious men had to give way, together with us, and we had to watch them die without finding replacement for them. In their place hundreds of different beliefs are arriving to hurl words at our ears we do not understand. They call each other liars, yet insist that without their teachings we cannot access the Eternal Hunting Grounds. And when we turn away, having tired of their bickering, they cry shame about us and say that they want to shake the dust from their feet and wash their hands in innocence. Then it will not take long for them to call in other palefaces who will push into our lands and take our horses' pastures. And if we then say that this should not be so, we will be ordered to move on. This is my reply to you. You will not like it, but you, if you were in my place, would speak even more harshly. Howgh!"

Using this final Indian word of affirmation he turned away from us and stepped a few paces aside, from where he gazed into the distance to overcome his aggravation.

While he had been speaking, his looks had been more on me than on Old Death. It appeared as if he had wanted to address me rather than the old man. Later, I learned from Winnetou that it had been his intention to enlighten me about the actual relationship between Whites and Reds. Soon, Winnetou walked back to us and said to Old Death:

"I held a long speech for my brother. He will agree with me, for he is a man who thinks right and fair. But let me admit that my heart does not thirst for blood. My soul is more merciful than my words. I thought the Comanche might dispatch a negotiator. Since they did not, I need not have mercy on them. Nevertheless, I will send a man to talk to them."

"I'm very glad," Old Death exclaimed. "I would have left this place in a very sad mood, had all these men been killed without making an attempt to save them. I also carry part of the guilt for them ending up in your hands."

"I can relieve you from this reproach, for I would have defeated them also without your help," Winnetou replied.

"But are you aware that a hundred are following them?"

"Winnetou knows. Remember that he had to make his way through them together with Good Man. They are only a hundred. I will surround them in this same valley and destroy them like the others if they do not freely surrender."

"Watch out then that they don't arrive too early. You must be finished with those here before the rest arrive."

"Winnetou is not at all afraid. But he will hurry."

"Do you have a man to negotiate with the Comanche?"

"I have many, but I would like it most if my brother would do this."

"I will be glad to. I will enter the valley for a short distance, then call for their chief. What are your conditions?"

"They must hand over five horses for each of the men they killed and for every one they put to the stake, ten horses."

"This is a bargain, but since there are no longer large herds of wild horses, it isn't easy to get a horse."

"We also demand the return of all other property they took from us. Furthermore, they must send us as many of their young girls as they robbed us of our women and daughters. We do not want any Comanche women. In addition, we want the children they took returned to us. Do you think this is hard?"

"No."

"And, finally, we ask that a place be established where the chiefs of the Apache and Comanche will gather to confer about a peace that is to last for thirty summers and winters."

"If they agree to this, I shall congratulate them," said Old Death.

"This valley, where their warriors are caught now, is to be the location of the council. Everything I demanded must be delivered here. Until this has been accomplished, the Comanche, who must surrender today, will remain our prisoners. I give them two moons to make the requested deliveries. If they have not done so by the end of this time, the prisoners will die."

"I do not think your demands are too high and will transmit them immediately."

He tossed the rifle over his shoulder and cut off a branch to indicate his position as a parliamentarian. Then he disappeared with the chief in the narrows of the entrance. It was not without danger for him to approach the Comanche, but the oldster simply knew no fear. I would have loved to accompany him to hear what the Comanche would reply, but he had been too fast. When I walked to the valley's entrance, I found only Winnetou; Old Death had already disappeared through the barricade. Winnetou now gave a somewhat complex signal up to the trail where his Apache warriors lay hidden, after which I noticed one arm after another relaying the signal down the line.

Indians possess a very clear sign language by which they can usually understand each other very well. They speak even over distance with each other, by day through smoke, and by night with fiery arrows. The smoke signals are made from a rise where a fire is lit which is nourished by damp wood to produce lots of smoke, held back by blankets suspended above the fire. When these are quickly removed, the smoke rises. Then the blankets are held once more over the fire, to be quickly pulled back again. In this way, individual smoke puffs are produced whose number, size and timing convey certain meanings. At night a similar small fire is lit. Dry grass is tied to arrows which are then shot high. From their number, direction and height the message's recipients can deduce their meaning. Much later did I learn the meaning of these signals, different among the various tribes, and whose meaning is, for obvious reasons, often changed. But, at the time, I was still ignorant, and Old Death explained to me that the signal of the raised arm had meant that anyone threatening him was to be shot. When Winnetou was certain that the scout had entered into a conversation with the leader of the Comanche, he walked back with us to take us to the recently arrived horses. These included a number of spare horses, some better, for use in exceptional tasks, others of normal quality, being spares.

"I promised my brothers to give them better horses," he said. "I will now select them. My young white brother, who spared my life, will get one of my own breeding. Old Death will instruct him how an Indian-schooled horse must be ridden."

He selected five horses. I was utterly delighted by the magnificent animal he brought to me. Standing next to it, he leaped onto its back and presented it to me, controlling it only by leg pressure and whistles. I had never seen an exquisite animal like it. The two Langes and Sam were also delighted about the steeds he choose for them. The Negro displayed all his teeth and exclaimed:

"Oh, oh, what horse Sam get! It be black like Sam and be just as splendid as Sam. Fit very well together, horse and Sam. Oh, oh!"

Several of the Apache guards switched saddles from our old horses to the new ones, then Winnetou asked me to mount mine. I was barely on it, when it kicked up first in back, then in front. Then it took a jump to the side, and I was on the ground – a real scandal! But the chief smiled only gently and said:

"No White, even if he were the best of horsemen, could keep himself on this horse if he does not know of its training. I shall now give my dear brother the necessary instructions."

He had known that I would be tossed, and yet had asked me to mount it! I could have broken my neck! A real Indian jest. Of course, among Indians two-year-old boys and girls ride like devils across the prairie and that on half-wild mustangs. Since one could assume that Old Death's negotiations with the Comanche's leader would require more than five minutes, Winnetou had enough time to give us a longer lesson, from which we learned enough to keep us in the saddles and to halfway control the horses.

Three quarters of an hour might have passed when the oldster returned. His face was serious. I had been convinced that the Comanche would agree to Winnetou's demands, but the scout's face led one to conclude the opposite.

"My brother will tell me what I expect," Winnetou said. "The Comanche do not want that which I asked for."

"Unfortunately, no."

"The Great Spirit slew them with deafness to punish them for what they did. He does not want them to find mercy. But what reasons did they give you?"

"They believe that they can still win."

"Did you tell them that more than five hundred Apache arrived, and where they posted themselves?"

"That, too. They did not believe it, but laughed at me."

"Then they are doomed to die; their other warriors will arrive much too late."

It caused my hair to rise thinking that so many people would, in just a few seconds, be killed from the face of the Earth!

"My brother is right. Winnetou knows no fear, but his back turns cold thinking of giving the signal for their destruction. I only need to raise my hand horizontally for the shots to fall, but I shall make a last attempt to prevent it. Maybe, the Great Spirit will provide them with some insight. I shall show myself and talk to them personally. My brothers may accompany me to the barricade. If my own words are not heard either, then the Great Spirit may not be angry with me when I execute his command."

We accompanied him to the barricade. Having arrived there, he climbed up on the lasso and walked upright along the trail for the Comanche to see him. He had not gone far yet, when arrows whizzed up, but fell short because of the distance. Then a shot cracked from White Beaver's rifle, fired by the new chief of the Comanche. But Winnetou kept walking quietly as if he had not heard the bullet that had impacted the rocks next to him. Then he stopped and raised his voice. What he said, I did not understand, since he used an Indian language. He might have spoken for about five minutes in a loud and urgent voice. In the midst of his speech he raised his hand, and we saw that every Apache, as far as we could see, which meant all around the valley, rose to show themselves to the Comanche. They had to realize that they were surrounded by a superior force. This was a sincere act of Winnetou's, his last attempt to move them to surrender. Then he continued speaking. When he fell silent, Old Death explained to me:

"He just said that he was awaiting their response . . . ah, by the devil!"

Just when the oldster spoke out, a second shot cracked, but Winnetou had dropped to the ground.

"The Comanche's leader fired at him again. That's his answer," Old Death said. "Winnetou noticed that the Comanche had loaded his rifle again and at the moment he aimed it at him, threw himself down. Now shall . . . oh, look!"

As quickly as Winnetou had dropped down, he rose, aimed his Silver Rifle and fired. Loud howls of the Comanche followed his shot.

"He killed their leader," Old Death explained.

Now, Winnetou raised his hand once more by pointing his hand flat-out. As far as we could see the Apache aimed their rifles. Far more than four hundred shots cracked –

"Come, gentlemen!" the oldster suggested, "let's not watch this. This is much too Indian for my old eyes, although I must say that the Comanche deserve it. Winnetou tried everything to prevent it."

We returned to our horses, where the oldster inspected his new steed. We heard one more salvo from the Apache, then their victory howls. A few minutes later Winnetou returned. His face was extraordinarily serious when he told us:

"There will be a great lament in the tents of the Comanche, for none of their warriors will return. The Great Spirit wanted our dead to be avenged."

He sat down where the fire had burned throughout the night and for a long time stared silently ahead. We were eager to depart, but could not show our impatience since we knew that he would take good care of us. Thus passed a quarter of an hour, half an hour, then even an entire hour. By then the Comanche's horses were brought from the valley and Winnetou rose to take us into the valley. There was no longer any trace of the barricades at both ends, and we saw no bodies lying about. Using lassos, they had been pulled them up to the trail.

At last, preparations were made for our departure. We were given meat and our water bags were filled. Then, ten men were assigned to accompany us.

"Ten?" Old Death questioned. "One's enough to show us the way."

"I do not assign them to you as guides, but for your protection," Winnetou explained.

"Protection? That we don't need. We are men enough to take care of ourselves."

"My brother is mistaken. I know him to be a courageous, a brave man, but presently the Mapimi swarms with hordes of Zacateco, Tshimarra and Concho, who are no one's friend and everybody's enemy."

"They are scoundrels, I need not fear! The Apache and Comanche are brave, but these semi-civilized rogues are cowardice in the saddle."

"My brother may consider that the most cowardly man can kill the most brave in an ambush. The young paleface I have to thank my life for must not die by the act of such a man."

"Well, if that's what you think, I am agreed. It's all right by me to assign us ten of your warriors."

"You will be satisfied with them. They are some of my best, and their leader is dear to me. I told him that he may not face me alive, if you encounter any injury; you can entrust yourselves to him."

"Well, I hope we can take him into our protection as well as he does us."

Old Death was not a man who liked to be told that he was going to be put in the protection of another. I, however, was very pleased that such a capable young warrior was going to accompany us. I hoped to learn from him, if only with respect to horsemanship. Then it was time to say goodbye. Indians do not care to display their feelings like Whites do; however, Winnetou made an exception. He embraced me, kissed me on my cheek, hung his calumet around my neck, and said:

"My heart is yours, also my arm. You carry already Good Man's totem, but Winnetou's peace pipe will protect you even better. Any Apache you show it to, will be willing to make his life a gift to you. Ride on, and may the Great Spirit protect you! I will tell him daily that I wish to meet you again. Should he bring us together once more, we shall become brothers, one like the other."

Once more he checked the dressing he had applied last night, shook my hand, then turned around and without looking back, walked into the valley. We mounted up and rode off, the ten Apache in the lead.

I was deeply touched by this farewell. Winnetou had left an indelible impression on me to last for a lifetime, even were I never to meet him again. Thus I rode, deep in thought, not paying attention to anything except to my contemplation of the image Winnetou had imparted on me. Finally, I had to look more after my horse, which started to give me trouble. Old Youngster, as the leader of Winnetou's men was called, noticed it and joined me to take me under his wing.

He was about my age and did not look that bold. Winnetou must have recommended me to him, since he was profusely friendly and attentive. He had crossed the Mapimi in all directions, insisted on knowing it exactly, and described his life there. I now learned more about this desert than I ever had before.

It stretches across the Mexican provinces of Chihuahua and Cohahuila, and forms an extensive plateau at an elevation above 3,600 feet. Except for the north, it is framed by steep limestone mountains, with numerous canyons separating it from the actual Mapimi. The plateau itself consists of undulating, treeless expanses covered by a meager growth of grasses, broken by large expanses of sand, with rarely a bush to be seen. At times, a solitary mountain rises from this miserable plain. Often, the ground is broken by deep canyons, making for long detours. But the Mapimi is not as waterless as I had thought. There are lakes which, although they lose most of their water during the hottest time of the year, still spread enough humidity to permit some good plant growth along their banks.

Our ride was taking us to one of these lakes, the Laguna de Santa Maria. From what Old Youngster was telling me, I concluded that this lake was located about ten miles from the valley we had departed from, making for a hard ride after a sleepless night. We rode almost exclusively through canyons, one after another, with no views.

For much of the day we were unable to see the sun, and when it was possible, only for a few moments. We rode to the left, then to the right, sometimes, seemingly, even backwards, so that without a compass I would have become totally turned around about the direction we actually had to follow.

It was towards evening that we arrived at the *laguna*[8], where the ground was

---

[8] Lagoon

sandy. No trees grew at the spot where we camped, only some bushes whose name I did not know. The *laguna*, with its brackish waters, was surrounded by sparse bushes, from which one looked out across a plain to a few low hills towards the west, behind which the sun had set already. But where we were, its beams had heated the soil mightily.

I had become almost cold in the deep, narrow, dark canyons. But up here the ground gave up such heat that one could have baked a cake on it. However, once the earth had released its heat to the air, the night was that much colder. By morning a wind passed over us, which drove us deeper into our blankets.

Early in the morning we continued our ride straight west, but soon numerous canyons required more detours. To get down into some of these precipitous, rocky canyons would be impossible had nature not been kind enough to provide breakneck, stair-like descents. And once down, one cannot get readily out without passing through ten and more other canyons, until one finds a spot where one can ascend to the surface, with danger threatening again. The horseman hangs onto his horse on the narrow trails, above him a small strip of sky and below him the horrible depth. And down there one can not find even a drop of water, only bare, dry, sharp-pointed rock rubble. High above swoop the vultures, accompanying the traveler from morning to evening. And once he lies down to rest, they settle a short distance away, only to accompany him again the next morning. They tell him by their shrill, hoarse screams that they only wait for him to drop from exhaustion or, because of his horse's misstep, falls into a canyon. At times one will see a skeletal jackal slinking around a rocky outcrop to disappear in its shadow, then to reappear behind the horseman to follow him hungrily, waiting like the vultures for a meal.

I learned from Old Youngster that it would take us four days to reach Chihuahua. He hoped, though, to catch up with Gibson and his companion still today. This helped me to suffer the terrible ride in a halfway decent mood.

By noon we had another terrible maze of canyons behind us and were crossing a grassy plain at a gallop. Suddenly, we noticed the tracks of more than ten horsemen coming from the right at an acute angle. Old Youngster claimed the tracks to be those of the group we were following. He even showed us the tracks of the shod hooves of the Whites' horses and the unshod ones of the two Apache Winnetou had assigned as guides. Old Death, too, was of the opinion that we were, without doubt, now following the right tracks. Unfortunately, it turned out that Gibson had a lead of at least six hours. His group must have traveled through the night, likely figuring on our pursuit.

Towards evening Old Death, who rode with smart Sam in the lead, stopped to let us, who had fallen back somewhat, catch up. Where he had stopped another set of tracks of between thirty to forty met the one we were following. This group had ridden behind each other, which made determining their number difficult. Their riding in a beeline and their unshod horses told us that they were Indians.

Coming from the left, they had turned in our direction, and from the almost similar age of the two tracks, we could assume that they had subsequently met the Whites. Old Death grumbled something that sounded like:

"What kind of Reds might they be? Certainly not Apache. We can't expect much friendliness from them."

"My brother is right," Old Youngster agreed. "There are no Apache here presently, and except for them, there are only the three hostile groups Winnetou mentioned. We must be on guard."

We continued our ride and soon reached the location where the Reds had met the Whites. Both groups had stopped and talked with each other. The result must have been advantageous for the Whites since they had joined the Reds, continuing their ride under their protection. Their previous guides, the two Apache we had originally got to know as Topia, had been released. The tracks of these two split here from the rest.

A while later, we arrived at a rise covered by grass and brush, and rare here, a tiny stream flowing down from it. The group ahead of us had stopped to water their horses. The brook's banks were bare, so that one could overlook its course for quite some distance, leading northwest. Old Death, standing by the bank, shaded his eyes, and looked in this direction. When he was asked what he was looking for, he said:

"I see two dots far ahead. I think they are wolves. But what's the reason for the beasts to sit there? If they are truly wolves, they would have run from us. No animal is as cowardly as these prairie wolves."

"My brothers may be quiet. I heard something," Old Youngster said.

We avoided making any noise, and truly, a weak shout sounded from the direction of the two dots.

"That's a man," Old Death exclaimed. "Let's hurry over there."

He mounted his horse with us following. When we came closer to the spot and dismounted, the two animals rose and ambled off. They had been sitting by the bank. In the midst of the brook we now saw a bare human head sticking from the water. His face swarmed with flies covering his eyes, ears, the nose and his lips.

"For God's sake, *Señores*, save me!" the mouth groaned. "I cannot bear this any longer."

Of course, we leaped from our horses.

"What happened to you?" Old Death asked in Spanish, since this was the language the man had spoken. "How did you get in there? Why don't you come out? It's barely two feet deep!"

"I am buried."

"Why? By the devil! To bury a human being! Who did that?"

"Indians and Whites."

In our hurry, we had missed the tracks that led here from the watering spot.

"This man must get out right away. Come on, gentlemen! Let's dig him out. Since we have no tools, we'll use our hands."

"There is a shovel behind me in the water. They covered it with sand," the man told us.

"A shovel?" How come you carry such a tool?"

"I am a *gambusino*[9]. We always carry a hoe and shovel with us."

We found the shovel, stepped into the water, and began our work. The creekbed's sand was easy to remove. Only now did we see that a spear had been dug in behind the man. From it, a rope was attached to his neck so that he was unable to bend his head forward. This kept his mouth only three inches from the water, making it impossible to take even a sip. In addition, his face had been smeared with bloody meat to attract insects to torment him. He had been unable to free himself since his hands and feet had been tied. The hole he was stuck in was close to five feet deep. When we finally got him out and had freed him from his bonds, no wonder, he collapsed unconscious. His tormentors had undressed him completely and beaten his back bloody.

---

[9] Prospector

6. At the Bonanza[10]

The poor man soon recovered. We carried him back to where we were going to camp alongside the creek. We first fed him, and afterwards I unpacked my spare shirt to dress him. Only now was he able to provide us with the desired information.

"I am a *gambusino* and last worked a *bonanza* in the mountains about a day's travel from here. I had a companion, a Yankee, by the name of Harton, who . . ."

"Harton?" Old Death impatiently interrupted him. "What's his first name?"

"Fred."

"Do you know where he was born and how old he is?"

"He was born in New York and may be about sixty years old."

"Did he talk about having a family?"

"His wife had died. He has a son, who plies some kind of trade in Frisco, I don't know which. Do you know the man?"

Old Death had spoken loudly. His eyes shone and his deeply sunken cheeks glowed. Now he made an effort to appear calm and replied in a lower voice:

"I met him some time ago. Supposedly, he had done well. Didn't he tell you anything about it?"

"Yes, he was the son of decent parents and became a merchant. Little by little, he built up a nice business. But he had a problem brother who attached himself like a leech and sucked him dry."

"Did you learn the brother's name?"

"Yes. His name was Henry."

"Right. I hope I'll manage to meet your Harton some time!"

"Hardly. He'll likely not live much longer. The rogues who buried me took him along."

Old Death looked as if he was going to jump up, but succeeded in controlling himself, and asked with a quiet voice:

"How did that happen?"

"I was just going to tell you when you interrupted me. As I said, Harton was a merchant, but was cheated by his brother for his entire wealth. I have the feeling he still loves this unscrupulous fellow, despite the fact that he took everything from him. After he became impoverished, he banged around at placers as a digger for some time, but never had any luck. Then he became a *vaquero*, in short, he did all kinds of things, but always without success, then, at last, joined the *gambusinos*. But he wasn't cut out to be an adventurer. As a *gambusino*, he did even worse than before."

"Then he shouldn't have become one!"

---

[10] Geological gold and silver placement

191

"It's easy for you to say, *Señor*. Millions of people don't become that for which they have talent, but for that which they are least able to. Maybe he had a secret reason to join the *gambusinos*. His brother became one, and a very fortunate one at that. He may have hoped to come across him that way."

"That's a contradiction. This miserable brother is supposed to be a lucky *gambusino*, and yet cheated his brother for his entire wealth? Doesn't a lucky gambusino have heaps of money?"

"Yes, but if he squanders it faster than he finds or earns it, then it's simply gone. He was a spendthrift to the highest degree! At last, Harton came to Chihuahua, where he was hired by my principal. There, I got to know and like him. This is rare, for you can easily imagine that *gambusinos* are highly jealous of each other. From then on, we went on explorations together."

"What's the name of your employer?"

"Davis."

"Really! Listen, *Señor*, do you also speak English?"

"As well as Spanish."

"Then be so kind and speak English. Here are two men, who don't speak Spanish, but will be very much interested in your story."

He pointed at the two Langes.

"Why would they be interested?" the *gambusino* asked.

"You'll find out in a minute. Listen, Mister Lange, this man is a gold prospector and works for a certain Davis in Chihuahua."

"What? Davis?" Lange exclaimed. "That's the employer of my son-in-law?"

"Not so fast, sir! There can be other Davises."

"If this gentleman means the Davis, who is engaged in the profitable business of buying gold and silver mines, then there is only one by that name," the *gambusino* insisted.

"Then it's him!" Lange exclaimed. "Do you know the gentleman, sir?"

"Of course! He's my employer."

"Do you also know my son-in-law?"

"Who is that?"

"A German by the name of Uhlmann. He studied in Freiburg."

"That is correct. He became the mine director and owns some nice profit shares. It looks as if he will shortly become a partner in the business. Are you his father-in-law?"

"Of course! His wife, Agnes, is my daughter."

"We call her *Señora* Inés. She's well known to us, sir! I heard that her parents live in Missouri. Are you going to visit your daughter?"

Lange confirmed it.

"Then you need not ride to Chihuahua, but to the *bonanza* I mentioned earlier. Did you not hear of it yet? It belongs to your son-in-law! Not too long ago he took a pleasure ride into the mountains and, in its course, discovered a silver deposit like none has been found before here. *Señor* Davis provided him with the workers to mine it immediately. They are very busy, and the results are such that one can guess that *Señor* Davis will offer him a partnership, which would be of great advantage to both of them."

"What do you say! Will, did you hear this?"

He had addressed his son, who, however, had remained silent. He was sobbing quietly, shedding tears of joy.

Of course, the rest of us were also happy for our companions' fortune. Old Death made all kinds of faces which made no sense to me, although I usually was able to understand them.

It took a while for the excitement to die down that Lange's son-in-law had discovered a *bonanza*. Eventually, the *gambusino* was able to continue:

"I helped Harton to get the operation at the *bonanza* started. Then we left to search in the Mapimi. We rode for three days without discovering any gold. This morning, we were still resting by the creek here. We had barely slept during the past night and were very tired, so that we fell asleep again without really wanting to. When we woke up, we were surrounded by a large group of white and red horsemen."

"What sort of Indians were they?"

"Tshimarra, forty of them, and ten Whites."

"Tshimarra! They are still the most brave of all these scoundrels. And they laid hands on you two poor devils? Why? Are they presently hostile to Whites?"

"One never knows what to think of them. They are neither friend nor foe. Although they avoid open hostility, for which they are too weak, they never develop a decent relationship with us that we can trust. And that is more dangerous than real enmity, since one never knows how to react."

"Then I would like to learn the reason why they treated you this way. Did you insult them?"

"Not in the least. But *Señor* Davis had equipped us well. Each of us had two horses, good weapons, ammunition, provisions, tools and everything one needs for a longer stay in this barren area."

"Hmm! That's, of course, more than sufficient reason for such people."

"They had us surrounded and asked who we were and what we were doing here. When we told them, they reacted angrily and claimed that everything in the Mapimi was theirs. Then they demanded that we hand over our belongings."

"And you did?"

"Not I. Harton was smarter than me. He dropped everything he owned, while I reached for my rifle, not to shoot, but only to intimidate; otherwise this would have been total folly with their superior numbers. But I was instantly overcome, pulled down and stripped down to my skin. The Whites did not help us, only asked questions. I did not answer, which is why I was whipped with a lasso. Harton was, again, smarter than me. He could not know their intentions.

He told them everything, even about *Señor* Uhlmann's *bonanza*. That's when their ears perked up, and he was asked to describe it. I interrupted him, so that he would keep quiet. At last, he noticed that they could not be trusted and gave no further information. Thereupon, I was tied up and buried, and Harton was beaten until he told everything. Since they were of the opinion that he might have lied to them after all, they took him along, threatening the most painful death if he would not lead them to the *bonanza* by tomorrow evening."

I had never seen Old Death's face as now, although I had experienced him in various kinds of moods. Now, he showed the most sinister, wildest and ruthless determination. He looked like he was ready to commit a murder, with no mercy for his victim. His voice sounded hoarse when he said:

"Do you think then that they headed for the *bonanza*?"

"Yes. They were going to attack the *bonanza* and plunder it. Great stores of munitions, provisions and other items are kept there, which would be of great value to the scoundrels. There's also plenty of silver."

"By the devil! They'll probably share the spoils, the Whites taking the silver and the Reds the rest. How far is it to there?"

"A good day's ride. They'll arrive there by tomorrow evening, provided Harton follows my advice."

"What did you tell him?"

"To take a detour. Against all hope, I hoped that someone might pass by here to free me. In that case I was going to ask the newcomer to hurry to the *bonanza* to warn the people. Of course, I could not have joined him, since I no longer have a horse."

The oldster gazed ahead for awhile, then said:

"I'd love to leave right away. If I'd leave now, I could follow the tracks of these rogues until dark. Can you describe the way well enough that I'd find it even at night?"

The man shook his head and warned against a nightly ride. Old Death decided therefore to wait for the following morning.

"The fifteen of us," he continued, "are dealing with forty Reds and ten Whites, making it fifty men. I don't think we need to be afraid. How were the Tshimarra armed?"

"They carried only spears, bows and arrows. But they took both our rifles and revolvers," the *gambusino* replied.

"That won't matter, since they don't know how to handle those weapons. Then we'll try everything, which, most of all, requires learning the location of the *bonanza*. You said that it can only be found by accident. I don't understand that. There must be water near a *bonanza*, flowing into some canyon. It must be easy to find in such an open, treeless area. Describe the place for me!"

"Imagine a canyon cut deeply into a forest. The canyon's steep limestone walls widen in the middle. The limestone is immensely rich in silver, copper and lead. The forest reaches from all sides right to the edge of the canyon, with some bushes and trees growing on its walls, and a good spring erupting in the back. The canyon, or you may call it also a valley, is about two miles long, but despite its length there isn't a spot where one can descend from above. The only entrance is where the creek empties from the valley. There, the rocks close in so tightly that there's only room between the creek and the rock wall for three men or two horsemen."

"Then the place is easily defended against an attack!"

"Certainly. There's no second entrance, at least not for non-residents of the valley. The mine is in the middle of the valley. For some reason it had been too cumbersome to walk for half an hour to get out of the valley, which is why *Señor* Uhlmann had a trail hewn into the rocks at an appropriate spot, where the rock doesn't rise vertically, but in steps. The *Señor* had trees felled and dropped at various places onto the rocky steps so that they lean against the walls. This produced a continuous mass of trunks and branches under whose cover steps were cut into the rock. No stranger would notice them."

"Oho! I'd say I could spot these stairs right away. It's given away by the tree cutting. Where trees have been cut, people must have been."

"When you get to the respective spot, you will find that the trees were lowered using ropes with great effort and peril. Understand! They were not felled as is common. No stumps can be seen. *Señor* Uhlmann had them uprooted, so that they slowly leaned into the canyon and took their entire root balls along. More than thirty men held onto each tree so that it would not tumble into the depth, but slid slowly until it came to rest on one of the rocky terraces."

"He has that many laborers?"

"Almost forty."

"Well, then we need not be concerned about an attack. How is his contact with the outside organized?"

"By mule trains, which arrive every two weeks to supply the valley with everything necessary, and then take the minerals away."

"Does the *Señor* have the entrance guarded?"

"Yes, during the night, when everyone's asleep. In addition, there's a hunter roaming the area during the day to provide the company with game. He won't miss anything."

"Did Uhlmann have any buildings erected?"

"No buildings. He lives in a large tent, where everyone gathers after work. Another tent holds supplies. Both butt up against the canyon walls. Huts for the workers, built from branches, surround the two tents in a semicircle."

"But someone standing at the edge of the valley could see the light-colored tents!"

"No, because they are covered by dense tree crowns and aren't made of white canvas, but rather a dark rubber material."

195

"That's better. And how are the men armed?"

"Very well. Each worker has a double-barreled rifle in addition to a knife and revolver."

"Well, then, the dear Tshimarra can come. Of course, that means we must arrive before them tomorrow. We'll need to push our horses. But let's try to find some sleep now. Considering what's expecting us tomorrow, we, as well as our horses, must be well rested."

Sleep did not come to me, although I had not slept for a moment during the previous night. The thought of catching Gibson tomorrow was too exciting. Old Death did not sleep either, tossing and turning from side to side. I was not used to seeing him do this. I heard him sigh and mumble softly at times, words I was unable to understand, although he lay right next to me. Something was troubling him. I had been struck by his behavior when the *gambusino* talked about Harton, but it could be explained by him knowing this man. Might he have some other relationship with this man than that of a mere acquaintance?

When we had lain for about three hours, I noticed him rise. He listened for our breathing, trying to convince himself that we were asleep. Then he rose fully and left, walking along the creek. Of course, our Indian guard did not hold him back. I waited. A quarter of an hour passed, another, then a third, with the oldster not returning. Then I also rose and walked after him.

He had gone some distance. It took me ten minutes to spot him, standing by the creek and staring at the moon with his back turned to me. I made no effort to approach silently, but the grass muffled my steps. Nevertheless, he should have heard me, had his thoughts not occupied him so much. I was almost standing behind him, when he jerked around. He ripped the revolver from his belt and snapped at me:

"By the devil! Who are you? Why are you sneaking up on me? You want me to shoot . . ."

He stopped. His mind must have been so far away that he recognized me only now.

"Ah, it's you!" he continued. "I almost shot you, thinking you to be a stranger. Why don't you sleep?"

"Because, thinking of Gibson and Ohlert won't let me rest."

"So? I believe you. Well, tomorrow the two will finally fall into our hands, or my name's not Old Death. I can't continue running after them, but must stay at the *bonanza*."

"Really? Why so? Is it a secret?"

"Yes."

"Well, then I don't want to intrude and bother you any longer. I heard your sighs and mumbling and thought I could help with whatever is troubling you. Good night, sir!"

I turned to leave. He let me walk off for a short distance, until I heard him call:

"Mister, don't run off. It is true that something's troubling me very much, but it won't come out. I got to know you as a discreet and goodhearted fellow who isn't likely going to judge me too severely. That's why I want to tell you what's bothering me. I don't need to tell you everything, only a few things; the rest you can easily figure out yourself."

He took me by my arm, then to walk slowly along the creek.

"What do you actually think of me?" he suddenly asked. "What do you think of my character of – of – well, of the moral Old Death?"

"You are a man of honor, which is why I like and respect you."

"Hmm! Did you ever commit a crime?"

"Hmm, I also mumbled now. "I annoyed my parents and teachers; crept through the neighbor's fence into his fruit orchard, and beat up other boys who weren't of my opinion, and so on."

"Don't blab stupid things! I'm speaking of real crimes, punishable by law."

"I can't think of any such things, of course."

"Then you are exceptionally fortunate, sir. I envy you, for it is a punishment to live with a bad conscience. Not even the gallows or penitentiary are equal to that!"

He said this with a voice that deeply touched me. Yes, this man's mind was bothered by the memory of a major crime, or he would not have spoken as badly as he did. I did not say anything and some time passed before he continued:

"Mister, don't ever forget: there is divine justice, against which the worldly one is mere child's play. Eternal justice stays on one's conscience and thunders its judgment into it day and night. It must come out; I must tell you. But why you, precisely? Because I put great trust in you, despite your youth and despite you being a veritable greenhorn. Also, because I have a feeling deep inside as if something's going to happen tomorrow which could prevent this old scout from confessing his sins."

"Are you out of your mind, sir? Are you saying that you have a premonition of death?"

"Yes, I do," he nodded. "You heard earlier what the *gambusino* said about the merchant Harton. What do you think of this man's brother?"

I figured what was coming, which is why I replied gently:

"At any rate, he was reckless."

"Pshaw! You say so only to be easy on me. Let me tell you, a reckless person is more dangerous than a truly malicious one. The evil one shows it already from afar, but the reckless one is often a charming fellow, which is why he is more of a danger than the former. A thousand bad people can be reformed, for wickedness has character on which discipline can gain a handle. But of a thousand reckless people hardly any can be reformed, for recklessness, carelessness, does not carry a handle to which discipline can latch on to. I wasn't actually really bad, but reckless, totally reckless, for this Henry Harton, who cheated his brother for everything he had, that was me, me!"

"But, sir, you gave me another name!"

"Obviously! I took another name, since I dishonored my original one. No criminal likes to talk of that which he has sinned against. Do you recall what I told you in New Orleans, which is that my good mother had put me onto the path to fortune, but that I looked for it in a totally different direction?"

"I recall it."

"Then I don't want to waste many words. My dying mother showed me the path to virtue, but I took the one to recklessness. I wanted to become rich, to own millions. I speculated without any sense and lost my inheritance and my business honor. That's when I went to the diggings. I was lucky and found plenty of gold, but squandered it as quickly as I gained it, because I was a passionate gambler. I labored for months in the diggings, only to put what I had won through hard labor onto a single number and gamble it away in five minutes. It wasn't enough for me. The mines didn't provide me with the sums the way I wanted them. I was so crazy that I wanted to bet a hundred thousand dollars just to bust the bank and after the first, all others. I went to Mexico and became a *gambusino* and had outrageous luck, but gambled it all away. This kind of life destroyed me physically. Additionally, I had become an opium smoker. I went all the way into the dumps without a way out. No one looked at me anymore, but every dog barked at me. That's when I happened to come across my brother who had some business in Frisco. He recognized me despite my misery and took me into his house. Had he only not done so! He should have let me rot! He would have missed all the misfortune, and I my pangs of guilt!"

He fell silent for awhile. I saw his chest heave and felt true pity for him.

"I was forced to be good," he continued. "My brother thought that I had completely mended my ways and offered me a position in his business. But the gambling devil was only slumbering, and when it awoke once more, it took hold of me harder than before. I reached into the till to force my luck. I issued bad checks, only to sacrifice the money to the Moloch of gambling. And I lost and lost and lost until there was no more to rescue me. Then I disappeared. My brother redeemed the false drafts and was made a beggar because of it. He, too, disappeared with his little son after he had buried his wife, who had died from sorrow. Of course, I learned this only years later, when I dared to visit Frisco. The impression made by this information turned me to better ways. Just prior to this, I had worked as a *gambusino* again and had been lucky. I had come back to pay compensation, but my brother had disappeared. From then on I looked for him everywhere, but never found him. This restless wandering turned me into a scout, which many people interpreted as being moral. I quit gambling, but not opium. I'm no longer smoking the stuff, but chew it, mixing it into the chewing tobacco, and these days enjoy it only in small quantities. So, there's my confession. Now, go spit at me and kick me; I won't mind, because I deserve it!"

He let go of my arm, sat down in the grass, put his elbows on his knees and covered his face with his hands. He sat like this for a long time without saying anything, with me standing next to him dealing with indescribable feelings. Finally, he jumped up again, stared madly at me, and asked:

"You're still standing here? Don't you shudder from this miserable human being?"

"Shudder? No. I feel sorry for you, sir. You sinned much, but also suffered much, and your remorse is real. How could I, even in silence, judge you? I am myself a sinner and do not yet know what life will bring me."

"Suffered much! Yes, there you're right, very much so! Oh, dear God, what are the sounds of all the world's trumpets against the never resting inner voice of a man aware of his serious moral guilt. I must suffer for it and make up for it as much as I can. Tomorrow, at last, I'm going to see my brother again. I feel as if a new sun is rising for me, but no earthly one. But all this is of no concern to you. There's something else I must tell you and ask you for. Will you fulfill my wish?"

"From the bottom of my heart!"

"Then listen to what I tell you! There is a good reason why I'm dragging my saddle along, even when I don't own a horse. If one cuts its lining one finds items destined for my brother, but only for him. Will you remember this, sir?"

"Your request is very modest.'

"Not at all. But, maybe, you'll learn yet the kind of trust I put in you by asking you not to forget it. And now, leave me be, sir! Leave me alone! I feel as if I must still study my debt register during the night. Tomorrow, there may be no time for it any more. There are presentiments, presentiments which, when they occur, one knows immediately that they tell the truth. I beg you, leave! In God's name, sleep; you do not have a bad conscience. Good night, sir!"

I walked slowly back to our camp and lay down again. It took me hours to finally fall asleep prior to daybreak, but the oldster had still not returned. But when everyone woke up, he was already on horseback, as if being in a rush to realize his premonition of death. The *gambusino* told us that, except for some back pains, he felt well enough to ride. He wrapped himself in a horse blanket and received a second blanket as a coat. An Apache took him on his horse; then we took off.

Once more, we traveled through canyons, in whose depths we rode till noon. Then, at least for the day, we left the difficult terrain behind. For hours we crossed grassy plains from which some individual mountains rose, always following the Tshimarras' tracks.

Eventually, the *gambusino* asked us to halt, and, satisfied, said:

"We must leave the tracks here. Harton followed my advice and took the detour. We will turn here to the right."

"Well! Then let's follow your direction."

To the northwest, in our direction, we saw some blue shadows. The *gambusino* explained that these were mountains. They were so distant though, that it took us hours to notice that we were coming closer. Shortly after noon we stopped for a brief respite, then continued with renewed speed. Finally, we saw the first, rather desiccated bush. Soon bushes proliferated, then we rode across green prairie where, at times, we had to ride around larger brush islands. We revived again, but our horses were truly admirable. Of course, these were quite different animals than those *Señor* Atanasio had given us. They kept trotting along as if they had just now left camp.

By now, we were close to the mountains. It was, however, also high time, since the sun was touching their peaks. That is when we saw the first tree, standing amidst the prairie, its branches shattered by storms. We greeted it, however, as a harbinger of the welcome forest. Soon, we rode under more trees, some forming groves. The rising ground took us to heights beyond which the terrain dropped steeply into a shallow valley. We had to get down and across it. On its opposite side, the valley's bare flank rose again to a substantial height, but at its crest carried green forest. Once up there, we rode under the trees along its ridge, only to descend again into another depression. Passing through a small canyon, we arrived on a small, treeless, grassy plain. Barely had we arrived there, when we saw a dark line cutting across the direction of our ride.

"Tracks!" the *gambusino* exclaimed. "Who may have passed here?"

He climbed off the fourth or fifth horse he had been on to check the tracks.

"I can see it without getting off," Old Death said angrily. "Tracks like these can only be made by a group counting more than forty horsemen. We are too late."

"Do you really think that these are the Tshimarras' tracks?"

"Yes, I sure think so, *Señor*!"

Old Youngster dismounted and for some distance walked along the tracks, then said:

"Ten palefaces and four times more Reds. They passed here about one hour ago."

"Well, what do you say to that, *Señor gambusino*?" Old Death asked.

"Even if that were true, we can still forestall them," the man replied. "In any case, they will reconnoiter prior to the attack, which will take them some time."

"They will force Harton to describe everything to them, so that they needn't waste time searching."

"But Indians attack only right before daybreak."

"Lay off with your daybreak story! Didn't I tell you that Whites are with them? They don't care about the Reds' habits. I'd bet that they will enter the *bonanza* in broad daylight. Let's get going, therefore!"

We applied our spurs now and galloped across the plain, but in a totally different direction from that of the Tshimarra. Harton had not led them to the entrance of the *bonanza*, but had deliberately taken them to the hindmost edge above the valley. We now tried to gain the entrance as quickly as possible. Unfortunately, darkness came too quickly. Once more we entered the forest and had to ride cautiously through the trees without any kind of trail, first up, then down again, and eventually had to rely on the eyes of our horses and the *gambusino* walking ahead. But branches were all too often still in our way, hitting our faces, even threatening to drop us out of our saddles. We therefore dismounted also to walk, pulling our horses behind us. In our free hand we held our revolvers at the ready, since we might face the enemy at any time. At last we heard the sound of rushing water.

"We have reached the entrance," the *gambusino* whispered. "Watch out! The creek is to the right. Walk singly and keep to the left along the wall!"

"That's all fine, but why hasn't a guard been posted here?"

"Not yet. It's not bedtime yet."

"Nice organization, this! And that for a *bonanza*! Where's the trail now? It's pitch dark."

"Straight ahead. The ground is level. There's no more obstacle until we get to the tents."

In the darkness we saw only that we had the level valley floor ahead of us. To the left, a sinister rock wall rose. To the right the water gurgled. We were unable to make out the opposite face of the valley, and just kept walking and pulling the horses by their reins. I was in the lead with Old Death and the *gambusino*. Suddenly, I thought I saw a figure darting like a dog between us and the rock wall, all happening in a moment. I called the others' attention to it. We stopped, but nothing could be heard.

"The darkness is deceiving," the *gambusino* said. "By the way, just behind us is the location where the hidden ascent is."

"Then the figure may have come down from there," I said.

"If that's the case, we need not worry; it would have been a friend. However, at this time, no resident of the valley has any business here. You must have been mistaken, *Señor*," the *gambusino* responded.

This exchange closed the issue, which would become so fateful, at least to one of us. A short while later, we saw the indistinct glow of lights penetrating the tent canvas. Voices sounded. The three of us were still ahead.

"Have the others wait in front of the tent until we have informed *Señor* Uhlmann of our coming," Old Death told the *gambusino*.

The hoof beats of our horses must have been heard inside the tent, nevertheless, its flaps were not opened.

"Come on in with me, sir!" the oldster told me. "Let's see the joy and surprise we'll bring."

Old Death, in front of me, opened the tent flaps to step in.

"There they are!" someone shouted. "Don't let them enter!"

While these words were said, a shot cracked. I saw how the Scout gripped the tent flap with both hands, and simultaneously became aware of several rifles being aimed at the entrance. The oldster was unable to stay upright and slid to the floor.

"My premonition – my brother – forgiveness – in my saddle – !" he groaned.

"*Señor* Uhlmann, for God's sake, don't shoot!" I screamed. "We are friends, Germans! Your father-in-law and brother-in-law are with us. We've come to warn you of an intended attack."

"By God! Germans!" it came from the back. "Is it true?"

"Yes. Don't shoot. Let me come in, just myself!"

"Come in, then, but no one else."

I entered. About twenty men faced me, all holding rifles. The scenery was illuminated by three lamps suspended from the ceiling. A young man stepped towards me. Next to him stood a totally down-and-out looking man.

"Was he with them, Harton?" the young man asked.

"No, *Señor!*"

"Quit fooling around!" I shouted, "and don't hold an examination. We are friends; the enemy is right behind us. They can arrive at any moment. You called this man Harton. Is he the one the Tshimarra dragged along?"

"Yes. He got away from them, just arrived two minutes ago."

"Then you stole past us, mister Harton. I saw you. My friends did not believe me. Who fired the shot?"

"I did," one of the men answered.

"God be thanked!" I breathed easier, thinking that one brother might have killed the other. "You killed an innocent man, a man you have to thank for being saved!"

Now the two Langes entered with the *gambusino*, who could no longer wait outside. A wild, loud scene of joy erupted. The remaining residents came from the surrounding huts. I had to put my foot down to have quiet return. Old Death was dead, shot through the heart. Our Negro Sam picked up his body and amidst loud wails, laid him down amidst us. Two women had appeared from behind the tent's division. One, the caretaker, carried a little boy. The other woman was embracing her father and brother.

Under the circumstances, I could rely only on myself. I asked Harton how he had succeeded in escaping. While the others talked and scrambled about, he explained to me:

"I led them astray by taking them along the ridge through the forest to the back of the valley. There, they set up camp while the chief went to reconnoiter. When it was dark they left, leaving their horses with some guards. I was left lying there with hands and feet tied, but succeeded in freeing them. Then I stole away to the secret stairs and down into the valley. I passed by you, thinking you to be the enemy and hurried here. I found most of the workers gathered and reported the impending attack. The first to enter was going to be shot."

"Had you only gotten lost! You caused great harm. According to what you say, the fellows could be here at any moment. We must establish some order."

Of course, I now turned to Uhlmann, the man who had stood next to Harton when I had entered. With great haste I informed him about how things stood, and with his help the necessary preparations were made within a couple of minutes. Our horses were taken towards the back of the valley, while the Apache posted themselves with Uhlmann's laborers behind the tent. Old Death's body was taken outside. A barrel of petroleum together with a bottle of gasoline, were carried to the creek. The lid of the barrel was removed and a man stood by who was ordered to pour the gasoline into the petroleum, and then light it when given the order. Once the barrel's content was aflame, he was to pour it into the creek, the purpose being to illuminate the valley.

Now, more than fifty men stood ready to await the enemy's arrival. We were the same number, but much better armed than they. A few smart and experienced workers were sent to the tent entrance to report the arrival of the enemy.

In the rear, the bottom fasteners of the tent were removed to get in and out.

Of course, the women and the child were taken to the back of the valley. Now, Uhlmann, the two Langes and I were alone in the tent. Sam had stayed with the Apache. About ten minutes might have passed, when one of the men from the front of the tent came in, reporting that two Whites had arrived, wanting to meet *Señor* Uhlmann. He said also that in the dark behind the two men had been more movement, from which one could conclude the entire group's arrival. The two were asked to come in, but before that, I and the two Langes hid behind the tent's division.

And who did I see entering? Gibson and William Ohlert. They were courteously greeted and invited to sit down, which they accepted. Gibson called himself Gavilano and presented himself as a geologist wanting to visit a colleague in the mountains. He said that he was camped nearby, when a certain Harton, a *gambusino,* had shown up, and he learned from him that better living conditions could be found here. He claimed that his comrade was sick, which is why he had Harton lead him here to ask *Señor* Uhlmann whether he would take them in for the night.

Whether this story was smart or silly, I did not take the time to judge and stepped from my hiding place. Seeing me, Gibson jerked up, and stared at me terrified.

"Are the Tshimarra who are following you also sick, Mr. Gibson?" I asked. "William Ohlert will not stay here, but come with me. And you, too."

As usual, Ohlert sat there totally disengaged, but Gibson caught himself quickly.

"You devil!" he screamed. "Pursuing honest people even here! I shall . . ."

"Shut up, fellow!" I interrupted him. "You are my prisoner!"

"Not yet!" he replied angrily. "First take this!"

He had held his rifle and now swung it butt-first. I caught his arm, causing him to make a half turn. The butt smashed down, hitting Ohlert's head, causing him to collapse. The next moment several workers pushed into the tent from behind, aiming their rifles at Gibson, whom I still had in my grip.

"Don't shoot!" I shouted, since I wanted him alive. But it was too late. A rifle went off and he collapsed into my arms, shot through the head.

"No hard feelings, mister! It's the custom here!" said the shooter.

As if the shot had been the signal, likely arranged between Gibson and his accomplices, wild Indian war whoops arose not far from the tent. The Tshimarra, with their White allies, had come already that close.

Uhlmann rushed outside, the others following. Shots cracked and men screamed and cursed. I was alone in the tent with Ohlert. I knelt next to him to check whether he was dead, but his heart was still beating., which reassured me. Now I could participate in the fight.

When I stepped outside, I found it was no longer necessary. The valley was almost in full daylight, illuminated by the petroleum burning in the creek. Our adversaries had been received very differently from what they had expected. Most of them lay on the ground; others had fled towards the valley's entrance and were pursued by the victors. Here and there, one of the attackers was still fighting against two or three of Uhlmann's men, but without hope of success.

Uhlmann stood next to the tent and sent one bullet after another to wherever he made out a target. I pointed out to him that it was advisable to send some of his men under Harton's guidance up the secret ascent to capture the enemy's horses. Once there, those who might manage to escape, could be caught. He agreed and right away dispatched several men.

Barely three minutes had passed since the first shot had been fired, and already the place had emptied.

I would love to skip over the following. Images which go against a man's heart, ought not to be painted by either pen or brush. True Christianity forbids even the victor to delight in his triumph.

The group, which had been sent up the ascent had easily been able to get hold of the horses and stayed there for the night. Only Harton returned. He had no idea who was dead on our side, or who had been killed in the course of a misunderstanding by the bullet of a friend. I walked with him out into the valley, where by now several fires had been lit. I stepped to a dark area, where we sat down, and I told him what he needed to know.

Like a child, he cried loudly and heartbreakingly. He had always loved his brother, had long since forgiven him, and had become a *gambusino* only in the hope of finding him among the prospectors. I had to tell him everything, beginning with my first meeting with Old Death to the last moment, when the bullet hit his remorseful brother. He wanted to hear every word that had been exchanged between his brother and me, and when, after more than an hour, we returned to the tent, he asked me to take him into my heart as I had his brother.

In the morning Old Death's saddle was fetched, and between the two of us, we cut through its lining. Inside we found a wallet, very thin, but nevertheless with a rich content. The deceased left to his brother several substantial bank drafts. However, the most important thing was a detailed description of a place in the Sonoran desert where Old Death had discovered a promising *bonanza*. From this moment on, Fred Harton was likely a very rich man.

It was impossible to find out what Gibson's plans had been with William Ohlert. Even Gibson's sister, Felisa Perillo, whom they had intended to visit, would likely not have been able to provide any insights. I found on William all the cash that had been withdrawn, of course, minus what had been expended on their travels.

Although Ohlert was alive, he did not seem to want to wake from having been stunned. I could expect that this would force a longer stay upon us, something I did not mind at all, since it allowed me to recover from the strain of events and getting to thoroughly know the activities at a *bonanza*. Eventually, Ohlert's condition would permit us to travel to Chihuahua to put him in the care of a good doctor.

Old Death was buried. Over his grave we erected a cross made of silver mineral. His brother quit Uhlmann's services in order to recover in Chihuahua from the strains of his life as a *gambusino*.

Uhlmann and his wife were most happy about the arrival of their two relatives. The Uhlmanns were dear, hospitable people; one could be glad for their happiness. When Fred Harton said his farewells, he asked me to accompany him in the search for his Sonoran *bonanza*; however, at the time, I was unable to give him a positive answer. Obviously, the Apache were richly provided and returned to their people with a heavy load of greetings to Winnetou.

Sam, the Negro, left with Harton, properly completing his task. Whether he returned to *Señor* Cortesio is unknown to me.

Two months later I sat together with the good monk, Benito, of the congregation *El Buen Pastor*, The Good Shepherd, in Chihuahua. I had brought my patient to him, the most famous doctor of the northern provinces, and he had succeeded in totally curing him. I said, 'totally,' because, together with his physical recovery, his mental well-being had also returned. It was as if the rifle butt's blow had extirpated the unfortunate monomania of being an insane poet. He was lively and well, at times even funny, and longed to see his father. I had not told him yet that I was expecting his father to arrive shortly. I had, of course, sent a report to New York, following which I was informed that he would come to pick up his son. As an aside, I had asked him to arrange for my discharge from Mr. Josy Taylor's organization. More and more, the thought of joining Harton on his trip into the Sonora had come to intrigue me.

Harton came daily to visit us and the good *padre*. He had developed an almost touching friendship for me, but was also delighted by my patient's recovery.

But I must say that a real miracle had happened to William; he no longer wanted to hear the word 'poet.' He was able to remember just about every hour of his life; however, the time from his escape with Gibson until his eventual reawakening at the *bonanza* was an empty page in his mind.

Today, we were sitting together again, the *padre*, Ohlert, Harton and myself, talking about our experiences and hopes. That's when a servant knocked, then opened the door to escort a gentleman in, at whose sight William exclaimed in joy. The kind of pain and sorrow he had given his father he knew only through me. Weeping, he threw himself into his father's arms. We others went silently outside.

There was time later to talk about everything, with father and son sitting with us hand-in-hand. Ohlert senior handed me my release from the Taylor organization, after which I told Harton right away that I wanted to accompany him. We would have enjoyed it even more, had a third person been able to join us. And with that I mean, of course, none other than the Scout.

ABOUT THE AUTHOR

Karl May (1842 - 1912) is today hailed a German literary genius. His unequaled imagination gave birth to a whole collection of characters that lived through exiting and realistic adventure tales that captivated generations of German readers both young and old. Yet his writings were never available to English readers.

ABOUT THE TRANSLATOR

Herbert Windolf was born in Wiesbaden, Germany, in 1936. In 1964 he immigrated to Canada with his family to provide his German employer with technical services for North America. In 1970 he was transferred to the United States and eventually became Managing Director, later Vice President, of the US affiliate. Retired, he resides these days in Prescott, Arizona, where, among other things, he has taught courses on scientific subjects at an adult education center, has written science essays and, widely traveled, miscellaneous travelogues. He is the Executive Vice President of the Planetary Studies Foundation. An astronomer friend has named an asteroid after him. He has translated a number of literary works from German to English, his first being Karl May's, "The Oil Prince", published by Washington State University Press.

Other Karl May Translations:

Title	Author	Publisher
The Oil Prince	by Herbert Windolf	Washington State Univ. Press
The Treasure of Silver Lake	by Herbert Windolf	Nemsi Books
The Ghost of Llano Estacado*	by Herbert Windolf	Nemsi Books
The Son of the Bear Hunter	by Herbert Windolf	Nemsi Books
Imaginary Journeys I	by Herbert Windolf	Nemsi Books
Imaginary Journeys II	by Herbert Windolf	Nemsi Books
Imaginary Journeys III	by Herbert Windolf	Nemsi Books
Pacific Shores	by Herbert Windolf	Nemsi Books
The Inca's Legacy	by Herbert Windolf	Nemsi Books
Thoughts of Heaven	by Herbert Windolf	Nemsi Books
Winnetou I	by Victor Epp	Nemsi Books
Winnetou II	by Victor Epp	Nemsi Books
Winnetou III	by Michael Michalak	Nemsi Books
Winnetou IV	by Herbert Windolf	Nemsi Books
Oriental Odyssey I	by Michael Michalak	Nemsi Books
Oriental Odyssey II	by Michael Michalak	Nemsi Books
Oriental Odyssey III	by Michael Michalak	Nemsi Books
Oriental Odyssey IV	by Michael Michalak	Nemsi Books
Oriental Odyssey V	by Michael Michalak	Nemsi Books
My Life and My Mission	by Michael Michalak	Nemsi Books
The Rock Castle	by Herbert V. Steiner	Nemsi Books
Krüger Bei	by Herbert V. Steiner	Nemsi Books
Satan and Iscariot	by Herbert V. Steiner	Nemsi Books
Along Unfamiliar Trails	by Kince October	Nemsi Books
The Legacy of the Inca	by Kince October	Nemsi Books
El Sendador I	by Kince October	Nemsi Books
El Sendador II	by Kince October	Nemsi Books
Old Surehand I	by Juergen Nett	Nemsi Books
Old Surehand II	by Juergen Nett	Nemsi Books
Old Surehand III	by Juergen Nett	Nemsi Books
Father of Victory	by Sergiy Marchenko	Nemsi Books

* abridged